THE MAD ARCHITECT

T.M. WOOD

Village Books Publishing
Bellingham, Washington

Paperback ISBN: 979-8-9930340-0-3
Hardcover ISBN: 979-8-9930340-1-0
E-book ISBN: 979-8-9930340-2-7
Library of Congress Control Number 2025919003

Cover Design by James Noble Frier
http://thenobleartist.com

Book Design by Jill Flores

Printed in the United States of America

First Edition

This story is dedicated to the people I've met around the world who inspired me—those who listened to me as I regaled them with my ideas. And most of all, to my father, the first person who gave me the confidence to believe this story is worth telling.

CONTENTS

MARTIAN YEAR 2019

(About Four Billion Years Ago)

*L*ong ago, before our own planet turned green and blue, Mars was a world filled with life, cultures, and conflicts.

Global tensions run high amongst the people of Mars. The civilians of the Aeternus Empire demand peace from their warmongering government of god-worshiping architect neophytes. The civil unrest in the nation of Ares doubles as the threat of war and mistreatment of civilians in their own country increases. Protests throughout the world seem to be a precursor for mass bloodshed. Who will strike first?

Chapter 1

THE FUEL

It was just another day on Mars. The impeccable flow of continuity remained undisturbed. Life as they know it, being as certain as you know it.

Thump thump thump! "I'm coming!" I rush to the door with a half-peeled banana in my hand and car keys in the other. I unlock it with a click, swing it open, and there stands Patrick, looking at me with his usual smug grin, like he knew I was gonna sleep in. His daughter, Laura, makes her way slowly from the car, dragging a duffel bag behind her.

Ushering my guests inside, I feel the warmth of the summer sun on my hand as I pull the door shut. "I know, I know … I should've set an alarm, but in my defense I went to sleep really late."

"You got distracted last night, didn't you?"

I check his expression. At what point does a grin become a smile? "I don't know what you're insinuating, but I went to bed last night at a decent hour."

He smiles with his arms crossed. His yellowish-gray eyes see right through me. "Four in the morning?" He rolls his eyes. "You went to sleep at the same time a nighttime commercial driver wakes up."

I point emphatically to the door leading into the garage. "But I had this idea for the car, and I wanted to try it out, and you know how complicated computers are."

I wait a moment for a response and I get nothing, just a smug smile. "Oh, I give up. I admit it, I have a problem."

He pats me on the shoulder. "Your only curse is that you think too much, but right now you don't have much to think about. My offer is still open. You know, the pay is decent, and I'd be right next door." As he walks inside, Laura skitters past us both and beelines into the kitchen.

I let out a little laugh and say, "Pat, out of the two of us, you're the only one capable of doing the special agent thing. Special Agent Patrick Reardan, one of the many people on the planet the magical and mystical monks over at the Order come to when they don't feel like doing the dirty work, which is nine out of ten cases."

It is true. His status as an agent in the Martian Center of Intelligence gives him authority that demands respect from everyone.

"I don't know about the Order of Genesis, but I'll be brutally honest right to the face of the president or the members of the senate." He shakes his head, swishing his thick, sandy-blonde hair all over the place. "All right, James, no politics today—at least not while Laura is here." I glance behind me to see his daughter sitting on one of the stools at my kitchen counter, eating cereal. Her bright, golden hair glows in the sunlight that streams through the window. Her little, fair face looks up at us, and she smiles innocently. Her pure golden eyes are warming my soul as per usual, but I still have to tease her.

"Uh, excuse me, miss? I believe that's my breakfast you're eating." I sit down next to her and stare. She just ignores me, and I can't help but smile. "Your dad has probably shown you how to cook, right? You at least know how to make your own bowl of cereal. I mean, what, you're like eight now, right?"

She glares at me with milk dripping off her upper lip. "Actually, I'm nine, and I'm turning ten in a few days."

I put my hand over my heart. "Oh, I'm sorry." I smile at Patrick, who seems to enjoy watching his daughter boss me around.

"So, you must know what goes in first, milk or cereal?"

She slurps up a third of my food in one go and makes eye contact as she gulps it down. "Who cares? As long as the last step is me eating it."

I look to Patrick for help. "Hey man . . ." He shrugs. "I would've said cereal first. If you put cereal in milk, it can splash and make a mess."

I clap my hands. "Thank you! A man with his sanity still intact." The kid clears her throat, and I turn back to Laura.

"Oh, and by the way," she says, "I can make spaghetti, grilled cheese, fried eggs, and puppy chow."

I put my hands up in surrender. "Ah! That officially makes you superior. Last time I tried to fry an egg, I swear I made an improvised biological weapon. Grilled cheese? More like cremated, but my spaghetti is, and will always be, the best."

"Yeah, well, try to keep her diet somewhat diverse while I'm gone, James," Patrick says.

I pick up a paper towel and wipe the milk off her face. "Don't worry, we won't just be eating spaghetti. We're also going to eat pizza, takeout, ice cream, hot chocolate, brown liquor, and bowls of sugar."

He scoffs at me and shakes my hand. "You're hilarious." I give him a smug smirk of my own. "Hey, it's one of my own few redeeming qualities. We can't all be superheroes."

"I'm not super," he says as he pokes his forearms. "No cosmic powers in these veins."

I blow a raspberry. "Who needs that? Never underestimate what a resourceful person can do."

"It's my job not to. It's the resourceful people with special power that you gotta watch out for." He opens the door, but then he holds up his hand, letting the sounds of the distant city of

Simeo inside. "And whatever you do, don't take her to school in the Subaru. It's too loud and flashy."

I grimace and look at Laura and then back at Patrick. "Yeah, about that..."

He laughs and leans his head back. "You broke it, didn't you?"

"I didn't break it! I sold it."

Patrick pretends to stroke an invisible beard, "Oh, really? And why's that?"

I twiddle my thumbs. "Because, third gear ... disappeared. But I got something even better!"

"Let me guess, a Lamborghini?"

I let out a dramatic gasp. "Patrick! You know I'm more responsible than that. It's an old BMW. Gloss black on the outside and black leather on the inside. And I've already improved it." And by "improved" I mean I've made it louder and faster, but it's probably best I withhold the specifics.

"Uh-huh, very practical," he says. "Well, as long as her booster seat fits, it doesn't matter, I guess."

He hugs Laura and returns to the door as a few cars go by outside. "You're so consistent and predictable. The only thing I can't predict about you is how fast you move about some things. I can always call it, but sometimes you've done it already."

"Well, actually, it's more like half done, I still need to—"

He puts his hand up to interrupt me. "I know, I know. Take the BMW. I would've preferred you got the Audi. Draws less attention."

"Hey, it's not as flashy as the Subaru, and it's not like I'm using the Nissan. I mean, I could, but ..." I scratch my head and pretend to get distracted by something.

"I'd probably have to arrest you or something."

I nod along. "Everything you say can and will be used in court so ... they can't use anything if you give them nothing. That way you don't get left with nothing."

"Well, as fun as this is, I need to get to work. Save some fun for me when I get back."

I call out to him as he walks to his car. "No promises. We run on fun, and with these prices, we gotta make do!"

Patrick gets into his car and rolls down his window. He must think he's pretty cool because he puts on his sunglasses and says, "That's because you got a lead foot," and drives off. I mean, with wit like that, how cool does he think he is?

I close the door and look back at Laura. She's putting her—*my*—now empty bowl into the sink. "Well, ma'am, are you all set for the weekend?"

"Yep!" she exclaims.

I put my hands on my hips. "Homework?"

She puts on a pouty face and nods. "I've got all of my assignments with me and the book we're supposed to read in class."

I stand on the opposite side of the counter and cross my arms. "Oh yeah? Is it a good book?"

She shrugs. "I don't know. You haven't read it to me yet."

"Aha! I see how it is. Well, I better start working on my vocal exercises. I wouldn't want you to leave a bad review and ruin my future in doing audiobooks." I start pretending to sing like an opera singer to make her laugh, which, of course, she does. You'd have to be a sad individual to not have the ability to make a child laugh. It will always be one of my most important powers.

Even though I don't have a daughter, and I'm still quite young, having a legacy is very important to me. It's not about being remembered or thanked for what you've done. It's just about being proud of what you're leaving behind. And having a child and a family—bundles of life that carry on after you die—from what I've seen, they are the best legacy you can have.

So, when Patrick asked me to look after Laura while he did some work for the Order of Genesis, I couldn't say no. I mean, he's my best friend. Laura is also his flesh and blood, his family, his legacy. So guarding their legacy is just one of those important things you can do for a friend.

I know, for the most part, I'm just overcomplicating something that all creatures are genetically programmed to value—the drive to leave something behind, a family, life, their DNA. We're designed to prolong the existence of life by any means necessary. And while it might be as simple as that—that is if you find genetics simple—I hope it's more than that. It shouldn't just be about survival. But I can't deny the fact that in some ways, it always will be.

Laura hops out of her chair. "So, when are you gonna teach me how to drive?"

I raise my eyebrows at her and point at myself. "Me? Teach you how to drive? We gotta slow down here. For one, you're too young, and none of my cars are appropriate for you to drive."

"Why? Do you think I'll crash?"

I pretend to stutter as she frowns at me. "I-well-no-it-it's just that your dad will be very mad if I teach you how to drive in a sports car."

Knock knock knock. "Oh good, saved by the bell," I say.

I go to answer the front door as Laura says, "This isn't over!"

Opening the door, I find a man knelt beside my Audi, seemingly admiring it. "Can I help you, sir?" I ask, wondering how he was able to ring the bell from all the way over there.

He looks at me and smiles, standing up with a grunt. "I think so. Patrick recommended that I come to you." His greasy black hair is long and frizzy; blue eyes almost pop out of his pale face. He walks over and shakes my hand, looking down on me just slightly as he stands at almost six feet tall.

"Oh? For something automobile related?" I ask as I open my garage with a remote.

He nods. "Yes, and no," he says, crossing his arms and nodding with approval as a yellow Nissan Skyline and a black BMW M3 are revealed from behind the now-open garage door.

"Well, I hope I'll be able to help you with both." I motion with my hand to bring him into the garage, where we find Laura sitting at one of the chairs at my desk.

She swivels around to face us and says, "I've been expecting you."

"Hey, Laura, I guess I just missed your dad then." She nods.

I blink and cannot help but frown a little. "I'm starting to feel like I'm the only one who doesn't know you, Mr. . . . ?"

"Stark, Leonidas Stark. But just call me Leo. Whenever people use my full name, it feels really official and like I'm in trouble." We shake hands and Laura gets up so that he can sit down.

"Like when your mom is mad at you!" Laura says.

He chuckles. "That too, Laura, that too."

I ruffle Laura's hair with my hand. "All right, sassy lady, you mind grabbing my notebook so I can help Mr. Stark?"

"Actually, I think it would be best if it's just you and I. The other matter Patrick wanted me to talk to you about is work related."

"Ah, I see. Well, in that case, Laura, that means you get to use the TV and the console. But no browsing."

"Woohoo!" She skips out of the garage and back into the house.

I wait for the door to click closed behind her before continuing. "Work related?"

"Yeah, he tells me that you'd be a great fit for a position like mine. I'm here to see if he's right."

Oh boy, here we go. I lean forward and interlock my fingers. "What position is that?"

He scratches his head. "Um, I'm sorry, I don't know how to explain this without giving you a little bit of context. But to start, I technically work for Patrick, as a sort of consultant."

"Okay, that means you're an expert in something he isn't?" I ask, relishing in this new information.

He nods. "I know a lot about the Order and what makes it tick."

"Order, like *the* Order? Order of Genesis? No one knows what goes on inside that temple. You'd have better luck having an angel over for dinner."

"Normally, you'd be right. But it just so happens I used to be a knight of Genesis, until I left."

"Left? Or escaped?"

Stark shrugs and pretends to be weighing things in his hands as if to say, *A bit of column A and a bit of column B.* "I was very young. I was able to sneak out with a shipment of goods to another colony and jump ship before anyone could notice me. The skills I learned from them have allowed me to survive, but I left their philosophy behind."

"Skills and philosophy?" I ask.

Stark nods and stands up. I sit up straight in anticipation, wondering what he is going to do.

"There are several universal currencies that the world runs on. Most are known to us, but not all of them. Most people harness them through technology: electronics and machines like cars, radios, computers, reactors, cameras . . . but then there are some people born with the ability to use their bodies as conductors for these currencies. People like us can master them by studying and experiencing them in proximity."

"What would be an example of one of these currencies?" I ask.

"The most common currency or cosmic force that a wielder can use is energy. The universe is soaked with it, and if you're powerful enough, all energy can be a resource for you, until you hit your limit." Stark pulls out a tissue from a tissue box and places it on the desk in front of him. He then pulls out a brass lighter and pauses to take a deep breath. He opens the lighter and strikes it three times. It doesn't make a sound, and no sparks or flames are produced. He then holds his empty hand out over the tissue and snaps his fingers. There's a flash as sparks fly from his fingertips, and small flames jump from his hand to the tissue, setting it ablaze.

"The most basic way someone like me can use energy is to take energy from one place to another."

I stand up and step closer to the tissue. "So you took the thermal energy from your lighter that normally would have produced a flame right then and there, but instead you harnessed and released it through your hand."

Stark looks at me, a little surprised at how quickly I am able to explain what I just saw. "Yes, that is correct. Did you observe anything else?"

I look away from the burning tissue. "I noticed that when you used your lighter the flame didn't instantly come out of your fingers. Where did the energy go?"

Stark looks impressed and holds his hand over the flames. "Energy cannot be created or destroyed. We can't break physics, only manipulate it. So, whenever we do anything with energy or any of the other cosmic forces, our bodies are the conductors."

"You're saying the thermal energy is stored inside you? That sounds like that could be dangerous."

"Yes, and no. Energy is energy. When I stored the energy from the lighter inside my body, it became a form of potential energy, a cosmic currency ready to be used for generating heat, movement, light electricity, or even nuclear energy. Whatever you can think of and are capable of."

"So one could technically absorb a huge amount of energy and then release it all at once?"

Stark nods. "You can see how, in theory, an extremely powerful member of the Order could be very dangerous if they were to go rogue."

I scratch my head. "Can this cosmic currency be used for anything else?"

Stark nods. "The other cosmic forces."

"Which are?" I ask as Stark extinguishes the flame with his bare hands.

Stark holds up a hand and wiggles all five fingers. "There have only ever been five cosmic forces recorded to have been used throughout history. The most common being energy. The second most common, but still extremely rare, is the ability to manipulate matter."

"Matter?" I blurt out. "Oh, sorry, I didn't mean to interrupt."

Stark smiles and says, "It's all right. Then there is time. There hasn't been a single person able to manipulate time in ... a couple thousand years, I think. Then there is information, which can be best described as the records or rules the universe itself and its contents adhere to. And last, there is space."

I speak, still staring at the charred tissue. "And ... I'm guessing you can't do any demonstrations of any of those." I pick up the black and crumbling tissue. I notice that it is completely cool, no evidence of there recently being a fire apart from the charred remains.

"No, it is incredibly rare for a wielder to have the ability to wield anything other than energy, and it is even rarer for someone to be able to wield more than one cosmic force at a time. The number of people in recorded history to have achieved that can be counted with your fingers. And some of them are angels and architects."

My brows knit together. "Architects? Like gods?" I start to remember the original purpose of Stark's visit.

"Yes, biologically speaking, angels, gods, wielders, and "normal" people are all human. But a wielder is like a modern sapien compared to a neanderthal. The Homo Sapien is the dominant version of humanity, but wielders are actually considered Homo Genesis, and the angels and architects are Homo Aedifex."

"Wait a minute, we're talking about people with superpowers. Angels and gods? And somehow my best friend thinks I should get involved?"

Stark looks at me with an unsure expression. "He wanted me to see if you have the same abilities as I do. He says he has reason to believe that you do."

I try to hold back a laugh. "Sorry to disappoint you, but I've never started a fire by snapping my fingers, or turned mud into gold, or something like that."

"Maybe not, but Patrick has had suspicions about your true nature but lacks the tools I have to accurately detect it. He says engines you work on generate unnatural amounts of power, your electricity bill is the cheapest in the city despite your banks of computers, and he has told me you don't dress appropriately for winter."

"That's not exactly extraordinary." I start to laugh slightly.

Stark shakes his head. "Not for a trained Genesis knight, but it is pretty interesting for a normal human being."

I cross my arms. "So, he wants you to test me? Because of that? All of those things don't sound all that weird to me."

Stark shakes his head. "I'd make for a poor teacher. He wants you to help me investigate intelligence reports using data from his own network of spies and information painstakingly gained from some very awkward interviews with the Order's upper council members. He believes the way you 'see the world' could be integral. And that you'd build your skills out of necessity. People like us make for good enforcers."

"This just keeps escalating." I sit down again, wondering if I am even comprehending the situation properly.

"The reports show a strange connection between the Aeternus Empire and a cult of fanatics that worship the architects. Rumor is that an angel and a rogue knight named Darius Vaughn are the leaders. Patrick and I believe that they and the architects have been commanding their neophytes to commit terrible atrocities. Several small cities and developing countries have been razed by their attacks. Men, women, and children have been used for things like experiments and breeding."

"Gods and angels are manipulating people, like proactively? I can't imagine you'd get a very positive response if you said any of this in front of a camera. There are several dominant religions throughout the world, but they each share a common fear and respect for the architects and their angel lieutenants when they come among us," I say.

"You, Patrick, and I and a handful of his superiors know about this mission. We need proof, infallible proof, because anything less would make sharing our findings with the world suicide."

"So you're telling me that Patrick wants to bring me aboard and have me help you investigate cultists, angels, architects, and potentially people with superpowers, and see if it's true that basically gods are commiting crimes against humanity."

Stark nods. "Gods that the majority of society has a faith in that they will defend violently."

I let out a nervous laugh. "Can't forget that, but who knows, maybe that could be useful if we're desperate. So, tell me about this cult. What's their deity? An architect? A person? A possessed cat?"

Stark chuckles. "The memory of their old emperor. He managed to convince everyone he was a god, until one day the architects paid him a visit. And with everyone watching, they exposed him for what he truly was. Nothing compared to them. Strange since they were the ones who granted him power in the first place."

I frown. "So his mistake was proclaiming himself to be a god. If he had said, 'emperor of the world,' they wouldn't have batted an eye?"

Stark nods. "It certainly seems that way." Stark paces for a few moments while I process the information. "The Empire has served as a sort of forced draft into the architect's armies for thousands of years. Their society revolves around their gods, so for the most part, they serve with passionate devotion. They extract blind loyalty from the weakest to the strongest people in their population. They have no real order or government like we do. No true councils or elected senates. Just one or two avatars to act out the wills of gods, and if they fail, they suffer the wrath of their absolute power."

"Ah, right. I've never been much of a history buff. Never knew where to start," I say before gripping the tissue. "Wait, have other people intentionally or unintentionally called out the architects like this? Or was this emperor the last or only one?"

Stark scratches his head. "Uhhh, I don't know, but I'm not sure how knowing that could help us."

I hold the smoking tissue out in front of Stark. "Smoke and mirrors. I'm willing to bet any person in a godlike position is going to feel the need to do whatever it takes to convince lower-status creatures to believe they are absolute. It's a key element of any government. It's hard to enforce anything if no one believes you have the right or power to do so."

Stark blinks like his eyelids are malfunctioning. "Now I'm starting to struggle with following *your* train of thought. What are you saying?"

I crush the smoldering tissue in my hands. "I'm saying that if I were in a position of truly absolute power, I would never feel the need to prove my abilities. Because if I were truly a god, for one, divine intervention would never appear necessary, because when I intervene, no mortal creature would be able to perceive or resist my influence. And if I allowed them to, then the mere sight of me should be enough to shake them to their core."

Stark starts twirling his hair in between his fingers. "So you're saying we call out the architects?"

I shake my head and wave my arms around. "No, no, no! I'm saying we call them *all* out with the world to see it. We start with the cult, eliminate the threat they pose, and understand the relationship between them and their deities. If it's true that an angel is one of their leaders, we can call them out and expose them too. And then, when there is absolutely nothing left of their cult and the angel that leads them, we call out their deity. Leaving no hope for faith."

"And what, fight them?" Stark asks.

"Not us, necessarily, but the Order could help with some proof." I squint. "We show the world that these beings we call gods are using people as proxies to commit atrocities and that they care more about saving face than saving us. We take away their faith and show that they're not absolute. That believing in them is a bad idea."

Either I'm crazy or Stark is (or maybe we both are), because he's slowly nodding as if my half-baked plan makes sense. "We're going to need some strong allies if we're going to go toe to toe with these people. I can introduce you to some. At the very least, until we can reasonably ally with the Order."

He places a small paper note on my desk and writes down a few names and phone numbers. "This is a list of people I haven't recruited yet but fit the profile for potential assets. Cops fed up with the government, assassins, and former knights like me."

He slides the paper to me, which I place in my pocket. "This will probably take years," Stark says.

"I hope so, because right now I can't even light a tissue on fire." I toss the tissue remains into the trash.

Stark claps me on the shoulder. "We'll get you there in no time. Patrick was right about you though. I think this was less about testing your abilities and more about getting us to meet. Even with what he said about you, he obviously knows something more than what he's telling me. But your observational skills and quick ability to accept what I've told you shows I need only trust our friend." He pauses and looks into my eyes for a few awkward seconds.

"Everything all right?" I ask.

He shakes his head. "It's nothing. I thought your eyes changed colour." He shrugs. "I gotta say, for a guy who spends most of his time driving sports cars and babysitting, you adjusted to this really quickly."

I point at my forehead to indicate I have a large brain. "I watch a lot of cartoons and documentaries."

Stark puts his hands over his ears. "I'd rather you don't try to explain it to me. In my experience, when someone starts to explain their abnormal behaviour, they start to sound crazy."

I shrug. "You think I'm crazy?"

Stark throws his arms up in the air. "I don't know. You welcomed the idea of conspiring against cultists and gods faster than most people pick up their phones when they ring, so maybe you're crazy or maybe I am. Or maybe the world is, and we're both sane. But as far as I'm concerned, for whatever reason, you're the perfect person to be talking to about all this."

"Well thank god for Patrick." I sit back down at my desk.

Stark gives me a thumbs up as he gets back into his car. "I'm gonna stick to thanking Patrick for now if that's all right."

As his car rumbles to life and rolls away, I pause and suddenly remember he never told me what work he wanted me to do on his car. Oops, sometimes I wonder how I stay in business. I mean, after all, the closest thing I have to an assistant is a nine-practically-ten-year-old girl who just wants to take my car for a joy ride.

I sit at my desk for what feels like forever. Not because I'm necessarily struggling to process the insane conversation I just had but because I'm expecting myself to wake up or come to from spacing out as a result of my ADHD deciding my imagination should distract me too. Though I don't think I could've made up today's events—not without some premeditation at least.

I lock up the garage and head back inside. I see little Laura playing games on my old console in the living room—some old zombie game from the looks of it. I smile as she makes various noises of enthusiasm in response to what is onscreen, not unlike the zombies she's fighting. I head down the hall and downstairs into the basement, flipping the switch to illuminate my lounge. I pour myself a small glass of water, but just before I take a sip, my eyes fall on something that gives me an idea: my model train set.

Setting down the glass and flipping the switch in the wall to give it power, I turn the trains on with a remote and watch them move around the table. Placing my fingertips on the rails allows me to feel the electrical current, like I'm being zapped by static electricity whilst hearing a strange buzzing in my ears. I have seen people touch the rails before, so it's not a strange thing to do, but perhaps if I focus . . . Stark did say people like him learn through close study and proximity.

The rails are what give power to the trains, the middle rail to be specific. That's where the current can be felt. Without taking my hand off the track, I carefully pull the plug powering the whole set out of the wall.

Silence, all of the trains have stopped. Not what I expected, but I can't say I have ever powered an electrical appliance with my hands before. I lift my fingers from the track and look at my hand. It must be more of a conscious than subconscious act to wield energy. If people could mess around with this stuff without even thinking, that could potentially be dangerous, or at the very least humbling. Then again, Stark did say one's ability to use these powers is determined by their familiarity. So wouldn't that mean a firefighter would have one of the highest potentials to control fire, given the amount of exposure to open flames? Or perhaps an arsonist would be more likely to use their power to start fires rather than suppress them.

I put my fingers back on the rails. If that's the case, if I can just focus, then ,in theory, if I can remember the experience of what happened when I touched the rails when they were already powered . . . I try to recall how it felt when the powered tracks buzzed when they came in contact with my skin.

Bzzzzp! As I hoped, along with the buzzing sensation of touching the powered rails, I feel a kind of force coursing through my body and out my fingertips. The rails hum and my trains buzz to life. I watch in disbelief as the little trains race around without being plugged in. But after about ten seconds of watching my trains operate, I start to feel dizzy and take my hand off the track.

The ceiling lamp flickers as I fight the urge to collapse. I slump down into a nearby armchair and catch my breath. I can't help but think I feel like a burnt-out light bulb, which seems appropriate. Stark failed to mention what would happen if I overextended myself. I should probably ask him about it the next time I see him. If powering a model train set can knock me out, I wonder what would happen if I tried to do something significant.

Chapter 2

THE FLAME

I slump down next to Laura and fight the urge to fall asleep. I know I got a good night's sleep last night, and yet I feel like I could pass out. I feel like I've pulled two all-nighters in a row. I can barely focus on the game Laura is playing right in front of me.

"Hey, Uncle J, are you okay?"

I blink several times and try to play it off as if I were daydreaming. "Yeah, I'm fine, just a little spaced out. I'm not used to long chats, so I guess I have more to think about than usual."

She hasn't taken her eyes off the screen. "More to think about?"

I nod. "Uh-huh, yeah, I get distracted easily."

"Do you fall asleep easily? Because you look half-awake."

I feel my head fall forward and I jolt myself awake, sort of. "I guess I didn't have as much energy as I thought. I guess I'm gonna need extra rest tonight."

"Aww! Does that mean I have to go to bed early too?!"

I laugh and pat her on the head. "No, but you still have to go to bed. So when I wake up in the morning I better not find out you've been playing past midnight. I don't want to send a . . . a zombie to school."

She outstretches her arms and starts to make weird slobbery sounds, which I suppose are zombie sounds.

"Whatever you say, drooling dead. See you in the morning."

"I will eat your flesh!" she says.

I wave my finger back and forth. "You always struck me more as a pancake-loving zombie."

And just like that, the zombie plague is cured. I leave her to enjoy herself while I crash in my bed face-first. I fall asleep before I can even adjust the covers.

A cool breeze on my face makes me open an eye to see if I left a window open, but what I see makes both of my eyes snap open. From all directions, I can see nothing but stars. The sun looks unusually large, or perhaps close—my body is fully illuminated by it. I look down to see . . . nothing. As far as I can tell, I am standing on nothing and can see the infinite void of the cosmos beneath my feet. Fighting the urge to keel over from dizziness, I adjust my stance, and as I do so, I realize I am standing on some kind of ethereal glass platform that shimmers like water when I move.

A voice disrupts the silence of space. "I was wondering when you'd visit. You must finally be opening your mind."

I look around for the source of the sound, but I can't find it. As I move, the stars around me start to seemingly move as well. It doesn't make sense. Sound isn't a naturally occurring phenomena in space; there's no atmosphere to give me a voice. Then again, I shouldn't be here either.

"Who's there?" I shout. Even though I can hear my own voice, it doesn't travel very far. Almost as if I'm standing in a small closet that is soundproofed. No matter how much I raise my voice, it will never truly reach anyone.

"Oh, come now, you're in a position to be asking some very good questions. Your true identity is leaking out from behind the mask you've been wearing all these years."

The glass beneath my feet begins to crack. I take a single, tiny step forward to try and avoid it, but the glass suddenly shatters completely. I fall through and the stars slowly begin to move around me.

"If you don't adapt soon and land on your feet, your legacy will be that of destruction."

The stars begin to speed up, eventually moving so fast that my field of vision is filled completely with bright light.

"Don't you dare look down! You know how to stand! So stand!" The voice rings in my ears as the universe itself speeds past me in a flashing blur. Which way is down? Even relative to me, I have no idea what is going on. Everything starts to move far away and compresses into a single point of light. I close my eyes and put one foot forward and lower it as if I were stepping off the last step of some stairs.

Tap! My eyes jolt open, and I discover that not only am I standing on solid ground again, but my surroundings have completely changed. I am standing on a strange white surface. The sky is a violet colour dotted with wispy black clouds. I kneel down and touch the ground with my hand. It's paper!

"A blank canvas."

I spin around to face a black-robed figure wearing a strange metal mask. The metal looks to be bare steel with gold plating on it. The gold is shaped in a way to resemble the skull of some strange animal, like a bull or a deer. Despite the mask, they are also wearing a hood, further obscuring their identity. Their voice is metallic and unnatural, but it has a bass to it that makes the air and ground vibrate.

"You are a blank canvas, infinite potential for greatness or disaster. Everything is about to change, so before you start your journey into the cosmic stage, I must warn you. You are like a sheet of paper, so beware. A page completely saturated with ink may as well be blank. A being soaked with infinite knowledge will be transformed by the cosmic chaos into a living corpse. A vessel of pure madness. Right now, you think you know nothing, but if you come to know everything, you will forever be the most empty you've ever been."

I squint to try and make out the features of whoever is standing before me. "Be careful, and when the time is right, turn the page. Just beware the urge to make your own edits."

Thunder cracks and the black clouds blot out the purple sky. Black rain begins to fall down, staining the paper surface beneath my feet.

"This ink will be the first entry in your story." The masked figure begins to dissolve like ink dissipating underwater. "At least try to last a few chapters—you're the main character after all. And beware the author of your pain."

The rain intensifies and becomes so intense that my ability to see cannot overcome the thick black downpour. Thunder again rumbles in the distance, until a great flash of purple light fills my field of vision. I feel my body burn and disintegrate as it is struck by lightning. Then I am weightless.

"Aaaah!" I shout. *Thump!* I feel dizzy and my head is pounding from slamming it into my bedside table. Apparently I managed to jolt myself out of bed and crash onto the floor.

I place my right hand on my forehead. "I swear if that leaves a mark . . ." Wait! I take my hand off my face. My hand feels sore and dry, and the reason why is immediately clear. Tattooed on the back of my right hand is the roman numeral IX. The symbol is surrounded by a nonagon, and on my index finger is a ring, a plain black band made of some kind of metal.

Something doesn't feel right; my hand doesn't feel the same. I have a strange sense something is off, but now that I'm looking at my hand and focusing on it, it reminds me of when I had surgery on my left knee. To use it feels strangely unfamiliar, like it isn't my hand anymore, yet it obeys my commands just fine. The tattoo is a deep black but doesn't feel unnatural to the touch. The odd ring feels weightless and almost as if it's neither hot nor cold, like it doesn't possess the properties of weight or temperature. The more I look at it, the more it looks familiar though. Maybe I just forgot I had it. Patrick said he sometimes forgets he is wearing his wedding ring. My ADHD could certainly make me forget a simple accessory.

"I don't remember this." I close my hand into a fist, and suddenly everything feels normal. "Hmm, feels fine now."

"What does?" My body chills when Laura's voice pulls me back into reality.

"I had a weird dream, I think." I snap my fingers. "Ready for breakfast?" I ask, with the least awake and confident voice imaginable.

While she's eating her breakfast I put one of my black driving gloves on my right hand to cover up the tattoo. I don't know why, but it feels like the right thing to do at the moment.

I splash my face with cool water in the hallway bathroom. My eyes are bloodshot red and have very visible darkness beneath them. I soak my messy brown hair and readjust my rectangular glasses and take a deep breath.

We clamber into the BMW. Laura is much more graceful due to it being a low and small car.

"When are you gonna get with the times and get an electric?" she asks.

I put the key in the ignition, and just as I'm about to turn it, I say, "When they sound as good as this."

The car rumbles to life. The lope of the idle makes the walls vibrate, and Laura covers her ears.

"You're gonna drive this every day?!" she shouts.

I roll up the windows and smile as we pull out of the garage. "No, I just enjoy making your dad nervous."

The drive to school is uneventful, but I may or may not have decided to show Laura how fast my car is amongst the electrics. Turns out, it isn't. I lose to a white SUV mom-mobile. At first I thought that they were following us, but it turned out they were headed to the same school as us. But I told Laura my car still sounded better.

Her response is, "How can you be in your twenties and still be such an old man?"

Oh well, you can't convince everyone. We get to her school, where many of the teachers and moms glare at us for arriving in a noisy machine. I smirk and back into a parking space. I notice the white SUV pulling up to the guard shack and see the driver point their finger at the gate aggressively and shout something at the guard. After a second of silence, the gate opens, and the guard watches the vehicle pull in. As the gate lowers itself, the guard begins to stumble and wobble like their legs have gone weak or something.

"Hey! Let me know how you do today. If you do good, I'll make carbonara for dinner."

She points at me. "I was planning on flunking, but I suppose I can get an A."

I give her a corny thumbs up. "Sounds good to me! Or I'll just have to eat it all."

She sticks her tongue out at me and heads inside. As I head back to my car, I spot the white SUV from earlier, which had just parked. A shorter woman is with her kid. She is struggling to put a jacket on them.

I announce myself. "Hello!" The woman pauses and then pats the child on the head and tells them to get back into her car.

I put my hands up. "I come in peace. I raced you at the light earlier and you beat me, so I thought I'd say hi." I wave at the child who has now buckled themselves into their seat. When they see me waving they give a slight wave back but quickly stop and look away. Poor kid doesn't look happy. The look on their face is a look of terror.

"Everything all right?" I ask.

The woman faces me directly. "Yes, he's not feeling well, so we're just heading home. Can I help you?"

I feel my eyes widen uncontrollably for a second before

I regain my composure. I could've sworn her accent was . . . Imperial.

I try to speak. "Oh, no, I just—" but she opens her car's door.

"And I really should be going," she says. She starts backing up, forcing me to move aside and watch as she drives off.

I sigh and think out loud to myself. "I've met cacti less prickly than her." I mentally pat myself on the back for the good joke. I head back to the car and make a point to leave the parking lot as loudly as possible. Why? I'm not sure. I think it has something to do with the fact that some people are annoyed by something that I enjoy. Knowing that when I enjoy myself more, it only irritates them more—it's like icing on a cake made just for me. That, or I like disrupting the peace.

I rush (within the law of course) to the market to get everything I need for the carbonara. As I turn the car off, I notice a woman who looks just like the one that brushed me off at the school going inside. Admittedly it isn't too weird, but the kid she had with her is no longer at her side. I notice her car isn't too far from mine, and I casually walk past it and look inside without stopping. No child in there. Am I being paranoid? At least she didn't ditch her kid in the car during the summer.

I pull out my phone and message Patrick: *Your friend forgot to give me his number. I wanted to give him an estimate for how much my work will cost him.* Patrick has told me in the past not to be too obvious or leave a digital trail that clearly shows what he's up to, so texting him about his work as an agent is a bit of a no-no.

I start looking for the ingredients I need to make the carbonara. I have most of what I need except for the cheese and eggs. *Ding!* Just as I'm grabbing the eggs, I get Stark's number, and I immediately call him.

He answers pretty quickly. "Hello?"

I look around. "Hey! It's James Diarkis. We never discussed the work you want done on your car."

"Oh, that's fine. I mostly wanted to discuss the other matter."

I think for a moment, realizing I'm probably being watched. "Well, I'd like to resolve that matter. Want to chat over dinner tonight? I'm making carbonara."

"Are you all right?" he asks.

I pause, trying not to raise suspicion. "Uh, yeah, you're not the only customer that made a unique impression today. Just had a repeat encounter with someone from Laura's school. And it would appear our mutual friend was right about me. I could be being paranoid, but I'd say her accent was from across the pond."

"I'll be there in fifteen minutes," he says, and hangs up.

I look around and freeze, when I see her again. It's definitely the same woman from the school. A man comes up to her and starts chatting. She smiles and directs him to what he is looking for. Awfully friendly for someone who nearly ran me over when I tried to say hi.

I pretend to be looking for something down the aisle the man went down. When I turn a corner, I see him talking to another man. Strange. If he asked her where the store carried something, why would his first action be to go and talk to someone? I grab some grape sodas off the shelf and then hurry to the checkout area. *I hate being paranoid.*

As I leave the store and get into my car, I notice the woman and the two men exit the store at the exact same time. I make a mental note. She appears to be about thirty years old, Asian, pale, short, with frizzy black hair. The two men look identical. Both are tall, with short, neat, dark brown hair and tan, olive skin.

I wait until they get into their cars. She gets into her white electric Ford SUV, and the two men get into a black Mercedes.

I start my car and calmly leave the parking lot. I drive normally until I reach a light turning red, and I floor it. The tires squeal and the engine roars. The exhaust makes a loud, gunshot-like bang sound as fire shoots out the back. I blast through the intersection before the traffic with actual right of way can even make it halfway through, looking in my mirror to see that, sure enough, the white Ford and black Mercedes got stuck at the light. They slam on their brakes like they were trying to cross as fast as possible but couldn't make it.

I keep checking my mirrors the whole way home. As I arrive I realize that I should probably let Patrick know what's going on and that I think I'm being followed. I don't know what I've gotten into, but I'm starting to think being a part of it is not my choice. Something about today is continuously giving me feelings of déjà vu, like everything I've learned and experienced so far are things I've experienced in the past. This would normally explain why it comes so naturally to me, but what perplexes me most is how calm I am, like experience is guiding my actions rather than instinct. And yet all of this is very unfamiliar to me, not to mention anxiety inducing.

Patrick tells me he'll be over soon. Once I'm home, I pull out everything and leave a few eggs out to warm to room temperature. I realize I need to make a choice: Is Laura safer at school, or should I go get her?

I stand staring at the three eggs in silence before I pound my hand on the counter. "Dammit." I grab the keys to the yellow Nissan Skyline and rush out of there.

The windows shake so violently they could shatter. The engine screams and the turbo is so loud it sounds like a plane taking off.

I disregard most traffic rules as I race to the school. When I get there and pull her out early, she asks what's going on. "Not 100 percent sure, but while we wait to find out, you're gonna cook with me. Passing the time until your dad gets back," I say.

"You're freaking me out a little," she says.

We speed away. "Don't worry. I'm not that bad of a cook."

She grips the door handle. "Not what I meant."

I look at her. "I know, I'm sorry."

When we get back to the house, I close and lock all the doors. I keep her busy by asking her to get the pasta started while I start whisking the eggs with some cheese and pepper.

We make the food in awkward silence while I wait for Stark or Patrick to arrive. Eventually, a knock at the front door breaks the silence but doesn't help with the tension.

A voice calls out from behind the front door. "It's Stark! Patrick told me he is on his way." I open the door and let him in quickly.

Once the door is closed behind him, I waste no time in bombarding him with questions. "You got any info on the cult members? Like appearance and names?"

He pulls out his phone. "Yeah, any info you can give me will help me check to verify your suspicions," he says.

I nod and start picturing the people I saw. "I want to be wrong, but I'm pretty paranoid these days I guess, and today I just had a bad feeling."

"No worries. It's better to be safe than sorry. And with everything going on, you only get to be sorry once."

I scratch my head. "The most memorable person was the woman. Mid-twenties to early thirties, Asian, short, pale, freckly skin, frizzy black hair."

Stark's brows knit together. "Wait a minute, are you sure?" he asks.

I nod. "Those are all the details I can remember."

Stark shows me a picture to which I nod in confirmation that the person in the picture is the same woman I saw at the school and the store. "Her name is Lana Smirnov. She is a full-fledged knight of the Genesis Order, a lieutenant in fact. And it looks like the commander has her first in line for the next captaincy position. And she's a part-time professor at the Genesis Academy."

"So a superpowered teacher basically," I say.

Stark shrugs. "A superpowered teacher that you suspect is following you. With no known connection to the cult," Stark adds.

I shrug. "She was with two big guys. Tall, both dirty blonde, olive skin, I suppose."

Stark glances up at me, looking surprised. "So, this is interesting. Was she obviously familiar with these two men?"

"Yes, it looked that way." Stark puts his phone away. "The Olsen twins are the two guys you saw, known enforcers of the cult. Smirnov, however, has no known ties to the cult. She wasn't even on our radar."

"I got the slight impression she was in charge." I peek around the corner to check and see how Laura is doing with the cooking.

Stark ponders for a moment. "That's not good. She's pretty influential, and she wasn't even on our radar as a suspected member. It's bad that they're following you. I didn't think they'd peg you as a target just for talking to me. Patrick thought it would be safe since you run a business out of your house, make it look like I'm a customer."

I look back at him. "So why infiltrate the knights? For power? Influence? What does the cult's activities consist of?"

Stark leans against the wall. "Killing people. Killing as many people as possible. And whenever their numbers seem to dwindle, they start abducting the children of powerful people. Knights and other wielders of powers similar to mine and yours."

I cross my arms. "To what end? To sow chaos? Do they have enemies?"

He shrugs. "I don't know. As far as we know, they kill just for the sake of it. Their actions never seem to follow a pattern that yields any result besides casualties on both sides. Yet they never stop."

I shake my head. "No, I don't think that's right. There has to be a reason. We are dealing with fanatics and the gods that they worship. There must be a reason. Death could be more than just an end, but also a means."

A new voice joins the chat. "You're right." Stark and I jump and face the new voice. It's Patrick. "Our two priorities are to break the endless cycle of bloodshed and to determine the reason why so much death is necessary."

"They could be following the designs of the architects without knowing the end goal … You think the cult would know the motivations of their masters?" Stark asks.

Patrick takes a deep breath. "I doubt it. Deities aren't historically known for being up front about their intentions. For the longest time, it was never clear if prayer actually did anything or if anyone was listening. Whenever a prayer was answered, they'd do it in a way where their influence wasn't clear."

Stark starts to pace. "Maybe we can ask them."

Patrick watches his friend walk back and forth.

"But if they don't know …" I start to say, "then we'll have to find a way to ask their masters, the one true primary source."

"Hey, Dad! You here for dinner?" We all turn to face Laura, proudly holding a messy bowl of steamy, cheesy-looking pasta. She finished it without me, not bad. She holds it up to show her father, beaming with pride.

Ziiing! Horror paralyzes Stark, Patrick, and I as a hole appears in Laura's chest. "Dad?"

Patrick moves first, followed quickly by me. He grabs her in his arms and pulls her into the other room. The bowl of pasta falls to the floor, shattering and splattering everywhere. I shut off the lights as quickly as I can.

"James!" Stark whispers. I look at him through the darkness. He is pulling one of my display katanas off the wall. I notice he is holding some kind of gun in his left hand and a sheathed sword in the other.

He passes my katana to me. "Do you have any guns?" I shake my head. "Well, be very careful. These people can be dangerous even when you're out of arm's reach. So don't hesitate."

I draw the sword slowly and inspect the blade. I've had it for a while, but I haven't cleaned it or sharpened it in a couple years.

There are a few spots on the blade that could be rust, and the edge barely feels sharp enough to cut paper. It won't be very optimal for fighting.

Crash! The front door bursts and breaks apart into tiny splintered fragments. Two tall figures enter the room. The Olsen twins. One is holding a large hammer with spikes on it and the other a large axe.

I keep as quiet and still as possible. Stark's gun, which looks like a big, bulky six-shooter revolver glints slightly in the dark with a gold sheen.

Patrick is holding a shivering Laura, whose shirt has been soaked completely with blood. Her face is contorted in pain and shock. It hurts to see her so panicked and confused. Patrick's expression looks just as helpless, the fatality of her wound being impossible to ignore.

I grip the hilt of my sword. Something isn't right. Where's the woman?

Zing! This time I see it, or at least I am facing in the right direction to see it just as it is too late. A bright, white light blinds me, and the next thing I see is Patrick bleeding from the same spot in his chest as Laura. The woman had snuck up on us and shot a bolt of light at him with her finger.

"No!" Stark fires his gun at her, and the flash lights up the room. I blink, wait . . . she's gone! In the instant the gun was fired, she disappeared.

Creak! I turn to the right but not fast enough, at the mercy of the blurred attack of the assassin. Luckily, Stark is faster. Somehow, he manages to draw his sword and block the attack faster than I can even turn my head.

Sparks fly as his sword clashes with a large hammer. I check Patrick and Laura. She's whimpering, and he's holding her, begging her to stay with us. "It's okay, Dad . . . it's okay . . . it's . . ." She gasps one final time and lets out a slow exhale. Her body goes limp. He gets up and reaches for something on his belt.

Bong! The twin with the hammer slams the large weapon in Patrick's chest and sends him careening across the room, crashing into the marble counter. The impact of the hammer with his body lets out a ring like a large tower bell.

"Ding-dong!" the twin says. Witnessing this causes something to wash over me. My thoughts stop for a moment to become more simple. My body shakes as if itching to do something. I can feel the shock setting into my core.

Something tells me I need to move. I grip my decorative sword and stand up as quickly as I can. And faster than I can blink, the large axe clashes with my sword. It's heavy and huge, bigger than my torso. Hilariously, I look even more visibly surprised than he does at the fact that my relatively tiny sword stopped his huge axe.

"Really?" he says. He changes the positioning of his hands on the hilt and pushes the blade of my sword out of the way and raises his axe upward.

I try to move to the right, but my body creaks and groans as I try to move quicker than I actually can. I have no choice but to try to block the attack.

He brings his axe down hard, and it cuts right through my sword, and if it weren't for the fact that I had stepped backward instinctively, I probably would've been cut in half or lost an arm.

"Huargh!" he shouts. The swing creates a blast of what feels like a small explosion of air, which knocks me back.

"No one told me the gearhead knew how to fight!" he says. The woman strikes Stark's chest with the palm of her hand. He gets knocked back but doesn't hit a wall or fall over. He recovers with a tiny hop and regains his footing.

"Don't underestimate my friends. It could be fatal!" Stark shouts.

I wince. "Yeah, to us perhaps," I say, and I spit out some blood.

Laura's body, which had been sitting up, falls over on its side. I try to sit up, and I feel a huge pain across my chest. I place my left hand on my body and feel my shirt being soaked with warm blood. I start to feel more and more dizzy. Looks like that dodge didn't save my life. It just made it a few minutes longer.

I look to the left and see Patrick sitting there, completely still, with dead, glassy eyes fixed on the corpse of his daughter. The tears on his face are still running. I wasn't even looking when he passed. He spent his final moments watching his daughter die, and then dying himself without being able to hold her. Something in me snaps. My mind empties itself completely, and my body shudders with cold rage.

I clench my right hand and feel my sword still there. The blade is snapped in half, but I manage to not drop it. Stark roars, charges at the woman, and tackles her, but before they hit the ground, the two disappear. In the split second they vanish, the walls around us explode in a loud boom that makes my ears ring as my body gets tossed like a grain of dust in a hurricane. I roll in the dirt and stop half-buried under some rubble and wood, not quite lying down. Instead I'm being propped up vertically.

My vision dimming with every second, I am still able to realize the axe wielder is hanging over me, raising his weapon. It becomes apparent that during the blast I lost my glasses, which obviously makes it harder to see clearly. I realize something as I clench my hands into fists. Our eyes meet. I'm pinned, but I may as well be standing up, so reaching him won't be hard.

I spit more blood in his direction. "You're not much of an executioner if you need to swing more than once." He stops and opens his mouth to say something, but I don't let him. I grip the hilt of my sword and run what remains of my blade through his neck. He gasps and exhales loudly, the air leaving his body almost as quickly as his life. I twist the blade around in his throat and whisper, "Ding-dong bitch. You're dead." And just as I do this, several armed men with assault rifles pour into what used to be my living room. My vision goes black. The last thing I hear is the remaining Olsen twin with the hammer shouting, "Garret!"

CHAPTER 3
THE FORGE

"Finally, it's about time you woke up."

I open my eyes. My arm is still outstretched with my sword in hand. The blade is no longer running through Garret's throat. Now it's stuck inside the neck of the hooded mask-wearing figure from earlier.

"We don't have much time, so let's get to work." His mask cracks and falls apart, and for a split second I make out parts of a face. Brown hair, purple eyes, pale skin, and a messy overgrown beard. It looks familiar, but not like anyone I know.

Before I can think more about it, his throat starts to ooze a molten liquid, like fiery hot metal. His body shudders and then explodes into a tsunami of the reddish-orange molten material. I brace myself, waiting to be burned alive. But as it passes over my body, it feels like warm bathwater. I drop my sword into it to test the heat. I watch it melt and evaporate instantly, like a drop of water on a hot pan.

The voice of the mask wearer echoes from the sky. "Relax and just keep an open mind. Be creative and resourceful."

I look around. This time the pages I was previously standing on are in the sky, and beneath my feet appears to be some kind of mirror. When I look up at the paper in the sky, I can see that they have words on them, but they're inverted. Looking down at their reflection in the mirror makes them more readable, but the words don't form any kind of sentence structure or obvious messages. I just see things like, Bear Witness, Ninth Chapter, Unstoppable, Horseman...

I look around and, as far as I can tell, it stretches infinitely beyond the horizon. I look at my reflection before it becomes obscured by the liquid metal.

"It isn't going to cool. It's actually going to get hotter." I kneel down and realize that when I put my hand near the liquid, it reacts strangely. As I try to touch the liquid, it moves away from me and starts to get hotter, like he said. But what is also strange is that the flames bursting from the bubbling lava seem to move in slow motion when my hand gets near them. I notice the ring and tattoo on my right hand are gone.

"Missing something? Find it."

I stand up and look around. "What is going on? Why am I here?" I shout.

"This is your one chance to survive. Being ordinary is no longer an option, but you can be something else. Though, if you act too slowly, you'll go mad. Remember."

"Go mad?" I ask. My ankles, wrists, and neck all begin to feel very heavy. Gold chains appear out of nowhere, wrapping themselves around my limbs and body, seemingly trying to pull me into the ground underneath the molten metal. "I suggest you find what you are looking for. Otherwise, the threat you pose out there will warrant you a cell in Hell." I frantically look around for anything. And then I notice it. As the metal gets hotter and brighter, my chains pull harder and harder.

I get down on both knees and place my right hand on the ground. The metal retreats from me. I close my eyes and think back to the feeling I had when I turned on my model trains. The feeling of the energy in my body, but also the energy I felt around me. I focus as best I can on the warmth of the lava as the chains pull harder and harder. The mirror beneath me begins to crack, but I ignore it to the best of my ability.

There! I can feel it, the heat of the metal. I can feel other forces affecting it, but if I can tell it to cool, they shouldn't matter, or at the very least, I'll be able to touch it. I focus on the heat of the metal. I can feel beads of sweat forming all over my body as I truly begin to feel the inferno of lava around me.

The pain makes me want to tense up and scream in pain, but instead I imagine the heat entering my body as I breathe in, and imagine it leaving as I breathe out. After nine breaths, the heat is gone, and the chains are no longer pulling on my limbs. Some, but not all, of the golden chains wither away like dead flowers in a time lapse. The lava turns black and wraps itself around my right index finger, cooling and becoming the same ring I was looking for. The tattoo is back too, but at first it looks like solid metal burned into my skin before returning to its black ink appearance and texture.

"Good, you did it. You've remembered your ability to use it. Remember, you have power, but your strength is determined by your resourcefulness. You have the power of the universe, but you're still bottlenecked by your mind."

I can feel the energy from all the molten metal inside my body, waiting to be used for anything, like a charged-up battery. I cross my arms and place my hands on opposite wrists over the cuffs connected to the chains that were pulling me down moments ago. I focus and compel the chains to melt away with the heat inside me.

The disembodied voice returns. "Those chains are a precaution against those with great potential to be powerful, and potential to be a threat. They can be made heavy enough to make even gods as restrained as humans, keeping them from ever knowing their true power. The fact that you can melt them so easily means you could be . . . well, at least that means you won't fall under Hell's jurisdiction."

"A threat to what?" I ask.

The voice continues. "The powers that be, the very object of your quest and the masters of the murderers that killed your friend and his child."

The shock of witnessing their deaths floods back into my body. The ground beneath me starts to crack and creak. "You have managed to keep madness at bay, but not forever."

"That's okay, maybe I'll find a use for it." I tense my right arm and close my hand but not quite all the way. The ring starts glowing crimson, and my veins start glowing as red light pulses through them. It looks a lot like electricity coursing through my body, with my veins acting as wires.

I focus on the feeling of the pulsing and of the energy inside me. I raise my hand skyward and begin to strain my body as much as possible as I compel all of it to obey my commands. I feel it bracing inside me, ready for release. I bring my hand down fast, like I'm swinging a sword downward to execute someone.

The light that follows is so blinding it goes straight through my eyelids. The images I see will haunt me for eternity. I see myself wearing smoking black robes, holding an unusual black sword with a zigzag-shaped blade. My face is pale and covered in burn scars. It looks as if my entire body has been drained of blood, making my skin almost look translucent. Then I'm standing behind a woman with reddish-auburn hair. She's wearing a long green coat with an *X* on the back, and she's holding a katana, which appears to have a blade made of emerald or a dark-green glass. Green flames surround her. Then I see a blue hand holding a gold dagger. The next few images flash by quickly. A landscape covered in charred corpses; glowing golden threads sprawling across the cosmos snapped in pieces; and a dark throne with a woman sitting on it. Her face is obscured, but I can make out her jet-black hair. Her face is blurry, but her eyes glow gold in the dark. And then a flash of purple light, and I feel myself standing in the world again.

The air burns around me, and I start to hear things crash and people scream as they're set on fire. I slowly open my eyes and look around. I'm back at my house.

Or what's left of it. The only things left standing are the garage and the front door. *Clump!* Okay, it just fell over. I take a step and look down. The ground is black and composed of a fine gray and black dust, like it's been seasoned with very fine pepper. I look at my right hand and open it. My sword is gone, and the glove is slightly torn up, but it is still intact.

"Gregor, you coward! Help us! Come back!"

My body tenses, and my eyes lock onto some kind of soldier lying on the ground. He is covered in several third-degree burns with his flesh sizzling like meat just thrown onto a grill. I look around and realize there are corpses everywhere. There are police cars outside that look like they've been half-melted. Others look like a giant has stepped on them. The electrical poles and lines are down and on the ground. I notice one other soldier that is alive and sort of moving.

I kneel down next to the man shouting for help. His black, SWAT-style armour is covered in blood and gore, but the golden trimmings and fastenings are somehow untouched. The Empire apparently can spare the expense to style their foot soldiers. "Tell me what happened here," I say.

He looks at me with a puzzled look. "What are you talking about? What happened here is that you—"

"Not that, you idiot. You think I can't figure that out by looking around? I'm talking about your mission, your purpose. What brought you here? I want to know everything."

"After what you did? I'm not telling you anything." He spits.

I hover my hand over his face. "Oh you definitely will. That is, if you want to change what *I'm* going to do to *you.*"

•   •   •

*C*RASH! Both Lana and Stark freeze for a moment. What was that huge release of thermal energy just now? It felt like it had come from James's house. Whatever it was, there's nothing to sense now.

Smirnov twirls a sword between her fingers. "Distracted? Aw, did you really get *that* attached to your acolyte already? Why? He didn't seem that special."

Stark lunges and thrusts his sword at her. She tries to parry, but he counters and their blades lock. Sparks fly where the sharp edges meet.

"He was a friend, not a drone like one of yours."

She smirks and brushes him aside with a swing of her sword. Stark's sword rings loudly as he jams it into the ground to stop the knockback from pushing him too far away.

She rests her other hand on the hilt of her offhand sword, which has been sheathed this whole time. "You're unbearably ignorant. Why didn't you become a knight? You'd fit right in."

"You cultists never look below the surface. Their code of ethics doesn't gel with me."

"Why not? I figured they'd love the goody-two-shoes type."

Instead of speaking, Stark attacks. For a moment, he disappears from Smirnov's field of view. She twirls her sword around her body and barely stops Stark's sword from cutting off her left leg. The cold steel still manages to slash her upper inner thigh.

Click. Her heart skips a beat, and she grabs her second sword. With a deafening bang, Stark fires his gun in his second hand, but to no avail. The blade stops the bullet from going through the middle of her back. It ricochets off into the ground and blows apart an unfortunate nearby tree. Angrily, she slashes both swords at him, but they don't reach him.

She sighs, having underestimated her opponent. She stands tall and serious with both her katana and her shorter wakizashi ready. "I stand corrected," she says as she turns to face him.

He's nowhere to be seen, but she can hear his voice. "You don't deserve to be standing at all, lieutenant." Her eyes widen as she sees her reflection get closer and closer. She puts both swords up to block the attack, but it doesn't matter. Their blades clash, and the sound of a distant gunshot rings in her ears. Her body goes into shock as a bullet passes through it.

He whispers in her ear. "You have the rank. I have the power. Only difference is, I don't have a rank to spoil how strong I am."

She grits her teeth and wobbles, fighting the urge to fall to one knee. "I told you . . ." he says. He presses the blade of his sword to her throat. "Underestimating us would be a fatal mistake."

In that moment, all colour disappears from their vision. The wind stops and all sound is muted completely. They both freeze. It's someone's cosmic presence. Stark searches their surroundings for the source of the power. It's so immense that the origin point is difficult to locate, like trying to tread water in a raging sea with waves hitting you from all directions. To make things more difficult, the aura is so overwhelming it starts to make Stark and Smirnov hallucinate. They start seeing people and fire; the sky flickers a purple colour, and stars begin to pop like fireworks. Whoever it is that they're near, they're so powerful, their very presence is chipping away at their sanity.

Smirnov doesn't hesitate, and she flees. Her body flickers into a blur and vanishes into the distance. Stark sheathes his sword and breathes as calmly as possible, the world still swirling around him like physics had been broken. He closes his eyes and focuses on slow, calm thoughts as best he can. The chaotic madness overwhelming his senses must have a source. What point is there in running? He doesn't know whose power this is or where they are. If he ran, there's a chance he could end up closer to whoever it is rather than farther away. So, he gets down and crosses his legs, with his sword resting in his lap, and he begins to meditate.

Desperately blocking out the outside world. Even with his eyes closed, his remaining four senses try their best to break his calm.

Screams, the roars of incomprehensible creatures, the smell of a thousand rotting corpses, the feeling of blood spattering on his face, something slick slithering up his arm, and the taste of something spoiled in his mouth. His mind feels more and more fragile as the seconds go on. Until finally, it all stops. He hears a sonic boom, and a blast of wind knocks him over and flips over several cars around him.

He opens his eyes, and everything is back to normal. The night sky is the same. There's nothing in his mouth or anything on his body. He takes in a deep breath and focuses for a moment.

"You really did flee, Lieutenant Smirnov." Stark stands up and heads back to James's house. There isn't much left. The cars are damaged; the BMW must've been completely obliterated. Or perhaps the cultists looted it, because it simply is nowhere to be seen. The Audi was melted to the ground, and the Skyline was blackened from the fire. Patrick's and Laura's corpses are nowhere to be seen; neither is James's. There is nothing but a giant, blood-caked crater and a few bodies. Wait a minute. Bodies?

He lands in the center, his eyes darting from one body to the next. "What happened here, ya bunch of cultist shits?" Stark inspects the four dead bodies scattered along the edges of the crater. Three of them look like Imperial special ops officers, but they are wearing armour with Atlas's insignia on them, a red planet with a forked bolt of lightning going through it. And the fourth body is even more perplexing.

Stark immediately recognizes it to be one of the twins. "Garret Olsen, the executioner. Even you couldn't escape the guillotine, could you?" He kneels down next to the body. There is an opening on the left side of his throat and one on the other. Someone managed to stab him before whatever happened here. Two holes in his throat are a brutal way to kill him, but not an easy way either. He frowns and looks around for the bodies of his friends.

"Strange that these are the only bodies left," he says out loud. There were other odd things he observed, but he had seen enough, and with the sounds of sirens getting closer, he had no choice but to leave.

• • •

*O*ne *Year Later.*

His old Mustang rumbles to life. Stark has just received a tip about a meeting where cultists will be giving speeches to their latest recruits, and that anyone who gets in will get to start their initiation at the penthouse suite of the Imperius Hotel downtown. *I suppose holding a cult meeting at the Imperial embassy would've been too obvious.* The hope is that a certain Professor/Lieutenant Smirnov will be there. Stark has been hunting her for months. She's unreachable within the temple at the capitol and untrackable when she leaves, though getting close enough to get her scent is extremely risky.

To make matters worse, whenever Stark has a lead on her or other cult members, they get assassinated or terrorized by a group of anonymous attackers that appeared out of nowhere six months ago. No official claim of responsibility, no declaration of an agenda ... just a series of assassinations and attacks on people that have and haven't already been blacklisted for cult activities.

The word is several former officers will also be there, whether it's police, government officials, or agents of intelligence bureaus— all of them being traitors of Stark's country: Ares. Stark has only been able to get a few of their names, and their involvement is a little concerning. The only things he could find on the officers were (depending on the officer) their resignation or termination for actively fighting the cult and their influence. Apparently their superiors didn't like them taking such independent actions whilst on their payroll. It's difficult to comprehend their presence there. Why would they work for them? Why would the cult allow them to be there? Whatever the reason, Stark had a funny feeling it would all become clear.

"All right Captain-to-Be Smirnov, let's knock you down a peg. Where do you go to party?" Stark pulls out of his garage. If she turns out to be there, the goal will be to neutralize any powerful cultists, arrest Smirnov, and find out what the cult's ulterior motive is . . . and then execute her. Not in the name of justice. Stark isn't delusional enough to confuse vengeance with justice, but he doesn't expect it to feel wrong when he finally does it. Another benefit will be that she won't become a captain of the Genesis knights. At first, when he fought her, he couldn't help but wonder why she seemed so weak. Stark knew his power was around the level of a lieutenant or a third officer in command. A captain's power is usually monstrous. That said, in hindsight, she always seemed to have an answer for his attacks. And when he finally did manage to wound her, it wasn't because he was better . . . it's because her guard was down. Stark doubts she will be as lax the next time they meet. But all the same, her power was still an advanced lieutenant's at best, so either she was really holding back, or she has friends in high places giving her a boost.

The other presence he felt, though, that power exceeded a captain's, easily—even a captain of the Order of Genesis, someone who needs to be a master of *at least* two cosmic forces to even be considered for the position. It is not customarily an individual capable of driving someone as strong as Stark mad just by being near them. That's the sort of thing Grand Master Koenig of Genesis Squad One would do, but it wasn't him. Was it an angel nearby? Perhaps providing support to his followers? Stark may never know. The presence was so unfamiliar and chaotic he could barely tell up from down.

Stark's informant, Marcus, is on the industrial side of town. He owns and operates a small railyard, so he'll be meeting him there. He's not one of his oldest and most trusted informants, but he has been the most fruitful. Stark met him soon after people all over the world began protesting the attacks. Still, governments did nothing. Stark has always kept him at arm's length because Marcus approached him first. In Stark's experience, he usually has to persuade someone to become an informant. They have never sought him out and volunteered before. Stark kept expecting something to go wrong or to fall into some trap, but he has always come through.

Stark's Mustang is a little out of place when he reaches Marcus' office. But not in the way you'd expect. Everyone that works here is driving some kind of really expensive sports car. Obviously, Marcus and his employees didn't pay for these with their railroad money, but whenever he thinks about bringing it up, he decides to drop it. One less thing to lie to the cops about.

Marcus Blackwell comes out from his mobile office to greet him, his huge arms and shoulders nearly bursting out from under his gray, collared shirt as he holds open the door for Leonidas. "Evening, Stark. Glad to see you're doing well." They shake hands and take their seats across from each other at his desk.

"Not as well as you," Stark says. Marcus smiles and begins to trim his beard using a small handheld mirror with Princess written on the top in pink.

"I didn't know you were royalty, Blackwell," Stark says.

Marcus smiles. "It was a gift from my daughter. She heard me say I wanted to get a mirror for my office here at work, so she gave me her favourite one on my birthday. I use it every day, not because I care about how I look but because of how happy she would be if she saw me using it."

He pulls out a bottle of wine from one of his desk drawers and gestures to the cars outside. "I'll admit my boss is a bit generous, but he calls it job security. He says that if he can spare enough money to keep me happy, he can spend just as much if not more on making my life hell."

Stark leans back and crosses his legs. "An interesting way of doing this; he sounds like an interesting guy. Is he your railroad boss, or is he your 'boss' boss?"

"The latter; he's everybody's boss. He likes trains and trucks, though; keeps asking me to commission crazy things for him. It's always a little scary telling him no."

Stark raises his eyebrows. "Really? Well I'd love to meet him."

Marcus pours them both a couple small glasses of deep, dark red wine. "You will. Tonight." Marcus spins around in his chair and stops to pull something out of the safe in his wall.

"You oughta put a painting over that," Stark says, holding up his drink.

"I don't know. I've considered it, but it feels like it would be obvious. Like a weird candle next to a bookcase full of books you never use. Might as well say, 'pick up candle for access into my monster lab,' or something more macabre." Marcus gulps a third of his glass, probably without even tasting it.

"What?" Stark asks, but his only reply is Marcus handing him a pair of white gloves and some cufflinks.

"What's this?" he asks, examining the items.

Marcus points at the gloves. "Those are so that you don't have to worry about fingerprints." He then points to the cufflinks. "And those are to help my boss and his men identify you as a friend if anything goes down. When the bouncer asks for your name, the boss wants you to say 'singular,' and they should let you in."

Stark turns the cufflinks over in his hands. They're gold and simple in design, a nonagon with the letters P.R. engraved on them.

"P.R.?" he asks.

Marcus's hands fall to his sides. "I don't know man. He just told me you'd get it. I didn't ask. But he did say to get a copy of the guest list. The physical copy will be in the underground parking garage."

Stark thinks about possible codes, locations, events, or even names it could be an abbreviation for. "I've always gotta apologize to you, Blackwell. You're always sitting on a lot of useful information. I hate to doubt someone who volunteers to help, but you know how it is with all these attacks," Stark says, sighing through his words.

Marcus shrugs. "Well, out of respect, I should at the very least let you know the man I work for is responsible for a lot of the anti-Imperial crap that's been going on lately. I didn't think that would bother you, though."

"What are his objectives tonight?"

Stark's question makes Marcus bluster like a horse. He scratches his pristine beard. "I don't know, but with all the instructions he's given me, meeting you has definitely got to be one of them. I guess he wants to make a good first impression."

"Sounds like a trap and a plan, par for the course at this rate." Stark rises from his chair. "Anything else?"

Marcus shakes his head. "Be safe, especially if you're going through downtown. Protestors are out today, and the cops are too. Things are getting stirred up. Try not to be there when bullets start flying. You don't want to become another statistic for the politicians to debate about whilst they pretend to care."

With one small sip of wine, he stands up from his seat. "I'll be all right, thanks."

They shake hands, and Stark returns to his car, which he plans on parking at the agency building Patrick's office was based at. Now it's Stark's headquarters. When he gets there, he makes sure he has everything he needs before departing. "Sorry, old girl, you'd be the life of the party. But showing up to a shindig like this one in a government car registered to ol' Patrick's branch would be what most undercover officers call . . . a bad idea." He pats the roof of the vehicle and takes a deep breath, hoping tonight will be different than the rest.

Stark gets dressed in a baby-blue collar shirt with a black tie and athletic pants made to look smart. When he puts the cufflinks on, he feels an odd sensation, as if someone powerful had made them, not an expensive smith somewhere in the city. Typically, if a cosmic wielder is strong and also sloppy enough, they can leave behind a trail of influence. Stark doesn't know anyone that is particularly powerful, and yet somehow it feels familiar. It suspiciously feels like that same enormous presence he felt the night he fought Lana Smirnov.

"Why do I have this bad feeling . . . that I'm walking into a trap?" Stark asks himself out loud. He begins his walk to the Imperius Hotel, a place that is so expensive and exclusive that not only do you need a big check but also a good name to write on that check to stay there.

Marcus was right about the unrest in the city. As Stark makes his way deeper into the city, the setting sun turns the sky orange, and the air becomes filled with chanting and whistling.

Today's protest was against the arrest and scheduled execution of a former police officer who had killed no fewer than six confirmed cultists. These six were members of a ten-man group of hunters who abducted and killed a hundred people when they took a neighbourhood hostage to conduct genetic experiments on, condemning numerous people, adults and children alike, to die.

The officer went into their homes and shot them dead . . . no warning or due process. And though one might think that would be the core of the case against him, instead he has been labelled a villain who executed them for their religion. That didn't go over very well with the public, given that the Empire has been at odds with Ares for centuries. The last open war was a few hundred years ago, but petty skirmishes and terror attacks from both sides have allowed both dominant Martian countries to escape peace indefinitely. It's either cold war or open war.

About forty civilians are standing at the bottom of the steps into the capitol building, where hundreds of heavily armed guards with all sorts of lethal weapons are stationed. Though, there are some officers amongst the people, and they are simply armed with shields. Thankfully, no one is antagonizing anyone … yet.

Stark tries to make his way past without getting caught up in it. But he can see a fight starting to break out before it has even started, between none of the protestors, a young woman in sweatpants and a loose sweater with her university's ball team on it, and a disgruntled cop.

"Save the one good cop!" she shouts, amongst other things. "Those who protect and serve don't get what they deserve!" The protestors call the officers on duty animals and cultists for standing guard for the officer's execution. The officer starts stepping up to her and getting into her space. She and a few others take notice and start to tell them to get back. He pushes harder until finally someone pushes on his shield, which he barely feels, but it is exactly what he wanted. A man with glasses tries to step in but is met with a shield getting slammed into his body.

Stark immediately starts walking toward the altercation before too many people take notice. The back of the man's head slams into the tarmac, causing him to gasp and convulse in pain. The cop draws a nightstick and raises it, but Stark quickly disarms him and grabs the back of his neck and drags the cop away with only a couple people noticing. No one tries to follow, instead tending to the injured protestor.

Stark tosses the officer onto the floor, but he quickly gets to his feet. Stark expects him to lunge, but instead he just stands there. He exhales, like he's relaxing. "Wasn't expecting a suit to be that strong. I thought it was one of my . . ." He points at Stark's clothes.

"Colleagues? Yeah if they're good people, any one of them would do what I did." Stark cracks his knuckles. "But good people don't do what I'm about to do to you."

The cop smiles, the perfect excuse on a silver platter. He dives for his shield and lunges. What he thought would be a successful charge is met with his shield shattering as Stark's fist passes through it like papier-mâché. The punch lands on the officer's mask, which, of course, also shatters, and the punch connects with his face, which also would've shattered had Stark not held back.

He falls over as if he has slipped on ice and crashes to the ground. He coughs and spits out a half-dozen teeth. Without skipping a beat, Stark rolls him onto his back and steps on the man's left knee, slowly putting pressure on it until he hears a distinct crunch. The officer lets out a gurgling, desperate scream, which Stark allows. He kneels beside him and considers inflicting more damage before taking a deep breath and deciding he's probably done enough. He inspects his clothes for any blood or damage and sees nothing of the sort.

"I appreciate you not fighting too hard. I didn't want to have to change." He exits the scene, leaving the officer to get used to the pain in private. It takes only fifteen minutes to arrive at the hotel after that. The huge skyscraper reaches high enough to only be second in height to a skyhook. The penthouse where the party is at is obscured by the clouds. The only reason Stark would have to go higher is if the Orbital Weather Station needed service, like the one time the planetary mirror stopped working and the day/night cycle froze. Having one half of the planet stuck in permanent day and the other in permanent night can apparently cause quite a bit of turmoil.

"Name?" the bouncer demands. Stark stands up straight and says, "Code . . . singular."

The bouncer checks his clipboard, hands Stark a metal

keycard, and ushers him in. "Use this in the elevator to access the penthouse suite. Have a good evening."

Stark nods thankfully and heads straight to the elevator. Just as he stands inside and swipes the card, thinking he's got it to himself, a young blonde woman slips in, black-and-red dress rippling as she swoops in. She swipes her card and chuckles after realizing he had already swiped his.

She looks at him; her face is sweaty from running it seems. "Sorry, I'm supposed to meet someone, but they told me to go to the party first. He likes making an entrance."

"Fashionably late type of guy?" Stark asks.

She shakes her head. "No, not usually. He just wants to be absolutely sure everyone is there before he arrives tonight. He doesn't like repeating himself when it's important." She takes off one of her white gloves and wipes the sweat off her forehead. Stark freezes for a moment and remembers.

"Ah, yes, that reminds me," he says, pulling out the gloves. He observes that she has the P.R. cufflinks pinned to the straps of her dress.

She stops shuffling around and gives him a knowing smile. "Oh, very nice. Glad to see another individual of good fashion sense. Best keep those on so that everyone can see what good taste you have." The elevator dings and the doors open, letting in the sounds of soft music and the buzz of a classy party.

"Have a nice night, sir," the woman says before walking off to talk to some other guests. Stark immediately begins looking around, glancing at people's hands every chance he gets whilst trying not to look too out of place. He makes his way over to the bar and asks for a champagne, which he takes a sip of.

The penthouse has two floors and a balcony with a pool, and the whole place is crawling with people. Nothing illicit is taking place, and yet Stark is surrounded with some of the most dangerous and influential people in the city. He sees the commissioner sitting with two women on his lap, several sergeants still in uniform having a drink with known underworld enforcers, even a few politicians, including one of the candidates for the city's next mayor. It's a site from a sci-fi film, people in ten-thousand-dollar suits interacting with others covered in tattoos, scars, and exposed cybernetic implants.

Stark strolls onto the balcony and takes one final sip of the champagne before spilling it into the pool. No sign of Smirnov at all so far. Stark leans on the guardrail and breathes in.

A voice makes him glance over his shoulder. "Even up here the air isn't clean, just thinner." A cop wearing a suit and his badge raises his glass, intentionally showing off his white glove and distinct cufflink.

"But the view sure is rich. The lights and the breeze are a different sort of experience." Stark nods in agreement as the officer joins him to admire the sunset.

"I can't quite get around the whole lifestyle myself. But when I pulled into the parking garage, the cars I saw down there were a good indicator that my blood is very out of place here."

Stark lets out a small laugh. "Yeah, I can believe it, I have an old, noisy Mustang. She ain't fast or modern, but it's fun."

"Nice! You should head down there and check it out. You might like what you see. I expected to see a bunch of electric junk, but half the cars down there are classics." Stark raises his eyebrows. The line between subtle and obvious is getting blurred a bit. But then again, it wouldn't hurt to go down there to check the guest list too.

Stark raises his glass. "Cheers." They clink glasses, and Stark begins to head back inside.

"Oh, by the way, since you like cars so much, I should let you know my boss will be here soon, and I can guarantee he'll appreciate your taste. So be sure to be back up here before he arrives."

Stark nods. *Yep, definitely not subtle.* The guard opens the elevator for him, and just as the doors close, Stark catches a glimpse of him putting on some white gloves.

"I hate conspiracies, especially when I'm part of one," he says under his breath. As the elevator goes down twenty stories, the floor beneath him shudders, and the lights flicker. The presence. Stark would recognize it anywhere. From that night and the same one he felt on the cufflinks . . . Something is coming.

Ding! The doors open to reveal a parking garage completely filled with hundreds of millions of dollars of exotic cars. Stark wolf whistles and admires before heading over to where the guest list is sitting on a pedestal, which is accompanied by one gaurd.

Before he can even ask, Stark says, "Code: singular. Just checking to see if a friend of mine has arrived." The guard nods and gestures toward the book of names. Stark flips through the pages; there are loads of people that shouldn't be here. If they were, the protests outside would turn to riots and civil war. Cops, politicians, military leaders, celebrities, doctors, Imperials . . . Stark shakes his head. If only he could get a copy of this book. He scans each page for Lana Smirnov but can't find her name anywhere.

"Wait a minute," he says by accident. There's a name in there that definitely shouldn't be there. Stark turns his wrist to look at the P.R. cufflink and now understands what the letters stand for. He stares at the page, and the name Patrick Reardan stares back at him—the name of a man he knows to be dead. His scattered remains were collected along with his daughter's.

Beside the name of each guest is a record of how they entered the building. Those who arrived by car have their parking space written down for valet purposes. Stark closes the book and hurries to space J9, where "Patrick" is parked. He almost trips when he lays eyes on a very unique car. A yellow Nissan Skyline, clean, pristine and definitely not melted from fire damage like he last saw it. Without saying anything or barely even thinking anything, Stark rushes back to the elevator, but when he presses the button, he realizes it is already on its way up.

It's gotta be him. The presence Stark has been feeling is the same person that made it possible for him to infiltrate this party. And his senses are telling him that he's here.

"Shit, gotta do this the old-fashioned way." He runs to the stairs and, like a wraith, bounds upward as fast as his powers will permit him. Barely even using the steps, he jumps off the walls using the railing for footing to launch himself up several floors.

By the time he reaches the top floor, several people are waiting for him outside the penthouse suite, ushering him in. They're all wearing the gloves and cufflinks. He speed walks through the doors and immediately begins searching for the real host of this party.

"Everyone, can I have your attention please?" A familiar voice makes everyone go silent and turn to pay attention. It's Gault, the lone surviving Olsen twin. "I know many of you members and new recruits were excited to be able to meet our leaders, Miss Smirnov, Master Vaughn, and Rytram, but they are on an important mission in the wilds. Instead, their ambassador, Gerrick Dale, will be your host."

Gerrick Dale? The war criminal? The guy who murdered families and launched the bodies at enemy troops to shock and demoralize them? *It's like bad people have an unspoken ability to group themselves together.*

Stark continues to look around until his eyes fall on the elevator. *Ding! Blam!* The doors fly off and soar across the room, crashing through the windows and off the side of the building, taking a few people with them. Stark tenses up as he hears several guns cock. All the people wearing white gloves start shooting Dale's cohorts in the backs of their heads. People scream and try to scramble, but most of them are unarmed. Any people who might've fought back were killed first. At first, Stark thinks the people with white gloves are only targeting the most dangerous and notorious attendees, but soon everyone is dropping to the floor, either dead or in shock.

There's a flash of purple light and a sonic boom makes everything made of glass explode. The remaining guests stumble and stop running. Some fall to the floor with their hands covering their ears.

The final and most anticipated guest announces his own entrance. "This is what I call crashing a party!"

Stark blinks and his eyes focus on the newest arrival coming out of the elevator. He's wearing a long, hooded, black, trench-style coat with purple trim. Underneath, Stark sees a light-pink collared shirt and a purple tie. His pants look just like Stark's, made to look fancy but flexible. His shoes are glossy black, and each step he takes lets out an unnatural, heavy thud, making the skyscraper creak and groan underneath them.

When Stark's eyes focus on his face, he doesn't know what to say. It's James Diarkis! Before he can ask him anything, Gerrick Dale comes out from behind the bar counter with a shotgun and opens fire. The shot clips several guests but misses James entirely. Then, for a moment, Stark loses sight of him, like he has disappeared from his senses. Suddenly, Gerrick falls over dead to reveal James standing behind him.

"So!" James claps his hands together. "Today we're gonna play a game called show and tell. Where you tell me what I want to know or I show you what it's like to be burned alive." He motions to his followers with the white gloves to round up the dozen or so survivors.

Stark steps forward. "Is it really you?"

James pauses for a moment and turns to face him. "Yes, and no; it's been a complicated year."

Stark nods slowly trying to decipher his words, though remains mostly dazed.

"Now then! Let's begin. How many of you are recruits? Raise your hands."

A few people do.

"All right, you can leave. You haven't ruined your lives yet, so it isn't my responsibility to end them." They all scramble for the elevator, pushing and shoving each other to get in. "Okay, anyone here should be an established member. Now it's time for you to tell me one of three things. The whereabouts of Lana Smirnov and the Angel Rytram, the plans of your gods, or the true identity of the Stranger."

"Isn't that four things?" asks a stern older gentleman.

James grabs him by the arm and pulls the old man to his feet. "Unless you've got something useful to say ..."

The portly man clenches his teeth and turns up his nose to James's question. James socks him in the face, thunder rolling in the sky as false teeth bounce across the floor. "Answer me this: o walking corpses such as yourself have families? Would anyone miss you? Would your loved ones prefer that you be scattered into the ocean? Or all over the street down below?"

One of the hostages, Gault Olsen, speaks up. "As if we'd betray our almi—mmph!" Stark watches in disbelief as the woman in the red dress from earlier kicks the back of Gault's knee and holds him down while covering his mouth in shiny red tape.

"Gault Olsen!" James shouts, doing a little excited hop. "So good to see you! How's your brother?"

Gault lets out a low, muffled grumble.

"Ha, that's okay, you can have a family reunion in a couple seconds. But first, can you answer any of my questions?"

Gault just stares at him defiantly.

James smiles and shrugs. "All right then, say hi to your brother for me!"

The woman starts to drag him away.

"Anyone else? If you tell me anything, I could be lenient. Better to be lenient than violent, right?" A few moments pass and he smirks. "Offer expires in ten seconds." *Crash!* The woman in the red dress yelps as Gault breaks free and charges at James.

Stark moves to intervene, but the cop from earlier grabs his shoulder and holds him back. "Watch," he says.

James extends his right arm and flicks his wrist, releasing several bolts of purple lightning into Gault's body, knocking him back and filling the room with the smell of cooked flesh. James looks at his watch, which Stark swears appears to be smashed and can't possibly be working, and says, "Well, times up. Let me show you how much better of an executioner I am than your brother."

James conjures a sword hilt from under his coat and draws a katana from an invisible sheathe. The blade sings as it is released into the open air. The hilt is black and wrapped in purple ray skin, and the guard is a black nonagon with brass trim.

Suddenly, the air pressure begins to change. The sound of a volcano erupting tears apart the room as James raises his sword and dark purple smoke begins to swirl around it like ink in water. Electricity arcs off the blade and shatters more windows and blasts apart any furniture still in one piece. James's cosmic presence is astounding!

Stark's vision begins to get blurry, but he is still able to comprehend what happens next. Everything suddenly goes quiet and freezes. James looks down on his victims. "Bear witness," he says with a whisper. He brings his sword down, and an inferno of purple fire and powerful winds come out of nowhere. Flames, smoke, electricity, and tons of violent kinetic energy push Stark and the rest of James's followers out of the penthouse. James's allies are allowed to slowly float through the air so they can safely witness his power.

Stark watches in horror as the entire top floor of the Imperius Hotel is blown apart and disintegrated along with the occupants. After the final thermal pulse is released, everyone scatters. Deciding to prioritize himself at least for the moment, Stark composes himself so that he can land safely on a nearby tall office building. Once he has caught his breath, he looks back to the remains of the hotel. The smoke has turned gray, and the flames have assumed a natural, yellow-orange colour.

James's voice makes Stark reflexively spin around like a ballerina. "I hope I made a good impression. Nice to see you again. Sorry I've been ghosting you all this time." He holds out his hand. Dazed and confused, Stark shakes it. He smiles at Stark. "These days, my name's Dalkanos Aioven."

Chapter 4

•

DALKANOS
AIOVEN

"A new name?" Stark asks.

James nods. "I figured the authorities would've wanted to ask me some questions had I used my old name. The monks at the Elder Monastery helped me find my new name. They said that it is tied to my new purpose."

"Taking down the cult," Stark says. Aioven smiles and pulls up a mask to hide the lower half of his face and obscures the rest with his hood. The sun falls behind the horizon, and the cityscape becomes illuminated solely by the streetlights and neon signs of the nightlife. Stark and Aioven stand a mile above the civilians below, but they can still hear the approaching sirens of the authorities coming to investigate Aioven's latest attack.

"So all this time, I've been investigating these terror attacks, and it's been you killing them? And you've only now decided to meet with me?" Stark asks.

Aioven turns his back to him. "I can't say I was entirely myself for those first few months of deciding what to do . . . with myself and the world. I was far too angry to be around anyone." He puts one foot up on the ledge and leans forward to look down.

Aioven looks off toward approaching helicopters. "Well, if you want to work together and stop these people, we should probably talk somewhere less windy." Aioven holds out his hand and slowly claws his fingers through the air, which somehow seems to drag a black fabric out of nowhere into existence, like he is tearing apart invisible wallpaper. With a final yank, the fabric forms into a large, hooded black robe. He holds it in front of Stark for him to take.

"You're still alive, and before you decide to become associated with a terrorist, I think you should wear this so that the public doesn't make the choice for you," Aioven says.

Stark takes the robe and puts it on, a perfect fit. "You missed your calling as a tailor," Stark says, wondering how he managed to materialize the robe in the first place.

Aioven steps back from the ledge and takes a stance as if he's about to run. "You know how to jump, right?"

Stark leans over the edge. "Yeah, why?"

Aioven points in the distance at some approaching helicopters. "Because our enemies can fly." As the spotlights of the police helicopters fall onto them, they both ready themselves to jump. "Follow my lead; get as much attention as you can. We're heading for the main square."

Stark barely has enough time to consciously process his instructions before Aioven is running toward the ledge. Stark observes as Aioven plants his right foot on the ledge of the building and launches himself into the air. Not wanting to be left behind, Stark sprints and leaps too.

With the wind pounding their bodies and screaming in their ears, they jump from building to building, soaring several dozen feet into the air. More and more helicopters converge on them, which normally wouldn't be the case, but Aioven is purposefully leaving a nice trail for them to follow, because with every jump he releases a pulse of kinetic energy that demolishes the roofs of each building.

As the buildings get smaller and shorter, the more they can hear the chaos of the police down below, desperately trying to keep up in their cars with the sirens screaming and the megaphones blaring. Eventually, they reach a short apartment building, and Aioven stops. "Let's jump down and make a sprint for the square."

Stark catches his breath. "All right, let's do it." They both drop off the side of the building and slam into the sidewalk, shocking a large crowd of people and knocking a few back with the blast of the landing. Several police cars and motorcycles come racing around a nearby corner.

"Oh dear, that's where we have to go." He starts walking toward their pursuers with big quick strides, almost hopping as he does. Stark feels Aioven coaxing out the energy around them before focusing on the police vehicles coming at them.

Aioven takes a deep breath. "Streets closed, boys; find another way home." He locks onto their kinetic energy and doesn't do anything except reverse their direction. He only has to simply hold up his hand as if to say, "Stop." And when he flicks his wrist, every vehicle, without pause or even slowing down, immediately speeds in the opposite direction, no doubt causing some serious whiplash.

Several officers are thrown off their motorcycles, and the drivers of the cars honk the horns with their faces. Most of the cars spin out or crash into parked vehicles. Stark and Aioven run past the cops as they try to make sense of what just happened. As they get closer and closer to the square, the sound of sirens and helicopters surrounding them gets louder and louder.

"How fast can you actually run, Stark?" Aioven shouts as they run across the tops of several cars.

"Pretty fast," He replies, looking up to see several helicopters circling the square. As they make it to the square, all exit streets are quickly barricaded. The pair slows down and stops in the center. Stark reaches behind his back to draw his sword, but Aioven stops him.

"We're not doing massacres like that today. We're just putting on a show," he says, looking around at all the LED signs and large TV screens surrounding them. "Time to see if these lovely people are brave enough to sleep without their night-lights."

Barricades are erected around them and special ops officers take cover behind their vehicles. An officer's voice echoes throughout the square. "We have you surrounded!"

Stark looks at Aioven. "Does he think we haven't noticed?"

Aioven shrugs cartoonishly. "Don't be too hard on him. He probably has to tell us that."

The officer's voice echoes again. "The knights are on their way! You have no chance of escape."

"If only you knew how trapped *you* are," Aioven says, as he kneels down and places his right hand on the ground. Stark notices that Aioven is wearing a ring on his index finger with three gemstones in it: one red , one blue, and one green. As Aioven focuses and starts to scout out the energy of the city's electricity grid, the red gem glows brighter and brighter. He starts sweating and tensing up as red lights race up his arm through his veins. He takes in one big breath through his mouth, and his veins begin to glow a deep purple as if he were oxidizing the harvested power. "Good night," he says. And as he exhales, the lights race back down his arm with a new purple hue.

With a low boom, the sounds of all the sirens are stopped, the lights of the helicopters and police cars shut off, and one by one the lights of the city are extinguished until the whole capital is plunged into darkness. The sounds of the bustling metropolis are gone, save for the panicked screams of a few thousand distant civilians and frantic police officers.

"Everything is going to turn back on in a few seconds. Time to sprint, Stark." The pair focus all the energy they have left in their bodies, whilst siphoning what they can from around them, and launch into a sprint out of the city.

They race to the Presidential Bridge, which takes them out of the capital of Atlas into the smaller city of Simeo. They remain completely unnoticed, leaping and bounding over confused people in stranded cars trying to figure out why they won't run or why the whole city in front of them went dark.

As they cross the bridge, they slow down and make their way to a Chinese food restaurant and head inside. Aioven snaps his fingers and his coat and Stark's robe disappear into a smoky vapor until they're gone completely.

Aioven, who is now dressed as an ordinary civilian, massages his left knee and stretches. "Now we're just two men that got off from a business meeting ordering Chinese from my good friend Sam. To the rest of the world, my name is still James Diarkis—a man who tragically is presumed dead, or he would be if anybody noticed or cared," he says lightheartedly.

As if on cue, a tall, orange-haired woman covered in freckles and wearing a dark-green T-shirt, cargo pants, and combat boots comes from the back office. "Successful night?" she asks as she pulls out several boxes of food. Stark blinks and tries not to stare at her huge arms.

Aioven gives her a thumbs up. "Should be after I eat some breaded chicken and white rice!" He invites Stark to sit with him on one of the stools at the counter. "This is Sam. She runs the intelligence side of things and handles our money."

Stark stops staring at the food hungrily. "Money?"

Aioven nods as he opens a box. "We run a few operations with varying degrees of legitimacy to fund our organization."

Sam leans forward, which makes Stark uncomfortable and forces him to look at the ceiling. "What kinds of businesses?" he asks, looking like he's talking to the ceiling tiles.

Aioven answers while he scoops some white rice and Tso's chicken into a bowl. "Casinos, strip clubs, restaurants, rigged street racing, boxing, assassination contracts, and arms dealing. I had to strong-arm my way into most of these industries. Most of the now-former bosses of the city work for us at my mercy. I was gracious enough to even create a few vacancies in leadership positions for more agreeable people."

"Jeez, man, how much does this pull in?" Stark asks. Aioven pauses with a mouthful of rice and looks at Sam. "Um . . ."

Sam answers him. "We made a million and a half last month," she says proudly, biting her lip at Stark.

"That much? Between this and tonight, you're gonna get attention from the knights and the Cultists," Stark says. Aioven pushes a bowl of ham lo mein toward Stark.

Aioven nods. "That's the plan—a slightly modified version of the one we started when we first met. The idea is this: to change the world, we have to get everyone involved. The good guys *and* the bad guys. And take care of anyone who poses a legitimate threat."

"And if the bad guys cause us too much grief?" Stark asks, twirling his noodles with his fork.

Aioven swallows a chunk of chicken and coughs. "Then we take them out of the equation completely. Our goals are the same. Figure out why the gods are encouraging violence and stop them from achieving whatever other goals they have. The death toll on their people and ours is catastrophic, but they've neglected to share their agenda or lay out any sort of manifesto. Casualties in war are regrettable but a little bit easier to comprehend. Mass murder under the order of religious fanatics starts to stink of things like sacrifice or genocide."

"You're worried they're up to something else? Could the architects actually be gaining something from all this bloodshed?" Stark asks through a mouthful of fried noodles.

Aioven stabs a piece of General Tso's chicken. "I hope not, but someone in that position of power, you'd think, once things get boring, they'll have no reason not to start over. Like a child in a sandbox of broken toys or disappointing castles. What if one day they decide it would be fun to release a plague onto us, or throw a meteor at our planet and destroy the planet's Climate Control Center?"

Stark tries picking up a noodle with some chopsticks and can't stop it from slipping away. "There's not much we could do about it," Stark says with a mouthful.

Aioven scoops up some rice. "Perhaps. I have a suspicion that's what they want us to think."

Stark sighs. "I feel like I'm part of a conspiracy crazy people talk about." Stark chuckles.

"Oh, you are. And I believe if we build up enough notoriety and call them out with all their followers watching, they'll be unable to resist a chance of killing us. Especially if we can convince them their acolytes can't do it."

Stark considers this idea, staring at his food, frustrated by his ineptitude with chopsticks. Aioven continues. "Think about it. They may be in charge of the universe, but we still get to interact with it and use its resources. I'm sure you've already noticed my resourcefulness of energy and matter."

Stark nods. "Yes, I have, though I can't understand how you accomplished such control over either one."

Aioven stands up, carrying his only empty plate. "I don't know how or why, but the Monks of Vyrkola took me to their temple and rescued me. My master was a veteran consular from the last Imperial war."

"Wait, a veteran of a war from six hundred years ago?" Stark's brows knit together so closely they resemble a unibrow.

"His mastery of the cosmic forces was deep—but passive. He wasn't a fighter, but his wisdom made him a great teacher. And he was more powerful than you or me. But he allowed the forces around him to influence him, rather than he influence them, like you and I."

Stark nods slowly. "That explains your katana, but not how he was alive."

Aioven picks up Stark's plate, shaking his head. "I already answered that question. His mastery over energy and matter allowed him to monitor and even sustain his own biology. He could use the energy and matter around him to increase his health span better than his body or any medicine could. Like cosmic rations or medicine to save his cells from senescence."

Stark blinks. "What, like . . . he can replace his cells and keep them from becoming senescent or cancer?"

Aioven nods. "Every single one of his cells is healthy. Granted, he isn't immune. He's just effectively ageless. Though he does not keep himself looking young, since they aren't very big on vanity."

"Are you gonna live forever too?" Stark jokes.

Aioven laughs as he rinses the dishes off before putting them in the washer. "I doubt the life I lead will allow us to test that. But I hope not. I just want to be alive until I'm happy with what I leave behind."

"Did he teach you anything else? Anything that I should know?" Stark asks as he places a tip for Sam on the counter. She winks and takes it.

Aioven holds up two fingers. "Two things. First, I was able to verify with legitimate tomes that the last emperor just before his fall claimed he would be given great power by the architects and granted the title of god as well."

Stark tilts his head. "How does that help us?"

Aioven smiles wildly. "Everything comes from nothing. My theory is that gods weren't always what they are today. If what the last emperor claimed was true, then we have much more in common with them than they want to admit. They might have to adhere to the same laws of physics, their minds could be similar, their biology might be similar . . ."

Stark's eyes light up. "That means they might be mortal like us too."

Aioven puts his right hand on Stark's shoulder. "Exactly! And hopefully they'll have the same fragile egos as us when we call them out. But I'll need your help in figuring out how to make the world lose faith in them."

Stark thinks for a moment. "Very well, I'll join you. If not for avenging Patrick and Laura, we would at least be doing some good if it all works out." Stark pauses and remembers something. "One last thing, what was the other thing he taught you?"

Aioven's face darkens. "Ah, yes. This I couldn't verify with any history books. But contrary to current beliefs, as far as I understand it, there are more than five cosmic forces."

Stark's eyes open up in shock, glaring at Aioven like he was just told gravity is a myth. Aioven nods and continues. "Most of them aren't recorded by any civilizations except for in three places: The elder Library of the temple where I was rescued and trained; the underground vault of the architect cult's Dark Temple, which, as far as I know, is also considered to be the Imperial capitol building in the city of Malista." Aioven pauses.

"And the third?" Stark leans forward.

Aioven takes a deep breath. "The Mother Temple."

Stark can't believe his ears. "But that place doesn't exist. It was a myth adults used to tell kids about. To explain where babies come from or where ghosts go to find peace before moving on. Heck, my school teachers pretended to threaten me with sending me there whenever I misbehaved."

Aioven beckons Stark to follow him out the back door. "My teachers used to threaten me with it too. 'Pay attention or we'll send you to the Mother on the moon to live with her forever.'"

Stark closes the door behind him. "We had wacky teachers, man."

Aioven snickers. He tosses a bag of trash into a dumpster. "Regardless, they probably wouldn't have told me about the temples if it weren't for the state I was in."

"State?" Stark asks, waving the smell of trash away.

Aioven closes the dumpster and sneezes. "After everything that happened. I was angry and confused, not sure what to do. Not sure what was real or how to feel. Eventually it started to feel like someone else was making choices for me—choices based on information that wasn't real. I was going mad."

Stark looks at his friend. "And the monks helped you? Healed your mind?"

Aioven shook his head. "Their elder subdued me and taught me the power of mind—one of the cosmic forces."

Stark begins to understand how everything played out. "One of which is in their records."

Aioven pulls out some car keys. "That's correct. Technically, my mind isn't healed. They just taught me how to control and calm my mind enough to not be a danger."

Stark follows him down an alleyway. "Did they teach you about the other cosmic forces?"

Aioven stops at a car under a cover. "No, they only knew about the power of mind. The Dark Temple holds the key to two others, and the Mother Temple carries the secrets to the last absolute force—the one that predates the earliest stages of the big bang, perhaps even before, if that's even possible." He turns to face Stark. "Will you help me?"

Stark looks at the skies. In a world full of superpowered people, angels, and gods . . . there are still things that take time to believe. But . . . "With the way the world is, I'd rather place my faith in you than anyone else. When we first met, you took no time in adjusting to the knowledge bombs I dropped on you. The least I can do is repay you with the same support and patience. And for what it's worth, most of what you're saying actually makes sense." Stark holds out his hand.

Aioven exhales with relief. "By the time this is over, I just hope you place most of your faith in yourself." They shake hands and Aioven makes the cover on the car disappear to reveal a purple

BMW race car. They hop in and Stark laughs a little. "Have you ever driven anything subtle?"

Aioven smiles proudly. "If you think this is outrageous, you should see my other cars. But I'm not a huge fan of subtlety. I'm a big fan of outward expression and theatricality." He turns the key, and the engine explodes to life, bouncing off the walls of the alley, making it even louder.

The engine grumbles at a low note as he accelerates and lets out a fluttering whistle as he takes his foot off the gas. "Now we're heading to the HQ, just a simple apartment building we use to launder some of the money. Lily will be there. She can help with filling you in."

"What's her role?" Stark asks, holding onto the roof handle. Aioven swerves around two cars and speeds past them. "She alternates between undercover work and being my field partner. Though it's mostly the undercover stuff."

"Was she the blonde woman in the red dress from earlier tonight?" Stark guesses, to which Aioven nods proudly.

Stark braces as they catch some air. "Speaking of which, the people you demanded information about tonight . . ."

"The demands didn't matter; the destruction did. I wanted to grab their attention. And yours. I said the names of their leaders just in case blowing up their penthouse wasn't enough to make them curious." A device hanging from the rearview mirror starts beeping, and Aioven puts the car into a higher gear and slams on the brakes. He slows down, making the car quieter, and waits a couple moments before passing a police car parked on the left-hand side of the road, hiding to catch speeders.

"Those people are our targets, but I never expected the party ambush to grant us any real intel," he says before downshifting and speeding back up.

"What were their names? I remember four," Stark says.

Aioven speeds up to beat a traffic light. "Not exactly. It's *three* people, and one of them is secretly the leader who calls himself the Stranger."

"Why is finding out the identity of the Stranger so important?" Stark asks.

"Because the Stranger is not only the mastermind and the key to calling out the deities but is also a massive threat. Whenever they strike, they don't leave any trace. No residual energies or matter. When they kill, their victims disappear. When they destroy, it's like they're carving matter out of existence."

Aioven thinks for a moment. "When you fought Smirnov, did she exhibit any kind of mastery over matter?"

"No," he replies. "Her abilities felt rather underwhelming for someone of her supposed rank, but I could tell she wasn't really breaking a sweat either."

Aioven ponders this new information. "So, she was holding back. We just don't know why."

"What about the others?" Stark asks.

"Darius Vaughn and the Angel Rytram," Aioven says.

Stark twists his body to face Aioven. "Surely it's the angel, right? As I understand it, angels possess powers that exceed even most knights."

"Don't read too much into what the churches try to tell us about these creatures. All angels, except for one, were once ordinary people with no cosmic abilities. Their minds were wiped and mortality scraped out of their bodies and programmed to serve eternally with pride. They are unfeeling corpses' vessels with wings, until they release all their power. Then they become monolithic monsters."

"All except for one?" Stark asks. "Angelus, the god and father of all angels. He serves the architects and is the head overseer of their armies."

Aioven exits the freeway and slows down as they enter a bright but small town. "Welcome to Simeo. University town and my base of operations." They pull behind a nine-story building and stop in front of a garage door.

"So, what's our current objective?" Stark asks. Aioven turns the radio to 95.10 and presses the button for the hazard lights. The radio comes to life. "Welcome to 951 Aedifex," a robotic Australian voice says. The garage door pulls open, and Aioven shifts into gear.

Aioven answers as they enter an underground parking garage filled with old, exotic vehicles. "Ascertain the whereabouts of one Alan Lee. A man whose ideals gel more with our own than Ares or the Empire. At least I hope so anyway."

Stark glares at Aioven. "Alan Lee . . . the war criminal?"

They pull into a parking place, and Aioven looks at Stark with a frown. "Surely you don't actually believe in the concept of war crimes . . ."

Stark is taken aback by the question.

They get out of the car as Aioven elaborates. "Isn't it more reasonable to say that war itself is a crime? And that the idea of calling anything a war crime is ridiculous? It draws attention away from the fact that war is a crime at its core. But then, some will argue that it is sometimes necessary to fight for your beliefs or your people. And if that's the case, why is it criminal to go the extra mile and do what is necessary?"

"He killed hundreds of civilians to stop one man from escaping," Stark says.

Aioven slams his door shut and looks Stark in the eye. "He was attacked and forced to duel a rogue Genesis captain. An enemy who refused to take the battle elsewhere and got several civilians caught in the crossfire."

"And how do you know that?" Stark asks.

Aioven steps into Stark's personal space, and his heart begins to race. "Because some of the survivors of that fight work for me. They told me the truth."

Stark starts to regret interrupting Aioven as the warmth leaves his body.

Aioven keeps talking. "Their children were being abducted and converted into acolytes. He went there to stop the traitor. Now the parents are here to return the favour. It would seem the Empire and its allies don't mind making parents outlive their children."

"How is this not public knowledge?" Stark asks less aggressively.

Aioven steps back, allowing Stark's body to warm up again. "My best guess—the Order and the capital don't want to admit that one of their most powerful officers committed treason. They aren't gods, but they do want unwavering faith. Otherwise, operating would be pretty difficult."

Stark follows him to the elevator, admiring the Lamborghinis and McLarens as they walk. "So, how do we find Alan Lee?"

Aioven presses the up button by the elevators. "We ask one of our newest friends." The doors open and they get in. With a push of a button, they quickly rise to the sixth floor. When the doors open, both men are facing the blonde woman from before.

"Welcome back, Aioven. And welcome to our humble headquarters, Leonidas Stark." This time she is wearing a loose, white T-shirt and tight, black, athletic pants. Her blonde hair is tied into two pigtails.

Aioven takes one of her hands and faces Stark. "Leonidas, this is Lilith Melrose, otherwise known as Lily, my partner."

"A pleasure." Stark bows his head.

Lily looks at Aioven. "Usually is."

Aioven flicks one of her pigtails. "Usually?"

Lily rolls her eyes. "As if I'd further inflate that big head of yours. Your guest is in room one." She pulls both men into the corridor and pushes her way into the elevator and giggles as the door closes behind them.

Aioven claps his hands together. "All right, let's go have a chat with our 'liberated' Imperial officer."

"Yes, right." Stark nods. "Wait what?" They begin walking down the hall, and Stark grabs Aioven's shoulder. "You captured an officer?"

Aioven enters some numbers into a keypad on a suite door. "We tracked him to a bar, drugged him, and brought him here. He's a prison overseer, so as our guest, he's right at home."

The door opens, and a man inside starts shouting. "You can't keep me here! I know my rights."

Stark and Aioven close the door behind them. Aioven flicks on the lights to reveal a man intricately cuffed and chained to a very shiny metal chair. The man's eyes are wild with panic, but he doesn't speak, as if he's expecting a response. He is dressed in a light yellow uniform that is covered in scuff marks and bloodstains.

Aioven finally breaks the silence. His voice is low and rumbles. "You're making demands to a dead man. The dead have no rights, and thus you don't either."

Stark sees Aioven's expression change to reveal his cruel enjoyment of the situation. A devilish smile, a slight frown, and bright excited eyes.

Aioven opens and closes his fists, making his knuckles crack. "Let's cut right to the chase, warden. You have information regarding the whereabouts of Alan Lee. You are going to lead us to him."

"I'm not helping you break that murderous captain out of prison!" The jailor spits in Aioven's face; he wipes it off and cleans his hands using the warden's jacket.

"Look, jailor," Aioven says, "I am a very violent man. I struggle with processing my emotions healthily. It takes a lot out of me to control myself these days."

The officer wriggles. "So go see a shrink!" Aioven slams his fist into the officer's face, permanently bending his nose to one side with a small *crack!*

"The situation isn't clear for you, is it? I can fix that. I have a great deal of experience with pain . . ." Aioven leans in close to the officer and exhales into his face. "You might say I'm an expert in pain." He pinches one of the warden's eyelids and tugs on it a little bit. "Maybe you need some help opening your eyes. I could get these eyelids out of your way free of charge.

He stands straight up to look down on the starved, quivering warden. "It's my understanding that you have a certain level of familiarity with the Empire's prison system. If you share your expertise with us, then I won't share my expertise with you." Aioven hovers an index finger over his hostage's left eye. "And trust me when I tell you, I'm always looking for an excuse."

Aioven pulls out a butterfly knife and twirls it around. The officer shivers as the warm steel is pressed gently against his cheeks. "These interrogations are always so fascinating. Sure, you learn intel about your enemy, but you also learn how many body parts people are willing to give up. Some more than others . . . I'm no psychologist, but perhaps that could be used as a metric to measure someone's character." He runs the tip of the blade down the man's leg and stops at the knee.

"Go to hell!" the officer barks. Without a word, Aioven sinks the knife just above the man's knee. Stark cringes as he watches him twist the blade around. The officer doesn't scream, but he does look like the wind was knocked out of him, barely conscious.

Aioven slaps him. "You better stay awake. If you fall asleep, I'm gonna pop your kneecap off with this knife."

Tears and snot start streaming down the man's face. He wheezes and coughs as he tries to speak. "What do you want from me?"

Aioven grits his teeth and twists the blade and yanks it out. He jams it into the officer's right shoulder. "Alan Lee's location! Where are you morons holding him?!"

"Nox! The Dark Tower! He's at the Dark Tower." Aioven yanks the knife out of his shoulder and holds it in front of the officer's face. The blood starts to bubble and float off the blade as if it were in zero gravity. With the blade cleaned and not even bloodstained he puts it away and blows the floating blood into the man's face, splattering it into his mouth and eyes.

"The Dark Tower, huh? Could be worse, I suppose. It's their second most secure prison, but at least we aren't trying to lay siege to Las Noches."

Stark kneels down next to the officer and looks at him for a moment. "What do you know about your leaders? Vaughn? Rytram?"

"Wha . . . ? Nothing! We as Imperial citizens live to serve as dutiful agents of the Empire."

Stark stands up and faces Aioven. "Now what?"

Aioven scratches his chin. "I might have an idea, but I'll have to sleep on it."

He beckons Stark out of the room, and just as they leave, the officer calls out to them. "What about me?"

"We'll let your colleagues figure that out when they find you."

The man yelps at the thought of being interrogated by his allies and starts screaming as Aioven closes the door.

Aioven waves as he joins Lily. "You can have room eight on this floor. Good night, Leonidas."

Lily, who is waiting for him outside, takes Aioven's hand and starts pulling him down the corridor.

"It's Leo! Don't be so formal," Stark shouts.

Aioven turns back to face him, stumbling as he walks backward. "You got it, Sir Leo!" he shouts with a salute. Stark rolls his eyes.

CHAPTER 5

VICTIM AND VILLAIN

Leonidas wakes with a start. A female voice and hard knocking is coming from outside. Not sure who it is or what they're saying, he hobbles over to the door to see who it is. When he opens it, the smell of fried food fills his nostrils. He blinks several times as he realizes it's Sam from last night in a gray tank top and flannel pants.

"You a late riser too, huh? It's almost noon. Aioven wanted me to wake you up and give you a tour." She holds out her hand. Leo blinks and takes what she's holding out of her hand. He takes a closer look to confirm that it is indeed the keys to his Mustang.

She winks. "Nice GT500, old school. The live axle cars are pretty raw. We'll be taking your car." Sure enough, when they return to the underground parking garage, his Mustang is there, along with several new cars. The purple and black BMW is now there, along with a bright-green Toyota Supra and candy-red Mazda RX7. The yellow Nissan Skyline is sitting off in the corner with its hood open and the engine hanging from a hoist next to it.

Freshly dressed and ready to go, they get into Stark's Mustang. "So why control the underground?" Stark asks as they pull out of the garage.

"Influence and resources to sustain his main quest of getting rid of every follower the gods have. And allies that don't care about jurisdictions help too." Sam rolls down her window and breathes in the fresh air.

"So he uses the revenue to fund his operation?" Leo asks as his brakes squeak to halt them at a stoplight.

Sam leans her head slightly to feel the breeze in her hair. "Yes, and the influence is useful too. He can use it to sow seeds of doubt and dissent. Get enough people to say the same thing, and people disagreeing with plans will become synonymous with denying science. He has even suggested the idea of doing something similar with other facets of society. You should know that, Leonidas Stark."

Leo thinks for a moment. It feels like either Sam isn't being 100 percent honest, or perhaps not even Aioven has fully revealed his plans to her. He could be wrong, but to him it feels like Aioven isn't just trying to stop people from placing their faith in deities but also to prepare the world for something new to believe in.

"What about when people no longer place their faith in deities?" Leo asks, curious what she might say.

"Only Aioven knows the answer to that," she says, glancing at him with a raised eyebrow. Leo raises his own in return, seeing that his questions are making them uneasy. Leo can see why such information might not be so readily given, but what if it's because people are expected to go along with it even when they don't know the big picture? Sounds a lot like blind faith to Stark. Perhaps to Aioven, blind faith is acceptable as long as it disrupts peace. Sounds like a slippery slope.

"Pull over here." She directs him to parallel park in a huge space in front of a fancy restaurant. "This is one of our recruitment centers. Head inside and order the carbonara, but make sure you're looking over the menu. Order a drink and say it quietly."

"Okay?" he says, shutting off the car.

"No, no, hand over the keys. I'm gonna drive this back to HQ and meet you here. From here, we walk."

He reluctantly hands her the keys. "Okay, just don't—"

She snatches them. "Scratch it? Seriously? I'm the one that got it to base safely before anyone could impound it."

Leo sighs and gets out of the car and watches as she gets in the driver's side and drives off. As he enters the restaurant, it becomes very clear that this isn't an Italian restaurant.

The sounds of knives cutting up raw fish and people speaking Japanese makes Leo very aware of the fact that what he will be ordering is not likely to be on the normal menu, which explains why it's a password that can't be mistaken for something else. A lady at the front takes him to a table and asks if he'd like anything to drink. He asks for a lemon-lime soda and for a few minutes to look over the menu. If it weren't for the fact that this is a recruitment process, he'd be tempted to order something real off the menu.

When the waitress comes back to see if he's ready to order, Leo asks her to come close. She does so, and he whispers, "I'll have the carbonara."

She stares at him, nods slightly, and rushes off. Stark hopes he didn't just make an unknowing waitress uncomfortable. When she returns, she is printing out a receipt. The only item on it being Spaghetti Carbonara with the Japanese character for nine (九) next to it .

She hands him a purple pen. "Please sign this for the records."

Leo does so, and she asks him to head into the kitchen with her. When they enter the kitchen, the staff pause what they're doing to watch as they head toward the freezer. She takes out a small, broken steak knife with patterns etched into both sides.

"Follow me," she says, opening the door to the freezer, where another door on the opposite end with a very thin keyhole faces them. She inserts the knife into the slit-sized keyhole and leaves it there.

"I can't turn it. Only those with the power can do that. I'll leave you to it." The main door seals with a satisfying *thunk,* and then he's alone with a silent audience of cold food to observe. Leo puts his hand on the hilt and tries to see if he can detect anything, but he doesn't. He removes the knife from the slot and examines it. The blade has been snapped in half, and upon closer inspection, he realizes that the scratches are actually patterns that have been etched in with an orange metal material. It almost looks like a piece of a motherboard from a computer.

He has an idea and inserts the knife back into the slot. He takes in a deep breath and attempts to twist the knife like he's turning a key. He feels it resist and starts focusing on the kinetic energy he normally would be putting into this act and turns it into electricity. The hairs on his arm stand up as the orange patterns on the knife start to glow red hot.

The knife turns, and the lock opens with a loud bang. Instead of the door opening forward, it quickly sinks into the ground, taking the knife with it. A grate covers up where the door went. A stairway leading deep underground is lit up by dim LEDs.

As soon as he crosses the threshold, the door shoots back up behind him and locks. With nowhere to go but down, Stark cautiously walks down the stairs until he reaches a dimly lit, large circular room with chairs lining the edge.

A voice reverberates off the walls. "Welcome, recruit!" The lights brighten to reveal more details of the room. The chairs themselves are all dark-purple cloth recliners with computers next to each one. Only two seats are occupied, both by women. Stark steps forward but stops near the center of the room when the voice speaks again.

"Your receipt, please." Stark turns around to see that a shirtless man in black pants coming down the same stairs he had just come down is the source of the voice. A little unsure how it is possible that they both came down the same set of stairs, Stark can't help but look a little confused. He holds out the receipt to him. The man walks over, his huge broad stature becoming apparent as he gets closer. He takes the paper, examines it, and looks up at Stark.

"You're Leonidas Stark. Master Aioven has been talking about recruiting you for months. He must be excited to finally have you here. Must've taken some persuading." He hands the paper to one of the women in the chairs. "Please enter his name into the system, Abita." One of the seated women reaches out with a dark almond hand, and she takes the slip of paper and types a few things before looking at the man with a perplexed expression.

"Jeremy . . . he's already in the system. He has a full profile with a rank and assignment already prepared." She turns the computer screen to show him.

"What's the assignment?" he asks. She tries to find out with a few clicks. "It looks like only a level eight officer can request this information."

"When was the mission assigned?" the recruiter asks.

"Eleven minutes ago," she answers.

The recruiter faces Stark. "The master has you in the system already. As his main lieutenant, no less. Tell me, are you willing to die for his cause? Are you capable of committing unquestioning loyalty to him? It sounds like he expects a lot from you."

Stark frowns. That doesn't sound right. "No, I don't. I'm here to fight against blind faith and villains whose faith makes them a threat." The recruiter glares at him. The two women look as if they're bracing for something to happen. Stark's right sword arm twitches as he mentally prepares for conflict.

"Perfect," the recruiter says. "The last thing Master Aioven wants is a bunch of yes men. He doesn't want to be a god. He wants to be questioned and to elevate those around him so that they too can have the opportunity to change the world."

Stark relaxes his sword arm. "It sounds like he already has a large amount of influence."

The recruiter sits down in one of the chairs. "In the lower parts of society, that he does, but he has very little say in the government and in the Order. He needs more influence to achieve his vision."

"What about the Empire?" Stark asks.

The recruiter crosses his legs. "There's no need for influence there. Aioven plans to raze their civilization and leave no opportunity for rebuilding."

A new voice joins the conversation. "Master Aioven will let you in on his secrets. He's been actively making it clear to everyone that you are to be a leader alongside him. I didn't realize he was so eager to create an account for you though." Everyone turns to see Sam standing at the bottom of the steps. "He trusts you because of something that happened 'before it all changed.' We've just been assuming you two know each other really well."

Stark raises his eyebrows. He can't honestly say they know each other that well, so he can't say with certainty that familiarity is the reason for his eagerness to trust him and induct him into his ranks. He'll just have to ask and hope he's up front with him. Sam sits down in one of the empty chairs.

"Is he all done here?" Sam asks the recruiter.

He nods. "Yep, the master did most of the work for us."

"Take a break then. As for you," she says directly to Stark, "Aioven requested that I take you to the mint."

"Mint? Like a currency mint?" Stark asks, bowing his head to the room before heading back up the stairs with Sam.

"In a sense, yes. What the master makes is very valuable to others, but much more so to him." She opens the door that takes them back into the freezer.

"That feels vague. So you're not making money?" he asks as he closes the door behind him.

"Aioven makes gold," she says.

Stark hops to catch up with her. "Makes it?"

They walk several blocks until they reach a main street in a city that shares space with a university campus. Students stare at them as they push past several new arrivals getting ready for their classes.

"Here we are," she says, stopping in front of a bar.

Stark looks around. "Strange location for a front, don't you think?"

Sam guides him down the front steps into the shop. "He thought it would be funny to have his storehouse of manufactured gold be surrounded by the front of higher learning."

Stark frowns. "Why's that? My time as a student taught me things I never would've learned elsewhere."

Sam snaps her fingers. "And that is all they truly have to offer. If you studied to learn and not because you think a piece of paper would guarantee you wealth, then he doesn't take issue."

They get to a service elevator in the back of the store. Stark watches as Sam zaps the buttons. "So, to him, there's no point in trying to study?"

"I tried." The pair jump and turn around to see Aioven standing right behind them, his long brown hair parted at one side, reaching past his eyebrows, the back touching his shoulders. Today, his glasses are black and rectangular.

He bows slightly. "I tried the whole 'go to school to find yourself' thing. Don't get me wrong, learning is fun, and I rarely care what I'm learning about. I just wasn't a very good student. And I thought I had it all figured out, but as time went on, I just felt wrong. Plus, it was expensive, which added to the frustrations."

"What did you study?" Stark asks.

Aioven shrugs. "English. And though I was passionate about it, I suppose you could say I was in it more for the creative capacity. I got frustrated with how little time I was spending brainstorming and thinking new things."

Stark speaks as they all get into the elevator. "What happened?"

"I quickly discovered that trying to study how to be creative with an outlet you love is a great way to make you not want to do it ever again. Actual creative work was a small fraction of the experience I had. And when I did get to be creative, there were too many rules."

He slowly waves his hand over the elevator buttons and the *M* button lights up. "These days I'm much happier than I was, and I feel my creativity is being put to good use too."

He looks at Stark. "What about you? What did you study?"

"Film. Cinematography, scriptwriting, and directing," Stark says proudly. It had been forever since he went to school.

"We should have a movie night," Aioven says. The doors open to a large, dingy basement filled with stacked metal crates, guns, and huge bars of gold.

"Welcome to the mint, my most devious scheme to date." He leaves the elevator first and picks up a rifle off a table.

"Okay, so what's the plan here?" Stark asks as he too picks up a minigun.

"Well, everything you see here is a part of our ongoing trade agreement with the cultists and the Empire," Aioven says as he disassembles the rifle and places the parts on the table. "We buy weapons from them in exchange for gold. Some of the weapons become part of our evidence collection if we deem the items proof of, well, intent for mass destruction." Aioven hands Stark a small bar of gold, which is somehow heavier than the massive minigun.

"Where does all the gold come from?" he asks as he drops the minigun to better hold the gold with two hands.

"I make the weapons into gold," Aioven answers plainly. "As you have already likely observed, I have the ability to control matter. I can influence it at the atomic level, which allows me to make gold out of anything."

Stark looks closer at the ingot in his hands. "So, what did this used to be?"

Aioven takes it from him and looks at it. "I think it used to be a few shotguns or something. Hence why it's so dense, which brings me to the other purpose of this operation."

He places the bar on a table and picks up a pistol. Stark watches in amazement as it shudders, shrinks, and morphs into a small golden coin.

"If I didn't know what I was doing, I would've lost a hand just now," Aioven says as he flips the coin.

"Because of density?" Stark asks, since Aioven mentioned density just moments ago.

Aioven nods. "Yes, in this tiny coin are a bunch of gold atoms that are packed way too tightly together, despite it being such a heavy element. If it weren't for my influence, this coin would've exploded like a grenade. Instead, the energy of them trying to get away from each other is contained and won't be released without my permission."

Stark looks around at the larger bars of gold. "And all of this gold ultimately ends up in the hands of the Empire?"

"That's right," Aioven says, looking pleased that Stark understands. He picks up a handful of bullets and morphs them into a smooth, golden sphere. "And we have moved 'millions' worth of gold' in exchange for weapons that can very easily be traced back to them."

"Expose them," Stark says.

Aioven puts the gold coin in his pocket. "And explode them." He holds the golden sphere in between his fingers and snaps them, splitting the golden ball perfectly in half before it pops with a loud bang and a bright flash.

Aioven and Stark say goodbye to Sam, and they start walking downtown. They stroll down the sidewalk for several minutes in silence before Stark speaks first. "How many forces can you wield?"

"Three," he says, holding out his right hand to show Stark his ring. On it are three gemstones. He points at the stones. "As far as I know, the stones represent my abilities. The red one represents energy, the blue one represents my influence over mind, and the green one is for my power over matter."

Stark had seen it before, and he couldn't believe his eyes then or now. "Aioven, those stones represent your mastery over the cosmic forces. Those are fully developed. For most people, it can take years or even decades for their stones to start showing."

Aioven looks at the ring for a moment. "Huh . . . I didn't know that. Each one appeared the moment I started to use a new power. Do most people not have stones like these even with powers?"

Leo shakes his head. "So that katana from earlier isn't your tool of fate?" Stark asks.

Aioven holds open his coat to partially expose the hilt of his sword. "You mean this?" The nine-sided guard has the same three gemstones on the points of the nonagon, with clear space for more stones.

"So you have both a handheld and a clad-type tool of fate?" Stark asks, amazed.

"I'm not sure what a tool of fate is," Aioven says, staring blankly as he closes his coat.

"Um . . ." Stark thinks about how to explain this. "The tool of fate acts as a focus—an inlet or outlet of your powers. It works in conjunction with your body, which acts as a conductor and storehouse for your power."

"And there are different types?" Aioven asks. His curiosity is piqued to the point that he has started walking a little faster, perhaps subconsciously out of excitement.

"Yes. The most common is the tool ype, which essentially means it can be an item like a weapon, a work tool, or basically anything that can be separated from your body whilst still being connected to you in some way."

Aioven looks at his teacher eagerly. "Any examples?"

"It can range from anything between a pen and a sword, though don't take my words as absolute," Stark says. "There are always exceptions."

"What are some of the most famous?" Aioven asks.

"I think the two most famous examples, though I'm not even sure they're real, are King Arthur's Excalibur and the wand of Merlin."

Aioven grabs Stark's arm. "You mean to tell me that Merlin was real? What about the other knights and the dragon?"

"Maybe, I don't know. There isn't much left today of the mythical world, assuming it ever existed. Chronos killed the last dragon and built his castle on its bones two thousand years ago. Merlin and Arthur lived several millennia before him, as much as ten thousand years ago." Stark shrugs. "No one has been able to find Merlin's grave, or Arthur's. These days it's just a distant myth."

"Hmm. So what are the other types?" Aioven asks, resuming their walk.

Stark pulls on his shirt's sleeve. "Second most common is the clad-type tool of fate. It can be anything from clothing to small accessories: robes, glasses, rings, or gloves . . ."

Aioven looks at his own ring, fascinated by how much he still doesn't know. He pulls out a glove and puts it on to cover it up. "Any others?" he asks.

Stark takes a deep breath. "The rarest is the internal or organic type. It doesn't have a clearly defined term for it. Instead of an item or something you wear, a part of your body has the same properties as a tool of fate. Your eyes, heart, skin, bones, hair . . . I've never met anyone with that type."

Aioven examines his hands. "A part of your body becomes a part of your powers?"

"That's right," Stark says.

Aioven chuckles. "Well, at least I'm not wildly extraordinary."

Stark laughs a little too. "In today's society, be glad you're not the internal type. Fanatics tend to hunt them down and kill them whenever they appear."

"Why?" Aioven asks.

Stark grips the hilt of his sword in anger at the mere thought of what he's about to say. "They believe it's some kind of affront to their gods. The churches tell us the gods have no need for tools to wield their power, and thus to mimic a god is blasphemous. Others just poach them for the gems, like harvesting pearls from oysters."

Aioven sighs. "Every day I'm given a new reason not to like these people."

Stark nods in agreement.

They walk for several blocks in silence before they reach a parking garage. They take the elevator to the top level, and Aioven pulls out a car key.

"Sorry about this. I was feeling a little conspicuous today," he says as he presses the button to make the car beep. Stark sees the lights of a purple-and-green Lamborghini with SVJ written on the side turn on.

Stark stands there and sighs. "Let me guess, you modded this too."

"I prefer the term personalized. But I'll be honest, I just got it because I could. I actually prefer the SV, but it's at the service center," he says as he almost clotheslines himself on the large rear wing. He presses a button on the remote, and both doors open and swing upward as the engine fires up.

"You are ridiculous," Stark says, and he clambers into the vehicle.

Aioven gets in and starts flipping switches. "Trust me, it's the world that has gone nuts. I'm actually quite sane." He revs the engine and sets off a few car alarms before closing the doors.

"Let's go plan a prison break," he says dramatically. The engine howls as he leaves the parking garage like it's on fire. Stark's head gets pushed back into his seat every time Aioven floors it.

Eventually, they make it to the highway, and Stark feels comfortable again, despite always going at least one hundred miles per hour.

Stark keeps his eyes on the speedometer. "This reminds me. Do you know what your penchant is?"

Aioven shifts into top gear to quiet the engine. "In the context of my powers? I can only guess what you mean by that."

Stark awkwardly readjusts himself in his seat. "Everyone that has powers like us has a penchant: an innate ability to perform a particular act with one's powers, regardless of the forces they wield. Basically, everyone has one thing that comes to them naturally."

"What's yours?" Aioven asks.

Stark points at the speedometer. "Doing things really fast. I can do things quickly once I've taken the time to understand what I'm trying to do. I can run fast, I can move objects very fast, and I can keep up with the speed of lightning."

Aioven tries to guess what his penchant might be. "Hmm … is it limited to one cosmic force?"

Stark shakes his head. "No, it applies to any absolute power you can wield."

Aioven reflects on everything he has done. "A lot of stuff comes naturally to me," he says, lost in thought.

"Well," Stark starts, "what is your signature move? What do you do really often and easily?"

Aioven scratches his beard. "I like to combine energy and matter into single attacks. I've even started using some of my mental influence in conjunction with my other powers as well."

Stark shakes his head again. "If you have to work on it in any way, it usually isn't a penchant." He snaps his finger. "It has to be as easy as snapping your fingers."

Aioven has a guess, but he doesn't say it. Instead he'll testify it the next time he encounters a new cosmic force. "Not sure what mine is, but I'll get back to you on that."

"Well, at least we can be pretty confident that Patrick was right," Stark says.

Aioven looks at him and nods but says nothing.

They arrive at a small building out in the countryside with a parking lot that wraps around the building. Beside it is a neon sign of a woman upside down hanging onto a pole.

"You're not married, right?" Aioven asks as he parks around back.

Stark shakes his head. "No, but aren't you … ?"

Aioven smirks. "Relax, Lily works here. Tax-free money for her and a way to pass information onto me. And she seems to enjoy it." He says that last part with a laugh.

They walk inside a gated back entrance before coming to an extremely sturdy-looking steel door. Stark notices there isn't a handle or a keyhole. Expecting him to use some special unlocking mechanism, Stark is rather surprised when the door slides into the ground when Aioven says the word, "Lilith."

They pass through and Stark watches the steel door slide back up. "A password seems a little basic for you, don't you think?"

Aioven readjusts his coat. "The more important the things behind a door are, the more significant security is."

Stark looks around and realizes they're in a locker room. The smells of perfume and alcohol are so strong that Stark could get a little buzzed from the vapors. When Aioven walks toward the door at the end of the room and opens it, loud hip-hop blasts through, and flashing red-and-purple lights make Stark wince a little bit.

As they cross the threshold, Stark understands where they are, a strip club. A few dancers walk past him, a little perturbed by the fact that he just came out of the locker room. None of the patrons noticed his entrance though. Realizing he got a little distracted by the scantily clad women around him, and almost got left behind, he hurries across the room to catch up with his chaperone. Aioven says something to the DJ that Stark can't even hear and out comes Lily wearing nothing but sparkly red bottoms and a black leather vest held together by laces.

Aioven puts his arm around her shoulder and points a finger at a gentleman sitting on a couch, staring at his phone. Stark notices he is wearing a uniform similar to the officer they interrogated yesterday but that is even more decorated. He looks like some kind of Imperial official, an emissary perhaps.

Lily nods and gives Aioven a thumbs up. He smacks her behind loud enough that Stark can hear it over the music.

Stark blinks and looks away as she undoes the laces of her vest. Aioven brings him to an office beside the DJ's booth. As the door closes behind them, Stark hears a hiss as it seals shut, blocking out the music completely, apart from the vibrations of the bass in the walls and floor.

"Okay, so …" Stark tries to form a sentence but fails.

"Why did I bring you here?" Aioven asks.

Stark nods as he drops into an office chair whilst Aioven digs through a fridge.

"We need information on the tower. And our best and quickest shot at getting that information is by having a chat with someone that works there, or at the very least used to." He hands Stark a soda in a glass bottle.

The door swings open as a very confused Imperial officer is manhandled into the room by a topless Lily. Aioven pulls out his butterfly knife and pops off the cap of his own drink.

Lily pushes the man so hard he falls flat on his face. Aioven takes a swig of soda. "He doesn't work at the Dark Tower, but he has toured the facility. And he just so happens to frequent my fine establishment."

Stark kneels down beside him. "What's your name, officer?" he asks as he slowly gets up on his arms and legs.

Lily pulls out a wallet. "Let's see . . ." Stark grabs the officer by his shoulder and pulls him to his feet.

Lily passes the man's ID to Aioven. "We are in the presence of Wesley Thane, a captain of the Imperial Navy." Aioven tosses the ID back to the captain, only for it to hit him in the face.

Lily pulls out some cash from the wallet. "Thanks for the tip!" She tosses the wallet to Aioven and starts to leave. Thane tries to lunge at her to get the money back, but Aioven intervenes by appearing between them, his hand resting on the hilt of his sword.

Captain Thane's face loses all of its colour, "You're—"

"See you later honey," Lily says, as she kisses him on the cheek. The door closes behind her, and then it's just Aioven, Stark, and the captain.

"You know," Stark starts, "the only captains I've ever met are from the Order of Genesis, but over there the monks don't really appreciate establishments like this."

Aioven takes a few steps into the captain's personal space. "You think your superiors would be proud of you? Hanging out in a strip club right in the middle of Simeo? Is this the behaviour of an Imperial admiral? Heck, I doubt our own politicians would endorse your actions, even though quite a few of them come here too."

Stark leans against the desk and watches Aioven circle the captain like a shark. He glimpses a flash of gold as Aioven slides the wallet back into the captain's pocket.

"We need you to shed some light on the defenses of Nox Tower," Aioven says soothingly.

"I don't know much. I've only visited," he says shakily.

Stark crosses his arms. "How many guards? What are they armed with? What is the building secured with?"

The captain begins to look on edge as Aioven continues to circle him. "Uh, well, the tower is surrounded by a three-story-tall wall with a few dozen snipers equipped with thermal scopes and goggles. There's only one gate in the wall and one entrance in the tower."

"What's the front door made of?" Aioven asks.

"Titanium-steel alloy," the captain says.

"That shouldn't be a problem," Stark says, "Anything else?"

The captain spins around and looks at Aioven. "The warden is a former apprentice of Rytram. He tends to also be the one to carry out incineration sentences."

"I have an idea." Stark motions to Aioven to come closer to him and whispers, "Once inside, we should be fine, but those snipers have to be dealt with quickly."

"What are you thinking?" Aioven asks.

Stark glances at the captain. "Can you use your mind powers on others to influence them? He could be a nice distraction," he says, alluding to the gold Aioven snuck into the officer's wallet.

Aioven gleams. He hadn't thought of trying such a thing. He turns to the officer. "Not what I had in mind, but your idea is much better. All right, captain, you're free to go. You can even tell your comrades about this interaction." Aioven moves like a blur and hovers his hand over his eyes. "On the one condition that you only do so at the entrance of the Dark Tower. Warn them as fast as you can, or I'll tell the whole world what you told me and where I heard it from."

Aioven feels into the man's mind. He can feel his desperation to stay alive, making it easy to break in. He urges his thoughts to become less tense, and the man relaxes as he is convinced of his new objective.

As Aioven feels things smooth over, he tries to search his thoughts for information but finds he is unable to read his thoughts. He pulls the captain in close and whispers in his ear.

The captain's face is contorted with horror. "Why would you want to go there? I don't know where that is!"

Aioven turns the officer around and ushers him to the door. "Then it is time for you to go. In nine days, go to the Dark Tower and tell them an attack is coming." He opens the door and lets him exit.

Once alone, Aioven turns to Stark. "Now then, you clearly have an idea. I'd like to hear it."

CHAPTER 6

THE DARK TOWER

Nine days later, deep within the Dark Temple.

Lana and Darius report to the Angel Rytram, who sits upon the Imperial throne. Lana devotedly kneels before him whilst Darius stands with one foot resting on the steps to the throne. His ragged, worn street clothes, extremely long, matted dark-green hair, and dirt-stained, sunburnt skin make him appear weak and disheveled.

"That's a lot to take in, I must admit." His voice echoes throughout the throne room. Lana and Darius look at each other; she is nervous and he's confused.

Darius steps forward toward his master, who sits on a throne atop a pedestal nearly fifty feet in the air. "With respect, Master, this individual has mounted several attacks. He leaves no survivors except for those he convinces to defect."

The angel smirks. "Sounds like someone I know, eh Vaughn?" With a huge whoosh that creates a powerful gust of wind, the angel slams into the ground before Darius.

"With respect? I do not sense respect in you for me," Rytram says.

"Then perhaps I only respect those you serve. Don't think too hard about it," Darius says plainly. "I still think the next time this individual attacks I should be there to investigate. We need to know more. I suspect that they are testing the water, to see what we can take before the real devastation comes."

The angel laughs as he flexes his golden glowing neon wings. "What makes you say that?"

Darius crosses his arms and stares down at the angel. "The intensity of the attacks hasn't increased. Instead, the level of devastation, while immense, has somewhat increased."

The angel sighs. "So what do they stand to gain? Our ranks are still strong, and our strongholds are secure."

Darius rolls his eyes. "They stand to gain everything we have: followers and influence. And so far that's what they've been getting. Even some of our own fear they could attack at any moment. We need to solve this before it's too late."

"What do you propose?" Lana asks.

Darius turns to face her. "I propose what I've been pushing for since the first attack: to meet them and discover their identity."

"That's a big risk," Lana mutters.

Darius grabs her throat and lifts her off the ground. "That's rich coming from the so-called captain-to-be who couldn't even kill Leonidas Stark, an academy dropout for fuck's sake." He tosses her across the room like a ragdoll.

Rytram takes a seat on the steps in front of the throne. "Don't underestimate Stark. He has very nearly the strength of a captain, even if he doesn't have the personality."

Something in Darius snaps. He reaches out without a single gesture and lifts the angel twenty feet up off the ground with his mind. "Don't underestimate him?! You've got to be kidding!"

The angel's wings flap frantically as he gasps for air. "You stupid bird, I've been telling you not to underestimate this unknown terrorist for months, and now you try to lecture *me?!*" Darius releases him and watches as he spirals to the floor and rolls down the steps to his feet.

Darius kneels down beside him. "Our gods prefer I don't kill you. Better for you to die at the hands of our enemies. They'd enjoy the conflict that follows."

Darius hears Lana stumble to her feet and says, "He is right about your personality. Stark is way more likable." He walks to the grand door that leads out of the throne room. "I will not be concealed, like a last-resort weapon or a trick hidden up your sleeves. Either we bring armageddon, or we don't."

Facing his wheezing comrades, he lets out a disappointed sigh. "The real fight isn't about peace or control. It's about the end of everything. And the only way to win is to be the one who destroys everything. Knocking everything down only to put it back together is the ultimate victory." And with that final remark, Darius leaves Lana and the angel to recover from his discipline.

• • •

*A*n hour later at Aioven's headquarters.

Aioven opens his eyes and remembers where he's at. His dreams are getting more and more vivid, a bit too much for him. He turns over to find Lily with her back to him and already awake.

He scoots closer to her and puts an arm around her. "Good morning," she says softly as he kisses her neck.

She doesn't turn to face him. "Don't take the Skyline today. The body kit and wheels arrived today." *That's right,* he thought. Today's the day he and Stark break out Lee, hopefully.

"We'll take one of the sedans," he says, pressing his hips into her from behind. She moans quietly. "I already let you sleep in. You gotta go soon."

He slides his hand down the front of her pants. "Well, let's make this quick, 'cause I'm gonna need all the luck for today."

He grabs her shoulder and flips her onto her stomach and

pulls down her pants. He takes her hips and lifts her up and presses into her.

"All right, if you can handle doing it fast, but I want something slow and savoury tonight," she says.

• • •

As they take a while to *wake up*, the other residents are starting their day in the lounge. "So, all these people? How does he find them?" Stark asks as he puts the flavour capsules in the coffee maker.

"What do you mean?" Sam asks as she desperately tries to tame her red hair with a brush missing most of its teeth.

He pulls out a couple of mugs. "Aioven has a network of followers, or allies, whatever you want to call them. Do most people seek him out, or does he find them?"

Sam gives up on brushing her hair when several of the teeth break off the brush. "As far as I know, it's just as complicated as how he recruited you. He's the one pulling the strings, but a lot of it is up to you. If you don't play by the rules, then you don't get to be in the game."

The coffee machine hums louder and louder. Stark grabs a jug of milk from the fridge. "So, the cause. What do we stand for?"

"Like us as a group?" she asks, tossing the brush in the trash.

"Sort of," he says as he takes out the pot of coffee. "I can see where Aioven is trying to go with all this, but I can only see the surface. What kind of world does he want to leave behind? What's left after he's done or dead?"

Sam stands beside Stark and watches as he pours the coffee. "I'm not sure. I don't think he's sure either."

Stark grabs a bag of sugar. "He wants revenge, or justice, or something along those lines. He's angry at the world. That much is clear."

Sam nods slightly. "Yes, that's true. But he wants his passion for change to mean something. He just doesn't know for sure what a better world looks like, or how to make one. Right now he's just trying to find something to direct his anger at."

"If you have any ideas, let me know, and I'll pass it on to him," she says. Stark accidentally dumps a whole cup of sugar into his coffee. As a show of courtesy, he gives Sam the unspoiled cup.

"I'll just put a few teaspoons in mine." She smiles, taking the cup.

Stark takes a sip of his, and the sugar is almost as strong as the coffee. "I don't know. I guess in order to figure it out, you'd have to be able to determine what the biggest problems with the world are. You can't fix everything, so we're gonna have to cherry pick." He pours out a little bit of his coffee and fills the rest of his cup up with milk.

"Only issue is, I don't think any of us have the perspective necessary to make such a judgment." He takes another sip of coffee and feels much better.

"He's right," Aioven says.

Everyone turns. When did Aioven show up *and* have enough time to pour himself a glass of milk with no one noticing?

He takes a gulp, and a third of his drink disappears. "Even before everything changed, I always figured the architects were the ones with the perspective needed to help the universe be a better place." He takes another gulp. "We need a god's eye view."

"It's strange, isn't it?" Sam says. "That we supposedly don't have the same perspective as the architects, and yet here we are with enough perspective to question them? Why allow us to have the free will to even doubt them?"

Stark puts down his coffee, unable to handle the sugar. "I don't think their perspective is anything special; they just have power. Just not as much as they would like us to think—at least that's my theory."

Aioven finishes his glass in one gulp. "Go on, Leo," he says.

"Well, think about it. We have the Order of Genesis, a whole organization filled with people like us, with dozens as powerful or more powerful than us. The Empire has emperors ascending to godhood and people becoming angels blessed with great power and 'divine' purpose. And then there's us, people with similar world-changing power, but we belong to no one."

Lily speaks before Aioven can. "But without our power, we wouldn't be able to fight."

Stark shrugs. "Without all this power between us and our enemies, would there really be any fighting? What difference would there be between us?"

Aioven pours and swirls a new drink like a glass of wine. "That makes sense to me. Power is so attainable for so many—it's bound to escalate things. As for the difference it makes . . . I'm not sure it matters."

Stark pours his sugar-saturated drink down the drain. "What if no one had power? What if everyone was limited to what their bodies could do and their minds could think of?"

Aioven heads over to the fridge, whilst Lily can't comprehend Stark's argument. "Then we'd all be powerless," she says.

Stark leans up against the counter. "Powerless compared to what? The natural machinations of the universe? Because I think we're all going to die out regardless of how strong we are."

Aioven hands Stark a glass of orange juice. "I'll be honest, Leo . . . I agree with you. Our ability to change the world would be reduced, but perhaps we wouldn't need to change it quite as much. We could just live. Everyone deserves a shot at living."

Lily scoffs and sits down to drink.

Aioven rolls his eyes. "Hey man, I'm gonna take a shower, and then we can get ready." Aioven walks away deep in thought. A universe without their absolute power? It's an interesting thought, but how would he take everyone's power away? It seems impossible to be able to change things like that, and would it ultimately save anyone? He gets to his bathroom and closes the door behind him.

He looks at his own hands. "A universe without power . . ." He looks at his reflection in the mirror. "The universe will probably die before I find a way to make that happen."

• • •

Sam drives them in her car for several hours before pulling off the freeway to park by a water tower in a small town. "Your bikes are at the top of the tower. Be careful you two."

The duo watch her drive away before leaping to the top of the tower. Stark is surprised by the fact that the two motorcycles look to be electric.

Stark looks over to Aioven to ask him about it but notices he is standing on the edge of the tower watching the sunrise. Stark extends his senses and feels the tension building within him.

"You don't need to do that, Leo," he says. "I don't mind being asked what I'm thinking." Stark stands beside him and looks onto the horizon.

Aioven's voice is lighter and almost shaky. "I don't know what purpose I used to have. I feel like the life I am living is not the one I was born with."

Stark looks at him concernedly. He puts a hand on his shoulder. Aioven tenses up before relaxing slightly. "I won't presume that you are my friend, but out of all the people I know, I want to befriend you the most," Aioven says.

"Why?" Stark asks.

"Because I believe you are capable and will not follow me— you will lead alongside me. It suits you."

Stark shakes his head and smiles. "I'm not sure I'm cut out for that."

Aioven puts his hand on Stark's shoulder too. "You are. You're the only one that speaks to me the way you do. You challenge me, and I need you to challenge me. Over the coming years, I don't expect many people to be honest with me."

"What good would that do?" Stark asks, retracting his arm, making Aioven almost look sad for a moment. "That is what this cause is all about. Challenging those who we are told shouldn't be scrutinized. I have no interest in being a god. Nothing would make me loathe myself more."

Stark puts his hands on his hips. "That sounds like something you should want your followers to know. Remember, you're telling *me* this."

Aioven's voice deepens and becomes gravelly. "I watched a child die, and I left my humanity when I punished the ones who killed her and her father." He grits his teeth. "I want to make a better world, I truly do, but I will also gladly fertilize the fields our seeds of civilization grow in with the corpses of anyone that would harm a child or threaten the legacy of life itself. I'd murder for peace, and I'm not sure that makes sense."

Stark realizes that he is seeing the man he was hoping to see all along. Not what most of his followers probably see: a symbol.

Aioven steps away from the edge. "I unlocked my powers the day I watched a child die. Now I have the power and the will to make monsters helpless."

Stark walks with him to their vehicles. "So, what are we going to do when we capture Smirnov?"

Aioven tilts his head and breathes in through his teeth. "Things that will scare angels enough to hide behind their wings." He mounts his motorcycle. "But their masters, they will truly know what it means to be powerless. I don't care what it takes. I will depict them as tyrannical, take away their faith, and decimate their power with all of Mars watching. The universe will know."

The ride to the prison takes them through several miles of

canyons before they stop at a T-junction that goes off onto a gravel foot trail. They hop off their bikes and toss them behind a boulder.

"So, why the bikes and the cars?" Stark asks as he winces from the sun beating directly down on them.

"To avoid detection," he says, pointing up at the sky. "Our powers depend on the resources the universe has to offer. When we use them, others like us can detect it, right? A bit like watching the water in a lake to find a fish or anything that could be hiding. Like a turtle, alligator . . ."

Stark stretches out his legs. "That's right. Though we may not always know for sure where something is, we can see the water reacting to them on the surface—air bubbles, ripples . . ."

Aioven takes off his coat and tosses it over the bikes. "Yes, and when someone like us uses our powers to travel quickly, someone could detect it, as long as they're paying attention."

They begin walking down the trail. Stark begins to feel right at home. He used to hike all the time in his hometown. "That way the Order doesn't find us? Or the Empire?"

"It's not just about *who* finds us but *when* they do," Aioven says before stumbling over a small rock.

Stark catches his arm. "You all right?"

Aioven laughs. "Yeah, I'm fine. I'm not the most dexterous individual. I've rolled my ankles in more unlikely places than I can count."

"I figured you could count pretty high," Stark says, letting go of his arm.

"Not r—*whoa!*" Aioven falls to the ground. "I'm good!" Stark takes his hand and pulls his companion back up. Aioven brushes himself off. "What did I trip on?"

Stark picks something up and holds it out in front of him—the small, smooth, gray rock he tripped over. "You weren't kidding," Stark says before placing it in Aioven's hand.

Aioven snaps it in half between his fingers. "I told ya!"

Stark keeps his pace slower than normal to make sure Aioven doesn't try to speed up. The deeper they go into the trail, the higher the rocks rise on either side.

Eventually, they reach a corner where Aioven says to stop. "Just around that corner is our opening into the valley of the Dark Tower. Let's take a look."

They both peek around the corner, and sure enough, the trench exits into a massive sand valley with tall mountains circling it. In the center of the circle is a tall, black tower with an octagonal wall surrounding it. Stark squints and can make out the sniper nests in the corners of the polygon.

Aioven leans up against the wall and slides down to the ground. "Now, we just have to wait for our Imperial captain to show up, and we can set your plan into motion. How're you feeling, Leo?"

Stark sits down next to him. "I'm feeling all right. You know, this'll put a lot of heat on us with the Empire."

Aioven nods. "You're right. I haven't quite figured out what personas we should show them—definitely not who we really are—at least not yet."

He holds out his hand, and the green stone starts to glow. Dust and rocks swirl above their heads before morphing together. Stark watches in amazement as a black scarf and cloak float down into his lap.

"Use that to hide your face for now," he says. Stark feels the thin, dark fabric in between his fingers, smooth but fragmented like an imperfect sort of silk.

"I really would love to learn how to do that," Stark says.

Aioven conjures a black hooded robe for himself. "I imagine we both still have plenty to learn."

They wait for almost half an hour. Aioven lays down to rest his eyes, allowing himself to take deep slow breaths. Stark had been spending most of the time looking at different rocks and wondering how changing them into something like the cloak and scarf even works.

Aioven opens his eyes. "Our captain is here." They both stand up and peek out the exit of the trench. Sure enough, an off-road vehicle is speeding toward the gate into the compound.

"He's really going for it," Stark says. Aioven puts his robe on and pulls the hood over his head. Stark follows suit and dons the cloak and wraps the scarf around the lower half of his face.

Aioven feels out to the captain with his senses and finds the gold coin he slipped in his wallet. He summons his katana and keeps it sheathed on his belt.

"When I snap my fingers, I want you to go down to the gate and put down the survivors. I'll handle the snipers and carry out your idea," Aioven says.

Stark nods and gets ready to launch himself. Aioven focuses on the dense gold coin miles away. He can feel the atoms pushing away from each other. He holds out his hand and snaps his fingers, signaling to the atoms that they have his permission to free themselves.

The explosion is visible from miles away. Alarms start blaring, and shouting can be heard. The flash and the smoke obscure most of what's going on at the gate now. Stark bends down and launches himself, moving so quickly that he breaks the sound barrier, causing Aioven to almost lose his balance.

"I thought I was fast," Aioven says before running at a few hundred miles an hour, with such control that he pretty much runs on thin air. Not that anyone would see, because to any ordinary human being, he would be a strange blur.

In a short moment he is at the first sniper tower. Standing behind the sniper, he draws his weapon and executes him with a swift decapitation. Aioven blurs to each of the eight towers and puts down every sniper in less than half a dozen seconds. Aioven takes their tripods and turns each gun to face inside the compound. With his part done, Aioven kneels out of view and waits.

Stark waits for the smoke to clear before walking toward the gate, which sits partially open. The car the captain came in is melting and on fire, and the captain is simply gone. The two remaining guards, mostly dazed and shocked, train their weapons on him. Without wasting a second and with both of his hands still hanging below his waist, Stark curls both of his index fingers, forcing the triggers of both rifles to be pulled. In the instant they fire, he redirects the bullets into their heads. The guards drop dead like ragdolls.

Stark places his hand in the flames of the burning car and exhausts all of the thermal energy, to the point that the fire is extinguished. With his sword still sheathed, he enters the compound with his hands above his head. Guards armed with automatic rifles and standard longswords surround him. Stark senses that the guards have some cosmic strength, but nowhere near enough for them to even gauge his own power.

As they step slowly toward him, Stark keeps his hands in the air, until he moves one of his hands slightly. All of the rifles, including the one beside Aioven, move to aim at a target. Aioven covers his ears and braces.

Stark waits until the guards stop moving. He makes eye contact with each enemy and counts ten targets. He curls one of his index fingers like he's pulling a trigger. The nearest guard with a rifle jerks his head back and flops to the ground. A gunshot echoes throughout the valley. The others look around confusedly as they realize he has been shot in the head. When they look at the seemingly unarmed Stark, all he does is shrug innocently. Stark pulls another invisible trigger and a swordwielder crumples into an awkward, dead heap.

Aioven smirks. "You crafty son of a bitch," he says as the gun beside him reloads itself.

Before Stark can allow the rest of them to realize what's happening, he closes both of his fists. Eight gunshots echo throughout the compound, and the remaining guards all die unceremoniously.

Aioven stands up and uses some of his energy to leap across the compound and lands between two prison buses. A few dozen more guards attempt to rush Stark, but Aioven flanks them with a column of purple fire, incinerating the three closest whilst the rest suffer third-degree burns.

Some try to ignore the pain and face him, but with a swish of his hand, he turns the rest to ash, as if they had become so delicate the wind could blow them apart. Now, being the one closer to the main door, Aioven is ahead of Stark. He strolls leisurely toward it as three more guards emerge: two with swords and another rifleman.

The first swordsman charges at him. Aioven unsheathes his katana with a diagonal, upward swing, cutting through the guard's sword and body like butter. The other guard attempts to rush him and thrust their blade into him, but Aioven side steps out of the way like a hummingbird. This time he swings his katana downward and releases a wave of purple fire, splitting the man in half before he too is turned to ash.

Aioven builds up a lightning storm inside him and unleashes it onto the rifleman, burning a hole through his chest. The smell of smouldering flesh and bone fills the air as the guard manages a few short breaths before the shock takes him down.

"You're brutal, you know that?" Stark says, standing beside Aioven.

"That's coming from the guy who put ten people down with mind-controlled guns." Aioven twirls his sword, making the blade ring through the air as if it is resisting its master's own commands and scraping against the air itself.

Aioven looks at the huge metal double doors in front of

them. "Do you prefer pushing doors in or pulling them out when opening them?"

"I say we push," he replies. They both twirl their swords into reverse grips and bend their knees. With their feet planted and their hands reeled back, they build up as much potential energy as they physically can, extinguishing some of the fires nearby as they feed off them where they can. Then they release it all with a simultaneous punch into the air.

The fifty-foot-tall metal doors crumple like cheap beer cans and are blasted open, getting knocked off their hinges and blown into the side of the building. Stark and Aioven can hear alarm bells ringing and people shouting. Not wanting to lose the element of surprise, they charge into the prison tower.

The pair each thrust their swords square into the chests of some stunned guards. They both quickly take in their surroundings. The inside of the circular tower is hollow, but the walls are lined with cells, miles into the sky. The roof of the tower is so high up that it's hard to make out with their own eyes. Guards start dropping by the dozen via grappling lines. Swords, rifles, and other gladiatorial weapons train on Stark and Aioven. The prisoners start banging on their cell doors and cheering.

They both brace and stop holding back. The sudden rise in cosmic pressure from their full release stuns the guards, allowing Stark and Aioven to start cutting them down. Most of the guards are killed before they can even attack. For the ones that do, their attempts never connect. Every sword is parried, every spear is caught, and every bullet is redirected to hit a guard.

With a twirl of his sword, Aioven's weapon is enveloped in dense black matter. When he swings the blade, the matter turns into tiny shards of hard, sharp material, shredding anyone who comes too close. Those who don't die instantly choke on their own blood and curl up onto the floor as the very act of breathing brings them closer to death.

Stark sees more guards coming, rappelling down with weapons drawn already. He points the tip of his weapon at the ropes. Bolts of bright blue lightning shoot from his sword and cut through all of the lines, causing several guards to fall nearly a hundred stories.

"Yikes, dude," Aioven says, before cutting down two swordsmen with a swing of black matter enveloped with purple fire, causing their bodies to break apart and then turn to dust and disappear.

"You have no room to talk," Stark says before sighing, "So, which one of these has Lee in it?"

A new challenger announces their own arrival. "You can join him after I cripple both of you." A tall, shirtless, muscular man appears out of nowhere. The light from outside reflects off of his pale bald head.

"Hey Leo, you think he's got an idea?" Aioven asks loudly.

Stark exhales loudly. "I don't know, man, it's taking a while for the light bulb to appear."

"Oh, that's not—" Aioven frowns. "Oh, that's his head. I thought that was a light bulb."

The man grits his teeth with a beastly growl and draws two rusty, bloodstained swords. "By the time I'm done with you, you'll be doomed to be a prisoner here forever!"

Stark elbows Aioven. "So his head really is brighter than our future?"

Aioven starts laughing. The man growls and charges. Aioven blocks both swords without even getting pushed back.

He spits in Aioven's face. "I am the warden of the Dark Tower. I will incarcerate you!"

Aioven pushes the warden back and adjusts his glasses under his hood. "You're more likely to blind me, warden. You missed your true calling. You should've gone into lighting."

The warden lunges again, this time with unforeseen speed and strength. Aioven steps out of the way, but the warden just stops and swings one of his swords at him. As their blades lock, Stark tries to take away his advantage of being a dual wielder by attempting to disarm his second sword arm.

Instead, the warden locks blades with both Aioven and Stark. Not liking where this is going, the warden pushes Stark back with a blast of kinetic energy, though it only knocks him back a few inches. He then proceeds to try and shock Aioven with electricity, but instead of knocking him back, it just makes him shudder for a split second. Aioven moves his shoulders around like they're sore as little bits of electricity visibly arc off of him, like he's shaking it off.

Aioven changes grip on his sword. "Static electricity is more lethal than that. That was like being covered in your hair after getting it cut—more scratchy and annoying than lethal." He twirls his sword around and spins the warden's weapon out of his hand. He then envelops his open hand with thousands of volts of electricity and backhands the warden across the jaw.

If the warden was an ordinary human, he probably would've died instantly, but the warden has powers of his own. He growls through his teeth and grips his sword with two hands.

Aioven looks at his stance before scoffing. "I may be a novice, but this isn't baseball. What kind of sword grip is that?"

Aioven puts one foot forward and the toes of the other just behind its heel. He loosens his body and lifts his heels a few millimeters off the ground. With one hand at the top of his sword hilt and the other at the bottom, he keeps the bottom of his hilt pointed at his stomach and the tip of his black pointed at the head of his enemy.

"*This* is swordplay," he says. The warden tenses up and grips his sword tighter. Stark raises his eyebrows. The monks must've taught him the basics of sword fighting in their own discipline.

With his rear foot to push him, and his front foot just scraping across the ground, Aioven takes one giant step and moves his sword like a lever, with his right sword hand acting as the pivot point at the top of the hilt. With minimum effort, the blade moves so quickly that the warden is forced on the defensive.

Despite all his efforts, Aioven simply augments his attacks with greater unnatural speed and strength, allowing his blade to escape the warden's senses and cut deep into his left shoulder.

Shocking both Aioven and Stark, the warden retaliates by thrusting his sword at Aioven's chest. Aioven parries and slams the hilt of his sword into the warden's face and breaks his nose.

"Nngh!" He stumbles back and points his sword at Stark. "You'll have to do worse than that. This pain is a shadow of what my masters are capable of."

Despite the condition of his shoulder, the warden reaches out and calls his second weapon back to his hand.

Aioven chuckles. "Not good enough?" He stops talking when he realizes the warden's ability to use his arm is supernatural. His eyes are glowing yellow, and Aioven can see thin, golden threads holding his shoulder together.

The warden points his weapons at both of them. "It doesn't matter if you kill us. They only stop pulling the strings when we are useless. Even a lifeless corpse can be a puppet to them."

"Let's test their limits then." Stark draws his revolver and shoots him right through his forehead." The man stumbles and his eyes glaze over. Stark and Aioven wait for something to happen, but nothing does. He drops to the floor, and the golden threads holding his shoulder together disappear, allowing his arm to fall off and roll away.

Stark looks at his gun like he's surprised that even worked. Aioven nudges the body with the tip of his sword. "Is it just me or was something supposed to happen?"

Stark looks at the body closely. "There definitely was a power inside him that could've been released. But it didn't follow his command. It was like it was following someone else's."

Aioven kicks the severed arm. "An architect's power maybe? Bestowed upon a follower?"

Stark looks at the man's eyes to check their colour, to see they're no longer a glowing yellow. "Regardless of its origin, why not let this guy use it against us?"

They both look at each other and come to the same conclusion. Whoever gave the warden that power decided that using it must have not been necessary. It could be because they deemed it impossible for the warden to win, or because . . .

"Someone else is coming," they both say in unison. For a split second, all colour leaves their vision, and in that same instant, everything is tinted green. As everything returns to normal, they look at each other and silently agree to hurry.

Aioven vanishes his sword and closes his eyes as he rotates slowly. Stark looks out the entrance as he hears wind and a strange, high-pitched thunder outside. For a moment he could've sworn that the sky flickered green.

Stark holsters his pistol. "Whoever is coming, we don't want to meet them," he says. Aioven opens his eyes.

"Looks like I've stirred the pot too much," Aioven says. "Their leaders are coming to meet us. Not the best day for an introduction, but not the worst. I hope you learned some improv skills whilst you studied film."

Aioven becomes a blur and disappears from Stark's senses. He looks up and sees something moving at the top of the building. It looks like a chandelier.

Stark jumps and soars upwards. As he slows down and reaches the top of the building, he realizes it's a giant birdcage covered in shards of glass and lights.

Stark grabs one of the many bars of the cage, carefully avoiding the glass. Aioven picks off one of the glass shards. "Hey Leo, do these look poisonous to you?" Stark pulls out a shard of his own and examines it. It's coated in an oily, transparent, black substance.

"It's an extract from the rivers of Hell." The voice of Alan Lee answers their questions from inside the cage. They peer in to see a dark-skinned man with thick, messy, black hair sitting cross-legged at the center of the cage. He looks back at them with wild eyes.

"You aren't knights. Are you captains?" he asks.

Aioven lets go of the poisonous shard. "We aren't from the Order or the Empire." Alan Lee looks surprised by this information and stands up.

"So what are you here for? If not for my execution?" Alan asks. Aioven frowns as he realizes how still Lee is standing.

"I could understand the Empire being a fan of capital punishment," Stark says, pausing to toss his shard, "but the Order?"

Lee's voice vibrates the cage. "The Order is just as insidious and brutal; they just care more about public relations than the Empire. Whenever they have PR concerns, they start eliminating people."

Stark floats back a little to get a good view of the entire cage up close. "Tell me something. My friend and I can sense how much power you're holding inside you. Escape from this facility would be easy for someone like you."

Aioven nods upon scanning Lee's body. "You've got a small atom bomb locked up inside you. Why not use it?"

Lee crosses his arms. "I could ask you the same thing, since you've got several. But I know better." He points at all the shards. "Any attempt to escape would send thousands of these shards flying, shredding anything and anyone in their path. If that doesn't kill you, the Stygian secretion will."

"All this will kill you?" Stark asks.

"And more importantly, all those imprisoned here," Lee says.

Aioven looks around at all the hundreds of cells. "Friends of yours?"

"Many of them are parents of gifted children like me, who do not want the likes of the Empire or the Order to take them away. Others are parents who couldn't stop them. Nothing wrong with having gifts when you live a normal life. But when those gifts draw you into dangerous battles, then what makes you special becomes what makes you disposable."

Aioven looks down. He can feel the potential energy begging his body to start falling. He takes a deep breath and puts out his foot and imagines the feeling of stepping on something solid.

With a low and long boom, he steps on nothing and realizes he can stand on air, unlike Stark, who seems to be kind of floating. He looks down and lets go of the cage, and instead of falling, he just stands there, suspended in space.

"What are you thinking?" Stark asks.

Aioven draws his sword. "I'm thinking let's start a prison riot. Stark, you catch anyone that can't land on their own."

Stark nods and starts dropping down. Aioven looks over his shoulder at Lee. "I only have two questions."

Silence from the cage.

"Can you wield matter like I can?" Aioven asks.

"Yes," he answers.

Aioven grips his sword. "How badly do you want revenge?"

"Almost as badly as you, Diarkis."

Aioven looks back at Lee.

Lee shrugs. "An investigating officer that worked your case was here a while back, though your fate wasn't of much interest to the authorities. I always thought it was odd that despite the destruction at your house, several bodies and cars were never recovered."

Aioven smirks. "I'm glad someone was paying attention."

"You weren't hiding?" Lee asks.

Aioven shakes his head. "Why hide when no one is looking?"

Aioven looks down to confirm that Stark has landed. "And I no longer identify as James Diarkis." He looks away from Lee and gets ready to start the riot. "These days I'm Dalkanos Aioven. A resurgent force of nature."

The whole tower shudders under the pressure of Aioven's cosmic power. He spins around, swinging his sword as he commands the matter of every cell door in the tower to convert and burst into a uniform black dust. He points the tip of his sword at Lee's cage. The smoke swirls around and solidifies into a dense iron shell.

Aioven shouts at the occupants of the tower, using his power to amplify his voice. "Everyone jump! Our friend here is about to let loose!"

"Seriously?" One of the inmates shouts. "Not all of us can fly!"

Aioven points down at the distant ground below. "My friend at the bottom will catch you. Anyone who can land on their own, stay a few moments to help catch those who can't."

They understand and start leaping like lemmings. Most of them are able to land without Stark's help. In a dozen seconds, hundreds of prisoners drop to the ground and start pairing up. Superpowered people pair up with those without power, and some with powers stay as individuals. They start running through the exit, blurring away at speeds their captors hopefully won't be able to track.

"All right, Lee, let's get you out of there. I'll catch the shards." Aioven starts compressing the metal with all his might. "It's a good thing iron can't fuse without the energy of a nova explosion, so there's no worry of something worse than a storm of poison shrapnel being released."

"Oh, great, I feel reassured now," Lee says.

Aioven smirks, but he's right—having a bunch of material bounce off a superdense iron core like that of a collapsing star is still very dangerous if done with enough force and material. Luckily, Aioven shouldn't have enough power to do that by accident. Beads of sweat start to drip down his face. The iron atoms put up an enormous fight, but he holds them in place. In all honesty, while what he is doing might be impressive to most, Aioven isn't sure he could even fuse hydrogen into helium if he wanted to. It feels like overkill. Even if he wanted to end the world. But it sure would make for a grand spectacle! All the same, he does his very best because he has no idea what to expect when Lee breaks free, only that he has a massive amount of power built up inside him. He has never had to counter another person's power before—at least not at a captain's level.

Despite his efforts, the superdense sphere starts to crack, letting sparks of orange light escape. He feels Lee inhale and hold his breath. Aioven strains as he braces for anything.

With a supersonic boom, the top of the tower is disintegrated. Aioven is knocked out of the air, and the iron sphere breaks open like an egg. White bolts of lightning circle around Lee in slow motion, arcing and forking as if they're searching for something to strike. As Aioven free-falls he sees little lights flashing around Lee and realizes all of the poison shards are still intact and are just turning in the air, reflecting light off of them. The deadly blades dance around Lee, flashing brightly like water in sunlight.

Not wanting to embarrass himself, Aioven twists his body and points his feet at the ground just in time. He lands with a gentle *tip!* and takes a moment to compose himself.

"You all right?" Stark asks, still rather shocked Aioven was knocked out of the air.

Aioven wants to speak but opts to just nod and catch his breath.

Lee silently appears between them, making Stark almost reach for his sword. Lee bows to Stark respectfully. "They always gave me the impression this place was guarded by an army."

Stark looks upward at the decimated top of the tower, seeing the sky where the roof should be. "We both expected the warden to put up a bigger fight."

Lee's eyes widened. "The avatar? You dispatched him that easily?"

The room is drained of its colour and fills with a golden glow. Aioven gasps as he is stabbed from behind. Both Lee and Stark are too slow to stop the warden from running a glowing, golden sword through his stomach.

"No!" Stark draws his sword and blurs right behind the attacker and swings wildly. Expecting the man to be cut in half, he is not ready for the searing pain of being slashed across the torso by a burning, hot sword. Somehow, the warden was able to move quickly enough to attack Stark without even needing to parry or block.

Stark and Aioven stumble; Lee shudders and tries to contain his power. The warden faces him. Lee can see straight through his forehead, thanks to Stark's supposed killing blow.

A dozen voices come from the corpse's mouth to speak in unison. "This one may not be able to kill or contain you, Lee. But we can." It points the glowing blade at him and flames as bright as the sun visible from Earth shoot out from the tip.

Stark grabs Aioven and blurs outside the tower to keep his friend safe. As he tries to move his shirt out of the way to check the wound, he grabs his hand, which shimmers and is briefly transparent for a moment. Stark stares into Aioven's eyes, who winks. Understanding the situation, Stark gets up to his feet.

"Lee! Draw him out here!" Stark shouts, stabbing the ground with his sword. Without wasting more than a few seconds, here is a flash of white light, and several shards whizz past Stark's head. The flaming body of the warden hurtles through the air and rolls several feet before extinguishing. Lee appears beside Stark, holding a huge, double-sided axe. The edges of the blades are extremely jagged, but what catches Stark's attention the most are the two huge gemstones in the center, between the blades, red and green. Stark truly is among some extraordinary people—extraordinarily dangerous.

"Now!" Stark shouts, pointing his sword skyward as he unleashes the fires from earlier and sends them spiraling toward the warden. Knowing the fire can only distract their enemy, Lee plants the bottom of his axe's hilt into the ground. The concrete cracks and hundreds of shards come out of the openings. The gems on his axe glow bright as he flies the shards at the warden with a push of his empty hand.

The warden counters Stark's fire with a gust of wind, but he isn't ready for the barrage of poisonous blades. Several shards go straight through him, and others embed themselves into his body. The hellish poison immediately starts to break down his flesh like a fast-acting, rotting plague. As his body begins to rot like a corpse in a timelapse, golden threads are again exposed, desperately holding the dead man together.

Stark and Lee change their stance as the warden begins to conjure a fireball. The warden shouts and points his sword toward the ground, but as he tries to thrust it into the floor, his wrist is caught.

"What?!" Lee can't believe his eyes. He looks over his shoulder, and Aioven's body isn't there. Instead, he has somehow managed to surprise everyone and slip past the warden's defenses.

Aioven moves the warden's arm out of the way. "You have no prisoners left, warden. You are relieved." He places the palm of his hand on the man's chest and then pulls back. Aioven remembers the night when Patrick died and how he first used his powers. That feeling . . .

He exhales and strikes the warden square in the chest with his palm. The warden's body explodes into a red mist, quickly dissipating into the air. The attack creates a shockwave that pushes Lee and Stark back.

Lee's grip on his axe loosens. "You know, despite having gotten in trouble with Imperials and cultists, you guys still seem like really bad news."

"Trust me," Aioven says, looking back at them, "we're the first good news Mars has seen in thousands of years."

The sky flickers green, and the wind gets knocked out of their bodies. Lee, who despite being so powerful has gotten rusty during his incarceration, has to fight to remain conscious. They all still have enough composure to realize the warden wasn't trying to stop them—just slow them down so someone else could finish them off.

"That was a nice trick!" The voice of the cosmic pressure's source booms throughout the compound. Aioven looks up to see a figure suspended a mile high in the air.

"Vaughn," Aioven growls. Darius Vaughn blurs away, escaping everyone's senses. Dalkanos Aioven is no fool. He turns sideways and points his sword outward. A split second later, just out of arm's reach, Vaughn appears and smirks with bemusement.

"So, you know me?" he asks, not perturbed by the katana pointed at him.

"That depends," Aioven says.

"On?" Vaughn takes a step closer. Aioven's sword ignites, and it is enveloped in swirling black matter and purple smoke.

"I think you know." Aioven smirks under his cloth mask.

Vaughn smiles with wild eyes and a wide smile. "A master of energy *and* matter. A rare sight unless your usual company consists of Genesis captains."

"We aren't of the Order," Stark barks as he pulls Lee to his feet.

Vaughn nods respectfully. "Of course not. You're too free thinking, not to mention quick to action. But I am still very interested in getting to know you." Lee and Stark stand on either side of Aioven saying nothing.

Vaughn's eyes flash red and green. "That's okay. I'm not interested in what you have to say. I want to know what each of you can do. Then we'll talk about why you're doing what you're doing."

Aioven senses Vaughn's influence washing over him. He can feel his will calling out to all the matter around them, probing the density and stability of the entire area.

"What are you up to?" Aioven asks, still ready to cut him down.

Vaughn extends both of his arms. "That question has too many answers, but I'll give you one if you share your identity with me."

Aioven, Stark, and Lee all sense the approach of others. Before they can be ambushed, they blur up into the air, where they stand together, suspended halfway up the height of the broken tower.

"What are you two doing here?" Vaughn asks in a low, calm voice. Stark and Aioven look in shock to see Lana Smirnov and the winged Angel Rytram blocking Vaughn's path.

The angel flutters his wings like a nervous pigeon. "Discipline us however you like, but our master told us to stop you from exposing yourself."

Vaughn shoves both of them out of the way. "As if I'd ever leave any survivors. And besides…" He looks up at the trio. "Their leader was about to share his name with me."

They join Stark, Lee, and Aioven in the air, but they keep their distance. Rytram steps forward first, his golden wings shining in the sunlight. "Stark and Lee, you both are known to us. But you…" He stares at Aioven. "I don't recognize your power."

Aioven spins his sword around his body. The air crackles as the blade slowly moves, as if the air itself is being burnt up. "Dalkanos Aioven." He pulls off his hood and reveals his face. His glasses flash as they reflect the sunlight, and his long hair flutters wildly as the wind blows through it.

Lana gasps. "That's impossible."

Vaughn pushes Rytram out of the way. "James Diarkis, one of the victims of Lana's last assignment. Looks like she missed something after all."

"Perhaps she's not captain material. She never returned to the scene," Aioven shouts.

Lana tries to charge at him, but Vaughn clotheslines her with a casual swing of his arm. "He may have a point, *Captain* Smirnov," he says.

Rytram draws a golden greatsword as wide and long as his body. "That's enough. We'll clean up this mess quickly and move on."

Aioven forces a maniacal laugh. "Ha! You're pretty confident for a pigeon."

Stark stands beside Aioven. "Are we going to fight them?"

Aioven takes a deep breath. "No . . . no, there's no point. Killing them now would be a waste. We need more witnesses." Aioven spins his sword around with his fingers. "Nothing wrong with scaring them though."

Lana and Rytram begin to call upon the power stored in their bodies. Rytram's sword ignites in blinding white fire, and Lana's body is surrounded by blue fire, flowing like water in slow motion around her.

Aioven points his sword at the smoking tower behind them. "Cute, but not enough."

With one swing, he compels the whole tower to break down. To the naked eye the whole thing just turns to a massive cloud of black metal dust, but Aioven has sharpened each tiny piece of metal into a blade so small and thin that it escapes the human eye on its own. Every grain of steel is shaped into imperceptibly small, razor-sharp discs.

The dark cloud starts circling Lee, Stark, and Aioven. As he directs the cloud with his sword, like a conductor of an orchestra, the cloud expands into a tornado stretching a mile wide.

Aioven looks over his shoulder at Stark. "Leo! Light it up!"

Squinting through the windstorm, Stark uses some of the kinetic energy of Aioven's cyclone to conjure up blue lightning.

The storm of metal and electricity grows larger and larger,

forcing Vaughn and his cohorts to back away to a safe distance.

"Stay back unless you want to get shredded," Vaughn says.

Aioven pats Lee on the shoulder and looks to Stark. "Take him to Sam's. He needs to get his strength back. I'll cover you."

Stark nods and takes hold of Lee, who struggles weakly. "I can run on my own."

"Not as fast as I can carry you," Stark says, gripping him. With his empty hand, Aioven creates a hole in the tornado for them to safely escape through. Once they escape and vanish from his senses, Aioven changes tactics. He turns Stark's lightning into purple fire and the steel shards into a black ink type of matter.

"Don't chase them," Vaughn commands. "Find Lee's family, and you'll catch up to Lee. Stark too, probably."

Lana becomes frustrated with their inaction. "What about Diarkis? He's here! We can stop him."

"We? Forgive me when I say I have zero confidence in you right now," Vaughn says.

Aioven releases a thermal pulse, igniting everything on the ground and setting parts of his enemies ablaze. Rytram's wings catch fire, and Lana's clothes burn, but Vaughn remains unaffected.

Aioven smirks. "Interesting." Rytram and Lana close in on him as the storm compresses around them. He looks Vaughn in the eye, taunting him with a knowing smile, and vanishes from all their senses. The matter compresses into a tiny, impossibly dense ball, and all the energy of the firestorm crashes into the center extremely fast. The extreme mass at the center starts to pull in random bits of debris that get crushed under the unnatural gravity.

Vaughn grabs his foolish compatriots and pulls them away as a catastrophic reaction occurs and the energy of a small thermonuclear weapon is released. The energy bouncing off the ball of dense matter is so enormous it knocks back all three witnesses. The initial blast is so bright that it appears to be the only source of light, outshining the sun. Everything else around it turns dark.

The explosion doesn't get more than a mile wide as Lana chokes the energy and forces it up into the sky. Lana, Rytram, and Vaughn watch the mushroom cloud form above them as the fire crashes into the upper borders of the atmosphere. The three Imperial leaders shuffle anxiously in the shadow of this destructive power, each of them trying to make sense of what they just witnessed.

"Let me get this straight," Vaughn says, facing his shocked followers. "Lana failed to kill a mechanic, and now he has powers that were previously never registered and is threatening our entire operation."

Lana gasps for air after fighting back the explosion. "He shouldn't be alive."

Rytram backhands her across the mouth. "He shouldn't be nuking us either! We can manipulate politics to keep the Order from getting involved, but we can't stop power-crazed vigilantes like these!"

Vaughn raises his eyebrows. "So, you didn't lie; you just failed to actually confirm the completion of your task. Maybe this guy is right. Maybe we shouldn't have let you become a captain."

"What's our next move?" Rytram asks.

Vaughn wiggles two of his fingers like he's dipping them in water. "Test the water, send one of our embedded assassins out to hunt Lee's family. We have more questions than answers after today, and after their demonstration of strength, we need to know their limits before they learn ours."

Lana and Rytram bow before blurring away. Vaughn turns back toward the mushroom cloud to admire it. "Dalkanos Aioven. You're far more interesting than you realize."

C̴ʜᴀᴘᴛᴇʀ 7

THE ORDER OF GENESIS

"Captain! You'll want to see this!" A young Order tech stumbles over his gray robes as he comes running down the hall to catch up to one of the few commanding officers in the order.

The tall, short-haired captain spins around, making his scarlet captain's cloak spin around like a twirling dancer's dress. "Relax, relax, what is it?" he asks, catching the young officer's shoulders.

He hands the captain a small digital tablet. "Captain Van Vuren, you asked me to monitor the fluctuations in cosmic power a few months back."

The captain unlocks the tablet. "You found something?" The tech nods, gasping for air. Captain Van Vuren taps the device and starts to look at the data. "Yes, but only if they exceeded the threshold I asked you to put in place."

The young officer zooms out on a graph showing energy levels. "And it did, sir. Someone used their power to release an explosion on par with the weapons used in the last war."

The captain stares at the massive spike in cosmic power. "An atom bomb? Or a release of personal energy?"

The officer shakes his head. "Neither, sir. The explosion was at a black prison site used by the Empire. Our readings indicate the whole building was broken down and then condensed at a super high speed to generate a huge explosion."

The captain hands the tablet back to the tech. "That seems like a rather indirect way to make an explosion. Why not just release the energy yourself?"

"I have a thought. Maybe he CAN'T release the energy. Maybe he is just a master of matter, and created a super dense ball that exploded!" the tech said. "They might not have been able to release energy at all."

The captain shakes his head. "I've never heard of a master of matter being able to push atoms together so tightly. You'd need to use kinetic energy in conjunction with your material control to do this sort of thing."

The technology officer takes and switches off the tablet. "If I may speak freely, sir. If I had his potential, I might still be learning what is possible, too . . . and I'd want some sort of safety net in case things backfire, like keeping enough power in reserve."

Captain Van Vuren blinks. His light hazel eyes dart to the ground while he scratches his head. "A good point. He could just be experimenting . . . or even just showing off."

"Showing off to who?" the tech asks.

"Anyone who is paying attention," Van Vuren says.

The tech keeps speaking, rather sheepishly. "Forgive me, sir. Even though it's not as destructive . . . isn't it similar to the death of a star?"

Van Vuren nods. "You think it's relevant?"

The tech shrugs. "It's so similar it can't be a coincidence."

He pats the tech on his shoulder. "A noteworthy observation. I'll be sure to include it in the council report." The captain thinks for a moment. "Do we have any intelligence on who was held at this site?"

The young officer swipes the screen a few times. "The criminal and former captain, Alan Lee."

The captain pulls out his phone. "That can't be good. Alan Lee is a powerful and dangerous man. His penchant was never the use of matter, at least not in this brute-force style. Someone rescued him. This is someone worse." He starts typing in a phone number. "His family is in protective custody, but he'll find them in no time if he's escaped."

A woman's sharp voice interrupts him just before he can make a call. "Don't worry about it. Your third in command is on the case." The captain turns off his phone, opting not to call his third seat just yet.

Van Vuren grits his teeth together. "And how can that be if I haven't given the order? Captain Smirnov?"

Her devilishly knowing smile curls as her fellow captain turns to seek answers from her. "Well, you see, planetary surveillance is your domain, but I happened to be passing by when the alert at the prison first popped up. I figured I'd send one of your best men to follow up, first to the scene of the surge and then to start with the leads we have." The tension in the air becomes heavy as she gets stared down by the captain of Squad Seven, a light breeze making her red captain's coat gently flap around.

Van Vuren grits his teeth and forces a smile. "So you told one of *my* officers to investigate Alan Lee? Are your people not capable? Or have their qualifications disappeared under your leadership? Or better yet, when did you receive the right to give orders to members of other divisions? Have you forgotten my squad also handles internal affairs?"

"Are you saying I shouldn't have been so proactive?" she asks, making a mock puppy dog face at him.

Van Vuren's knuckles crack as his hands shakily form into fists. "I'm saying that if something happens at the Department of Surveillance that demands a response, then the head of that department—*myself*—should have been notified immediately."

Suddenly, both captains feel their muscles tense up, like a full-body cramp from dehydration. All colour leaves their vision and they break out into cold sweats as the wind is knocked out of them.

A booming but calm voice breaks up their little spat. "I do not remember inviting children into my temple. If you wish to bicker like fools, then perhaps you should join the senate or go back to kindergarten."

The newcomer relieves the two young captains of his influence. "Such captains you are, arguing over jurisdictions. Not to mention, I shouldn't be able to make you forget how to breathe so easily. Especially you, Van Vuren. I expect better from you."

Van Vuren turns and bows to his superior. "I apologize, Master Koenig. I let my emotions get the better of me." The head leader of the entire Order of Genesis stands over both of them, his cosmic power weighing so heavily on his subordinates that their bodies begin to creak like old wooden structures. His white captain's coat flows through the air in slow motion, the gold trimmings glinting as they reflect light, and the solid black *1* on his back signifying that he is indeed the fearsome commander of Squad One. His dark, gold hair reaches down past his shoulders, and his beard shines with a glossy, glass-like finish.

"That you did."

Smirnov smirks watching her colleague get reprimanded, but her smile quickly disappears when Koenig looks at her, the Grand Master staring into her soul with his piercing golden eyes makes her feel light headed. "And you, while your intentions may appear good on the surface, even as a captain you do not have the authority to just order anyone around. You are in charge of covert operations. You should be spending your time doing your job and not doing the jobs of others—badly, I might add. And in situations such as these, I expect to be in the loop. Or do you think my role in the Order is not essential?"

She bows. "I am sorry, Grand Master. I meant only to help and provide a swift response to a dire situation."

Koenig sighs and motions for her to stand up straight. "I'm sure, but you still overstepped yourself. Captain Van Vuren, contact your officer and let him know you're joining him."

"Yes sir, I will leave immediately." As he turns to leave, Koenig continues to speak. "And if you can, try to make contact with whoever destroyed that prison. There's a chance that whomever is behind it may not be our enemy. But they are powerful. So much so that only our captains and masters can match them."

Van Vuren nods. "I'm not concerned, Master. I will resolve this as quickly as possible." He pulls out his phone and starts dialing his third seat.

The grand master crosses his arms. "Just be cautious. Like you said, it is possible this was a case of showboating rather than a truthful display of power. Don't make any assumptions about what you're up against."

* * *

Hundreds of miles away, back in the parking garage of Aioven's headquarters, Stark, panting and hobbling, slumps Lee onto a couch and lies down flat on the floor, sweaty and hyperventilating. Not seconds later, the emergency exit door swings open and slams shut as Aioven races in. He too stumbles to a stop and has to kneel down and catch his breath.

Stark grunts as he struggles to turn his head. "What the hell was that, man? I didn't know we were in the business of creating lightning death storms."

Aioven puts his hands up. "Sorry, spur of the moment... I just ... improvised." He takes a few more deep breaths. "I got carried away."

Stark crawls to a chair and slumps into it. "And you showed them your face! Isn't that like breaking rule number one of the superhero rulebook?"

In a similar ungainly fashion, Aioven flops into a beanbag chair. "Don't worry about that. I did that for a reason."

Stark raises his eyebrows as if to say, "*Which is?*"

Aioven exhales and puts his hand on his chest to feel his heart racing. "They can't share that information with anyone, and even if they did, they'll have quite a bit of difficulty trying to label us as anything but enemies of the Empire. Which will make any interactions with the Order of Genesis quite easy for us."

"You think Smirnov will be able to resist the temptation to attack you amongst her peers in the Order?" Stark asks.

Aioven leans back and stares at the ceiling. "It wouldn't be good for her cover. If she blows it, that's good for us, but it also works in our favour to be able to taunt her out in the open. It will frustrate her and her allies, which hopefully will make them impatient and reckless."

"Um, hello? I'm also here," Lee says. "And I'm not 100 percent sure why I'm here. I'm the big bad 'war criminal' who everyone wants to execute but never does for some reason."

Aioven lets out a dry, tired laugh. "I think you can safely assume we don't care about that. And I personally don't subscribe to the idea of 'war crimes' anyways. War is a crime, but that's okay since we don't shy away from the morally abhorrent."

Lee leans forward. "So, then why break me out? To recruit me? I won't work for anyone until I see my family."

Stark shakes his head. "Your family is in witness protection, under guard of the Order. It might take weeks—"

Aioven pulls the lever on his chair and lies flat on his back. "Sam found them yesterday. We figured it would be a good bargaining chip on top of breaking you out of an Imperial prison. You can see them as soon as you like, though I'd recommend a shower before you hug your wife."

Lee crosses his arms. "And if I joined you, what is the endgame?"

Stark stands up before Aioven can answer Lee's question.

"Hold on, Aioven. You seem to know more about this than I do. So I'll bite. What did Lee do to get locked up? Because it wasn't just the Imperials racing to lock him up. Captain Koenig branded him a war criminal himself."

"A fair question, Lee. Share your dark deeds with us." Aioven closes his eyes and stretches himself out.

"Um, well . . ." He looks at Stark since he seems to be the most interested. "Back when I was still captain of Squad Eight I was in charge of a small detachment escorting some explorers to set up a colony on an island. The island is rumored to have an entrance to a temple, said to hold treasures that belonged to some old demigod: Rei Iven."

"What happened to the colony?" Stark asks, having never heard of such a place.

Lee shook his head. "They never even planted their damn flag. Aeternus Imperial troops and their sorcerers descended on us in droves. Mowing down civilians, doctors, cooks, and whole families. It was like a nuke hitting a thatch hut. They took me to the island and interrogated me, days of torture to get information out of me."

"Information about what?" Stark asks.

"The location of the temple," Aioven says, reminding them that he's not asleep.

"Yes, we had old runestones left behind by entities that predate our current gods, the architects. The Department of Development deciphered them to be instructions on how to find and safely enter a temple."

Stark slowly turns to Aioven. "A temple, Aioven. Isn't that a coincidence?"

Aioven lets out a wheezing laugh and a cough. "It isn't." Aioven pulls the lever on his chair and forces himself to sit up straight.

"Alan Lee, I am hunting for knowledge that would level the playing field between us and the Aeternus armies, as well as their architect cultists. Powers so rare that they have not been recorded in history. I believe the temple on your failed island colony is similar to one that I seek: the Mother Temple."

Lee puts his face in his hands. "So your endgame is power."

Aioven stands up quickly, causing Stark to tense and put his guard up.

"I am not some power-hungry warlord. By all accounts I should be dead. I should have died at the hands of those drunk on their power, alongside several others I cared about. So believe me, if getting the justice I seek was as simple as taking the villains to court or shooting them in their sleep, I'd do it. But we're dealing with cultists, demigods, and gods. I have power, but you and I both know it's not enough."

Aioven storms off, the lights flickering with each step.

Lee looks at Stark. "Sorry, I've served a lot of power-hungry people. I made an unfair assumption."

Stark wipes the sweat off his forehead with his sleeve. "Relax, he'll come 'round. It wasn't unfair. I think he wants to prove his quest for power isn't about the power itself. I think that he is frustrated that he's not convinced himself. Let's stay focused: I want to hear your story."

"Well, after they figured out I wasn't going to tell them anything, they just let me go." Lee scratches his nose.

"Go on," Stark says.

Lee starts picking at his fingernails. "When I returned to my home, I found them waiting there with my wife and daughter, with guns pointed at their hearts and knives at their throats. They demanded I tell them how to find the temple."

"Soldiers or cultists?" Stark asks.

Lee shakes his head. "Inquisitors. The Imperial military had started recruiting those crazy fucks. Any special assignments that need skills like yours or mine, the inquisitors would be sent. They were doing some kind of archaeological dig to find the resting place of their last emperor."

They both pause for a moment, before Lee is ready to share what happened next. "I was the captain in charge of the Development Division, but my specialty was augmentation and cybernetics. My daughter lost her arm in an accident, and I designed the replacement. My technology has since evolved to help retired veterans and those out in the field."

"Sorry, I'm not following," Stark says.

"I design state-of-the-art pacemakers. I am more familiar with the human heart than most people. So when I saw them threatening my family, I lost control and just . . . gave them all heart attacks until they burst. Apparently it was considered cruel and unusual to make people explode from the inside rather than incapacitate them. And because I didn't immediately report back to the council, I was detained, and due to the scene I left at my home, they weren't eager to let me go. It wasn't long after that the Empire's spies started spreading lies about how my carelessness got the colonists killed and how I unethically executed people I thought were spies. The Empire even managed to make up some crazy story about me throwing the bodies of their fallen soldiers at them to hurt their morale, which Koenig accepted as the truth."

Stark couldn't help but be flabbergasted. "The grand master actually fell for all that?"

Lee nods. "Somehow, yeah. It was insane. But he still branded me a traitor, so I went into exile. I was almost immediately captured by the Empire."

Stark looks off to where Aioven went. "You know, I can see why Aioven wanted you as an ally now."

Lee frowns like he doesn't understand, to which Stark just says, "Ask him yourself. Your motivations are rather similar. I'll get you to your family soon. Before we leave, I need to talk with Sam."

•　•　•

Aioven walks down the hall in a daze and accidentally bumps into Lily. "Oh! Hey. I was just heading to bed. You want to join me?"

She makes a *tsk* sound through her teeth. "Can't, sorry. Sam asked me to go on a recruitment escort."

Aioven nods slowly, a little disappointed. "Ah, gotcha, that's okay. I'm pretty tired, so it's probably for the best. Which name is it?"

"Oh, it's a new find, so you won't find him on the list," she says while getting out her phone and hurriedly writing something down.

"So who—" he starts, but she ignores him and rushes off.

"Sorry! I gotta go. I'm already running behind." He watches her rush down the hall before opening his apartment door and heading inside.

When he slumps face-first onto the bed, he doesn't even bother grabbing the sheets or changing clothes. He closes his eyes and feels every part of him relax and decompress into the soft mattress. His thoughts become more and more vivid as his sense of reality dims. Eventually his thoughts slow down until finally ... *I'm back.*

Aioven opens his eyes, coughing. It's still dark, but he definitely isn't home. His vision adjusts, and he realizes he's in a dense forest, surrounded by trees that are as tall as skyscrapers and just as thick. Their branches have no leaves, so there is little to no obscuring of the night sky, which is unnaturally colourful with galaxies and stars seeming to be very close and visible.

Aioven hears a faint, hypnotic version of his own voice through the trees. "Madness is a slippery slope, and you've already begun to fall. But how did this begin? Did you jump? Or were you pushed?"

A faint creaking sound echoes from far away, like old floorboards being stepped on by someone trying to be stealthy.

The voice speaks again, the creaking getting closer. "Everyone has a monster inside them, and that monster is born from personal fears. Everyone is afraid of something. That's one of the weaknesses of imagination. It allows us to always be the best at tormenting ourselves."

Aioven slowly and quietly gets to his knees, and pauses to listen for anything nearby. His heart skips a beat, and he holds his breath when he sees movement in the distance. A tall silhouette is walking with long strides, each step taken as quietly as a mouse despite the crunchy grass all around. It pauses for about a second between each stride and twitches violently. Aioven squints. It looks like an animal standing on its hind legs. He begins to feel uneasy from either holding his breath or beginning to make out what the creature looks like.

It looks to be a giant, mutant deer, standing on its hind legs and towering up to ten feet tall, with long arms that almost reach the ground with its huge, five-fingered claws. Its feet look like huge eagle talons, and its massive antlers have bits of rotten meat hanging from them. The way it moves makes Aioven wonder how grounded in reality it is. Between each long stride it twitches violently like a crude stop-motion animation. When the starlight catches it, he can see that the entire creature looks to be in a state of decay. Most of its flesh has decomposed, exposing bones and mushy insides, and wherever there is skin, it looks sunken in.

"You could have a talent for instilling madness into the cores of your enemies at the very sight of you, but be wary. The path to becoming a monster is dangerous, and you could very well come to fear yourself as they do. Medusa looking into a mirror or Midas touching the world could become your problem too. In your efforts to save the world, you might just consume it."

The creature tilts its head back, and the creaking sound echoes loudly through the trees. Looking up at the stars it lets out a haunting howl, which can best be described as a hollow, distorted train whistle. The pitch is low and metallic, not a sound a living thing should be able to create.

It looks straight at Aioven, and the creaking becomes so loud until it builds to a loud crack and Aioven's eyes open suddenly. His eyes adjust to the darkness only to freeze in horror upon realizing the creature is in his room, suspended above him. With its claws and talons, it defies gravity with its back on the ceiling, still as a statue and staring down at Aioven in bed. Aioven is completely paralyzed.

He can't understand why. He knows his fear is irrational, but his confidence abandons him, and the shock is too much. He feels himself break down. He doesn't have a fear of deer or monsters specifically, so why this nightmare?

Aioven hears his own voice again. "Everyone needs a guide." He blinks, and he's suddenly in a field, face-to-face with a beautiful black horse. "Before you become too lucid, I must warn you. You will face what you fear most, and it will break you. It is inevitable, but be careful in your strides to prevent your destiny, or your only companion will be madness."

The horse huffs and clops toward him. Aioven feels compelled to reach out and stroke it, but as he does so, the horse rapidly decays and bites down hard on his hand.

Images flash in his mind: Several worlds being turned into lifeless deserts as an unseen force turns them stale. A green sword clashes with Aioven's, and stars explode. Golden threads wire the universe together and all converge at a distant point. A disembodied blue hand holding a black-and-gold dagger stabs him in the chest. A glowing gold pearl falls to the ground and shatters.

"The apocalypse is inevitable. Fight it all you like. Put enough effort into trying to stop it, and you'll create a new apocalypse yourself."

For a moment there is darkness, and then Aioven's body is

engulfed in a green inferno. The searing heat of the flames eats away at his flesh with each lick.

"Aioven!" Everything zooms into focus. He is back in his room, awoken by the feeling of someone touching his arm. He inhales sharply and sits up so fast he crashes into the face of the person who came to check on him.

"Ah! Jesus, man, you trying to break my nose?!" Aioven's vision comes back into focus as he recovers from being light-headed.

Aioven gasps. "Sam!" Sam had come to check on him, and now had her head tilted back with one hand pinching her nose.

"You were shouting like you were fighting someone. When I came in here you weren't even breathing," she says with a nasal voice.

Aioven takes a deep breath, as if he's breathing new life into a corpse. His whole body is sore. He stands up slowly and looks at his hands as he closes them into fists. It's faint, but he can hear the same low creaking sound as he did in the dream. All three gems on his ring start to glow: red, green, and blue.

"Sorry about your nose, Sam, but I need you for something. Normally I'd ask Lily, but she said you asked her to go recruit someone."

Sam frowns, a little confused, like what he said doesn't make sense. "Um …" She watches as Aioven walks over to his bathroom and looks at himself in the mirror.

"I have an idea," he says, staring into his own eyes, trying to imagine himself as a stranger. "It might be just the thing—exactly what I need to be the best version of myself."

• • •

Stark and Lee come skidding to a halt after running at super high speeds for nearly half an hour. Stark grabs a nearby streetlight to catch his breath and looks around. They're downtown. A construction site for a skyscraper sits on one side of the dead street and an alleyway between two dingy apartments on the other. The sun has just begun to set, casting an eerie orange glow over the pair as they make their way into what should be a safe house for Lee's family.

Not wanting to make things awkward with small talk, Stark stays a few steps behind Lee as they climb the steps up to the top floor. Their destination is a door on the landing facing the stairs. They both walk up to it.

"All yours." Stark gestures for him to open the door. Lee takes a deep breath and closes his eyes. Feeling the internals of the locking mechanism as he closes his hand around the doorknob, he wills it to open for him as if he had the key. After a few clicks come from the lock, they both enter the apartment. There are no immediate noises or signs of movement as the door shuts behind them. They wait to see if they can hear anything and look at each other after several moments of silence.

Stark taps Lee on the shoulder. "Body heat," he whispers, pointing at a door. They both approach it, their footsteps seeming to make the whole building creak.

Lee speaks in a soft voice, "Jess? Daniel? It's me, Alan. It's Dad." He reaches for the door handle but stops when the door clicks, and it slowly opens. A woman shaking with a boy hiding behind her is there to greet them. She is holding a kitchen knife that has been broken in half, with a little bit of blood dripping from the tip.

"Alan? Is it really … how are you here?" she asks, lowering but not dropping the knife. Lee holds out his hands slowly. "I haven't quite worked it out yet myself, but I need to get you out of here. I don't see how 'escaping' has made me any new friends."

"Well, it might've just a little bit," Stark interjects.

Lee squats down and holds his arms out to his son, who peeks out from behind his mom. "I thought you were gone." says the boy.

Lee smiles. "I was, but — well when I heard about your sister I thought I had lost all of you."

A voice from somewhere in the room ruins the moment.

Blood drips onto the floor as the hidden assassin speaks again. "He was, but don't worry, kiddo. This time it will be permanent."

Stark and Lee draw their weapons to face the speaker. They see a man wearing Genesis knight robes for a few split seconds before the air itself is set on fire. Stark and Lee manage to make out that the man has a cut on his right cheek from the knife Lee's wife is holding. Before they can do anything, the whole top floor of the apartment gets blown away, sending Stark crashing into one of the rooms of the apartment building on the opposite side of the alley. Lee tumbles and crashes through the fire escape and lands in a big heap between both buildings.

Dazed but desperate to save his family, Lee rushes to his feet and swings his axe, releasing a wave of kinetic energy at the fast-moving opponent, who is forced to stop and plant themself into the ground to avoid being blown away.

"Whew! They weren't kidding about you, Captain Lee! Or should I say *ex*-Captain?"

Stark hops out of a window and lands beside Lee. "For a third officer, you move rather quickly!" Stark says.

The man steps into the light, illuminating his sandy blonde hair and tan skin. "Let's not put too much weight into those ranks, shall we? Anyways, I've got a job to do." He reveals and pats Lee's son, Daniel, on the shoulder and holds a knife to his throat.

The blood drains from Stark's face. He grips his sword with two hands. "Let the boy go, before you make a mistake." He won't allow another innocent to die on his watch.

The young officer laughs. "Why? You'll just kill me anyways. That is if you *could*. I'm here to apprehend you, Alan Lee. It's time for you to go back to your prison."

Stark points his sword at him. "Are we to believe that's really your purpose here? I didn't realize the Order was training its knights to take hostages."

A gunshot sound bounces off the walls, and the officer dodges out of the way, dragging Lee's son with him.

A voice Stark recognizes to be Van Vuren's shortly follows. "No, he isn't here on his captain's orders. What are you up to, officer? What is Smirnov wanting you to do?"

Captain Van Vuren appears before the officer, making him yelp with surprise. "I don't work for Smirnov! I serve a higher purpose!" the man shrieks, making Daniel whimper.

Stark and Lee stand ready to fight just behind Van Vuren; the rogue knight continues to keep the child as a hostage. The captain rests a bolt action hunting rifle on his shoulder. "Third Officer Mark Wesley, you answer to me as of this very moment, or it could be your last."

Stark double takes. Where'd the gun come from? He notices the wooden stock is shimmering and that the metal of the barrel is dark with glowing green flecks in it. He looks closer and sees a single large green gemstone embedded in the stock of the weapon.

"I don't answer to anyone but my master! You have no authority over me!" He presses the blade of his knife into Daniel's throat, beginning to draw a little blood.

Stark, Lee, and Captain Van Vuren all point their weapons at him. "Unhand that boy now! Or we will do it for you. I didn't come all this way to kill anyone, just to talk. But if you hurt that child, you may as well give up on the idea of leaving here alive."

"That is unnecessary." A metallic voice rolls through the alley, coming from behind the trio, somewhere in the dark of the unfinished building structure.

It's Aioven! Stark can't mistake that cosmic presence for anything else. Aioven's chilling voice continues. "His refusal to release the boy makes little difference. He can stay in his grip, because when I'm done, his hands will be only things left near him."

A shadow looms over all of them, and a low creaking of the exposed steel beams and fire escapes unsettles everyone present. The warmth is sucked out of the air and everyone's bodies, making them all shiver as an unfamiliar cosmic presence washes over them.

Everyone turns their backs on Wesley to face the darkness of the alley, straining their eyes to see what is hiding just beyond the light. "All who threaten children fall under my jurisdiction, kidnapper. Would you like to hazard a guess as to what your sentence is?"

The creaking gets louder and more frequent, until they all hear a loud snap. Wesley shrieks behind them, and when everyone turns to see what is happening, all they see is a panicked knight swinging his arms through the air, sending huge arcs of electricity and bolts of lightning everywhere in a desperate bid to escape Aioven's invisible grip. Amidst the chaos, Daniel runs back to Lee.

"Dad!" The moment he picks up his son, the officer freezes in space.

The voice speaks from the shadows again. "I will not let you harm another child under my watch."

"Oh no . . ." Stark whispers, as a cloaked figure steps into the light. Under his black hood he is wearing a black-and-purple metal mask with a *Y* shape in it, presumably for him to see out of, as it looks like a tinted lens. He is wearing a black tunic and pants, with what looks like a tarnished gold chestplate, which seems to have been melted and cooled numerous times, as it looks uneven in some places.

In his hand is a sword with the hilt of his katana and a black blade of cruel design. Halfway up the blade it zigzags and then curves into a massive, curved hook at an acute angle. It is the last sword anyone would ever want to be stabbed with because it looks like it'd be just as good at cutting as it would be tearing one apart.

"You're a waste of space." Aioven flicks his empty hand at the officer, and black chains appear out of nowhere and flail at the frozen knight, like tentacles thrashing around at prey. As the chains reach him, he unfreezes and begins to struggle. Most wrap around his limbs, but some chains pierce his body and attach themselves to his insides. The masked newcomer raises his hand upward and slowly closes his hand into a fist. "You're not even worth interrogating."

The trio flinch as officer Mark Wesley is slowly crunched and compressed into a bloody ball the size of an apple. When released, the dense mass of flesh plops to the ground with a wet *splat*.

"Sorry you had to see that. I have a weak spot for kids," Aioven says, breaking the awkward silence. Captain Van Vuren considers pointing his weapon at the masked man, raising his rifle slightly. Aiovens sheathes his sword into an invisible scabbard. "Peace, Captain. I have no quarrel with you, only those that would stoop so low as to harm a child."

The captain, whose original goal was to learn the truth, decides to lower his guard a little and return his rifle back to the holster on his back.

"I take it you and Stark are responsible for Lee's escape," the captain says.

Aioven nods. "Indeed we are. We're trying to make as many friends as possible. Our cause is not the kind that can succeed with a small fellowship." The masked man holds out his hand. "My name is Dalkanos Aioven. I lead the movement to free the world of Imperial and architect influence." The captain shakes his hand slowly.

"The what-to-what?" the Captain blurts out. "Well, at least what you're saying is you're not an enemy of the Order or the High Nation of Ares."

Aioven shakes his head. "Absolutely not. In fact, I actually wanted to establish communications with your council of masters and captains, but I hadn't worked out the details yet. But this works, as it gets introductions mostly out of the way. I hope I made a good first impression."

"Well . . ." Captain Van Vuren nods slowly. "But now I have to report all this back to the council. Captain Koenig personally ordered me to come out here."

Aioven kneels down beside Lee's son to inspect the shallow cut on his throat. "Exactly. You'll be introducing us instead. It's always better to have someone introduce you than when you have to be the one to introduce yourself. It can help with your credibility."

The captain crosses his arms. "I'm not sure how the council will feel about an escaped but still rogue ex-captain, a former assassin, and some mystery masked guy going around dispensing their own version of justice. Especially after your little demonstration in dismantling that prison tower."

"One moment. You can come out now, he's safe." Aioven beckons Lee's wife to join them from inside the apartment. He had covered the entrance door in chains to keep her from getting involved. When she opens the door they disappear, thus allowing the whole family to be back together. "In exchange for wiping out their enemies, I'm sure they'll be able to make an exception. But we'll try not to break all of the rules."

"And what are your demands?" The captain frowns.

Aioven opens and closes his hands like a novel. "I was hoping in exchange for our services I could check out a book from your library, or perhaps do a bit of light reading in your temple."

The captain gets impatient and speaks specifically. "And what do you seek? Why do you seek an alliance with us?"

"I seek three temples. I have already visited the Elder Temple, I intend to pillage the Dark Temple, but I must still locate the Mother Temple."

The captain smirks. "The Mother Temple? That place is a legend . . . a myth. It never existed."

Aioven shrugs. "Neither did I until about a year ago."

The captain rolls his eyes. "Why would you want to go there? It's a place known for being so mysterious that no one knows who built it, what's in it, or where it is. No one knows if it's safe, dangerous, or holds treasure or certain death."

"So? That basically means you have nothing to lose but potentially *everything* to gain!"

"Hey, Aioven." Lee pats his son on the head. "We're going to head back to your place to patch Daniel up if that's all right."

Aioven motions like he's shooing them away. "I would never say otherwise. You all go ahead, we'll catch up." He faces the captain. "And I'm afraid our conversation must end, as I'd like to discuss some things with my friends." Stark remains silent.

The captain nods and bows respectfully. "Until we meet again, Dalkanos Aioven. But please, do not take too long, as I'll be wasting no time in reporting this." The captain's body flickers and disappears from their senses with a rush of warm air passing over them.

Stark turns to face Aioven. "Nothing to lose but everything to gain? So when are you going to get into public speaking?"

"What do you mean?" he asks, as his armour and cloak dissipate, revealing his normal street clothes of a T-shirt and jeans.

Stark throws his arms up in the air. "You could seriously speed up your recruitment process with some rallies. Get all flashy with your powers and persuade them with that silver tongue of yours."

Aioven thinks about it, imagining the influence he could have as a public figure rather than a murky, mysterious terrorist with an undeclared agenda. "It's not a bad idea, but if I'm going to give speeches, I'd like to be prepared. And I think some . . . *dirt* on our enemies would help sway people to our cause."

Stark claps him on the shoulder. "Well, let's chat about it back home." Aioven agrees, and they head off.

Chapter 8

THEY REMEMBERED THE ANNIVERSARY

"Make sure to let those eggs get to room temperature," Sam says to Daniel, who is precariously holding a few eggs, running across the kitchen to put them in a bowl.

Alan calls out to his son. "Boy! Those aren't your eggs, so quit acting like a chicken!"

Daniel giggles and puts the eggs in the bowl.

"Good! Now we need . . ."

The door into the kitchen clicks shut. "What's all this?" Stark asks as he and Aioven enter the room.

Aioven fist-bumps Sam and picks up a box of uncooked spaghetti. "I asked them to help with making carbonara tonight."

Stark processes for a moment before realizing what's going on. He catches Alan and his wife all over each other and coughs conspicuously. "You know, if you two want some privacy, you can take any room you like. We got Daniel under control. He'll be okay."

Alan restrains himself and stops devouring his wife's face for a moment. "You gonna be good, Daniel?"

"Yep!" he chirps.

Eager to resume, Lee grabs his wife's hand and says, "Well let's go, Jessie. I need a shower."

Sam starts whisking a mixture together in a bowl. "He's my sous chef!"

The kitchen door slowly opens, and everyone looks over to see Lily, who clearly is trying to be sneaky. "Oh! Sorry, I was just wondering if we needed anything and was gonna check in the fridge."

Aioven smiles when he sees her. "Um, I'm not sure. Sam, are we out of anything?"

Sam opens the fridge. "It's not too bad, but someone drank all my soda and ate my macaroni salad!"

"That might've been me," Stark admits.

"All right then, you and Aioven can get some more. I'll text you if I think of anything."

"Okay, I'll just head to bed then," Lily says before quickly blowing Aioven a kiss and disappearing.

"Wait I thought you said—" Aioven says as the door closes. "Man she's been pretty weird ever since she started recruiting people."

"Um, I actually wanted to talk to you about that," Sam says.

"Okay, is it all right if we talk later? I'd like to go for a drive. Leo, you in?" Aioven asks, to which Stark nods.

They leave the kitchen to look up and down the hallway but see no sign of Lily. "You know, Aioven, your girlfriend behaves pretty weirdly," says Stark.

He shrugs. "I don't know why. She's usually pretty clingy, but then again, so am I. Maybe she's just tired and needs some space."

They get in the elevator and start heading down to the parking garage. "So, I can't help but notice . . ."

"That we're having the same thing for dinner that we were going to have when Patrick and Laura died?" Aioven says grimly.

"Yeah," Stark says. Aioven pulls out his phone and shows him the current date on the calendar. "Today is June 4th, the day they died. The day James Diarkis died, and I was born." They both climb into Aioven's Lamborghini.

"I just . . ." Aioven grips his steering wheel. "I think I have it mostly figured out, man, but I also definitely have no idea what I'm doing. I think this is a good cause, but I don't know what my goal is."

Stark puts on his seatbelt. "What are you saying?"

Aioven looks at the ring with three gemstones on his right hand. "I should be dead, but for some reason I've got these awesome powers, so I was able to survive. And I think I'm more angry about the fact I survived than the fact that I watched my friend and his child die. I feel as though I should be using my power for something, or it's a waste, so I came up with this half-baked plan to put together a group of people to fight whoever it was that killed Patrick and Laura. But now it's the beginning of a movement, and I'm not sure what the goal is. Most of the time I'm angry and want revenge. When I'm calm and tired, I suddenly don't have any direction."

"What was your goal initially?" Stark asks.

"Well, when I met Sam, it was just to find out who did it. And kill them and their associates as brutally as possible," Aioven says.

Stark shakes his head. "That's not what I mean. I mean the moment you got your powers and did whatever you did to Garret Olsen. What was driving you?

"Revenge. I wanted to kill everyone in sight."

Stark nods. "Okay, is any of that feeling still there?"

Aioven looks at his friend. "Yeah . . ."

Stark slaps the dashboard. "Then use that to figure it out. You're taking today to commemorate your friends. You still feel that primal need for revenge. That's James Diarkis talking, not Dalkanos Aioven. You need to use that as the foundation for your cause, even if you don't share that name with anyone. Vengeance can be the fuel you need to rally others against injustice."

Aioven chuckles. "That's a very problematic sentence, dude."

Stark smirks. "Hmph, maybe, but I think you are more likely

to relate to how James Diarkis would feel than Dalkanos Aioven. Aioven is a figure for people to follow, a useful tool for influence, but James Diarkis is who you are, who you *still* are. I mean, look at all these cars. Are you really gonna tell me 'Master Aioven' likes to spend his spare time and resources collecting super cars? That's for you."

Stark looks at his friend as he seemingly spaces out. Aioven fiddles with the shifting paddles on the steering wheel. "I do still want to hunt them down. I want to get rid of the Empire. I want to stop the gods from being a reason for all these atrocities."

"Tell me why," Stark says.

"Because I hate them for what they did, and I know I have the power to hurt them," Aioven says.

Stark asks again. "Tell me why. Why might others want those same things? What motivations could they have apart from yours?"

Aioven sighs. "Freedom from oppression? To escape conflict? To be able to choose who or what you place your faith in?"

"That's it." Stark claps.

It finally clicks in Aioven's mind. "Stark, you're a genius. You just gave me an idea for a speech."

Stark shuffles in his seat. "Well, let's hurry up with this grocery run, and get you back home, so you can write it down."

Aioven takes off his seatbelt. "Nah, I need to write this down now. You drive, and I'll make some notes on my phone."

They swap seats, and Stark takes a few moments to familiarize himself with the controls. "Since nobody else is going to ask about earlier . . . Where did that whole mask and robe getup come from?"

Aioven looks up as they pull out of the garage. "I don't know how to explain it in a way that makes sense. I saw it one time in a dream, and I haven't been able to forget it. And each time I think back to it, for some reason, in my mind, I feel like I'm looking in a mirror. When I call upon a certain amount of power, the mask gets drawn out too."

"In the dream, do you think it was you behind the mask?" Stark asks.

"Maybe." Aioven taps away on his phone. "But it doesn't feel like that. It felt more like the mask itself was looking back at me, rather than with my eyes behind it."

"So the mask is sentient?" Stark accelerates onto a main road, pushing them both into their seats.

Aioven responds as the engine quiets down. "I'm not sure, but I had a weird nightmare earlier today, one of my worst ones. And some weird part of me thought it was a good idea to combine what I saw in my dream and what frightened me … Well, you saw what happened."

"It was like you became someone else entirely," Stark says.

Aioven nods. "A creature in the shape of a man, but with the restraint of a monster."

"What use is that to you?" Stark asks, coming to a stop at an intersection.

"James Diarkis is a man with a face, but Dalkanos Aioven could be the nightmare that keeps my enemies awake at night—something that frightens them so terribly that facing it would make them lose their sanity. I shared a little bit of my madness with that third officer guy, and I got a bit carried away."

Stark guffaws. "James, you almost made him as dense as a neutron star."

Aioven hesitates for a moment, like he can't process what Stark has said. "Yeah, in hindsight, probably not what I should've done in front of Lee's son. I feel bad for doing that with him watching."

Stark shakes his head. "Have a chat with Lee later, and see how he's doing. Don't worry about it. You saved us and the captain from having to fight with a kid in the mix."

"I'll do that. I appreciate the suggestion."

They drive along in silence as Aioven jots down some bullet points and cool-sounding phrases for a rally speech. Eventually his phone dings. "Well, that's all I could think of for the speech," he says as he pockets his phone.

"Send me what you have. I'll review it for you," Stark says.

Aioven unbuckles his seatbelt. "You sure? You've been so eager to step up and do way more than your fair share."

Stark shuts the car once parked in front of the grocery store. "You and I both have witnessed firsthand what happens when the wrong people have power. I've spent a lot of my life being frustrated and helpless as I watched family and friends be detained, exiled, or harassed because they made those around them uncomfortable."

Aioven's head tilts like a curious puppy. Stark pulls off his seatbelt too. "My family name used to mean something. My grandfather was the captain of the Fifth Division. My father was a master and taught and trained many future generations of knights. Until one day he decided to retire and marry."

"I didn't know you could retire from the Order. Or marry . . ." Aioven says.

Stark shakes his head. "You can't. Not really. I can really only think of one person in history that ever 'retired.' Rei Iven, same guy Lee was talking about earlier, though I think the leaders of Squad Four are his direct descendants, so I guess the exile wasn't hereditary."

"Well, what happened?" Aioven asks.

"My dad did everything he could to document his knowledge— his findings from research and all his wisdom. They destroyed everything he gave them and sent him and his fiancée to prison."

"Then how do you exist?" Aioven asks awkwardly.

"His fiancée, my mother, was pregnant with me. When they found out, they released her but told her they'd take me at the age of nine for training. And so, on my ninth birthday, they took me, and I never saw her again."

Aioven let out a shocked exhale. "I can't imagine you were very cooperative."

Stark bites his tongue before speaking. "No, I wasn't, but I didn't even realize my father was alive. It was only when I made the rank of knight that I found out, because knights are allowed to use the temple computers. I found out through their closed network that my father was somewhere in the prisons under their temple."

"Do they know that you found out?" Aioven asks as they climb out of the car.

"Yeah, but they didn't know I existed anymore—not after I removed every trace of me. At least not until our new captain friend showed up. My birth wasn't common knowledge in the temple despite being called Stark."

"How do you know our newly acquainted captain?" Aioven asks as Stark closes and locks the car.

"Victor was a sparring partner I practiced a lot with at the academy. Really smart and really strong. He and I were the only ones to graduate in our class, then I went ran away to film school we never saw each other again," Stark says.

"The academy is *that* rough?" Aioven asks.

Stark tosses Aioven the key fob. "Yeah, man, each class has like a dozen people in it. The age range is huge too: some kids as young as fourteen to full-grown adults in their thirties. But in the end, either no one graduates, or just a few people make it through."

Aioven crosses his arms. "Wow, Leo! I didn't realize that you were a degreed scholar!"

Stark smirks. "Pfft, all I did was succeed at making myself appear to be more useful to them than the rest."

Aioven puts his hand on Stark's shoulder. "I'm sorry, man. Kids—heck, *people* in general—should never be treated like resources."

"Well, as you can see, I've moved on," Stark says. Aioven looks at the distant cityscape of tall skyscrapers. "Now it's their turn to move on."

Stark shrugs. "I don't think they will. Not without a push."

"I'm pretty good at pushing." Aioven laughs as he pulls a shopping cart out of a cart corral. "You can be the good guy and catch them. I just need you to keep me from getting carried away."

"Like a good cop/bad cop routine?" Stark asks, smiling.

Aioven pulls out his phone. "Yeah, a lot like that. Whaddaya say, Leo? Us against the world? Together I think we'd make it."

Stark holds out his hand. "Question is, will the world make it?" They grab each other's forearms with a Spartan handshake, solidifying their brotherhood.

"With our help? It just might," Aioven says.

•　•　•

*D*eep underground in the temple of the Order of Genesis.

"You're telling me Stark is alive? I thought he was killed when he got caught up in that terrorist campaign against the Empire."

"That's right, Master Koenig, sir," Van Vuren confirms, still kneeling and looking at the ground.

The grand master tells the captain to stand up with a motion of his hand. "And what of his new companion and very obvious leader?"

"Sir, he appeared to everyone's surprise and freed Lee's child from Wesley's grip and killed him."

Koenig strokes his golden beard. "Why would he do such a thing?"

Van Vuren struggles to understand what his superior is getting at. "Why did he kill my officer?"

Koenig slaps the back of Van Vuren's head. "Don't ask such

ignorant questions. One of our men went to one of our safe houses and proceeded to endanger the lives of a mother and her child. It is important we ask ourselves why and under whose authority."

Van Vuren thinks back to what the late Mark Wesley said shortly before his demise. "He spoke of a master he served, but…" Then his memories roll further back.

Koenig looks intently at his comrade. "You've remembered something?"

The Captain nods. "Not long before I departed to intervene, Captain Smirnov took the credit for sending my officer out there."

The grand master stares at Van Vuren, puzzling over this difficult-to-grasp information. "Are you implying what I think you're implying?" Without speaking a word, Van Vuren nods like a child being questioned by their parents. "And you have no clue as to her motivations?"

Van Vuren sighs. "I have only guesses as to her intentions. She has shared none. This in contrast to the masked knight, who said he wants to eliminate both Imperial and Architect influence."

Koenig raises his eyebrows. "Who doesn't? But then, that might be the hint we need in understanding tonight's events. See if you can make contact with them again."

"Should we trust them? He says he seeks the secrets of the Mother Temple. If history has taught us anything, it is not to underestimate people like this masked knight who seems to know what the Temple holds."

"Well then, I should ask you: Is he strong?" the master asks plainly.

"Umm…" Van Vuren clicks his tongue. "I mean, he took down my third seat easily, and with a lot of theatricality. But the energy I sensed in him just barely exceeded that of a second-in-command."

Koenig's eyebrows knit together so tightly they almost form a unibrow. "Are you sure? A man who can barely beat a lieutenant wants to challenge Imperials and gods? Sounds like a madman."

Van Vuren scratches his head. "He didn't carry himself like a knight or even someone who is familiar with the Order. But he thinks we have information that he needs."

The grand master paces before finally sitting down at his desk. "I agree with you. He is likely to be very dangerous—but only potentially. I will not make the same mistake as my predecessor and pursue unnecessary allies. We don't need another emperor. I've managed to lead the Order for a thousand years without repeating her mistakes."

"Yes, Master. I will seek them out, or find a way to make myself clearly available for contact." Van Vuren bows and departs the office. As he's leaving, he bumps shoulders with Captain Smirnov herself.

"Sorry to hear about your man," she says. "Had I known it was going to be so dangerous, I would've gone myself."

Van Vuren restrains himself and turns to face her fully. "Why *did* you send him, Captain Smirnov? The Lee family usually gets escorted by lieutenants and captains."

Smirnov looks at the floor with a guilty look on her face. "I admit I do feel responsible for the outcome of what took place. He told me you rarely assigned him on any missions of significance, so when I heard that the prison where Lee was at had been attacked, I sent him . . . as a favour. I thought it would be a good opportunity for him to prove himself since that seemed to be what he wanted."

"I see." Van Vuren looks at the floor, pretending to accept her explanation. "Very well. Good night, Captain." As he leaves her behind, he senses an unusual amount of tension in her as he walks by. But she doesn't relax as he would expect her to when he turns a corner down the hall. Instead, her anxiety is increasing like she's about to do something important. As he considers masking his presence and stalking her, he fails to realize that she has disappeared from his senses without a trace. He rushes back to catch her, but she is nowhere to be found. "For someone with nothing to hide, you certainly are good at disappearing," Van Vuren mutters.

• • •

"Well, we went to the store to get a couple of things and instead got a full cart," Stark says. "Mars take me, how are we going to get this into your car?"

"Don't worry about it. There's some space in the front trunk." Aioven unlocks and opens up the car so he and Stark can start stuffing cans, bags, and jugs of drinks into the highly impractical Aventador.

"I've been curious. What's the difference between captains and masters in the Order?" Aioven asks.

"Um . . ." Stark pushes and clicks the hood shut. "They're all members of the Grand Master's Council, but their philosophies are usually very different."

Aioven pulls open the driver's side door. "Does having different philosophies mean that the play different roles?"

Stark rests his arms on the roof of the car. "Kinda . . . Captains are typically the highest ranking and most freakishly powerful military leaders, who answer to the grand master. The grand master only answers to our head of government. He is not supposed to directly intervene unless he believes the nation is under existential threat. Doing otherwise could be disastrous for Mars. He and the captains use the military divisions to maintain order, protect territory, and also wage war where necessary."

"Who is the current grand master?" Aioven asks.

"His name's Adam Koenig, he's, ah, a few centuries old, and he has done nothing but spend those years collecting knowledge, wisdom, and power. Not to mention, respect through his accomplishments. He was a normal captain when Emperor Atlas fell a thousand years ago and led the Order through the last war with the Empire six hundred years ago, and he witnessed the exile of Iven and is still alive today. He is living breathing Martian history," Stark says.

Aioven picks his nails as he tries to imagine how nightmarishly powerful the grand master is. "I see. And what about the masters?"

"They're more like sages or monks. They're less about combat and more about just making things better. Sometimes through combat or healing, but the goal is to make any fight brief and free of unnecessary harm. Which, I should say, is something the captains were also trained to do, but with different disciplines."

"They're trained to make battles short but decisive?" Aioven asks.

Stark nods and looks Aioven dead in the eyes. "Right now, my friend, there are only two things that separate them from us. Their power and experience and . . ." Stark pats the roof of the Lamborghini. "They aren't dramatic. You're a strong guy, no doubt about that. You'd probably give a third officer or a lieutenant a run for their money, but you'd need to be quick, efficient, and precise. Heck, you'd probably do some damage to a captain if you put all your strength into one attack." Stark waves his arms around. "No tornadoes of fire, no wasting energy on theatrics. These people will make you into sliced lunch meat so thin a flashlight could shine through you, all 'cause you wanted to twirl your sword."

Aioven opens his mouth to say something but stops as if he forgot how to speak.

"James, I don't mean any disrespect. You asked, and I know these people."

"You think Smirnov is just as capable as a captain?" Aioven asks finally.

Stark groans. "Well, she wasn't that strong when I first met her. Somehow she's stronger. And someone with immense power can hide it from others far more easily than they can fake having more than they do."

"That's nice," Aioven says defeatedly.

Stark snaps his fingers. "You've grown to be so strong in such a short amount of time. Usually, if someone's maximum potential is high, that leads to what can be perceived as a high growth rate."

Aioven's eyes light up. "So you think I can get stronger?"

Stark shrugs. "I would think so. It's what I was taught. One percent of a neutron star's energy output is going to be a fuck ton more than one percent of an atom bomb's energy output. In theory, the same principle should be applicable to you. You have insane potential, so you've been getting stronger and stronger without any need for training. Your excess power has been a safety net for you to figure it out on your own. Most people can't afford to mess around, make mistakes, and experiment in the heat of battle—not when they're starting out."

Aioven lets out a nervous laugh. "So long as I don't piss off a captain or worse."

Stark dismisses his friend's comment with a slow wave. "Nah, don't worry about them, we've got other—"

TTSSSiiiing! A familiar whistle cuts through the air, and the high pitch makes both Aioven and Stark's ears ring. They draw their swords, but as Aioven tries to transform into his armour, the attempt to do so knocks the wind out of him. He feels warm liquid soak his shirt from the middle of his upper back and chest.

"Aioven!" Stark shouts as the air is compressed violently by someone's presence. Aioven falls on his behind like a toddler too tired to walk. Stark looks around, feeling out for the source of the monstrous power, but to no avail. The longer he tries to search, the more Stark struggles to stay calm and steady his breath. He may not be able to see his attacker, but he knows her identity. "Steroids aren't very becoming of a captain. Nor is attacking civilians, Captain Smirnov!"

Another whistle and Aioven's car explodes, distorting Stark's hearing and all-around spatial awareness. He hears the muffled screams of witnesses fleeing, cars burning their tires as they try to escape, only for a few to crash into each other in panic. Amidst the shouting and car alarms, Stark senses the low crunch of footsteps as Smirnov approaches.

The moment he reaches for his sword, Stark gets the side of his head stomped into the ground by a captain's boot.

Smirnov grabs the hair on the back of his head and lifts him up like a mother dog does to a pup. "Hard to believe you're Arthur Stark's son. You look more like a cosplayer to me."

Stark laughs and spits blood in her face. "Says the imp narc wearing a captain's cape."

Lana smiles devilishly without even bothering to wipe the blood off her face. The light of the flaming Lamborghini is reflected into Stark's eyes by a silver necklace with a round pendant hanging from Smirnov's neck.

"At least I can back up what I say," Stark says through bloody teeth. She lifts him to his feet and pushes him backward.

"Your father's fusion reactor station was a cool project, and he was a hell of a captain. Which is why I had him imprisoned. The architects don't like it when their subjects try to leave the sandbox."

Stark wills his sword back to his hands and takes a two-handed duelling stance. "I figured your all-knowing architects would know that diversity is the spice of life."

Lana looks at the ground. "A rematch? Hardly a fair fight now that I'm a captain."

Stark takes a deep breath to find his center. "When I last saw you, you were barely a third officer." Stark's legs wobble as Smirnov proceeds to almost knock the wind out of him with her presence alone.

Smirnov rolls her eyes. "After I eliminated Reardan and his kid, my masters made sure I was up to the task of being a captain."

Stark inhales through his nose sharply and relaxes his body. Lana smirks and draws just one of her swords, and as Stark charges at her, the smouldering ruin of Aioven's car suddenly rolls and crashes into Lana. The surprise attack stops Stark in his tracks, but it hardly moves Lana. Still, it has served a purpose anyway, as Aioven is able to tackle her to the ground. He stabs her in her left knee with his butterfly knife and leaves it there. Blinded by rage and pain, he grabs her head with both hands and slams it into the ground, the impact putting a dent into the pavement.

"This," Aioven says, catching his breath, "has been a long time coming." He puts both hands on her throat and begins to squeeze, but his fingers struggle to put any pressure on her windpipe. It's like her neck muscles are flexing to resist being choked. Realizing the inevitable just barely too late, Aioven claws at her as she pushes him away. He tries to land on his feet, but his body gives way, and he resigns to rolling a couple times before stopping face-first, breathing into the pavement. Unable to get up, he coughs and wheezes helplessly.

Lana clears her throat and grips her sword. "You're not very patient for a dead guy. You'll have to wait before you get to choke me. That's a third-date activity."

Aioven lets out a hysterical laugh as Stark pulls him to his feet. "Ha! Don't worry about it, dear, you're not my type. I've tried crazy two too many times."

Stark hits Aioven on the shoulder. "Hey! Focus. Captains, remember?" Aioven watches as Stark returns to his two-handed fighting stance and finally takes a deep breath and does the same. No theatrics.

Lana puts her hand on the hilt of her sheathed secondary sword. "A semi-trained veteran and a novice pretending to be a superhero. Gee, I wonder how this'll go."

Not wanting to give her any openings, Aioven follows Stark's lead so that their steps are taken at the same pace. When they're within range of her, they both stop and start circling her until they're facing each other with her in the middle.

"Oh, you thinking you're being clever!" They charge at Lana. Aioven swings for her head, and Stark aims for her weakened leg. Moving as if her attackers are in slow motion, she stomps the blade of Stark's sword into the ground whilst parrying Aioven's attack and slamming the metal guard of her katana into his face. Then, with a twirl, she slashes open Stark's shoulder and follows through with a swipe at Aioven's left leg, which isn't severed, but his knee buckles, and he falls to the ground once again. Stark winces and clenches his teeth and tries to take a one-handed stance. Aioven returns to being helpless as the tendons holding his knee together fall apart.

"Dude, really? You'd be better off playing possum." With a flick of her sword, Lana knocks Stark's weapon out of his hand. She moves to skewer him only to feel an electric shock course up her leg and through her body. Despite this, she absorbs it and turns to face Aioven. "We know you're strong now. You can't surprise us twice."

"Wanna bet?" Aioven spits. Without even responding, Smirnov walks right up to her helpless victim and runs her sword through the side of his neck

"This time, stay dead," she snarls through gritted teeth. Aioven smirks at her remark, coughs, and splutters blood before letting out one final breath. She yanks the sword out of her kill and turns to face Stark, only to find . . . nothing. Just a pool of blood where he used to be. She goes into alert mode and grips her sword, rotating slowly enough to maintain a sturdy stance.

Aioven's voice bounces around in Lana's skull. "You still have to kill me first, ha ha ha!" She looks down, wincing and squinting through blurred vision and the worst migraine she has ever felt, only to see that Aioven's body is gone too. The wind starts to pick up, and the flames of the burning Lamborghini get bigger and bigger as Lana feels them being fed huge amounts of oxygen. Eventually, the winds get so strong that breathing becomes a struggle.

A voice makes her freeze. "I didn't know you could be *made* a captain. I thought you had to *become* one." Lana turns to face the speaker and draws both of her swords. "I may be an old vet, Captain Smirnov, but even my jailors knew better than to call me anything other than . . . Captain." It is the former captain of Squad Eight, Alan Lee.

Lee says, "You people are very noisy. I was in the middle of a . . . shower. Can we resolve this so I can get back to what I was doing?"

Lee steps into the beam of a streetlight and pounds the pommel of his axe into the ground. Smirnov recognizes the weapon: an axe with blades that make it as wide as a car and a hilt as long as the wielder is tall.

"You aren't a captain anymore, Alan Lee," Smirnov says, resisting the urge to take a step back.

"You want to see what happens when I disagree?" Lee picks up his huge weapon like it's made of styrofoam.

Lana lets out a slow exhale. "Damn you," she says and disappears.

Lee juts the end of his axe's hilt back into the ground, and the wind stops completely, as if it had been given a command. "You gents all right?" he asks, turning around to face Stark and Aioven, who had reappeared.

He kneels down beside a weakened, pale Aioven, with Stark putting pressure on his wound. "That's a neat trick. Must be pretty clever to make illusions like that."

Aioven wheezes and smiles. "You give me too much credit. I'm not clever enough to make a mirage out of matter and energy. It's more like a form of hypnosis or induced hallucinations. Rather difficult to do on people stronger than me, and exhausting when I'm injured."

Aioven holds out an open hand, revealing Lana's locket sitting in his palm. Stark tilts his head and curiously takes it and opens it.

Stark squints. "It's a picture of a woman with red hair and green eyes. Pale, looks to be in her late twenties or early thirties I guess."

"Is she definitely Caucasian?" Lee asks, "because that sounds like Lieutenant Rose Carpenter, or at least she was a lieutenant last I saw her."

Stark hands the locket to Lee who nods. "Yep, that's her."

"Something worth looking into?" Stark asks.

Aioven lies down flat on his back. "You may say it's a good lead or possibly even leverage. But Sam'll probably say it's an opportunity to make things personal. Give it to her and she can look into it."

"Why? Might I ask?" Stark asks as he pulls Aioven to his feet.

"Well, we need to get an understanding of the scope of the Empire's infiltration into the Ares government and the Order. And whoever that is in that locket is either an Imperial, a cultist, or a close companion that may have been told too much during some pillow talk. So an opportunity to gain some info or leverage on the not-so-good Captain Smirnov and her cohorts."

"That was your immediate thought upon stealing the locket?" Lee asks suspiciously.

Aioven nods. "Being a terrorist has taught me something: People respond very differently to the same things. Choose wrongly, and someone can seem immune to torture. Choose wisely, and their capacity to resist seems nonexistent."

Lee takes Aioven's arm over his shoulder and helps him over to a nearby bench. "And the other thing?"

Aioven slumps onto the bench and his eyelids begin to feel heavy. "That cruelty and creativity go hand in hand. Some things still make me grit my teeth just at the mere thought of them, but

I never imagined hurting another living thing would be so easy. Not fun—just easy."

Stark puts his hand on Aioven's forehead. "Sometimes, I don't know whether you're trying too hard to be profound or just sound crazy."

Aioven leans his head back and looks into the sky. "I'm probably just mad." He exhales and then his entire body goes limp. Lee and Stark watch their comrade lie there for a moment before realizing that the almighty Dalkanos Aioven has just passed out on a streetside bench.

"I don't get it," Lee says, crossing his arms.

Stark gets out his phone to text Sam. "What's up?"

"There's very little about this man that makes sense. You met him before he became all of this, didn't you? That's what Sam said, though she wouldn't say anymore."

Stark sits down next to Aioven. "When I met him he was just a regular guy. Living by himself, he worked on cars, though mostly just classics and almost exclusively internal combustion engine cars."

Lee frowns. "Well, that doesn't explain anything at all. How did you come to know him?"

Stark twiddles his thumbs. "Well I came into contact with him because Patrick Reardan asked me to recruit him for an op. He was an MCI agent who was a friend of mine that I also worked for in a sort of freelance capacity."

"He was?" Lee says, sensing he is getting close to the answers he is looking for.

Stark nods. "Yeah, Aioven—though he went by a different name back then—was looking after Patrick's daughter for him while he was out undercover in the Empire as a, um ... well, I'm not sure actually. Something that kept him from being killed upon entering their territory."

Lee raised his eyebrows like he was impressed. "Why did

he want to recruit him? Did he have training or experience of some kind?"

Stark shakes his head as he sends a text to Sam for her to pick them up. "None that I knew of, and he did nothing to make a case for him other than saying, 'He's meant for it. I know it. I know he has gifts, but it's more than that.' And he wouldn't really explain it further than that."

"Like a gut feeling or an instinct?" Lee sits down to rest his legs too.

"No," Stark says. "He made it sound like he knew something but didn't have the words to say it. My only lead to what his motivations were is that he wanted me to reach out to Aioven after his final visit to the Empire."

"I'd be surprised if it wasn't connected somehow," Lee says, leaning forward to stretch his back.

"Yeah, well, unfortunately I can't ask him anything about it. Patrick and his daughter were killed by Lana and a few of her imps. They tried to kill Aioven too. But for some reason, his death didn't take, and he came back with power. He doesn't understand why, and nor do I, but his growth rate is so fast that he has almost masterful control over three cosmic forces."

Lee jerks his head and spins it around to look at Stark. "*Three?!* You're saying this green bean motherfucker is more cosmically flexible than a captain, yet he almost got completely iced by one?"

"Energy, matter, and mind," Stark says.

Lee frowns. "Huh, well I didn't know 'mind' was a cosmic force. If he's begun to master these powers so quickly, how could he possibly know what his penchant is? 'Cause I mean mine's more or less energy since my father was a meteorologist and a part-time storm chaser."

Stark raises his eyebrows. "That's neat that you can trace yours back to him. I imagine you and I would work as an interesting team if it came down to it. My penchant is likened to that of a hummingbird. I can do things I'm skillful at very quickly, even for a cosmic-forcewielder. I can move fast enough to evade the human eye, and I can perceive a much larger amount of information at once than a normal person."

Lee leans back, looking rather curious. "So you could watch a lightning storm in slow motion and track the arcs of electricity?"

Stark nods. "Unless you've found a way to exceed the speed of light, I should still be able to keep my eyes on you. Unless you know how to manipulate space or time."

Lee whistles. "No, I thought Captain Koenig was the only guy that knew how to do that because it was an impossible skill to teach?"

"My father was close to figuring out how to do it himself. His theory was that you'd be better off learning the skills in the wild than from a person. That's why he set up facilities to observe black holes and neutron stars. Observing their effects on the space around them allowed him to, at the very least, better sense the universe around him. Not to mention, he was also really close to building a commercially viable fusion reactor," Stark says, reminiscing about the days of researching his father's studies.

"What stopped him?" Lee asks.

"He got arrested for getting married."

Lee rolls his eyes. "Pffft, if that isn't the council in a nutshell, I don't know what is."

CHAPTER 9

•

PIGEONS ON A PYRE

"Get in here, Melrose! Hallman!" Sam is shouting orders at everyone as their leader is wheeled into their trauma room, which is filled with medicine, medical equipment, bandages, and everything they were able to gather as civilians.

Lily and a never-before-seen gentleman dart into the room looking disheveled and confused. "What the hell happened?! What's wrong with him?!" Lily asks, panting.

"Captain Smirnov took a certain dislike to him for surviving her last attack," Stark says as he and Lee lift him into the hospital bed.

"Do we have a doctor in the building?' Stark asks. Sam puts on some gloves and a mask. "Not quite. I was an ER tech for a few years until I met James."

She tears open his shirt and starts cleaning his wounds with various materials and liquids. Mostly just bruises and cuts, but the most concerning being a hole in the center of his chest.

"I guess Captain Narc has a talent for plasma. These look like plasma burns to me." Sam gets out a flashlight and shines it down the hole and lets out an unenthusiastic sigh. "Well, this could take a couple days. The attack went straight through and clipped his heart and a few other things."

"How the hell is he alive?" Lily gasps.

Sam shoots her a glare. "You should be thankful. His heart looks like it's struggling, but it's still beating, just too fast. I'll see what I can do to revert everything back to the way it should be. In the meantime, I'm going to sedate him."

"Revert everything? Is that a medical term?" Stark asks.

Sam pulls off her gloves. "My powers are the reason why James noticed me. I'd use them whenever I could to save our more tragic patients."

She rolls Aioven onto his side to look at the exit wound and holds out both of her hands with the palms facing out. In complete and utter disbelief, Lee and Stark watch as the hole in Aioven's back closes, with no trace of damage remaining, no burn marks or even a scar.

Stark inhales sharply. "That's not something I've seen before."

Lee kneels down and looks closer at where the wound used to be. "I'm pretty sure no one has seen this before. I'd guess that the Order would be shocked as well."

The two men look at Sam. "You can speed up the healing process? Is that your penchant?"

Sam shakes her head. "No, my main power is reversion. I can return anything to its original state so long as I have an adequate understanding of the state I want something to return to."

"So, you aren't technically healing," Lee says, standing up.

Sam lays Aioven onto his back again. "No, I'm simply restoring his body to a previous and much healthier state."

Stark watches as Sam shines her flashlight into Aioven's chest wound and begins restoring his internal organs. "That's got to be the most remarkable thing I've ever seen."

"Aioven said something similar," Sam says, focusing hard on her work.

"I imagine he recruited you right away, once he discovered your abilities," Lee says.

Sam cringes a little as bits of seared flesh and organs regenerate with nasty squelching sounds. "Actually, no, he took his sweet time. It took him a while to even understand what kind of powers I had. But he spent more time trying to figure out what kind of person I am."

"What was he waiting for?" Stark asks.

"After a month of talking to me whenever I wasn't busy, he told me about who he was and what he planned to do. And he said that he might not be able to save the world by himself, and that someone like me could make all the difference in undoing irreversible damage," she says, as Aioven's blood seeps back into his body.

Everyone watches quietly to give Sam the peace she needs to focus on healing Aioven. Sam takes a deep breath to pause and close her eyes. "Lily, I need you to contact Captain Van Vuren. Aioven left me a note that he was going to want to have a meeting with him to discuss some kind of partnership with the Order. In exchange for the services we provide, they provide us with their library and your father's freedom."

"Erm . . . that doesn't sound like something they would go for," Lee says hesitantly.

"That's what Aioven said. He's still working on the details of persuasion, but if all else fails, we can just raid the temple and break out your father."

"Ha! I think I'm gonna sit down. At least before Aioven's blood or your crazy ideas make me pass out from hysteria." Stark slumps into a chair in the corner of the room.

"Lee, I appreciate your help. You should go back to your family. And Lily, please go and do what I asked you to do as quickly as possible. I'll let you know when James wakes up."

"You sure? Right now?" She groans.

Sam immediately stands up and gets in Lily's face. "Melrose, you will get out there and do what I fucking asked you to do. I'm sure James is sorry for getting injured at an inconvenient time for you, but unfortunately for you, I don't give a damn. So instead of spreading those legs for once, use them to run."

Stark blinks and crosses his legs and retreats into his chair as much as he physically can. Lily's mouth and eyes twitch as she glares at Sam, who doesn't back down. Lily finally turns around and starts to leave.

"And take your friend with you. You may as well since you two have been inseparable for days now," Sam says, gesturing to the gentleman trying his hardest to not make a sound during the whole scene.

Lily grabs him by the shoulder and drags him away. Sam exhales and returns to Aioven's side. "I swear, James, if I didn't know how stubborn you are, I'd tell you she's a walking time bomb of disappointment. But she's the only one that can teach you that.

"I don't trust her at the best of times," Sam says, "but ever since she brought this Hayton Hallman guy on board, the two haven't split. And you should hear the way she talks about him around James."

"Does she make fun of him or something?" Stark asks.

"No, she makes these weird comments. Eh, you'll just have to see for yourself. I don't want to come off as a crazy by reading too much into things."

Aioven groans and shuffles around in his sleep.

"How long does it usually take to heal wounds like this?" Stark asks, noticing the hole in Aioven's chest is still there.

"Not usually that long. I'm just being slow and cautious since his heart was clipped by the plasma," Sam says.

Stark grimaces as he watches strands of flesh knit themselves back together like alien worms. "Any idea how he's still alive?"

"I think he's been trying to figure that out for a while now—for like a year," Sam says softly.

Both fall silent as Aioven talks in his sleep. "The mission . . ."

he whispers. Aioven jolts around, and all the windows and light bulbs shatter.

• • •

Aioven's mind is in even greater turmoil than his body. Dozens of voices speak in his head at once: men, women, children, all in unison. "A third moon orbits Mars. Fear and dread preceded by death. A legacy of dust awaits the world whose keeper lost their own. The final mission. No orders. Just an innate purpose." Images flash through Aioven's mind of cityscapes dissolving into ash-like debris with no smoke or flames; green fields and blue oceans dry up to become a red-orange desert.

The voices continue. "You have no control, but you can fight if you'd rather die standing than on your knees." Aioven sees people running from a distant burst of gold light, like a sunrise that just keeps getting bigger and bigger. The ground shakes as the golden tidal wave washes over every single living thing, breaking them down into a black mist. The screams of workers, mothers and their children, and officers trying to console people in their final moments. And then, nothing. No trace, no corpses, no remains of the dead or ruins of civilization.

A single voice speaks. "We have been bored before. This is usually how we clean our sandbox. But the way things are going, we might not have to."

The voice shoots a thrashing migraine into Aioven's skull, unable to wake up despite knowing he's asleep.

"If you plan on being entertaining, I suggest you get your hands dirty," the voice whispers. Aioven holds up his hands when he feels a dry crusty substance all over them, ancient blood. The screams of billions begin to echo, pulsating through his brain so violently he loses control over his thoughts. As he sees that the dried blood covers not just his arms but his entire body, he realizes what's happening.

He feels the final moments of each and every death simultaneously—the fear, confusion, guilt, and anger. Aioven's own emotions get drowned out by all the noise until finally, suddenly, everything is muffled. His body feels numb. The voices have become muted. And they no longer convey any sense of anger. His own emotions intertwine with billions of others; he may as well not have any.

Aioven hears his own voice. "Cruelty and creativity." A purple beam of light shoots from the dead planet and blasts into the surface of another nearby world. The planet is molten, toxic, radioactive, and constantly being collided into by asteroids.

An unknown but familiar voice speaks. "Be a better architect. Use their sand against them." In a flash of green light, Aioven wakes up with a start, choking on his own spit.

"James!" Stark rushes over to sit him up and claps him on the back. Sam grabs him a cup of ice water, which is subsequently inhaled by Aioven, who then proceeds to chew on the ice.

Sam tries to resist the urge to stop him. "Are you okay? The sedatives should've kept you under for a little longer."

Aioven gulps down some ice. "Yeah, I just—" His eyes roll back, and he slumps back down.

Sam takes the cup of ice out of his hand. "I guess he needs a different dosage." As she sets the cup back down, Lily comes bursting back into the room.

"Aaaaah!" Aioven screams and jerks out of bed. Seeing everyone's startled faces, he forces himself to stillness. "I think I've had enough dreams for today, or night. Whichever it is."

Lily nods slowly and then looks to Sam. "Hey, Van Vuren is on his way. I told him you'd meet him at a travel center."

"How far?" Sam asks.

"About fifteen miles, just to avoid the dense population of downtown."

Aioven adjusts his clothes. "Good thinking. A few sleeping truck drivers aren't going to bother us. Let's just try not to bother them."

They all go down the hall, and as they're heading to the elevator, Lee catches up to them. "Where are y'all headin'?" he asks.

"You don't need to come. You can stay with your family," Aioven says.

Lee looks up and down at Aioven. "I'm pretty sure you need more babysitting than my son does."

"Fair enough. I can't really argue otherwise, can I?" Everyone harmoniously agrees and then all continue downstairs and depart in a convoy of vehicles. Aioven and Lily leave in his yellow Skyline; Sam rides with Stark in his Mustang; and Lee borrows Aioven's Redeye.

"You got something against having back seats?" Lee asks as Aioven passes him the keys.

Aioven shrugs. "Not really, but it does make for a good moocher deterrent when I tell them they can go in the trunk."

They all zoom out of the city, with their engines vibrating the buildings like a lion's roar in the night as they each race onto the motorway.

"So, how's Hallman doing? Is he useful?" Aioven asks as he lets Stark get out in front as he fiddles with his GPS.

Lily nods. "He's been super eager and helpful. He reminds me of you in a lot of ways."

Aioven raises his eyebrows. "Is that a good thing?"

"He's pretty creative like you, but he's really good at painting, and he's a bit of a car guy, though a bit more up to date." She gets out her phone and shows him a picture of a Tesla sitting low to the ground.

"Ah . . ." Aioven clicks his tongue. "I wonder what sound it makes when he honks his horn."

Lily sighs. "Oh, whatever. It drove real nice. He gave me a ride in it, much more smooth than this thing."

"Sounds like an interesting guy," Aioven says flatly.

"Why does he bother you? Do you feel insecure or something?" she asks.

Aioven doesn't look at her, but he cracks a smile, eventually beginning to chuckle before laughing forcefully.

Lily leans away from him. "Can you stop? You're making me uncomfortable."

Aioven shifts down a gear, revving up the engine. "Geee!" He taps his GPS, and it starts showing them their route.

"Yo, I'll see you guys in a bit. I'm gonna need some fuel." Lily peers over at the fuel gauge to see it's three-quarters to full. But before she can say anything, Aioven floors it.

Aioven woohoos as the engine howls. "Sorry! I guess she's a little thirsty. There's not much I can do about it!"

A fireball shoots out the exhaust with a gunshot noise as it flies past Stark and Sam. "Drat! What's got into him?" Stark asks as the loud bang startles him.

Sam takes off her shoes and puts her feet on the dash. "That's what happens when you sit in a car with her and you neglect to tape her mouth shut."

"You're not her biggest fan, are you?" he asks as he puts his foot down to keep up with Aioven.

Sam chuckles for a few seconds before saying, "I'd love to introduce her to a big fan, or just put her through it, I dunno."

When they finally arrive, they come to find Captain Van Vuren waiting for them already, sticking out like a sore thumb in his black robes and scarlet captain's cloak.

Aioven gets out of his car, having magically transformed into his mask and armour, and opens his arms to the waiting captain. "Everyone, I'd like you to meet the esteemed and very friendly Captain Van Vuren."

Van Vuren smiles softly and waves. "Hello everyone. As I understand it, you want to start a dialogue about a sort of partnership with the Order?"

Stark nods. "Yes, in return for aiding in the conflict with the Empire, we would like access to your temple's libraries."

Van Vuren strokes his chin. "To what ultimate purpose does this serve?" Aioven holds out his hand and summons a small, swirling cloud of black-and-purple smoke, with arcs of purple electricity zipping off of it, and everyone except Sam looks into the swirling matter and energy and begins to feel sleepy. As soon as Aioven makes it disappear, everyone snaps back to being fully awake.

"I have already mastered three cosmic absolutes, though not entirely on purpose, and more so I have stumbled onto an odd truth. There are definitely more than five cosmic absolutes to be wielded in this universe. And in a war where gods and angels are on the battlefield, knowing what they are would be of great benefit to us."

"So you seek power?" Van Vuren asks cautiously.

"I seek to give the people the tools they need to take charge of their own destinies," Aioven says.

Van Vuren nods, understanding the sentiment, but is still clearly hesitant. "So I ask again, you do not seek ultimate power? As someone who wields three already, why should you stop there?"

Aioven, remaining calm and patient, answers back. "Because if I had all the power, then I'd have all the responsibility. I do not want to be responsible for everyone. The very thought gives me anxiety."

Van Vuren gestures to Aioven's attire. "Then why the mask and dramatic garb? It looks like you're trying to look intimidating and powerful."

"That is partly the purpose of my mask and armour, though it is mainly to allow me to navigate your society as an ordinary person, without the general public being aware of what I am capable of. Dalkanos Aioven is a forcewielder ready to do whatever is necessary to do what he thinks is right, whereas my other face allows me to have the priorities and concerns of an innocent civilian and get a realistic feel for how my actions affect people."

"So you're saying you're completely selfless?" Van Vuren frowns doubtfully.

Aioven shakes his head. "No, no, no. I don't believe in selflessness. But I do believe that because I'm alive when I shouldn't be that means I should help people who might not be so lucky when the Empire comes knocking."

Van Vuren takes a deep breath and finally smiles. "Captain Koenig will appreciate your eloquence, and if you truly are speaking with candor, then I think the library masters and Captain Grizwald will also allow you to peruse through their tomes."

"Captain who?" Lee blurts out, making everyone look at him. "Sorry, it's just been a while."

"Horatio Grizwald, a bit eccentric but a fun man to chat with. A very talented librarian and historian. Captain Koenig promoted him when Captain Stark was incarcerated."

"I look forward to meeting him," Aioven says.

"Just one more thing." Van Vuren begins. "How do you know there are more than five cosmic forces? How do you even know where to look?"

Aioven hesitates to answer, making everyone stare with curious eyes. "I had a vision, or I should say *visions*. And they aren't just about the cosmic forces either. They also led me to where Lee was being held."

"So what do you know then, from these visions?" Van Vuren asks.

Aioven looks at the ground with his hands on his hips. "Not a lot. They're not really clear. It's usually a lot of doom and gloom stuff, but I've managed to figure out some of the stuff pertaining to the forces. I know that beyond energy, matter, space, information, and time there is the force of mental influence, which I mastered at the Elder Temple with the help of the monks there, which allowed me to regain my sanity."

"That's personal experience though. What did your visions tell you?" Van Vuren asks urgently.

"That the secrets of two more cosmic forces are hidden deep within the Imperial Dark Temple, where the last emperor ruled from. And I believe your archives hold the secrets to finding the last and most important cosmic force, hidden in the Mother Temple."

"Which has never been found. What force lies there?" Van Vuren asks again.

"I do not know. I only know it holds the secrets to creating a doorway to a universe where no mortal has gone before," Aioven says.

Van Vuren blinks. "Where?"

Aioven points skyward. "To the throne room of the heavens."

Van Vuren looks as if he's struggling to process the conversation. "What kind of doorway would you have to make to get there?"

Sam steps in. "The kind that allows matter to travel from one point in space to another, without having to actually travel the necessary distance. A quantum gate, which is what you could consider to be a man-made wormhole. The kind my father used to write theories about."

Aioven nods. "Which brings me to my final point. In return for our help, we request that you release Arthur Stark to help us in our research. Imprisoning a man so intelligent and talented seems a bit of a waste."

"I don't know if the other captains would go for that, but I'll vote in your favour. I never liked what happened to your father anyway." Van Vuren nods toward young Stark.

"My father found a way to reverse engineer an architect's quantum gate in order to create our own artificial ones, allowing for interstellar travel and the close observation of black holes and neutron stars. The reason for his arrest: he got married."

Aioven puts his hand on Stark's shoulder. "We'll get him back, and you can voice your opinion to those responsible soon."

Van Vuren scratches his head. "Well, I don't know if that's—"

Fwump fwump fwump! The winds suddenly pick up to the sounds of large, beating wings.

A voice echoes across the parking lot. "You hear that? The cosplayer wants to storm the throne room, but he doesn't even know how to open the front door!"

Everyone draws their weapons as more than a dozen angels land hard on the ground, surrounding them in a big circle. The shockwave of their landings creates a huge but short-lived torrent of violent wind, making some members of the group struggle to keep their balance.

"Dalkanos Aioven, how good to see you again. I never got to pay you back for letting my bird out of its cage." An angel steps forward, wearing golden armour and wielding a gold greatsword as wide and tall as his body. It's Rytram.

Aioven draws his sword with a twirl. "It's the head pigeon, Rytram himself. Did Vaughn send you to get your wings clipped?"

"No, he sent us to see if we would be enough to kill you," Rytram says.

"Oh, so you're like a canary in a mineshaft," Aioven says. One of the angels flies at him, attacking from behind with the help of his wings flinging him forward. This angel is wielding a smaller but still golden longsword, and Aioven is forced to stop trash-talking and block the attack. Not missing a beat, two more angels charge with their swords drawn too. Aioven pushes the first angel back and sidesteps away from one attacker to parry the other.

Not wasting any time, he punches them and turns to move on the offensive with the angel he dodged.

"James!" Stark shouts.

Aioven winces in pain as an angel shoots him in the lower part of his left knee with a glowing-hot red arrow.

"Motherfucker!" Aioven conjures a jagged chain out of nowhere and flings it at the shooter, allowing him to yank and reel them in and grab them by the throat. With one hand he crushes the angel's throat, but before he can toss the limp body aside, Rytram charges at him.

"Hyah!" Sam blocks Rytram's sword with an equally massive katana, which she wields as if it were as light and wind resistant as a small twig. She pushes him away and sweeps the large blade at him, which pushes the angel back with such force that his feet get burrowed into the ground.

A gust of wind and lightning blasts a hole into one of Aioven's attackers and carries them away like a leaf in autumn. Twirling his greataxe, Lee joins the fray, leaping into the air and kicking a surprised flying angel in the head, causing them to fall like a limp ragdoll.

Without a chance to catch his breath, another angel charges at Aioven, which he swings his sword at, sending a wave of black matter into the flying assailant faster than they can dodge.

A dozen angels leap into the air, beating their wings. Without even thinking, Aioven pushes off the ground and hangs there motionless.

"We outnumber you, blasphemer!" Rytram shouts, pushing Sam out of the way to fly up and attack Aioven from underneath. Aioven just barely dodges the attack and tries to swing his sword as he flies by. To Aioven's surprise, Rytram is suddenly stationary and not only blocks Aioven's sword but also parries it and stabs him in the shoulder as he tries to get away.

"Ha! You may be strong, but you have no experience! All that power, and you barely know how to use it." Rytram points his left index finger at Aioven and shoots a bright golden beam at him, which hits him like a train, making him lose grip of his sword. The angel slams him into the ground, churning up the dirt and crops of the field below.

"Aioven!" Stark shouts before quickly turning to Van Vuren, who is dealing with two angels. With a quick blurring attack, Stark manages to stab one angel in the back, allowing Van Vuren to sucker punch the other one to death.

"You've gotta get help! Go!" Stark shouts. Two more angels land by them and attack. Stark pulls their attention to him, allowing the captain to nod and escape. He pulls out possibly a phone or a walkie talkie, hopefully to summon the reinforcements they need before it's too late.

Lilith, dual-wielding a shortsword and a longsword, engages one of Stark's attackers, but her surprise attack isn't enough to defeat them. Stark, despite his best efforts, also has found himself locked in a duel that is stopping him from aiding Aioven.

And their help would've been very welcome. As Aioven wobbles to his feet, two dozen angels hover above him in a circle—Rytram included—all drawing glowing golden bows with white hot arrows nocked and ready to fire.

Rytram shouts down at Aioven. "Too bad! You should never have tried to talk such a big game. Then this wouldn't be so embarrassing!"

Aioven lets out an inhuman growl and throws his arms up into the air with a howling scream, releasing a final desperate wave of kinetic and electric energy. But before it can do anything, Aioven is shot down by more than twenty arrows. The heat melts his skin away but somehow doesn't cauterize his wounds, allowing him to bleed like a punctured water balloon only for his blood to boil away, causing him to be literally blinded by pain and the blood in his eyes. Unable to even breathe or scream, his body paralyzes him with the ultimate sensation of pain before finally shutting down.

"No!" Stark tries to get around his opponent but is thwarted as the angel knocks him aside by smacking him with one of his wings.

Aioven's body falls dead on the ground, quickly soaking the soil with his blood. Everyone's angels pull away from their duel and join their brethren in the sky. Rytram rests his sword on his shoulder. "He beat death once. I don't see him beating it a second time. What do you think, captains?" Rytram says to an unseen listener.

An unknown man's voice cheerfully calls out. "Here I thought we had the element of surprise!"

Van Vuren lands beside Stark to brush him off. "Look, Stark! Above us!" Stark looks to where Van Vuren is pointing to see multiple people hovering in the air, two of whom are wearing captain's cloaks.

The lead captain calls out to the angels. "You aren't in Imperial territory, Rytram. You're in our jurisdiction!"

"It's captains Venturi and Kingswood! Along with their lieutenants!" Van Vuren shouts.

Their cloaks flow slowly in the wind until they finally rest as the new arrival of cosmic power disturbs the air. On the back of Kingswood's white-and-red coat is a large red number 2, and on Venturi's black coat a white 6.

Kingswood, a broad-shouldered, grizzly-bearded man in a dark-brown cowboy hat draws a pair of revolvers from under his coat and twirls them. The chambers in them start to glow bright red and spin around, emanating a sort of mechanical whining sound like a supercharger in a muscle car.

Venturi, a very smartly groomed, golden-blonde gentleman, simply cracks his knuckles, causing gemstones on his hands to light up: a red one on the palm of his right hand and a green one on the back of his left. As Stark looks closer, he realizes they're duelling gloves.

Venturi closes his left hand into a fist, and his body slowly becomes covered in some kind of synthetic armour He tosses aside his captain's cloak, which is caught by his subordinate. He conjures an ornate rapier and grips it in his right hand. As he does so, the blade starts to glow orange-white as it gets as hot as it would have been had it just been pulled out of the forge.

"Captains! Not so punctual now, are we?" Rytram calls out.

"Hey, cockhead!" Kingswood barks. "How do you like your chicken?" He pulls back the hammers on his pistols. "I'm a fried kinda guy myself."

The whole sky lights up with two bright red flashes, and the air fills with sounds of lightning striking. Before anyone can say or do anything, two singed angels fall out of the sky as if they'd flown too close to the sun—still alive but unable to fly, and writhing in pain as their wings burn away.

Rytram lunges at Kingswood as he lets his guns cool down. But a sudden breeze makes him hesitate, and just in time. If it weren't for the fact he had noticed Venturi was gone, he'd probably have a skinny sword blade through his eyeball. Tilting his head to the side, he narrowly escapes impalement as Venturi's sword grazes his cheekbone. Venturi tries to swing the weapon at him, but the angel plants his foot into the air and leaps away.

Rolling and trying to hop to a safe distance, Rytram can barely stay out of Venturi's reach as he quickly thrusts his sword at him over and over again. Unable to move his sword fast enough to attack back, he is forced to avoid taking damage.

Kingswood looks down at the gawkers below. "Quit looking up my skirt like it's some sort of peep show and get up here! I ain't dancing for ya!"

Sam is the first to jump into the fray. With her sword pointing at her target, she slices through the air and immediately puts her enemy on the defensive. Unlike Rytram, Sam can swing her massive sword around with no effort, making her attacks heavy and unfairly fast.

Lee churns up the air under the wings of two angels and pushes them around, whilst messing with their ability to fly, like kites.

Stark zaps holes in their wings with a couple well-placed shots of small fireballs. Even with these successful dispatchings of angels, the swarm is still nearly twenty strong.

The fighting continues as the bodies drop to the floor, some still with life left in them. As the fallen angels groan and crawl, a low, unnatural rumble shakes through the ground. The floor begins to pulse intermittently, and everyone's ears start to ring and roar like they've been plunged underwater. The pulsing gets faster and faster until it becomes so loud and powerful that the clouds in the overcast sky are progressively cleared away with each beat. Streaks of dark ink race across the heavens, dyeing the sky a deep purple as they saturate it.

Despite the warnings, no one knows what carnage is about to be wrought onto the world. The deep bass akin to branches and tree trunks creaking and snapping accompanies the horror rising above the helpless angels.

Eclipsing the moons with unnatural posture is the undead, mutated corpse of Dalkanos Aioven. Half the flesh on his body has been melted away by the arrows of the angels. His organs continue to function as his heart beats within its exposed cage. The blood he has lost retreats from the dirt, returning to the awoken zombie's insides, allowing the body to regenerate.

Sam uses the distraction to slice her angel in half and sandwich Rytram between herself and Venturi. "From the looks of things, Aioven isn't the only one that's finding themself face-to-face with death."

Venturi twirls his sword. "What in the name of the cosmos is going on?! Van Vuren!"

"I don't fucking know!" Van Vuren shouts before turning to Stark.

"Hey, don't look at me, I just started working with the guy," he says with a knowing smile and his hands held up in surrender.

The angels stuck on the ground scramble and begin to run away. Despite the rapid healing of his body, Aioven's head and face are still deformed, which can be seen thanks to the fact that half of his mask has been destroyed. A large, black antler protrudes outward from one side of his skull, with a shorter one on the other side. His eyes are sunken and shriveled like dry raisins; a gray spot sits in the middle, which might be what's left of his pupils.

He extends his arms to watch his skin, muscles, and veins slither to his fingertips like grotesque, parasitic worms taking root in their host. When the bones are once again covered by flesh, he closes his hands into fists, cracking all of his knuckles at once. His veins glow a bright gold colour, bright enough to shine through the skin already covering his body. From his fingertips, golden threads appear in his hands, leading to all the angels on the ground around him fleeing. He closes his demonic fists around the threads, and the angels burst into flame, with purple fire escaping from every orifice on their bodies. They screech and flap their ruined wings desperately as their insides are hollowed out until nothing remains but a thick golden vapor.

The angels, captains, Sam, and Stark watch completely motionless as the monster steps into the golden mist and inhales it with one big breath. As the gold remains are absorbed, his body heals even faster, until, within a matter of seconds, all physical damage to his body has been healed. Without any scars present, the only indication of what happened is the fact that his skin appears pink, tender, and baby smooth. He looks up at the onlookers above, still clearly wild and certainly not the Aioven everyone has come to know.

"You dare take the power of our masters for yourself?! Heathen!" Rytram swings his sword downward, launching an arc of golden light at the recently risen zombie. Before the light even crashes into the planet's surface, the sound of chains rattling behind Rytram makes him spin around, only to receive a brutal backhand smack across the face. The attack knocks out several teeth and splits open his lip. Aioven had effortlessly penetrated the angel's defense, and rather than kill him right away, he'd rather play with his food.

Acting on pure instinct, Aioven lassos several angels with red-hot chains, severely burning them as he thrashes them around like yoyos. Occasionally he yanks one toward him to punch them in the head, which decapitates them more efficiently than a guillotine. Some angels are so unlucky as to get caught between two chains only to be pulled apart. This carnage continues until Aioven has brutalized half a dozen angels before their leader comes to.

Rytram points his sword at Aioven. "Angels! Restrain this demon!" The remaining dozen and a half or so angels all point and fire their bows at him. And instead of dodging, or even blocking them, he allows them to hit his body. Only this time, they have little to no effect. As each arrow lands, they are seemingly extinguished, and everyone can feel where the power is going. A swirling vortex of high winds and purple electricity begins to swirl around Aioven and the angels.

Stark hurries over to Captains Venturi and Kingswood. "We all need to surround Aioven and brace ourselves as quickly as possible!"

"Why? He seems to be doing just fine," Kingswood says, holding onto his hat so it doesn't blow away.

Stark sheathes his sword. "Because he's not in control! He isn't trained in combat, and he's not very good at managing his power. His restraint causes him lots of problems, but it saves us all from him going nuclear. He'll be fine, but we won't be!"

"He's right!" Lee says. "I've seen him let loose a little bit. It made these guys piss their pants before, and he was still holding back. That's why they sent so many of these fuckers to kill him."

Sam shakes her head, trying to keep her hair out of her face. "Whatever we do, we need to hurry, or we're going to die coming up with a plan."

Venturi nods. "We should send whatever he releases skyward. The atmosphere will take it much better than the surface."

Golden threads connecting the arrows to the angels become visible, and the pressure in the air along with the high winds make it difficult for even the captains to breathe. They all form a circle just on the edge of the main storm. Aioven's horns decay into dust as he extends his arms once more, this time setting every single angel ablaze with blinding purple fire. As nearly two dozen captain-level angels are exterminated, he crosses his arms over his chest and pulls in his legs, like he's floating in the fetal position. The stolen energies, the electrical storm, everything is pulled toward Aioven until time seemingly stops.

"Brace!" Sam shouts. Aioven's body becomes ground zero for one of the hottest points in the universe, releasing a glowing juggernaut bubble of biblical power and pushing the pressure of the air out of the way as if there was nothing there. Rytram disappears just in time to escape certain death as the ground ripples and cracks. The shockwave sets everyone's clothes and hair on fire as they go head-to-head with the power of a full-blown atomic explosion. Everyone knows it would be suicide to try and push the explosion back with brute force, so all they can manage is redirecting it skyward, creating a mushroom cloud dozens of miles wide and all but entirely blocking out the sky for anyone in the immediate area. The intense heat turns the crops on the ground to instant ash, and the sounds of nearby raid alarms and the screams of panicked civilians are an indication that while this is terrifying, it at least didn't result in innocent fatalities.

Though, if it weren't for their resistance, there's no telling how big of a radius the explosion could've had.

"Is it over?" Kingswood asks, as everyone peers into the dissipating smoke until, finally, the still-standing and floating figure of Aioven is revealed with his back to them. His cloak flows in the wind in slow motion with deep rippling sounds like a heavy flag at half-mast after a battle. The cosmic pressure in the air quickly lifts as he looks over his shoulder at his frightened friends. His face is exposed for a few moments before his mask hides his brown eyes.

"It is not over. But this has been an unfortunate step in the right direction. I understand that now is not the right time for me to explain—the pain is too fresh. I will do so soon. And I will invite everyone to hear my words and understand why I have done what I have done. For a better future. For them."

Venturi puts away his sword and crosses his arms. "Such declarations for a man who won't even stick around to explain himself." Lee, Sam, and Stark, along with the three captains, all find themselves unable to breathe as they're forced to their knees.

The source of this immense cosmic pressure speaks casually before anyone can see them. "If it's all right with you lot, I'd like to have a little chat of our own. Before the whole planet becomes some sort of nuclear battlefield."

Standing before them in black robes and a gold-trimmed white captain's coat, is the one man officially recognised as the most powerful forcewielder on the planet: Head Captain Adam Koenig of the First Division, grand master of the Order of Genesis.

Stark and Sam have to avoid eye contact with him in order to remain conscious. It's like staring into a moon as it gets closer and closer to the planet. The sheer sense of scale for this man's power is so overwhelming.

"Took your time, eh boss?" Kingswood says as he holsters his

Chapter 10

LEGACY OF ASH

pistols.

The man's face and golden hair remain still. "It took some aggressive negotiations with the senate to permit my release. Two atomic scale detonations helped my case. Now, what is going on here, Victor?"

Van Vuren stands at attention. "Sir! I was acting as an ambassador to negotiate an alliance with Dalkanos Aioven and his followers."

Koenig pulls out an ornate cane on it with three jewels, their hues being too dark to make out their actual colour. "Well, it would appear negotiations went rather poorly."

Venturi steps forward beside Van Vuren. "In his defence, Head Captain, the angels were interlopers. I can't imagine they helped."

Van Vuren nods emphatically. "And we were just about to reach an accord. I was going to relay their terms to the council for review."

Koenig puts his cane back into his coat. "Very well, Victor, I accept this explanation of these events more easily than you being the one responsible. Now I would like to know who is— who unleashed such power? An archangel? Rytram?"

Kingswood starts smoking a cigar. "From the look o'things, almost every angel here was an archangel."

"Archangel?" Sam whispers to Lee, who whispers back, "A captain-level angel, usually."

Koenig puts his hands together in his sleeves. "And I'm assuming the explosion wasn't one of you? I'd be forced to reprimand you for such recklessness. And yet, there are no knights present that are capable of such destruction."

Van Vuren looks apologetically at Sam, Stark, and Lee who are all still stuck kneeling. "It wasn't a knight, sir, it was Aioven. The man we suspected to be responsible for the breakout at the Dark Tower."

Koenig paces in front of the trio. "Well that explains Lee's presence. And while it's a pleasant surprise to see Stark again," he stops before Sam, "I have no idea who you are."

Sam grits her teeth and says nothing.

Van Vuren continues to share what he knows. "Her name is Sam Parks, and from what I gather, she is a kind of second in command or advisor to Aioven."

Sam speaks in an unwavering, stern voice. "I don't speak to people that force me to my knees."

"Very well, you can answer my questions on your feet." Koenig pulls her up with his mind, not using a single gesture to make it look effortless.

"Your master has a lot to answer for. Engaging the Empire, having this much power without declaring himself to the senate or to the Order. Such destructive potential must be monitored."

Sam smirks. "So he can end up like a dog on a leash like you?"

"If he were anything like me, he'd be here to explain himself. He's clearly capable of leaving a serious impression," says Koenig.

Sam rolls her eyes. "He isn't some domesticated pup like you to do what is expected of him."

Stark quickly adds to her sentence to draw his attention to him. "He's a monster, the likes of which you've never encountered."

Koenig grunts a small laugh. "I can only assume he will be as cooperative as you. I'm afraid I cannot permit an alliance with you children. This war doesn't need wild cards like you messing everything up. Official policy on Aioven will be to detain him or kill him if he becomes too great a threat."

Stark, Lee, and Sam all get locked into a T-pose. "As for you three, if you don't wish to be executed, you'll rethink your defiance."

A distant boom emanates from the west, and everyone but Koenig waits silently, looking into the horizon. The group ducks as cosmic pressure washes over them, Aioven's power. But it's distant. Aioven is releasing a lot of power, but this time it's far away.

Van Vuren reads a message on his phone. "Sir! Wait. The Empire! There's a riot happening in the capital."

"That isn't our business," Koenig says as he remains unaffected by Aioven's power.

Stark sneers. "Oh, please. The great head captain doesn't think that maybe Aioven is there? Or do you need Mom and Dad's permission to hit the town?"

Suddenly, all the colour in the world becomes muted and darker, with the once again bright-blue sky becoming a midnight purple.

"Quiet your minds and listen closely." Aioven's voice booms in the skulls of everyone—not just the captains and Aioven's friends present at the scorched battlefield but everyone in the world.

• • •

In places like Atlas, the huge screens of the main square flicker. The large TV overlooking the pedestrian-packed intersection cuts to the masked and hooded face of Aioven.

"Halt your thoughts. Look to your phones and television screens. Close your eyes and see my face. This is a message to the good people of the world. And indeed, the good people of the Empire too. I have grown tired of waiting to wage war with your military and its leaders. I am sick of your masters and their misdeeds, both on the surface and above us in the heavens. Your civilization is poisoned by corruption, cruelty, and power lust."

The screen cuts to a massive temple with huge, golden angel statues standing in front of the pillars and stairs that lead inside—a building of immense size, as long and wide as a football field.

"Behold, the Dark Temple of the architects and their angels." An explosion of purple fire originating from inside the temple blasts apart the walls, causing the colossal-sized building to collapse. The statues partially melt to become grotesque, distorted versions of themselves, and the pillars at the front fall to perfectly block the entrance.

"The Capital will be destroyed in nine hours. Everyone who remains will die. To those of you who are innocent, I say to you: Leave Now. To all others—the politicians, the angels and architects, the powerful lurking in the shadows—I say to you: You will not escape. I will not stop until your Empire is reduced to ash." When I am finished here, the Empire's legacy will be nothing but ash. You have nine hours. This is your only warning."

Aioven's threat seems to work in the Empire too. The protestors that had gathered in front of the Dark Temple scramble despite the police trying to tear-gas them.

Captain Koenig releases Stark, Sam, and Lee to focus on evacuation efforts while they look for Aioven. "If Aioven is responsible for this, it is now your job to prevent any unnecessary death." Flying toward the Imperial capital city of Malista, the trio gather on a rooftop overlooking the chaos on a main street.

"You think he's still in control?" Lee asks, watching the smoke from Aioven's attack on the temple rise in the distance.

Sam grimaces, watching the violence unfold below. "I don't know. I knew he wanted to raid their temple, but I thought we'd all be involved to make that happen."

Stark pulls out some binoculars. "I remember him saying that he'd kept some energy in reserve to stay sane. I'm guessing that destroying the temple used too much power . . . and his sanity slipped."

Lee watches explosions pop up throughout the city. "That explains why he was suddenly so much stronger. He wasn't trying to stop himself from going nuts, so he had tons of power to spare."

The ground shakes as Aioven's presence crushes the city. Everyone looks frantically for their friend, but he's nowhere to be seen.

• • •

Remarkably, Aioven is much closer than they realize.

"Hmm . . ." Aioven, once again fully dressed in his robes and armour, is hovering above Malista, watching in disgust as people are dragged into police vans, likely to never be seen again.

He didn't want to get involved in the chaos too much since the Order's knights had shown up. At least until he saw that the captains and other knights were not trying to rescue anyone! As for Imperial forces, only the city police are present—no angels or forcewielders anywhere.

He takes a deep breath and allows himself to fall out of the sky, landing directly onto the windshield of a police van and crushing the driver. Few people notice or bother to take the time to acknowledge what just happened, so Aioven continues to hop to the ground and pull the officer out of the vehicle.

"Which capitol building is used by your intelligence agency?" Aioven demands. The officer squints through his own bloodied face at Aioven like he's in a trance. "The place where your minister of intelligence runs to hide! Where is it?!" Aioven asks again.

As his eyes start to roll back into his head, he points at a large, black skyscraper a few miles away from the city center.

Aioven nods and says, "Thank you for your service," and slams his head into the van, leaving a nice, head-sized dent in its side. After releasing the occupants of this van and several others in a similar fashion, Aioven goes to scope out the intelligence headquarters. The armoured doors with keypads next to them dissuade Aioven from thinking he'll be discreet about this. Kneeling down, he waits to see if there are any knights or captains nearby. So far, so good.

• • •

"Hold on," Stark says, pulling out a gold coin from his pocket. "If Aioven lost control, then why are these still stable?" Sam snatches the coin out of Stark's hand and looks at it carefully. "How many of these trapped coins has Aioven snuck into this city?" Stark asks.

Sam struggles to compose herself. "I, um, hundreds of millions of dollars worth . . . But if they haven't gone off yet . . ."

Stark finishes her sentence. "Then we're all very lucky, or we're standing in ground zero."

Lee groans. "Hey, remember that time Aioven warned everyone he was going to raze this place? Like three minutes ago?"

Sam stands on the edge and looks down at the bubbling mass of panicking people. "I think trying to stop him would be a bad idea. For one, I don't think we would be able to, and two . . . I think we should help the civilians evacuate. I don't think he's interested in harming innocents."

They all agree and hastily jump off the building and start directing people and saving stragglers.

• • •

Aioven stands up and strains his eyes as a woman and a child open the front doors of the intelligence building and rush inside.

"That's interesting," Aioven says, and just before standing up, two Genesis knights approach the door and blast it open amidst all the chaos. They both hurry inside, looking behind themselves to make sure they aren't being followed.

"I've got a bad feeling about that," Aioven says, hopping across the street. He enters the building and begins to move as carefully and quietly as possible. At first there's silence, until he hears a ding come from down a hallway. Peeking around the corner, he sees two sets of elevators, one having just arrived at the top floor. With a slow and steady motion with his hands, he wills the elevator's double doors to slowly and quietly open.

Like a character in a platformer video game, Aioven leaps forward and plants one foot on the wall and launches himself several dozen stories upward, only to surge upward again with the help of his other foot pushing away from the opposite wall. He stops at the door of the top floor, with the back halves of both feet hanging off the edge. He inhales and holds his breath as he places his hands on the doors and opens them as quiet as a mouse. He notices that the elevator sitting at this floor is sparking and appears to no longer be functional. As the doors close behind him, he presses the call button to bring an elevator up to the top floor.

Tip-toeing down the hall, he can hear low voices, which confuses Aioven at first, because wouldn't these knights be under the impression that they're alone? He hears a sword slide into its sheath, and Aioven instinctively draws his. There's an unusual amount of aggression that he can sense down the hall.

Aioven reaches an office door made of fogged glass. He presses his back to the wall beside it and focuses his hearing.

He can hear two men arguing. "Did you have to get so carried away? Corpses aren't fun, you necrophiliac. I've gotta draw the line somewhere." Aioven closes his eyes and breathes as he struggles to maintain composure.

The sound of two bodies slumping to the floor makes Aioven twitch, as he can tell one is much lighter than the other. Another male voice responds. "Don't worry about it. This whole place is going to shit anyways. No one will know we were here. I didn't sign up for this celibacy crap when I was born."

"But, dude, seriously," the first man says.

"Well, just don't watch then. We've done worse than this."

Aioven has heard enough. He places his pinky finger on the frosted glass and causes the whole thing to crack. In an instant, the glass breaks into tiny invisible pieces and tears into the room. The sounds of papers, surprised shouting, and windows breaking fill the room quickly and then cease just as quickly.

"Gentlemen!" Aioven enters the room, with papers flying around in shreds or being pulled off the large desk in the center by the breeze of the now-destroyed windows. "I would've hoped that you and your fellow knights would want to help these people get to safety."

He looks down at the bodies of the mother and child on the floor and feels a heat fill his veins as his hands become unnaturally steady with focus. Aioven kneels beside the mother, who is in a state of undress, and does his best to cover her up. He looks over at the child and almost reflexively gasps when he sees her body shift as she breathes. His knuckles crack as his hands close into fists.

"I'm sorry, but I'm afraid it's still my turn to be the monster." Aioven kicks the large desk out the window to expose the two knights who had been taking cover.

Aioven has an idea, seeing this encounter as an opportunity. "Do either of you have any familiarity with Arthur Stark and the dungeons of your temple?"

The two knights look at each other before one finally says, "I don't know much about him, and I've never been to the cells. I've only—"

Aioven liberates the knight's head from his shoulders and pushes him out the window.

Shaking as he watches his comrade splatter onto the pavement below, the other knight manages a more useful answer. "Since his offense wasn't all that severe, the council just put him in one of the upper holding cells. He can do whatever he likes in there; he just can't use his powers. Most didn't want to punish him, so the council basically just supervises him."

Aioven rests the bloodstained blade of his sword on the knight's sword. "That was almost helpful. How can I get to him?"

Trying not to look at the blood, the knight continues. "The presidential seal on the floor in the main hall. His cell is right below that."

Aioven nods. "Seems simple enough. Now I know where I'm needed next when I am done here."

He raises his sword long enough for the knight to start begging, only to sweep him away with an electrically charged swing, sending the blackened corpse careening into the air. Aioven watches as the body breaks into pieces when it hits the ground.

He hears a groaning behind him and immediately sheathes his sword and transforms his appearance. His robes turn black and brown. As his sword clicks into place, it returns to its more standard katana state. He rushes over to the little girl and looks her over.

"Hey, take it easy. How hurt are you?" he asks quietly. She looks at him and then at her mother. She screams and runs over to her, stumbling as she struggles with a clearly broken leg.

She grabs her mother's shoulder tightly, causing her head to slump to one side. "Mom! Mom! Wake up! You gotta wake up!" Aioven feels frozen like a deer caught in headlights, not sure how to help. Her screams get louder and more incoherent as her hope fades. Eventually she starts coughing and curls up with her mom, quietly sobbing.

Aioven stands up slowly and looks out the window, the sounds of panicked shouting and screaming finally reaching his ears.

"What have I done?" he says, looking down onto the chaos of the streets below. He turns back to the girl and says, "Hey, I don't want to rush you, but it won't be safe here for much longer. Do you have any other parents or guardians?"

She sniffles and continues to sob. "I want my daddy! Mommy!"

He kneels down next to her. "We should find your dad. He needs to make sure you're safe."

She starts to let go of her mom's body. "But what about my mom? I can't leave her."

Aioven reaches out and closes her mother's eyes with his hands. "If you want me to, I can bring her to you once I've made sure you're safe, okay?"

She leaps onto him, wrapping her arms and legs around him. "It's okay, shush," he whispers as he picks her up and gets to his feet. She can't be much more than five. He pulls out his phone. "A few hours ahead of schedule, but I'm not in a patient mood today."

"Imperials, angels, knights . . ." His voice echoes throughout the city in a prerecorded message. "Those of you that are here, I hope you're here to help those who deserve to survive. In ten minutes, I will be turning this place to ash. Imperials, meet me at your emperor's final resting place, where you can negotiate your legacy with me."

• • •

"Shit, Aioven, what the hell are you thinking?" Stark asks out loud.

Sam slaps the back of a vehicle as it speeds away. "What's wrong?"

Stark pulls on his hair in anxiety. "What do you mean, 'What's wrong?' Aioven is terrorizing this city in order to . . . to . . . I'm not even sure."

"The empire pushed him too far, didn't they? They nearly killed him!" Sam shouts.

Lee puts his hand up. "Um, guys?"

Stark replies more calmly. "I agree with Aioven that the Empire has to go, but by burning this place to the ground and sending all these people into a frenzy, what will our legacy be?"

"I'll admit the idea sounded a lot better in my head. I guess that's why it's good to run your thoughts by people you trust." Aioven, without his armour, announces his presence to his companions. "I wanted to get what I need from their temple and learn about their spy network. I did the first thing, but when I visited the intelligence agency, all I found were two knights taking advantage of the chaos I created."

Lee frowns. "Knights in the intelligence tower? Like captains or . . . ?"

Aioven shakes his head. "I doubt it. Just a couple of losers."

"What were they doing there?" Sam asked.

Aioven grits his teeth. "Taking advantage," he says, holding the now-sleeping girl tightly in his arms. "From what I could find, this is the minister's daughter."

He sighs. "Just get the rest of these people out of here. We need to get to work on more important things. This will be over soon." In a flash, he vanishes in a blur, leaving the trio in his dust.

"You didn't lecture him on why this is wrong," Sam says to Stark, who just looks around.

Stark sighs. "I don't think he needs me to tell him that. He's literally carrying his guilt in his arms.

• • •

Aioven arrives atop a grassy hill with a statue of a hooded, winged figure at the top. Beneath it lay a tombstone marked as King Emperor Atlas of Fear and Dread, Master of Death. Phobos, Deimos, Mortis. The Last Absolute.

"Wait a minute." Aioven stares at the words and mouths them over and over. "Hmm, that's helpful," he says. He holds out his hand and molds the ground into a comfortable kind of cradle to lay the girl in. As he sets her down the rest of the aircraft evacuating civilians leave the Imperial city's airspace, likely headed toward their nearest city of Zion. Feeling several presences approaching him, he adorns his armour and mask once more.

"Aioven!" a man shouts. Being so close to detonation, Aioven has to conserve as much energy as possible, otherwise he might lose control. Several bullets bounce off his armour as a man on a jet pack soars into the air, peppering Aioven with strange ammunition from an assault rifle. At first Aioven is able to dodge most of the bullets, until they start curving toward him. Not interested in a long-winded fight, Aioven lassos the ambusher with a chain and pulls him to the ground.

Aioven kicks the man's weapon out of his hand and puts his sword to his throat. "Name and affiliation with the Empire! Now!"

He spits. "Jaxx Hosney, head minister of intelligence."

Aioven lowers his sword. "My condolences to you, sir."

"What?" Jaxx asks, but before Aioven can explain himself, two more try to ambush him. Twisting his body left and right, he catches two spears out of the air and jams both of them into the ground. With a simple duck and weave, he escapes a desperate superman punch and a clothesline from the two spearmen.

"Teh!" Aioven grabs their heads and slams them together and lets them fall limp to the floor. A pop rings out in the distance, and a bullet hits him in the chest, knocking him down to one knee. He looks up just in time to see the muzzle flash about a mile away in the distance behind another hill. Despite anything he can do, the bullet hits him square in the forehead.

His head is knocked back, straining the muscles in his neck. "Agh!" He pulls out his sword and focuses his mind down to the rhythm of a hummingbird. The sounds of the world are muffled as everything becomes motionless. As he allows his senses to take in enormous amounts of information, he is able to perceive the world around him as if time were stopped. He scans the landscape and braces when he sees the muzzle flash again, slowly followed by the sound of the sniper's gun firing.

This time he sees the bullet coming, still very quickly, and puts his blade between it and his heart. It ricochets into the ground, causing massive sparks to shower all over Aioven's incapacitated opponents. There's a pause, and Aioven starts taking steps toward the shooter. Another shot is fired, which he blocks. Then another and another. Aioven begins to run as the shooter starts firing faster and faster, with the accuracy of each shot worsening. Using his powers, Aioven starts to run extremely fast, whilst swiping rifle bullets out of the air like tennis balls. Eventually, he begins to run faster than the bullets and is on top of the sniper in an instant.

He leaps several feet up to pounce on the sniper, but they're ready. They roll out of the way as Aioven lands and thrusts his sword into the ground. As he tries to move to attack, a minigun turret rises from under a pile of rocks. The sniper grabs it and starts spooling it up. Not interested in seeing its effectiveness, he raises his sword to throw it at the sniper, but they're ready. Before even Aioven can catch it, he is hit in the neck with a taser so strong it causes his whole body to spasm.

The minigun opens fire and begins pounding into his armour, for the first time leaving actual dents in it. As he desperately tries to curve the armour-piercing rounds away from hitting his weak spots, he falls to one knee again, though this time he has his assassin within reach. He grabs the wire of the taser and sends a current of electricity tantamount to a bolt of lightning into the body of the sniper. With a loud crash and a bright flash, they are completely blown away. As Aioven regains his faculties, he raises his hand toward the minigun and melts the rotating barrel by turning its kinetic energy into heat.

Ping. Another bullet bounces off of his helmet. Without looking, he whips out a chain toward where it came from and yanks the shooter to his feet. They're wearing simple street clothes, a hood and a balaclava. Aioven rips it off to reveal a woman with deep black eyes and olive skin. "Not bad," he says, before punching her unconscious with one blow.

Upon returning to the others, he tosses the now-chained-up sniper beside the other Imperials. "So, these are the patriots that have come to witness the end of their world as they know it?"

One of the Imperials with orange hair spits at him. "As if you could wipe out the Empire. You'd need—"

"The explosive power of a dozen nuclear weapons? Way ahead of you." He pulls out one of his golden coins and tosses it in front of the orange-haired Imperial. "What's your name, sir?" Aioven asks.

"I am Imperial Captain Kal Yeager," he says, puffing out his chest despite being on his knees and still being very sore.

"I wasn't expecting you to volunteer your title so easily," Aioven says.

Yeager huffs at him. "It's good etiquette to at least introduce yourself to the person you plan on killing."

"In standard practice I'd usually agree with you, but in this case, I'd advise against killing me altogether. Because if you kill me, who's to stop this from happening?"

With a smooth motion of his hand, he levitates the coin and drops it at the feet of the Emperor's statue. "Let's remodel. He needs some work done." He snaps his fingers and the impossibly dense gold atoms in the coin are finally allowed to push away from each other, and in doing so release so much violent energy that it creates a crater a quarter-mile wide, sending Aioven's hostages flying and tumbling partially down the hill. No recognizable remnants of the Emperor's grave remain.

When they stop, Aioven is waiting for them. "Captain Yeager, did you recognize that coin? You should, since I traded with you using those."

Yeager looks up at him and snarls. "You bastard!" Aioven claps for him and pulls him to his feet to brush off his shoulders. "I can see why they made you a captain. You must be good at crossword puzzles. Would you like to explain to your companions what this all means?"

Yeager spits again, this time getting it on the visor of Aioven's mask. Aioven puts both of his hands on the captain's face and squeezes his cheeks hard and shakes him. "You know, that makes it really hard for me to see what I'm doing."

He proceeds to punch him in the face three times, making a gust of wind with each blow and leaving a very noticeable dent in Yeager's face. Holding him up on his feet by the throat, he says, "I know I'm not a very good cook, but I appreciate you being so enthusiastic about being fed my signature dish." He tosses him to the ground, looking at the other hostages. "Teeth, fresh from your own mouths! And if someone doesn't speak now, it's going to be tongues for dessert."

"You'd fit right in in the Empire, you know that?" the assassin says with a smirk.

Aioven twirls his sword and points it at her. "Never! I'd be running the Empire, but burning it is more fun." He grabs the other spearman and raises him to his feet. "How's it going? You must be feeling pretty good. Out of the two of you, you're the good-looking one now. So tell me, handsome, what's your name and rank?"

The older, gray-haired gentleman blinks confusedly. "Uh, Marc Webb."

Aioven nods emphatically. "And? What do you do?" he asks again.

"I'm a member of the senate," he says.

Aioven crosses his arms and laughs. "A politician with a spear. I didn't think you people could be any more untrustworthy."

Aioven puts him back on the ground, motioning him to sit, which the senator does. "And then there's you." He makes the chains restraining Jaxx Hosney disappear, and Hosney looks up at him, confused.

Aioven points at Hosney. "You aren't on my list, but I am glad you're here." He holds out his hand to him, and with trepidation, the Imperial minister takes it and stands up. Aioven points to the cradle of dirt and lets him walk toward it on his own.

He starts running so hard he kicks up dirt with each stride. "Sarah! Oh my god, Sarah!" He picks up the girl and holds her tightly in his arms.

He spins around and turns to face Aioven. "What the hell is she doing here?!" he demands.

Aioven points at the smoking city. "Would you rather her be in the city I'm about to destroy?"

Jaxx almost drops the girl upon hearing this question, making Aioven almost lunge forward to catch her. "Careful!" he says.

Hosney holds his daughter tightly. "What are you talking about?"

Aioven groans. "Are none of you paying attention?" He pulls out another gold coin. "Your city is *filled* with these, millions of them!"

His hostages stare at him without saying anything. Aioven shakes his head. "Why is it a thing for the bad guys to tell their master plan right before they do something big? It's not as satisfying as I thought it'd be."

"Huh?" the senator asks.

"Shut up. Now look at me, Jaxx. I'm assuming you're this girl's father, yes? I promised her I'd get her to safety."

Minister Hosney nods. "Yes, I am. I'm Jaxx Hosney. This is my daughter, Sarah. Her mother, my wife—" Still holding his daughter he moves aggressively into Aioven's personal space. "Her mother! Where is her mother?!" he shouts.

Aioven puts his hands on Hosney's shoulders and takes a step back. "That's what I wanted to talk to you about. You aren't on my list, but I did promise your daughter that I'd get her mother too."

"Well, where is she?!" Hosney shouts.

Aioven calmly replies. "I'll take you to her, but you should let the little one rest here. I think she's seen enough today."

Jaxx looks around. "Out here by herself?" Several heavy footsteps accompany the arrival of Stark, Sam, and Lee.

"We'll watch her. She'll be safe, I promise." Stark says.

The minister looks at Aioven, who nods. He places the girl in Stark's arms. "Thank you, Leo," Aioven says.

Stark adjusts his hold on her and looks at Aioven. "As much as I'd like to say you're welcome, we're all rather uneasy about this, so just do what you have to do."

"Fair enough. Let's go, Hosney." He takes Jaxx's hand and they almost instantly travel back to the intelligence tower, but this time entering through the broken window of Jaxx's office.

Aioven starts pacing, kicking scattered papers around. "When I started this mess, I did it to accomplish three things." Jaxx stumbles a little bit, like someone trying to keep their composure after coming ashore from being on a ship for a long time.

"The first was to raze the Dark Temple of your angels and cultists." He pulls out a laptop from under some binders and folders and holds it out to him. "The second was to find someone like you and ask you how many spies you have in the Ares capital and under the esteemed noses of the Order of Genesis."

Jaxx takes the laptop. "And the third?"

Aioven looks out the window. "Third, burn this city to the ground as an example to all of Mars, not just the Empire."

"Lea!" Jaxx runs over to the corpse of his late wife.

Aioven lets him grieve and sits down on the floor with his legs crossed.

"Why? *Why?!* Who did this?!" Hosney howls, choking on his own voice.

Aioven points at the laptop in Jaxx's hand. "That's why I gave you that. I figured you'd know how to look at the security cameras here."

•　•　•

Back on the hilltop, some unwelcome guests arrive to find Stark, Sam, and Lee standing amongst several Imperial officials.

Several captains and lieutenants appear with their capes flowing in the wind. "What is the meaning of this?!" Koenig roars.

Stark sets down the girl in Aioven's cradle. "We're here making sure the innocent are safely evacuated. As I'm sure you've been too."

Koenig's short temper and patience immediately expire, and he draws his sword. "Don't play games with me, you dropout! You were supposed to find Aioven!"

Stark draws his own sword, and storm clouds crackle above their heads. "Oh, so now we work for you? I didn't realize you were gonna pay us!"

"Where is Aioven?!" Captain Koenig ignites his blade in stellar white flames, contrasting the sky to a dark blue. The little cane sword has transformed into a huge greatsword; the blade is pearl white and wrapped in blue flames.

Chapter 11

THE STRANGER

"The guys that killed my wife," Jaxx says as Aioven picks up his wife's body. "They weren't just knights." He points at the screen. "This guy here, the chubby one, is Bobby—or Robert—Yaxley. He's a lieutenant under Captain Venturi."

"Somehow I can't picture those two being compatible," Aioven says as he hands Jaxx's wife to him.

Jaxx grunts and wraps his arms around her and takes a deep breath. His voice falters only slightly. His tone is emotionless probably as the shock settles in. "Yeah, Robert isn't much of a knight or a lieutenant for that matter. He's had HR called on him multiple times."

"Didn't know they had an HR." Aioven laughs a little.

Jaxx shakes his head as if to say yes and no. "They believe themselves beyond personal accountability. No vigilante will be tolerated," he says.

"Well, what about the other guy?" Aioven asks.

Jaxx frowns. "That guy is Peyton Shelton. He's one of Lord Xenos's spies."

Aioven leans in toward the laptop's screen. "Lord who?"

Jaxx nods. "I believe your people call him the Stranger. According to rumors, he was given his title due to his unique powers. And if he succeeds in destroying the Order of Genesis, he'd be granted the title of god-emperor."

"Granted by who?" Aioven picks up the laptop and zooms in on Peyton's face.

"Nomor, one of the architects," Hosney says.

Having never even heard an architect's name before, Aioven reflects on how much he does not know. And how much he might learn from Jaxx, the Empire's most trusted secret keeper.

Aioven holds out his hand as an offer. "In return for the safety of your daughter, would you be willing to share the identities of Xenos's spies?"

Jaxx shakes his head at first. "I don't fully understand why Shelton allowed or even directed Yaxley to try and do the things he did. Perhaps to make the Order look like the bad guys amidst your attack, to make it seem like they were a part of it. Usually Xenos would ask us to pin the blame on the Order for our attacks."

Aioven scratches his head. "I hate to say this, but I think they were *both* into it."

Jaxx closes the laptop and hands it to Aioven, who nods and takes it from him. "Not a bad tactic. It makes it easier to write the history books when the conflict is over."

The Imperial spymaster looks at his wife's face and shakes his head. "Only if you win. But eventually, the truth comes out."

An interesting choice of words. "Well, my friend, I am in the business of legacies. If you give me a chance, I'm sure I can help you get the future you want for your daughter."

Jaxx looks at Aioven's outstretched hand and shakes it. "That honestly sounds like a nice change for me. I have hoped to do more good than my present circumstances allow."

"Well, technically, just so you know, you aren't swearing allegiance to the Order of Genesis. My people and I are independent, and I imagine the Order aren't big fans of us either." Aioven pulls out a metal sort of business card and hands it to the now-former minister of intelligence.

"Use that to find your way to one of my safe houses. I'll let Sam know you're coming. She'll take care of you and your daughter. But before you go, I need one more thing." He holds out Smirnov's locket and opens it to show the picture inside. "Who is this person? What is her affiliation with the Empire? And how important is she to Smirnov?"

• • •

Back on the hill beside the desecrated grave of Atlas, Stark and Koenig stand opposed with their weapons drawn. Sam checks her wristwatch and sees that she has received instructions to take the girl to a safe place. When she picks up the girl, one of the captains in a black-and-white coat draws a three-foot-long retractable baton. "Hey!"

Lee stands between them as she picks up the girl. "She's taking her somewhere safe, 'cause you see, we're in the business of helping people. Something you wouldn't know anything about, *Captain* Iven."

Sam disappears with the girl, and Lee takes a step back and smiles. "You guys were too busy to help with the evacuation effort, so I don't see why it matters."

"Indeed." The wind whistles as everyone realizes that Aioven is standing in the middle between both groups. "My, my! All of you captains here in one place? Aren't you leaving everyone at the temple vulnerable to attack?" He grins. Would your home be able to withstand an attack with your forces nearly cut in half?"

Koenig whips his sword through the air and points it at him. "Aioven! Your threat has been allowed to continue long enough."

"My threat of what? Am I threatening something you're protecting?" Aioven asks, nonchalantly stepping toward the still-chained hostages. "And since Lee was just talking about your contribution to the saving of innocents, I must say you're actually in the red." He tightens the chains around Webb and Yeager and grips his swords with two hands. "Your lieutenants Shelton and Yaxley tried to do some pretty terrible things."

Captain Venturi wakes up from seemingly spacing out. "My lieutenants? What things?"

Aioven cuts the chains off of the assassin. "You're free to go. Your client is about to die and so your contract ended. I won't interfere with your work as long as it doesn't interfere with mine. No hard feelings."

"The name's Jeena if you ever need to find me," she says, massaging her wrists.

"I won't," Aioven states bluntly. "Unless you plan on working with me and not *for* me."

She raises an eyebrow, looks at him like he's crazy, and scurries off. Aioven pauses and looks at the assorted captains. "You'll chase a child but not an assassin? Hmm."

"Hey! Hood-head!" Venturi shouts. "What did you mean by what my lieutenant tried to do?"

"I'll be sure to include it in my speech to the public," Aioven says as he turns his hostages to face the city. "You think I only want to kill you. I want to do more than that. I want people to see who you are and what you've done. I want history to forget everything about you."

"Enough! You are stalling! Submit or be destroyed!" Koenig commands.

Aioven pulls out a chrome purple coin, identical to the golden ones save for its colour. "Apologies, I was savouring the moment."

He stands in front of everyone, snaps the coin in two, and tosses it into the air and extends his arm like a bird of prey spreading its wings. "Behold, the future legacies of all my enemies."

The coin dissipates and the ground shakes. Distant pops and booms can be heard as buildings explode behind him. The destruction and explosions escalate with each passing second, and just as one of the skyscrapers in the city center starts to fall, everyone is blinded by an intense light and heat. The ground gets set on fire, and everyone is knocked into the air.

Almost a hundred miles back, the captains land with their uniforms all slightly singed, save for Captain Koenig. They all look up as the towering mushroom cloud races up into the atmosphere, casting a dark shadow over all of them. Not that there was anything left to cast into darkness. The Imperial capital had been completely flattened.

"Hey, look on the bright side!" Aioven claps Koenig on the shoulder. "It wasn't nuclear, so there's no fallout! It's basically free real estate now!"

"At what cost?!" Koenig swings his sword, carving and melting away miles of terrain. When the flames disappear, Aioven is standing in the rubble, somehow unscathed. "Look, Captain— I think that you misunderstand me. We would both come to regret fighting each other today. I ask you to give me a few more days, and then I will share what I've learned with the world. Decide then if we are truly enemies."

Koenig moves to swing his sword again, and Aioven gets ready to avoid his attack, but they and everyone else suddenly become perfectly still as they sense a disturbance in the world around them. An influence has washed over the land and their bodies, filling their minds with bizarre feelings.

An incorporeal voice fills the air. "Did I miss my invitation? No worries, I love being a gate-crasher!" The sky turns to a glowing, verdant hue, and the ground turns black as Darius Vaughn makes everyone aware of his arrival. His surprisingly weak-looking appearance glows in the bright-green moonlight: his pasty white skin, tall and skinny body, and his strange, dark-green hair. His black pupils dance around excitedly as he makes eye contact with everyone present.

He pulls on two black, rubber-like gloves, covered in

glowing green gemstones on each knuckle. "I enjoyed watching your performance at the prison break. I heard that you were spectacular in dispatching my birds, too! But it is my turn in the spotlight! I expect to impress you in turn."

Dirt, stone, and grass start getting lifted into the air in long, thick streams as they are converted into something weird. Aioven is distracted by what he senses in the changes happening to the matter around him and what is now beginning to swirl above Vaughn's head. The density of everything is becoming the same. Aioven is disoriented by what he senses happening around him. As he watches Vaughn direct the strange matter around him, he sees everything it touches emulsifying into more strange matter. Within moments, tons and tons of the terrain around them has been converted into this odd matter, now circling and arcing over Vaughn in slow motion.

"Still confused? Hold out your hand. It won't kill you per se, but if it did, it would only make you … *stranger!*" The matter begins to glow bright-green to illuminate the bubbling mass of apocalyptic goo that's about to be unleashed on them.

Strange . . . Aioven tenses and faces everyone behind him. "*Run!*" he shouts at all of the captains. Without even moving a muscle, Vaughn sends the green matter streaming toward everyone, and Aioven's realization has come too late for many. Dozens of knights are crushed by the torrent of matter, and those that aren't instantly killed are melted and morphed into the same green goo. Aioven grabs Stark and Lee and pushes them forward. "Go! I'll slow it down if I can!"

For once, he's not holding anything back. Aioven swings his sword and releases an arc of purple fire and black matter so large it disrupts the clouds above. Despite this impressive feat, the green matter passes through it like smoke, blowing it apart like a harmless illusion. Everyone, even the captains, continues to flee, the last one to leave being a hesitant Captain Koenig.

"Stranger!" Aioven releases a storm of lightning, desperately trying to reach around the fast-approaching wave of bubbling matter. Vaughn closes one hand into a fist and then opens it, causing the bubbling matter to contract and then explode out into hundreds of tiny tendrils that catch and absorb Aioven's lightning. The huge droplets glow purple a little bit and then continue advancing toward him.

"You're strong, Aioven. But I am a god to be! You can't win!" Vaughn shouts from behind the wave. *If I can't win, then there's only one thing I can do,* Aioven thinks to himself.

Vaughn hears Aioven's voice behind him. "So you're the Stranger, emperor to be, Xenos himself." The would-be god-emperor looks over his shoulder in shock. "*What?*"

Aioven's attack lifts up dirt and stone behind Xenos as the energy is directed away from him by a small chunk of green matter. "That was foolish, boy. I was beginning to think you knew what my power was. Oh, well."

Before he can react, the green matter latches itself onto Aioven's sword and quickly begins to convert it. Not wanting to be taken over, he throws his sword onto the ground. "Now you're truly helpless," the newly self-proclaimed Emperor Xenos says.

Xenos runs him through the middle of his chest with a jagged, glowing green spear of rock. "You can't escape my strange matter. It's absolute. Whatever I touch is mine to control, and now you and your power will be mine."

Aioven stumbles backward and looks at the strange matter around them and then at the god of strangeness. "You may wield the most dangerous substance in the universe, but your mind isn't ready for the madness I could unleash unto you. If you were absolute, you would have caught me."

Aioven's image shimmers and explodes into a hundred shards of glass and then boils away into an invisible mist. Darius, now knowing his identity has been exposed as Xenos the Stranger, curses Aioven's name and talks into his open right hand. "Rytram, contact Nomor. He'll want to hear of this. I might be able to give him some more information regarding this Aioven character. Apparently he has the power to hypnotize people."

• • •

Almost fifty miles in the distance, stumbling and crashing into a farm field devoid of crops, Lee and Stark finally stop fleeing and collapse from exhaustion. Stark splutters as he falls face-first into what he hopes isn't fertilized soil. Lee crumples into a heap, spitting and spraying sweat out of his mouth while trying to coax some life back into his lungs.

Lee rolls Stark onto his back and puts his hand onto his chest to check his heart rate. "I heard you were fast Stark, but are you feeling all right?"

"I'm more of a sprinter, to be honest," he says, coughing and choking on his own spit.

"So, what the hell was that?" Lee asks, looking straight up into the sky. "I've never seen powers like that before."

Thunder rolls in the distance with a flicker of purple light on the horizon. Lee points in the direction of the thunder. "He probably knows."

"Maybe," Lee says. "Or maybe it was just unfamiliar enough to make him nervous."

Stark shakes his head. "No, if he doesn't know for sure yet, then he at least has a good idea. He told us to run before Vaughn started attacking. He was puzzling it out."

"It was strange for sure," Lee says, and then having his eyes light up, he clambers to his feet. "That's it!"

Stark's phone starts buzzing and making an unusual morse code warbling beep sound. "Hold that thought." He pulls it out and hops to his feet. "Someone's at the safe house."

"Who?" Stark asks. "The Imperial guy, Sam, and the kid."

"What about Aioven?" Lee asks, pulling Stark to his feet.

"I don't see him," he says. "Any idea where he could be? I'm sure all those captains would love to know."

Stark looks in the distance toward where the flash of purple light came from. "You're right. They're all probably still out looking for him." The events of Aioven's attack on the Empire still fresh in their minds, they puzzle over everything Aioven said, guessing at his intentions.

Aioven's first words when he suddenly appeared echo in their minds. "My, my! Is it common practice for this many captains to be this far from the temple?" Thunder rumbled again in the direction of the capital.

Lee looks at Stark. "You don't think he'd be crazy enough to raid the Genesis Temple, would he?"

"To get information on the remaining absolutes?" Stark asks. "I don't think we can rule it out. Not after what just happened."

"Should we warn them?" Lee asks.

Stark folds his arms and thinks for a moment, recalling Captain Koenig's behaviour. "Nah," Stark says. "I think it's time we head home. I can't imagine James has much left on his itinerary."

• • •

Aioven's friends were right. He had just one more objective for the day. Atop a hill a few miles away from the temple, Aioven basks in the golden glow of the monument as the sun rises behind it. "It's been a while since I last visited a place of *higher* learning."

He steps forward and starts skidding down the hill like he's riding an invisible snowboard, gaining huge amounts of speed before leaping off the ground. Like a skipping stone with infinite momentum, he hops across the landscape, gaining speed with each step and covering miles in moments.

He comes to a stop at the bottom of the temple steps. Two guards with pikes walk up to him, and blades of white-hot plasma ignite from the top ends. They cross the blades and obstruct Aioven's path.

"I will be very plain," Aioven says, pointing toward the mushroom cloud in the distance. "You see that?" The two guards frown, confused about where he's going with this. "*That* is my handiwork. Or perhaps it would be better for me to say that is what is left of the Empire after I snapped my fingers."

Aioven tenses all of his fingers in his right hand and paralyzes the two guards. "Just *imagine* what I could do to you." He releases them and they wobble slightly as they breathe frantically like they've just surfaced from being underwater for a long time.

"You don't strike me as curious, because, as we all know, cats who are curious…" He brandishes his black, jagged sword inches away from their faces. "They get atomized."

The two guards look at each other and step aside. "And no one will think less of you. And even if they did, at least there'll be something *left* of you."

Now standing before the several-foot-tall, grand, double-entrance doors of one of the most secure religious buildings of the world, Aioven jams his sword into the gap between the doors and twists it to the left like a key. As if it had lost all structural integrity, the stone doors crumble slowly into a pile of gray sand. In a blasting cloud of dust, Aioven clears the entrance and strolls inside, alarm bells now ringing as knights and monks appear all around him.

"A very fine building," Aioven says, his voice echoing throughout the entrance hall. He looks around at the grand marble-and-granite structures that fill the football-field-sized space— marble pillars with runes scattered haphazardly across them; the dark granite floor has golden hieroglyphs stretching across it. The whole place is quite ornate, surprisingly expensive even for Aioven's tastes. He looks around his immediate surroundings and finds himself standing in a circle with an arrow pointing out of it. "The presidential seal," he says.

"Keep your hands where I can see them!" a guard shouts as he points a pike with an ignited blade of plasma at him. Dozens of knights and guards come together to form a circle around him.

"Why?" Aioven says. The guards and the knights surrounding Aioven all look at each other. "It matters not whether you can see my hands. I can kill you just the same."

A knight steps forward, holding a rifle covered in glowing red gemstones. "Threatening members of the Order in our own temple is rather brave of you, sir."

Aioven shakes his head. "Actually, that wasn't a threat. This is: I am here to release the one and only Arthur Stark. I will deal harshly with anyone who tries to stop me. As for the remark of my so-called bravery, bravery is facing down fear and defeating it. Do I look even remotely afraid?"

The knight quick draws and fires his weapon. A bolt of red-hot plasma hits Aioven at the speed of a bullet and explodes like a hand grenade. Everyone takes a step back as the smoke clears to reveal Aioven completely unaffected.

Aioven brushes dust off his shoulder. "In my experience, I have yet to kill anyone that is 'brave,' just stupid. I have defeated many who failed to understand my power. Still others did come to understand—and I have watched them run or beg for their lives. In any case, none demonstrated any true 'bravery.'"

He drags the tip of his sword across the floor, superheating the granite and turning it molten. "Tell me, sir knight, are you willing to be the first brave man I kill?"

The knight shivers as the weight of his own gun becomes almost unbearable. Aioven spins around in a circle, pointing the tip of his blade at everyone. "This goes for everyone. Absolute power corrupts absolutely. And madness awaits those who face it, too."

Aioven jams his sword into the center of the presidential seal, melting and subsequently lifting the red-hot molten rock away to expose a large, fish-bowl-type structure of super-thick glass beneath the floor. Aioven hops onto the top of the glass dome and peers inside. The frosted glass makes it difficult to see its contents. Despite this, he can sense a powerful presence inside, very similar to Stark's. "Dad's coming home."

Aioven stomps on the glass and an electric shock runs up his legs and stuns him for a moment. He yelps and shakes his head. "Mom always said not to tap the glass." He returns the favour and unleashes blinding currents of electricity into the glass, this time also controlling the security currents as well. The glass starts to warp and bubble as it gets heated to temperatures north of three thousand degrees. Aioven feels the sweat boiling off his face from under his mask, internally impressed by the integrity of the holding cell. Eventually, like a bizarre, molten egg yolk, the dome finally splits open and spills hot-orange lava everywhere before quickly cooling into what some would call glassy modern art.

Amidst the heat waves and indeed waves of molten glass stands a man who is an older, spitting image of Stark. "Jesus, man! If you're gonna rescue someone, cooking them alive kinda defeats the whole purpose," he says, stepping into the lava pools like they're nothing and walking over to Aioven.

Aioven shrugs. "I'll be honest, I didn't have much of a plan in terms of rescuing you. It's been a sporadic day, and your breakout was more of a spur-of-the-moment thing. I was originally here for the library archives."

"The archives? Who are you?" Arthur asks. Aioven holds out his hand. "Dalkanos Aioven, a friend of your son's."

Arthur raises his bushy gray eyebrows. "I see, and what has he gotten himself into?"

Aioven claps him on the shoulder. "Your son has joined

my conspiracy against the Empire and the gods it worships. Nothing serious."

The man absorbs the information and almost immediately guffaws. "Ha! At least he ain't getting married!"

Aioven clips his sword to his belt. "I think I may have found something even more deadly." He beckons Arthur to follow him out of the hole and back into the entrance hall, where nearly a hundred knights stand waiting, clearly in shock that anyone would be brazen enough to do this in broad daylight.

One of the pikestaff-wielding guards shouts, "We cannot permit you to leave! Arthur is a prisoner of the Order."

Aioven claps his hands together. "Is he now? Tell me, Mr. Stark. How do you feel?" Arthur begins to stretch like an olympian getting ready for a hundred-meter dash. "You know, I gotta tell ya, I feel great. I feel like enjoying some fresh air and going for a run. I don't feel like a prisoner at all now."

Aioven hands Arthur a card with coordinates on it. "That's a fantastic idea. I'll join you." Arthur, clearly the benefactor of Leo's speed, zooms away, far into the horizon, creating multiple sonic booms. The knights all look at each other and back at Aioven.

"What?" Aioven asks. "Did you expect me to leave too? I wanted to see if your library was open. I'm not actually here to kill you."

"It isn't open." A voice comes from behind some of the guards to reveal a woman fully decked out in glowing steel armour, with a double-bladed staff already ignited.

Aioven faces the challenger. "And to whom do I have the pleasure of speaking?"

The female guard spins her staff and assumes a fighting stance. "Neela Thane, commander of the temple guard. Your arrest or extermination is my ultimate responsibility." Aioven puts one foot forward before the other and starts to slightly stand on his toes. Despite Aioven's lack of sword, the commander recognizes the duelling stance and whistles to signal the knights and guards to attack.

The battle of the temple begins, and Aioven changes fighting styles continuously to prevent casualties. Restraining himself from using any of his powers to summon storms or energy or matter, he instead duels the occupants of the temple whilst augmenting his physical abilities.

The first few guards he just trips and clotheslines out of commission, but eventually Aioven does draw his sword. His unorthodox swordplay of constantly twirling and spinning makes the intentions of his attacks and counters unclear. In any normal duel, this kind of fighting style would be suicidal or at least very inefficient—not to mention the vulnerability of such ostentatiousness. But to his trained opponents' surprise, Aioven's mad, untrained fighting style proves impossible to overcome. He overwhelms first one, then another foe. All are left alive, but unable to press any advantage before being dispatched.

Commander Thane has seen enough. She sends a current of electricity through the floor, hoping to stun the intruder.

"Hup!" Aioven spins through the air, leaping over Thane and landing behind her. "I don't want to kill any of you. I just want to read a few books."

"If you don't want to kill us, then sheathe your sword!" she shouts, lunging at him and fanning the air with her staff. Aioven blocks the first two attacks, but she manages to hit him in the head with the hilt section of her staff. As she tries to take advantage of this opening, Aioven instinctively stumbles backward and thrusts his sword forward, leaving a shallow cut in her side. Despite being grazed on the right side of her waist, she presses her attack and stabs Aioven in the chest, though his armour stops it just short of reaching his heart.

Aioven hisses through his teeth beneath his metal mask and

grips her throat. "As far as you're concerned, it doesn't matter what I'm holding. I could be dual-wielding flyswatters. What matters is my intent."

"And what is your intent, Aioven?" A captain has entered the fray, and the customary, immense cosmic pressure on the air and distinct sound of a captain's cloak makes for a memorable entrance. Aioven grips his sword with two hands and faces "Captain" Lana Smirnov.

"Captain! Now that you're here, I'm inclined to do things differently," he says.

"Oh?" Lana draws her weapons.

Aioven sheathes his sword into nothingness. "I could explain our history to your 'comrades,' but before I turn the world against you, I'd like to destroy your sense of security as you did mine."

"Captain, what is he talking about?" Thane shouts, still keeping her staff pointed at Aioven.

"We all have a weakness. You took mine, and now I have none. Now it's my turn to do you the same favour." Aioven vanishes in a sonic blast, knocking over a handful of guards and briefly stunning Captain Smirnov and Commander Thane.

As everyone calms down and starts checking on each other, Lana steps outside over the ruined entrance and peers into the distance, unaware of where Aioven is going. It isn't home—at least not to him.

Returning home, miles away near the city center, Lee and Stark drain themselves of all their energy.

"Really wish we could've taken the Lambo!" Lee shouts, skipping from one street lamp to another.

Stark catches his breath on a high-rise stone wall, startling a cat and making it scurry away. "We took out a whole bunch of cars, remember?

Finally landing on the roof of their apartment headquarters, they can relax their muscles and hobble inside.

Stark calls out as they come down the stairs. "Sam! It's Leo and, um, Alan!"

"I'd rather you stick to calling me Lee. And why can't we use the elevator?"

They burst into the common room to find everyone calm and sitting on the L-shaped couch. Sam is beside the Hosney girl, checking her for wounds while her father holds her hand.

Lee looks around for his family whilst Stark is perplexed by the absence of their leader. "Sam? Where's Aioven?"

"So that's his name, huh? 'Aioven' is the guy who broke me out?"

Stark feels a familiar presence, like he's just visited his childhood home, but the memories are suddenly not so hazy and repressed. He spins around to find himself facing his father for the first time in almost a decade.

"Son . . . Leonidas . . ." Arthur Stark holds out his arms and lets his son approach him on his own.

Starks stares at his father with unbelieving eyes. "Dad?"

"It's me." Arthur nods, using as few words as possible as he chokes back tears. "I haven't seen you since you were a boy."

"I was fourteen," Stark says, now standing at arm's length from his father.

Arthur's arms start to fall. "I'm so sorry I've missed so much of your life. I didn't—"

Leo embraces his father but doesn't say a word. Arthur shakily inhales and just holds his son.

Sam whispers to Hosney and his daughter to usher them out of the room. Once they're alone, they release each other.

Arthur looks around and asks hesitantly, "Where's your mother?"

Leo's face darkens. "She died."

Arthur's cosmic pressure starts to shake the whole room. "What?! It was Koenig, wasn't it?!"

Sam rushes back into the room as pictures fall off the walls and glasses of water spill onto the floor.

Leo grabs his father by the shoulders and shouts, "It was cancer! It was cancer, Dad. She got it visiting one of your stations to collect your research data as a bargaining chip for your freedom."

The room becomes still again and Arthur falls to his knees. "I could have treated her—they knew that!"

Leo sits down on the floor in front of Arthur and tries to look him in the eyes. "Did Aioven—the guy who freed you—tell you why he got you?"

Sam starts picking up pictures from the floor and rehanging them. "You think it was for a reason?"

Leo drags his father to the couch and lets him sink into the cushions. "As much as I appreciate Aioven's actions, his original plan was to free my father through diplomacy, not force."

Sam crosses her arms. "Something to do with Vaughn?"

Arthur perks up. "Vaughn? Darius Vaughn? The pipsqueak deserter who ran off to join the Empire?"

Leo cleans up the spilled water and knocked-over glasses and places it all in the sink. "I didn't know he was a deserter, but you got the name right."

The disgruntled dad rearranges himself on the couch and runs his hands through his greasy, long, pepper-gray hair. "Yeah, little punk was an officer, but he didn't make a numbered rank or anything like that. Didn't stop him from having big aspirations though."

Leo sits across from his father on the opposite couch. "Well 'god-emperor' is a hell of a life goal."

Arthur looks at his son with a bemused smile. "What? The kid could barely light things with matches. He was almost talentless."

Sam closes the fridge holding a juice pouch in her hand. "What about his skills with matter?"

Arthur teeters his hand back and forth. "He was decent. He

could rearrange carbon atoms with a little bit of external help from things like furnaces and pressure chambers."

Leo stands up and looks out the window into the night sky, unable to see the stars amidst the bright lights of the city. "I think I know why Aioven brought you here. Vaughn isn't a nobody anymore, and he is more than just capable with matter now."

"That's right," Aioven says, having clearly heard most of the conversation. The door into the lounge closes behind Aioven, still wearing his armour. Everyone stands up as he enters the room, pulling off his armour and making it dissolve into black smoke as it hits the floor. "He is more than just talented. Tell me something, Arthur. Are there any recorded individuals in history capable of controlling quarks? That is to say, beyond up and down quarks?"

Arthur shakes his head almost immediately. "No, as far as we know, all six quark types can only exist in the most extreme environments in the universe. In layman's terms, outside of such environments they would decay into up and down quarks, the types found in protons and neutrons. I'm not sure anyone has ever truly found a way to control elementary particles, let alone any of the variants besides the up and down quarks."

Aioven hangs his cloak on a bar stool beside the island in the kitchen. "Well, history has indeed been made. I do not know how, but Darius Vaughn, otherwise known as the Stranger, has achieved mastery over strange matter."

Arthur's eyes widen with a wild look of disbelief. "That's impossible. In order to gain such a power, one would have to be in a place where strange matter can form."

Leo buries his hands inside his face and sits back down. "Inside a neutron star, one of the very things you used to study in your stations, Dad."

Aioven nods apologetically. "Yes, I'm afraid your freedom came sooner not out of charity but of necessity. I am sorry if this offends either of you, but I did not want to wait until we had leverage on the council."

Arthur and Leo look at each other. "Is he trustworthy?" Arthur asks.

Leo nods. "He is. His methods are extreme, but I like his goals."

Leo's father looks back to Aioven. "What are your goals, sir?"

"I want to rid the universe of the architects. I want new, better leaders to step forward. I want to step back and lead a normal life."

"You seek power." Arthur crosses his arms.

Aioven walks over to Leo and puts his hand on his shoulder. "Not exactly."

Chapter 12

•

POWERS BEYOND THE HORIZON

Aioven puts his arm around Leo's shoulders. "Sam, I want you to escort the former Captain Stark. Pick whatever vehicle you like; just make sure it's discreet."

"What are we doing?" Sam asks.

Aioven points out the window. "We're going to space. And we are going to help the Starks find a way to counter Vaughn's powers."

Leo pushes Aioven away. "What are you talking about? We don't have a shuttle."

Arthur holds up his hand like a child in a classroom. "Well, actually, my stations can't be economically reached using conventional ships. Even at light speed, they would take years. We're actually using reverse-engineered architect technology."

Aioven and Leo both look at Arthur in surprise. Arthur looks at both of them confusedly. "Do you two not realize how space works? We don't even have light-speed capable ships, and you think we've been traveling thousands of light years to get to and from my stations?"

Leo snaps his fingers. "You found another way? A shortcut?"

Sam and Aioven look at each other before Sam speaks up. "Um . . . like wormholes or teleportation?"

Arthur interlocks his fingers together. "More like a Rosen Bridge of sorts. Though we can't really take the credit—it's the architects who developed the technology. We just sorta took it apart and put it back together."

"Why would gods need such technology?" Aioven asks.

"They needed a mode of transport to get them from here to their kingdom," Arthur says.

Leo, Sam, and Aioven share unsteady looks, unable to reconcile Arthur's revelation with everything they'd thought they knew about Architects.

Leo shakes his head as if to wake himself up. "Culture shock aside, we need more of a plan than 'going to space.' What kind of counter are we trying to come up with? Strange matter takes over and converts everything it comes into contact with. Its properties are so powerful that whatever it touches can be absorbed and made uniform—to the point of making anything it touches have the same 'perfect' stability and density."

Sam throws her juice pouch into the trash can. "Well, it's still only matter, right? Isn't there something else, some other force, that can defeat it?"

Aioven opens a drawer full of car keys and lets Sam pick one. "Yes, I do think there is a solution. But I struggle to imagine how we will control it once created. It seems impossible! But we must try!" He picks up a key fob for a Lamborghini and says, "Let me go get changed into something more comfortable."

As Aioven leaves to get changed, Sam and Leo look at Arthur, who is scratching his beard and furrowing his eyebrows in deep thought.

"What is he talking about?" Leo asks.

Arthur barely looks up before saying, "Either your friend is very powerful, or we're about to do something impossible."

Sam nods. "He's talking about black holes, isn't he?"

Leo's father heads over to the fridge and pours himself a small glass of tequila.

"What're you doing?" Leo asks. "You won't find many drinks in my cell, but given what we're about to do, I doubt there will be any in a black hole. So, I figured I'd get a swig of one before potentially going past the point of no return."

"I'll drive then," Sam says.

After receiving coordinates from Arthur, everyone sets off. Sam drives a very reasonable electric Toyota SUV in a matte gray. Aioven is back at the helm of a chrome purple Lamborghini that looks like a baby version of the last one that blew up.

"A Huracan, James? Very inconspicuous," Leo says sarcastically.

Aioven laughs. "I guess my love for cars was one of the few things that survived almost dying. I'm not usually the one engaging in covert operations."

Leo twists his body as he suddenly remembers something. "By the way, what about those other cars we brought out when we met up with Van Vuren?"

James waves his hand nonchalantly. "Lily and some of our friends are taking care of that. She's got our latest addition handling security at the apartment in the meantime."

"The Hayton kid?" Leo asks.

James revs the car's engine and flies past Sam and Arthur. "Yeah, she said she met him when she was working and decided to give him a shot when he started 'bitching about the Empire,' as she put it."

"Hmm ... weird," Leo says.

Aioven nods at him emphatically, "Ya think? I tried to ask her more about him since he was being recruited into my little world, and she didn't tell me much before she started acting like I was interrogating her or something."

"And were you?" Leo asks.

"No, not at first, but by the end I was. All I learned is that he's a poet and likes the cars that she likes."

Leo squints. "You said they met while she was working?"

Aioven shrugs. "She didn't specify where; she didn't have reception wherever she was either."

"She didn't—oh boy." Leo facepalms.

"Look I know how it sounds—" Aioven starts.

Leo holds up his hand to make Aioven stop talking. "Before you try to convince yourself that your girlfriend isn't cheating on you . . . If it walks like a duck, and quacks like a duck, then it's probably a duck. The dog in *Duck Hunt* would be laughing at how much you're missing right now."

"The what?" Aioven asks.

"You never played NES?" Leo asks.

Aioven shakes his head and throws his arms up in the air.

"Well, you're gonna need a hobby," Leo says.

"I could always hit the gym," Aioven says, laughing forcibly.

"A bit cliche. I thought you said you didn't want more power," Leo says, elbowing Aioven in the arm.

Aioven holds up his index finger. "Funny, though I meant that when I said it. I don't want any more power—not solely for myself. If I wanted power for myself, I wouldn't have gone out of my way to gather so many extraordinary people. If one man changes the world, then what is he going to do when entire nations of people turn against him? Who's going to vouch for him and his actions? Where will his credibility come from? I'm not clever enough to come up with a good answer to those questions."

Leo nods. "Makes sense, but I meant more so right now. We're going to my father's space station to find a counter to *strange matter*, and . . . I don't understand how figuring that out doesn't make you stronger."

Aioven shakes his head. "Because I won't be the one getting the power to beat him. I'm going to let you and Sam do most of the studying, and I will just be observing and supporting you."

Leo stretches out his legs and leans forward trying to reach the dashboard as Aioven gets close to their destination somewhere in a national park. "You would give up the opportunity to gain something from this excursion? You'd rather us study neutron stars and black holes than do it yourself?"

"Absolutely!" Aioven says immediately as they pull up to a parking lot after passing a sign that says Reclaimed Imperial Memorial Park. Aioven nods emphatically. "All right, neat place. Not exactly the launch center I was expecting."

"You know, my dad failed to mention how we were going to get into deep space," Leo says as they unbuckle themselves.

"I noticed that too. He just said, 'reverse-engineered architect technology.' Sam seemed to be close with her guess, though; maybe it is wormholes."

Stark smirks a little. "You know, I'm really glad my dad didn't disappear one day just to come back fifteen years later and say, 'Sorry, son, I went in the wrong wormhole.' Being in prison is more believable."

Aioven laughs. "If I heard someone tell me that, I'd just think they tried anal and it went wrong."

They laugh for a few minutes, exchanging jokes of a similar nature until Sam and Arthur show up.

"All right, everyone!" he says in a low but low, mechanical voice. "Ready to use a quantum gate?"

Sam slips the car key into her pocket. "A gate? To another dimension or another point in space?"

Arthur walks up to the mouth of a cave in a hill beside the car park. "Just another point in space. I'm taking you to one of the gates we built. Artificial wormholes can only be created with both sides next to each other. Then we move them around to make traveling between two points easier. We don't really know how interdimensional travel works. From what we understand, you can either do it or you can't."

Leo peers inside the cave dimly lit by flickering ceiling LEDs. "And yet somehow the architects can do it? Allegedly?"

Arthur stops just before the threshold of the cave entrance. "Yes, perks of being gods, I guess."

Aioven places his hand on the inner wall and notices something strange. He feels a slight resistance of a force trying to push away his hand from the stone surface, like when the wrong ends of a magnet are forced to be too close to each other.

Aioven presses his palm into the wall and focuses his senses. "How does one open a portal?"

Arthur notices Aioven's fixation on a point in the wall. "By mastering the properties of a yet-to-be-named substance, which we just call exotic matter. An extreme material with negative mass."

Leo frowns. "Negative mass? Why is that necessary?"

Arthur cracks his knuckles as if he's about to do something. "It keeps the door from collapsing into a black hole." He taps his right index finger on a seemingly random point in the wall, and a hole with blue light coming through starts to slowly open.

Aioven speechlessly stands beside Arthur as a circular gateway opens up, letting in light from the other side to show them the interior of a large room made of what appears to be stainless steel. Peering inside the portal, everyone can see a huge window that reveals the vastness of open space to them—the only difference being the alarming fact that the brightest and biggest object visible in the window isn't a star or a planet but rather the blue-and-white glow of a black hole. As the portal opens up completely, they all feel the huge object's gravitational pull, even without crossing over to the other side of the gateway.

"How does one gain this power?" Aioven asks eagerly, excited by the thought of teleportation.

Arthur raps his knuckles on the cave walls, causing a maze of golden wiring covering the whole interior of the cave to light up. The golden threads all link up where Arthur had tapped his finger.

"No one has the power to teleport themselves. Instead you activate the gate's mechanisms with a small input of your cosmic power. Then the gate will open as long as you don't tell it to close, or as long as your heart is beating." Everyone tenses as a breeze of cool, stale air comes through the portal.

Leo puts his hand through the portal, the cool air coating his skin, reminiscent of how it would feel to submerge one's hand in a pool of ice water. "How does the portal work?"

Arthur waves grandiose gestures at all the glowing golden wires on the inner cave walls. "The inversion motor, that is what generates the exotic matter. It's a bubbling machine composed of, well, a kind of plasma or a similar sort of thing. It isn't mechanical or electrical, and it's barely physical. The task of reverse engineering this stuff requires a cosmic master of matter, such as the grand master of the Order of Genesis, Adam Koenig. We may have designed each gate, but we needed him to put it together."

Aioven touches his ring to one of the vein-like wires, causing it to glow brighter and pulse. "So, few people can build portal gates and no one can teleport without them?"

"No, it is impossible," Arthur says, gripping the edges of the portal like he's verifying its sturdiness. "If it's a phenomena in the universe, in theory, our minds can unravel the mystery."

"Well, is that what you want us to work on?" Stark asks.

Aioven shakes his head. "No, but more importantly, let's see what we have to work with on the other side."

Arthur ushers them through the portal and allows it to close, letting the golden light leave the cave and plunge the tunnels back into darkness.

• • •

"**M**aster!" Rytram, Lana, and Darius all stand together beside a dark steel throne in deep conversation as a woman wearing black Genesis robes hurries into their large hall. They all say nothing as the lady catches her breath and kneels. "My lords, one of our agents has come to us with news on Dalkanos Aioven. Specifically, his current whereabouts and the location of his base."

Darius beckons the spy to stand up. "So, we now know his base of operations? And that he is not there?"

"Yes, Master," she says.

Darius looks at his compatriots. "Well then! *Captain* Smirnov, I imagine you'll be very interested in hearing this."

The false knight drops to her knees and begins her report. "Dalkanos Aioven's headquarters is in Simeo, near the city center in the tallest apartment building. He bought the whole building out and uses it to launder money and keeps it as a safe house for his followers and himself."

Darius smiles. "How very interesting." The hall groans and expands like a person's chest when taking in a deep breath. A hollow voice looms over the Imperial rulers. A shadow extinguishes the candle-lit chandeliers, passing over the only four occupants of the cyclopean throne room. The doors on the opposite end from the chair had opened to release blinding yellow light, like a piece of the sun had been dropped on the planet's surface. The figure casting the shadow is difficult to see, but it is cloaked in perfectly black robes that reflect no light.

"Almighty Nomor!" Rytram kneels before the silhouette of the architect. "To what do we owe the pleasure of your presence?"

The obscured god strolls toward the throne, taking long, silent footsteps. "Exorsio wanted me to ask you why you allowed an entire city to be reduced to rubble. Are you at war? Or was it terrorists?"

Darius kneels beside Rytram. "A fanatic with a grudge, your grace. He was collateral damage in one of Smirnov's assignments."

The throaty god's voice growls. "He clearly wasn't damaged *enough*. I thought you controlled the market on uranium and that all warheads were destroyed?"

Lana finally kneels too. "Lord Nomor, I have made it my sole purpose to defeat him."

The god conjures golden strings out of thin air to raise his neophytes to their feet like puppets. "Have you now? I am not impressed. When my siblings and I designed this universe, we did not allow for this man to interfere in those desires. He IS merely 'collateral damage.'"

"He has great power, Master," Rytram says. The architect removes his hood to reveal dark tan skin and shiny, smooth black hair, tied into braids and laced with natural curls. His pupils glow like small yellow suns surrounded by black starry scleras.

The deity stares at the angel with cold disdain. "Greater than yours? I ought to take your wings right now if you can't put them to good use."

Darius steps forward. "Lord Nomor, I possess a power that Aioven can't beat."

The god grips the angel by the wings, making his feather shrivel up and blacken like wilting flowers. "None of you possess power. You possess nothing. Your abilities exist only by the grace of Exorsio. Even yours, Xenos. You still have a ways to go before you ascend. In the meantime, deal with these interlopers. This conflict is more entertaining than anything you could ever come up with. But—if you cannot control this war, we can always return to do the work ourselves. A lifeless universe is boring."

●　●　●

Arthur gestures broadly out the window at the cosmic

spectacles so close to the facility their influence can be felt by every spectator present. "Before us, and graciously spinning us around, is a black hole with less than half the mass of our sun. As you can see, it is growing, however."

Aioven, Sam, and Leo all press themselves against the glass to stare into the most energetic phenomena they will ever see: a black hole with a glowing blue accretion disc feeding on a small, blue neutron star that is being thrown around like paper in the wind. The blue light swirling around the deathly silhouette makes it look like a cosmic drain sucking in a whirlpool of bright-blue light.

Arthur leans on the glass. "The neutron star being thrown around it is old. It was likely a rogue before it got caught in this maelstrom."

Sam gazes in with wonder upon the baby-blue stream of matter sinking into the black hole like water in a drain. "I didn't know neutron stars could go rogue. Apart from spinning, I thought they were stationary."

"Nothing in the universe is static," Arthur says before turning to Aioven. "So now you see the focus of our studies. We sought to unlock the potential of the singularity and harness the strength of the neutron star. Skip the whole Dyson sphere concept and go straight to the ultimate energy source."

"Today . . ." Aioven looks back and forth between Leo and Sam. "Today we shall see if our bodies are truly meant to wield the power of the cosmos. Sam will attempt to achieve some kind of familiarity with the neutron star, to see if its insides have anything to offer. And Leonidas here will try to understand the trapdoor in space that is the event horizon."

"To serve what purpose?" Arthur asks.

Aioven pulls out a pair of leather gloves and melts them into a churning spiral of bubbling matter in the air. "Our enemy, Darius, who is soon to be Xenos, the god of strangeness, wields strange matter. Something that theoretically can only be created in the cores of neutron stars."

Leo peers into the center of the eerie sphere of darkness. "And what interest is the black hole to us?"

The swirling matter wraps itself around his hands and returns to its original leather state, perfectly fitted to his hands. "Singularities are the only things in the universe that can contain or even destroy strange matter. It is the only counter the universe has to offer."

Arthur crosses his arms. "And what do you have to gain?"

Aioven puts his hands on the shoulders of Leo and Sam. "I'll have a master of matter and a master of energy at my side. We'll be the most unstoppable team that the world has ever seen."

• • •

The group pauses to looks at each other, as the moment's gravity sinks in. Failure will almost certainly be fatal, or worse. Each grows quiet and steels themselves to the task. In that moment, they are oblivious to the threat approaching their home on the other side of the universe.

"You know, I never was a man of materialistic leanings," Alan says as he paces the rows and rows of exotic vehicles in Aioven's stable with his son at his side.

"But they're so cool," little Daniel Lee says.

Alan faces the young boy with a raised eyebrow. "Oh? Couldn't Aioven use his resources to save people rather than buy half-million-dollar gas-guzzling super cars?"

Daniel stops at an old green Toyota Supra. "Do you think he wants to help people? He blew up a city."

Alan pauses. "You know, that's a good point."

"Have you seen what Master Aioven can do?" Daniel asks, staring into his father's eyes.

"Yes, I have, son, but—"

Daniel opens the car's driver-side door. "I think that he likes killing people."

Alan wonders whether he should speak freely to his son. "He is the man who saved you," he says. His child looks at him with a look of disappointment akin to a father's when their young fail to sneak into the house past curfew.

The boy pulls out the car's key and pushes it into the ignition. "Dad, are you lying? Do you think he wants to help people? Do you think he's doing his best?"

Alan Lee sighs and sits on the fender of the car, unable to look at his child. "Dalkanos Aioven is as powerful as he is passionate. Sometimes he is giving it all he's got, or at least he thinks he is. Other times he abandons all urgency to play with his kills like it's a game. I understand your unease. He shouldn't taunt them, insult them and then dispatch them like it's a light show."

Daniel leaves the key in the ignition and gets out of the car and forces his father out of the way. "I don't like hurting people. The good guys should save people. But Master Aioven's killing, I think it helps, but I don't like it." Daniel's hands tighten into fists as he struggles to understand his own feelings on such a complex issue.

Alan stutters as his son begins to exude an energy he never detected before. "A boy barely a teen shouldn't be talking about things like this."

Daniel rests his hand on the hilt of a sword Alan had never seen before. "Dad, you were just like him before you went away. Maybe we should all be glad Aioven has his cars."

Alan hisses through gritted teeth. "Why? Because questioning your master would be foolish?"

Daniel leans in despite his father's reaction. "That's not what I'm saying. I think that he is a better person because he CARES about being seen as the good guy. And playing with fancy cars seems to distract him from revenge killing."

Alan's posture falters and almost slouches to hear his son speak like such a fanatic. "And what's that, my boy?"

"The world," Daniel says before finally turning away from his father to leave him alone with Aioven's distractions.

Alan looks around at all the personalized vehicles and almost curses the very name of the man who reunited him with his family. That is until his thoughts are blown away by the heavy breathing and stomping of a strapping lad rushing into the garage.

"Master Lee! I've come to warn you. Our spies and the city's cameras have all but confirmed the Empire has come to Simeo."

"To do what, Hayton? Where are they headed?" Alan asks, patting the man on the back as he coughs.

The young man whistles as he catches his breath. "Here, sir, they are heading here. And I sense Captain Smirnov but nothing else, just lots of enemies."

Alan inshales so sharply his lungs almost bleed. "Lana? How in the hell did she find us?" He looks at the young man. "Do I know you?"

The man bows theatrically. "Hayton Hallman, Lily's right hand."

Alan grabs his shoulder and forces him back upright. "Oh good, another thespian."

"Sir?" Hayton asks.

Alan begins walking toward the exit but not before looking over his shoulder at Hayton. "Oh, and just so you know, her name is Lilith. You would be wise to call her that in Aioven's presence. I have seen what he does to his enemies. I would love to see what he does to those who threaten what little he has. Acting so familiar could give the wrong impression."

Hayton croaks as he stutters. "I do not—"

Alan holds up his hand. "Just send an alarm to Sam. She's with Aioven—"

"And the Starks," Hayton says.

Alan draws his axe and points it at Hayton. "Your ability to finish my sentences gives me pause. You must be very observant—and lucky to have Lilith Melrose as your keeper."

Quickly gathered at the top of the building, Alan stands beside his son and several more of Aioven's followers, waiting for the Empire's avengers. "Well, men, whilst Aioven seeks a way to beat the powers that be, we must defend his keep in his stead. We must band together—strangers, children, parents, warriors, young, and old."

The fighters all look at Alan Lee and then at each other, unsure of themselves and their chances. Alan slams his axe into the roof. "Doesn't sound like much today! But I swear to you in less than a year our enemies will tremble at the sounds of approaching Dalkanonian knights! An army who has no allegiance to gods, emperors, kings, presidents, or overbearing spouses. We fight for the delicate flame of life! And we burn those who would snuff it out!"

"*Yeah!*" The loyal men of Aioven's rebellion cheer and raise their weapons into the air. Anyone with even a small talent for cosmic awareness would find the display of strength impressive, were it not for the invaders standing in the air like vultures on invisible branches. They were floating above them, possibly watching the whole time.

Captain Smirnov steps down onto the roof like she's using an invisible staircase. "And here I thought you savages possessed no charisma!"

A teen steps forward, with rough, greasy hair and the body of a seasoned linebacker. "You should see my charisma up close!" The males of the group laugh as the speaker adjusts his pants with a hard pull.

Lana rolls her eyes. "I'd need a magnifying glass to see your charisma."

The men laugh even louder. "The two-faced bitch has got you there, Cory!"

Cory bows. "Apologies *Captain* Smirnov, but last I checked, my charisma was so big it could be seen from space!"

"Shut it, boy!" Lee shouts, gripping the hilt of his axe with two hands. "This one is here to fight."

Lana draws her two swords and starts pointing the tips at various targets. "Yes, I'm here to burn your home as you have burned mine." Her red-and-black captain's coat whips around violently as the force of her power is released, making everyone adjust their footing to stay standing.

"You mean the city we burned?" Lee asks.

Lana grips her weapons so tightly her knuckles turn white, her gold-armoured companions landing beside her like birds on a perch. "No, this is personal for me, as it is for these men. Yes, your master burned our capital, but he also burned my house and took what I was fighting for."

"What?" Lee asks, faltering in his stance.

Lana bends her knees. "You don't know, and I don't care. I'll just leave him to find what I found."

· · ·

Aioven stands behind Sam and puts both of his hands on her shoulders. "I'm afraid I'm not much of a teacher. When I learn something new it comes to me too quickly to understand how I. . . understand it."

Arthur holds his hands behind his back and looks at the pair with a smile. "You may learn things quickly, Master Aioven, but you still do it the same way as the rest of us: through experience."

Aioven gazes out the window at the almighty neutron star, his eyes straining from its brilliant light. "Whenever I learn something new, it's because I felt something previously hidden away from my senses, something I was only unconsciously aware of before. Whether it was a natural phenomena, like thunder and lightning, or a man-made fire fuelled by gasoline."

Leo steps forward. "Haven't others attempted this before?"

Arthur shakes his head and looks at his confused son. "No, say what you will about Grand Master Koenig, but he did have the foresight to only employ intelligent men without our gifts to this station—to avoid the risk of any who would attempt to harvest such power. Few would even try to do so. The near certainty of burning up is a powerful disincentive."

Aioven steps away from Sam. "Sam, I want you to go carefully. Try to get a sense of what is involved. We need to use just enough to defeat Xenos."

"Aye," Arthur says. If you bite off more than you can chew in this space is especially dangerous. There is no need to go fast."

"He's right." Aioven nods. "Siphon what you can, but don't overdo it. You are far too important. And its easy to draw too much power here."

Sam closes her eyes and reaches out with her arms and thoughts, feeling out the star's influence on reality. Despite its energetic shine, the power of its spin and the gravity that fails to collapse it is far greater. She feels it spinning almost a thousand times per second. And the material beneath its hard, cruel crust is so dense that trying to make sense of it makes her feel the same sort of strain she would if she stared into the sun. She knows from her high school classes that the core is an extreme place, but her senses tell her it is a void hidden away.

"Be cautious, Sam, take it slow," Aioven says, returning one of his hands to her shoulder. The moment his hand rests on her, the star suddenly transforms in her mind. It's as if his presence draws everything into focus and calms things down. Sam wonders if he's even helping her on purpose, though she tries not to get distracted.

Within the star churns plasma and matter being violently compacted to the point that she can't discern the difference between matter and energy. It's like they're the same stuff. The core is strangely enveloped in sheets of matter so solid that she can't see through them.

"Tell us, do you see anything?" Aioven asks.

Sam nods. "I see . . . matter fighting to escape, matter so neatly compressed into layers, like flat sheets."

"Incredible. What you're seeing is nuclear pasta. Neutron stars are the second most extreme things in the universe. They compress things so violently that phenomenas that would normally be impossible in normal space can occur. Energy and matter can be pressed so tightly together that they become the same thing. Strange quarks can appear, and nuclear pasta can also be made. If that really is what you're seeing, you could be looking at the single strongest material in the universe," Arthur says.

Aioven claps his hands. "I'm not a scientist, and I still think this is exciting. I wish I could see what you're seeing, Sam. But please, be careful."

Despite his hand being removed from her, Sam keeps speaking. "I also see some of the core."

Aioven turns, restraining his shocked tone despite having just praised her. "The core? What do you see?"

Her breath grows shaky and congested sounding. "The quarks, most are stable . . ." Blood begins to leave from her mouth and nose. "Others are changing and changing others to be like them."

"Sam, open your eyes, please," Aioven says. Sam tries but feels her eyes gluing themselves shut as blood begins to seep out of them and her ears.

She wobbles and crumbles gracelessly into Aioven's arms. "Sam!" Leo and Arthur kneel beside them.

Arthur places a hand on her forehead. "Careful, don't shake her up too much. Forcing yourself to learn something faster than you're meant to is a hard thing on the mind."

"Too fast?" Aioven finds the concept a surprise.

Arthur nods. "Yes, Master Aioven, you are blessed with a fast-learning mind, but even so, the mind is more of a sponge than anything else to a cosmic forcewielder."

Aioven gently sits Sam upright against the wall. "What do you mean, Arthur? Is she going to be all right?"

Arthur removes his jacket and uses it to clean some of the blood off Sam's face. "She didn't explode, so she won't die, but her brain almost started to leak out of her head."

"What?" Leo reels away from Sam, wiping his hands on his pant legs.

Arthur rolls his eyes at his son. "Calm yourself, boy, you weren't so squeamish back when you made bowls of worm pasta for your mom and I."

"Arthur." Aioven regains Arthur's attention. "What do you mean our minds are like sponges?"

Arthur looks at the ground as if he wants to kneel. "I don't presume to know your mind, but for most people, even the most gifted among us, their minds soak up knowledge over time—enough for a lifetime. As we forget things and learn new things, there is a certain balance that is maintained without us even knowing. But if one were to learn too much too quickly and reach total saturation of our consciousness, well, the mind will try to maintain itself by emptying its contents just as quickly."

Aioven's eyes widen, and he places his hand on his closest advisor's head. "You say that far too calmly." For once, he discards all of his destructive powers and dives into Sam's thoughts, urging her sanity to not leave her like his did. Childhood memories had already begun to escape, along with experiences with lost family, proud moments at school, and . . . the day her child was born. Aioven's resolve to hold his friend together keeps her thoughts from escaping any further. He then reaches into her, the same way he does to himself to keep the monsters away, and pushes her mind to grow, so she may have room. Aioven's mind had to be expanded to contain the remains of his identity as well as the monsters bred by his madness, whereas Sam's mind contains her one-of-a-kind personality, and now . . . knowledge that gods wouldn't dare freely share with just anyone.

The bleeding stops and Sam opens her eyes, partially blinded by blood. "Not the worst thing you asked me to do," she says.

"Maybe, but usually you say no when I ask you for crazy things. At this point I may just stop asking." Aioven smiles and turns to Arthur. "Let's clean her up," he says.

"The strange matter in the core," she says, making them all freeze. "I can't make it or wield it, but it is contained in the pasta."

"Really?" Leo asks.

Aioven strokes his chin. "How interesting."

"The strange quarks weren't converting the layers of pasta?" Arthur asks.

Sam blinks a few times, still unable to see clearly. "The pasta's effects on gravity seems to keep the strangeness from converting it, but it doesn't destroy it."

Aioven kisses the top of her head proudly. "A suitable material for a god's trap, but we still need information from the star's more massive cousin to build a guillotine fit for a deity."

"The singularity," Leo guesses out loud.

Aioven turns to his friend. "Not exactly," he says. "If you can figure out how to create or destroy singularities, that would be beyond anything that I know. Or imagine possible."

Sam grabs Arthur's arm and pulls herself up. "A star is one thing. I feel like my veins are filled with burning fuel, but black holes are the most powerful things in the universe. More massive than anything else. How can we hope to even scratch the surface of their power?"

Leo stares into the swirling mass of glowing particles, observing its absolute power over everything that gets too close.

"The event horizon could give us a few hints," he says.

"Please elaborate," Aioven says as he wanders over to the gate they entered the station from, feeling its edges.

Stark removes his coat and massages his arms. "Empty space isn't truly empty. It's filled with particles forming from nothing and destroying each other. But when a pair of particles is born close enough to a singularity for one to be swallowed but not both, the survivor steals a bit of the black hole's mass. These monsters radiate themselves away by losing their mass like this. I could, at the very least, study this process to see if there's any hints on what lies beyond the horizon. A stretch I know, but I'd rather start with knowing how to remove these one-way trapdoors before knowing how to open them. Understanding their mass radiation and finding a way to speed up the process could prove useful."

Aioven's arms fall limp at his side. "Well, that confirms one thing. Had I died that night, I have no doubt you'd have put yourself in the position I am in now. You have the strength, and you have more wisdom than I do. I expect if you were leading my people, you'd be much further along."

"Then they wouldn't be your people, they'd be mine. I can't gather followers like you." Leo points at himself. "And I appreciate your vote of confidence, but it was you who recruited me."

Aioven dips his fingertips through the threshold of the portal. "You forget how we met. Before I even had my powers, it was you who sought me out and succeeded in getting me involved."

Leo sits down on the floor and crosses his legs. "I think Smirnov needs to take the credit for giving you the motivation. You didn't have all this anger back then. Maybe you could've joined us without it and these powers . . . well I guess we'll never know."

Dalkanos Aioven glances up for a moment and looks toward his friends. Arthur frowns, looking from face to face for an explanation but receives none. Aioven continues to meditate on the influence of the quantum gate, feeling the sensation of weight but somehow in an inverted sense. Near the portal the feeling of heaviness is the same, but when he holds out something like his sword, the weight pushes the sword away from the gate and slightly upward.

Meanwhile, Leo holds out his hands, how someone might when warming themselves in front of a fire. He cautiously extends his senses toward the heat of the glowing blue accretion disc.

He doesn't try to siphon any of the kinetic energy. "I can sense the immense kinetic power, a near-infinite source of energy even compared to the nuclear fusion of stars. But I dare not try and take any for myself. I'd be lucky if a melted brain is all I get for my efforts."

"The rest of you would melt as well," his father says.

Leo sends his mind careening into the cosmic whirlpool, speeding up to what can only be described as a fraction of the speed of light. He starts to take short, rapid breaths with his eyes rolling into the back of his head. He begins to gasp as air and drool race out of his mouth.

"Son!" Arthur falls on his knees beside Leo. Unable to even gasp for air, Leo manages a few weak croaking sounds before curling up onto the ground like a fetus in the womb. His mind succumbs to the pull of the event horizon and feels as if he is being carried toward a waterfall, unable to swim to safety.

"Boy!" Arthur grips his child's hands and immediately starts choking as well. His pupils disappear, and he sprays saliva everywhere as he stands up straight, only to fall backward like a plank of wood.

Sam tries to move to catch him but stumbles. She and Aioven watch as Leo's father crashes into the floor and becomes motionless.

Before either of them can think of how to treat Arthur, Leo convulses and begins to roll around, unable to breathe or scream.

Aioven looks at him, trying to sense what is happening, but Sam grabs his wrist. "He can't do it alone!" she says.

Aioven sees Leo's face turn blue, and without even fully understanding the repercussions, he grabs his friend's hand only to find himself now sharing in the same torture. He begins to feel a pulling from all directions on his body, and a shrill howling fills his mind as his own atoms fight being pulled apart into streams of plasma. Leo retches still, but less violently than before. Sam, who is still recovering from her peek into a neutron star, grabs Leo's other hand. The trio, linked together now, all must shoulder the weight of the most violent force in the universe and survive.

Their bodies may be at a safe distance, but they know that the pull of the singularity could still indeed separate their consciousness from their physical vessels, leaving behind vacant, but still technically alive, shells. Leo's breathing calms, deep through his nose and out slowly through his mouth, knowing full well that no matter which direction they go, any effort would bring them closer to the center. Aioven and Sam helplessly go along with their friend, who takes them toward the forbidden core.

What happens cannot and will never be possible to explain. For a moment, everything freezes, and then the entire universe is compressed into a small spot before turning red and fading away. Sensations of time, gravity, temperature, or movement simply vanish from their senses. Before Aioven can panic or despair in his helplessness, he blinks, and in the next perceivable moment, he has returned to his body. Sam and Aioven yank their arms away from Leo, light-headed from some kind of motion sickness. Sam sits up in a daze, her vision flickering like the world is moving in fast forward. As reality slows down, she is able to wobble to her feet and get beside Arthur Stark, who still remains motionless.

Dalkanos Aioven slams his hand into the floor as he gags on his own breath. "I'd rather crash a car on purpose than do that again." Aioven keels over and vomits what little he has in his body.

Sam takes Arthur's wrist and grips it, waiting a few moments before breathing a sigh of relief. "He's alive," she announces and lies down on the hard floor.

"It's a shock that any of us are," Aioven says before gagging on acid reflux and puking all over the floor.

Sam removes the outer layer of her robe and uses it to make a pillow to support Arthur's head, and then she starts walking toward her sick leader.

Leo stands up, as if he were suddenly weightless. "You may want to postpone feeling sorry for yourselves, or you'll never have the chance to be sorry again."

Aioven and Sam both look out the window when they realize that everything outside is different. The neutron star is now losing huge chunks of itself to the black hole, falling into it so fast that not all of it can be absorbed fast enough. Bright jets of red light are now being emitted from the black hole's poles.

"Gamma ray bursts," Aioven says.

Leo nods. "We may have accidentally sped up this behemoth's meal. That star will disappear, and then, when the singularity has nothing left to feed on, it will radiate away and blow us all to pieces. What normally would've taken billions of years is now going to happen in a few minutes."

Aioven stares at Leo. "That fast? Shouldn't that be impossible?"

Leo picks his sword up off the floor and examines the hilt before presenting it to Aioven. Three stones sit on the guard of the hilt: red and green gems on either side and a new black one in the center.

Aioven's eyes light up with pride, and he can't hold back his smile. "You did it. Both of you did it."

Sam points out the window. "Not yet." The star disintegrates completely, and its light disappears into the event horizon. Almost as quickly as it disappeared, the accretion disc dims slightly and turns purple, just before beginning to sink into the shrinking black hole.

Sam starts trying to wake up Arthur. "Aioven, we have only a few moments. What should we do?"

Aioven looks around, gazing back at the gate, which is still closed, and the black hole, which is moments away from going into apocalypse mode. "Can you slow it down again?" he asks.

Leo looks at his friend like he's mad. "All I did was light the fuse. I don't know how to put it out!"

Aioven braces. Unable to think of a solution, he holds out his arms and braces.

"James, *No!*" Sam shouts, running toward him. The black hole destabilizes and releases its torrents of energy like a dying star. The station around them boils away like water dropped on a hot skillet. Aioven conjures a shield that deflects most of the heat, but every part of their bodies starts to slowly cook. Their skin and hair quickly begin to singe and burn.

"Gaaahhhhh!" Aioven stops redirecting the energy and starts to absorb it.

"You need to go!" he shouts. What little howling air remains barely carries his voice to his comrades. Sam looks to Arthur and back at Aioven hopelessly. Leo struggles toward Aioven and joins him in his effort to deflect the blast away from them. Aioven looks back at the portal gate, which is still closed and yet somehow still intact. *That's it.* Somehow, the explosion can't reach the gate. Nothing can touch or damage it. Sam and Leo, almost in perfect unison, grip Aioven's shoulders to absorb the blast together. Aioven takes one hand away from the shield and reaches for the gate to activate it.

Leo's knees almost buckle as the void of space tries to crush them. "James! Hurry!" Their arms begin to blacken and melt as the universe fights to put them to extinction. Aioven remembers the sensation of stepping through the portal, willing or even begging it to open so they may lunge through it. And then, the gate crumbles away and all the exotic matter he can sense disappears. For a second, he almost makes peace with his mortality but realizes that the fact he is even able to detect the absence of the exotic matter means he felt the loss of the negative mass necessary to open a portal. And if he can sense something, it's a resource he can use and recreate.

Aioven turns toward the explosion, and instead of willing the energy away or absorbing it, he focuses on the particles in space that would normally be forming and annihilating themselves and instead freezes them as they're born. Stuck in a stasis, he only gives them permission to annihilate themselves if the matter is allowed to have negative mass.

"Open!" he shouts, as his bones begin to be exposed. The empty space around them begins to bubble and seemingly gather to one point. Before it's too late, Aioven flings the swirling matter behind the group away from the explosion and sends the energy of the blast into the new door, using his body as a conductor. The gate opens, and as his body finally starts to lose its integrity, he lets go of the shield, and the party is swept away into his gateway.

CHAPTER 13

•

ENEMIES OF THE THREE

Gunfire, flaming arrows, spears, and all manner of supercharged, seemingly archaic weaponry flood the air. Those with melee weapons clash on the ground and indeed the sky— Aioven's followers versus Smirnov's crew of undercover agents, all still dressed in their Genesis garb.

Daniel darts from fight to fight in order to support the group as a whole. Meanwhile, his father faces down the false captain herself. His large axe sweeps through the air almost as quickly as her comparatively smaller swords do, keeping her from going on the complete offensive. Whenever she thinks she sees an opening to swing or thrust her blades into Alan's body, he parries, sidesteps, or grabs her arm to redirect her and trip her like a child.

"Wearing a captain's coat doesn't mean you fight like a captain," he says, blasting her with a sudden gust of cold wind.

She is knocked over but recovers with a combat roll and sticks both swords into the ground. "You're right. I don't."

She points a finger at him and shoots a high-intensity beam of gamma radiation at him. He blocks it with his axe, but it instantly disarms him and puts a very clear hole through the front of his shoulder and out of his back. Not even falling to one knee, he breaks the windows of the buildings around him and sends the hand-sized shards straight to Lana. She pulls her swords out of the ground and starts spinning the blades so fast that it looks like she's holding two transparent, circular shields. Lee's eyes see only slightly silver steel blurs flickering around her as the glass hits a shield and turns to sand.

Now surrounded by a pile of white sand, she points her offhand sword at him. "I don't need to fight like a captain. My masters granted me enough power to ensure my victories from this point onward."

"So you're saying they weren't happy with your performance?" Lee asks as his axe returns to his hand. She throws one sword at him, which he dodges easily, but he recognizes the trap too late. Lana charges at him with her remaining sword and locks their weapons together, whilst the other sword returns like a boomerang. Unable to dodge in time, the second sword slices his left knee open. He stumbles and Lana takes advantage immediately by burying her sword in his stomach.

"No!" A bolt of blue lightning smites Lana and destroys her offhand sword in a barrage of steel shrapnel. The splintered pieces of her sword disappear into her body and lodge themselves into nearly every internal organ except her brain and heart. She starts coughing up blood and gasping for air as the act of breathing becomes a painful chore with sword shards in her lungs. Daniel lands between her and his father, sword pointed at her and his blade coursing with arcing blue electricity.

"You'll be fine, but she won't." He raises his sword skyward and grips it tightly, holding it with one hand. "Bye, lady."

Another gamma bolt shoots through the air, again coming from Lana's finger, which was hidden under her cloak. The bolt leaves a fist-sized, sizzling hole in the center of Daniel's chest, making it possible to see through his body. His eyes glaze over, and he falls limp in front of Alan. Now with only one sword left, still barely able to breathe, and with only one remaining male of the Lee legacy, Lana grips her tool of execution with two hands and rests the blade on the hopeless Alan Lee.

She pauses for a moment, twitches her head like she heard something, and spins around and blocks a bolt of white light with her sword. Before she can look around for the source, several bolts from all directions force her to move away from the Lees. Suddenly, the ground turns to a sort of wet concrete, swallowing her feet only to solidify instantly. A huge column of white fire engulfs her, forcing out a gurgling scream as she both burns alive and drowns in her own blood.

The savior lands beside the Lees to reveal that it is Captain Van Vuren, holding his rifle. He first places his hand over Daniel's wound and seals away his insides from the elements with a shield, but he is unable to remove the hole in his chest. He turns to Alan and closes the wound in his shoulder and knee.

"That's a neat healing trick you got there," Alan says.

Van Vuren pulls him off the ground and over to his son. "I can't say I healed you per se. All I did was stop you from leaking anywhere. Can you stand?"

"Barely!" Alan says as he stands awkwardly, like a doll with unnaturally bent limbs.

Van Vuren grips his rifle. "You'll need to carry your son to safety. I'll handle these jokers." He looks up into the sky at the false knights fighting Aioven's men.

"You'll need to kill me first!" The smoke clears to reveal Lana Smirnov, fully healed and now armed with a black katana gilded in some sort of glowing gold. Van Vuren aims his rifle and fires at her, only this time she swipes away his attack with her bare hand. His senses have to be deceiving him, but it is like her energy levels have increased several times over, well beyond his own, in an instant.

"I told you my masters would not allow another defeat." She steps forward to attack when everyone present feels a sensation they have never felt before, like the environment around them started to move in a way invisible to the naked eye. Matter, energy, and everything else starts to bend and then suddenly tear. From a random point in the sky, the apocalypse is unleashed. A hellstorm of purple lightning and hot-blue fire explodes from nothing and sweeps all over the battlefield. Anyone in Aioven's organization experiences the flames and electricity like bathwater or caffeine reinvigorating them, but everyone else is burnt to a crisp by the bolts and turned to ash by the fire. Out of the rift in space come three figures: Sam Parks, who wields a glowing red sword as large as her body; Leonidas Stark, holding his own sword, which has notably changed in colour to a crystal, cobalt blue; and standing between them, Dalkanos Aioven is fully outfitted from head to toe in pristine, shining silver armour, the edges accented with what looks like purple neon lights and gold patterns of nonagons.

Ashes rain down on them. Aioven starts walking and proceeds to jog and then run at Lana. "I'll kill you before they realize how powerless you are!" With a swing of his sword, an arc of bright purple light stops Lana in her tracks, blocked by her own sword but unable to cut through it. Too busy trying to avoid getting steamrolled by his attack, she is unable to stop him from stabbing her in the back with light, undetectable speed. Her grip on her sword falters, and the arc of plasma slams into her body, searing and melting her skin. Abandoning her defenses, she swings at Aioven and creates the opportunity to get out of harm's way.

"You are stronger, Captain Smirnov," Aioven says mockingly. She howls and resists the urge to touch her wounds. What happens next is something they've never seen before. The wounds heal, and her skin restores itself to near perfect condition in a matter of seconds.

She struts around and flaunts her healed body at them. "One of the many powers Lord Exorsio granted me. As long as I have power, I will heal from any wound. So do not disrespect me by burning a serva—"

Before she can talk about her grand masters, her nose has been broken, crushed under the force of Aioven's palm striking her face. With his fingers latched onto her head, he carries her up and far away from civilization in seconds and releases her, throwing her at supersonic speeds downward, vaporizing the ground to make a half-mile-wide crater upon impact. Her broken bones crunch back together, and her skin and muscles rewrap themselves back over her bones. She had to have been going faster than the speed of sound to do that much damage. Aioven lands at the end of the crater, looking down on her. The gentle sound of his feet gingerly patting onto the rocky surface seems almost silent compared to her landing.

"Let's see what strength your masters will trust you with. I bet it won't be enough." Aioven stands before her with his zigzag sword at the ready, inviting her to attack first. She stands up and takes a deep breath to center herself. Aioven remains still, not taking a fighting stance as she slowly steps around him. With two hands gripping her sword, she charges, hoping to stab at him from the side. He parries her as if she's moving in slow motion and grabs her neck with his open hand.

He gently shoves her back a few steps and swishes his sword nonchalantly through the air. "Come on now, Captain. Surely you can do better than that. I mean, yes, I want to prove how much stronger I am than you, but you could at least get my heart rate up."

Lana once again charges, this time swinging her sword as hard as possible, starting down low and slashing upward. This being exactly what Aioven wanted her to do, he catches her attack with his sword, parries it, and sweeps her away with such kinetic force that rocks and nearby hills disintegrate and flatten themselves.

"Oh, you're not dead." Aioven points his sword at her. "Try

again," he commands. She looks at her own katana and curses under her breath. "Are your masters not going to grant you the power you need? I'm not unstoppable."

She looks up at him and grips her sword with two hands.

Aioven sighs. "I guess they don't care, or they're not watching."

Lana's hands start to tremble, contemplating how to approach him or make her next move.

Aioven kicks the dirt. "I'm not sensing any changes in you. If your masters want you to die, then so be it."

Cracks splinter across the ground, eventually opening up into a narrow crevice so deep that the darkness below hides the bottom. The sudden abyss opens up just a few steps away from where Lana is standing. Aioven holds out a hand. "Your masters have a talent for cruelty that I admit I share with them. Though I'd like to think I'm a touch more creative." He closes his fingers around something invisible, yanks hard, and thousands of black, jagged chains shoot out of the fissure in the ground and fill the sky. The chains nearly block out the sky as they jingle before curling and racing toward Lana like a swarm of metal snakes. Some wrap themselves around her body, but others seemingly temporarily osmose through her flesh in order for the links to connect with her body. Chains bury themselves inside her, connecting to things like wrist bones, ribs, and so many other excruciatingly painful and uncomfortable places. Without gritting his teeth or grimacing at all, Aioven yanks on the chains and starts to pull her toward the crevice. "I'll be back for you, and when I return, you'll wish this had killed you."

The shrieking she manages as the planet swallows her and the crevice seals would have haunted Aioven had it not been for the fact that he had been planning this moment since the day Patrick and Laura had died. Perhaps it will haunt him one day, but not today.

He looks upon the horizon and then into the sky to see that

the sun would not be going down for some time. His work is far from done.

Not even allowing him a moment to savour his victory, the Order arrives. "Ah . . . the esteemed *Master* Aioven joins us at last." Aioven is greeted by the all-too-predictable sight of every captain and master in the Order of Genesis. A colossal collection of power. And at the front, Grand Master Koenig greets Aioven and his people.

Aioven says nothing but stands in front of his people as well, to make sure he is the first thing between them and the Order. Koenig rests his hand on his sword hilt. "Will you come quietly?" he asks.

Aioven does nothing. Koenig partially draws his sword. "Your power and independence cannot be allowed to continue. For the sake of the world and the creatures clinging to its surface, I ask that you peacefully surrender."

"How about this," Aioven says. "I invite you all to my formal speech at the Royal Mars Circular Hall. I promise no violence will befall anyone until after I have made my intentions clear and our alliance is made."

"Alliance? Why would you want to work with us?" Koenig asks.

Aioven holds out his hand and turns it like a key, opening a rift behind him and his comrades. "Because we can help each other for the betterment of the world. You have traitors and monsters in your midst. Without me, they'll take you down from the inside."

Koenig laughs and looks at his subordinates, who all remain stoic. "My people were all handpicked for their strength and loyalty."

Aioven steps into the portal. "After today, I can say for certain, loyalty isn't guaranteed." The portal closes, hiding their current whereabouts from the Order.

"Captain!" Van Vuren rushes to stand before his commander. "Shall I track them?"

Koenig waves him away with his hand. "There's no need. We know where they'll be."

The grand master looks around. "Where's Smirnov?"

•   •   •

Captain Smirnov is somewhere far away, deep underground beyond everyone's senses. She awakens, or at least she thinks she does, because she is surrounded by total darkness. She waits for a few minutes to let her eyes adjust, but it doesn't do her any good. Wherever she is, there is no light or sound, so as her eyes try to adjust themselves, her ears do as well. Eventually the silence fades away as the sound of her own pulse gets louder and louder. She hesitates to breathe as it starts to become deafening. Just as she thinks about using her powers to create a light, she gets an uneasy feeling that she isn't alone.

Aioven speaks softly to break the silence, overpowering the sound of her blood rushing through her body. "You should be thankful. I could've left you somewhere with no oxygen to die."

He lights a small candle and places it on the floor. The floor is uneven stone, and the dim candlelight flickers across the walls of the cave they are in. Smirnov tries to move but stops when she realizes the chains from before are still attached to her body and have zero slack in them, meaning any movement would cause extreme pain and discomfort, as the links buried in her body would start to pull on her bones. Even without moving, the itchiness of the chains latched onto her insides is otherworldly.

She opens her dry mouth but has to lick her lips before speaking. "Are you going to kill me?"

Aioven dissolves his mask and armour to return to his normal street clothes. He fixes his hair and puts on his glasses and places his katana on the floor beside the candle. "Do you have any idea how long it has been? How hard I have fought to get to this moment? Killing you would be like preparing a Michelin-star meal and then eating it in seconds. I want to savour this."

Lana looks at the fire and focuses on it, causing it to flicker and swirl. Aioven raises his eyebrows and looks at the candle and back to her. "You sure you want to do that?"

She tenses, and when she tries to turn the flame into a raging inferno, instead of her thermal energy being fed to the fire, it is instead transferred to the chains in her body. The jagged metal starts to glow red hot, searing her flesh with a loud hissing and crackling sound. Lana stops and starts screaming.

Aioven places tape over her mouth. "Ugh, I don't enjoy this any more than you do! You smell like a spitted pig. Not that I don't like pork; but you smelling good is just bad."

Lana's eyelids start to droop as she slips in and out of consciousness. Aioven rips the tape off her mouth to wake her up. "Well, I still have work to do. And I'm not done with you. You have too much potential. But first I must root out your network of spies, to replace them with my own agents." Aioven picks up the candle and holds the flame close to her face. "You and your masters could've had the world. But you broke into the wrong house and killed the wrong child. Not that there was any way you could've known. I certainly didn't, but here we are anyway."

Lana winces as the candle burns one of her cheeks. Aioven smirks and pulls the flame away from her. "Well, before I go, do you want me to leave this here so you can see?"

She looks away from him and closes her eyes, trying to steady her breathing whilst ignoring the pain as best she can.

Aioven nods. "I guess the humane thing to do would be to put out the flame. Wouldn't want to use up what little oxygen you have." He blows out the candle and then . . . nothing. Lana waits for him to say something else, but she hears nothing, not even the shuffling of his clothes as he leaves. She can't sense his presence, so she has no idea if he has left or not. Unable to use her powers without the chains cooking her insides, all she can do is awkwardly contort herself to get into a comfortable, cross-legged position and close her eyes. She grips her jagged chains, embracing the pain. Lana resolves to escape and one day deliver vengeance to her captor.

•   •   •

Stark and Sam return to their home base, with everyone there except Aioven. Alan is mostly healed, with his shoulder bandaged. Daniel sits on the couch with his mother, wiping tears from her face as he tries to reassure her. Cory McGregor brings them both glasses of water and pats the teen on the shoulder. Lily and Hayton are there too, waiting in anticipation for what's next after Lana's attack.

Leo steps forward and sees his father covered in bandages, sitting in one of the lounge chairs. Arthur nods at his son.

"This is it," Leo says. "Let's let the world know who's in charge now."

Right on cue, screens all over the planet are forced to broadcast the same message. Aioven's masked face appears on screen, his voice more metallic and distorted than usual. "Good people of Mars, I have come before you to answer for my actions. I have killed, destroyed, and conspired against those in control of our nations. I want you to join me at the Royal Martian Amphitheater. I will explain myself. I am not afraid to face your judgment, because I believe that you will find my actions just."

Despite Aioven's claim to not hide behind screens, he maintains his control over the world's broadcasts, hijacking even closed-circuit TV systems. This is to allow those who cannot be present to witness what is about to happen.

Within the hour, people pour into the theatre, some taking seats and others quite content to stand. The huge structure is like a gargantuan, indoor coliseum. At the center is a round stage with space for almost one hundred thousand people.

On the circular stage, stands Sam and Leo, watching as thousands of people exceed their venue's capacity. Amidst the crowd are the captains of the Order of Genesis, brandishing their weapons and standing out in their white coats.

Koenig stands before his subordinates before they all disperse into the crowd. "We'll allow him this speech, let him say his piece, and when I give you the order, we end this here and now." Some officers go to guard the exits whilst most of the captains stand or sit in the front row.

"Peace!" Stark shouts, holding up his hand. "Or silence! Whichever is best suited to you, my friends." His supernaturally amplified voice cues the audience to be quiet, and everyone's eyes fall on the stage.

"My name is Leonidas Stark. This is my friend, Sam Parks." He gestures for her to step forward.

She bows to the audience. "We come before you today to make it known what role we wish to play in the world."

Stark nods. People have been suffering. Dying. Changes need to be made. Individuals held accountable. But those in power have chosen not to do so."

Sam shrugs. "Why not? What explanation have they given for their inaction? None. They remain unmoved by your suffering. And so we offer another choice. A better one. We promise to explain all that we do, transparently."

Stark gestures into the crowd. "We do not pretend to have all the answers. Instead, we offer you the chance to discover them with us. And to tell you more, here is our leader. Good people of Mars, I give you . . . Dalkanos Aioven."

A tear in the open air bubbles and boils as purple flames usher Aioven onto the stage. He steps through the rift in space like a curtain being raised. Fully armoured, masked and cloaked, his presence blankets the audience. Many find it difficult to look directly at him, disoriented by waves of power. Others begin to clap and cheer, encouraged by his destruction of the Imperial capital. He turns slowly around, bearing witness to how many have come to listen. He sees people who are interested in supporting the cause. Others who appear open, curious to learn more. And still others with angry eyes, intent on seeing him punished for his 'crimes.'

"Not long ago, I was one of you. I lived a normal life, content at living each day one-to-the -next. I was unaware of many things. I did not know that my life was not mine; I was another's pawn in a game I did not choose to play. One day, without explanation, I watched my best friends slaughtered. I, too, was killed. But I was reborn! And became the man before you. I am more, but a part of me died that day."

He beckons Sam and Stark over to him, putting his arms around their shoulders. "You do not need to remember my name. Remember me because of what I've done, and what I will do. Judge me for the company that I keep."

He looks first at Sam, and then at Stark, smiling. They nod and depart the stage, leaving him alone to face the crowds. "Architect fanatics. Imperial servants. They came into my home and assassinated my friends. I was collateral damage." He pauses, and his voice raises, "My life was ended. But I was granted a second chance! And I've chosen to dedicate myself to opposing tyrants and neophytes, deities and monsters." He unsheathes his glossy black, zigzag-shaped sword and points it skyward. "Join me! Together we will rid the world of these oppressors who have too long enjoyed toying with our lives! They will no longer rule our fates—those will be our own!"

He looks around and spots several Genesis captains working their way toward him in the crowd. "Listen to me! You may be judging me falsely."

Aioven sheathes his sword and lights flicker across the theatre. "There are refugees amongst us today, survivors of the Imperial capital. Take them into your homes. Welcome them into your communities. When I razed the city, I made sure that only the guilty died. These are not your oppressors; they are your comrades."

He points his finger straight at Adam Koenig as the spotlights in the facility highlight each and every captain in the crowd. "We have also been graced with the rare presences of fully-fledged captains of the Order of Genesis, here to no doubt arrest me for trying to change the world. Who can blame them?"

He extends his closed hands forward, palms down. "They believe themselves here for your protection. But you are not in any danger from me. I know that you see the same injustices that I do. Individuals are disappearing from their homes. Religion is being used to justify crimes on children. Mass murder happens with regularity. Even peaceful protests are being met with violence. All without any cause. Social norms are eroding and investments that could benefit us all are no longer being made. The technologies being sold as being for our benefit instead threaten the survival of our species! The only people benefitting are those few who see themselves as above us all, who would sacrifice us without a second thought."

The captains all hold positions on Adam's signal. Aioven nods at him as if acknowledging him, allowing him to speak. "You don't matter to them. You could be an Imperial, a captain, or even an angel. We all live in their sandbox, or at least that's what they want us to think. Because the moment we start believing we should have more control over our lives is the moment they start losing their power."

Aioven levitates his sword into the air without even a gesture. "And here's how I feel about power . . ." He closes his hands into fists, and the whole theatre darkens and is filled with a deep-purple-hued light. "I have powers. I did not seek them out, I do not crave more. Whatever powers granted me, I will use them to make a better world."

The walls creak as colour returns to the world. "I remember my life from before. I had dreams—I know that you do, too. You deserve the chance to pursue those dreams without others bending you to their wills. I won't pretend to be selfless, but I believe that you can be more without me becoming less. And if I am successful in creating these opportunities, by defeating those whose mission has been oppressing us all, I hope that you seize on the chance to be free! To know that you have the potential to be more."

Aioven begins shouting. "No more power-hungry politicians! No more bloodthirsty neophytes or scheming to consolidate wealth for a select few! All I offer is: your thoughts, your life, and your freedom—your true rights." He gets down on his knees and rests his hands in his lap. "I invite you to see with your own eyes what I have seen, and I hope you will judge me honestly and fairly."

Aioven inhales and closes his eyes. "See for yourselves." He exhales and fills the stadium with a blue mist, traveling into the crowds in a matter of seconds. As it reaches them, it floods the minds of everyone present with images of vivid memories from Aioven's past: the deaths of the Reardans, Mark Wesley holding Daniel Lee hostage, and the two knights attacking the Imperial minister's family. Visions of angels trying to kill him, and even the attack on their home base. The voices of the traitors and spies echoing throughout the hall.

"You may have noticed that several of those despicable people were wearing the uniforms of Genesis knights. You'll be relieved to hear that each and every one of those people are either dead or spies working for the architects. The rest are here with us today, acting under the orders of the false captain, Lana Smirnov, who is in my custody and will be returned to the Order when I see fit. But what about these fine folk?" The theatre spotlights every knight and captain that was present during the attack in Simeo.

Aioven stands up and steps into the center of the stage. "Order of Genesis: your actions right now will be remembered! You can see clearly those amongst you who are traitors to humanity. Will you act justly?" The crowd begins to panic and chaos erupts. As one, both traitors and members face off and draw their weapons. Aioven smiles, spreading his arms, "You've chosen wisely."

With a whirling spin of his sword, and a three-hundred-and-sixty-degree spin of his body, he fills the room with a vortex of purple fire and black smoke. To the captains and innocent bystanders, it feels like cool mist, but to the enemies of Aioven, it feels as though bones and flesh were being torn apart. But the firestorm's effect is solely in their minds. The captains seize on the moment to disarm the traitors, who struggle desperately. Most are quickly subdued. Some fight on despite the pain and threaten to escape.

"Come now, you can't bind them without my help?" Aioven flicks his wrists and chains twist and turn through the air, digging themselves into the flesh of their targets and hooking onto their insides and lifting them up into the air—some by their necks, others by their ankles.

"People of Mars! Civilians, Martians, Imperials: join me. We can root out the monsters like the ones you see here. Together, we can build a new society. If you can do so, join my ranks here on this center stage. I'll welcome Genesis knights and anyone else who is unhappy with the cards they've been dealt!"

Needless to say, Aioven's previous recruitment tactic never managed to yield as many interested parties as this speech. Some almost immediately run onto the stage to join him. Others look at their friends and elect to climb the stage together. Even some knights stand by him, and none other than Captain Van Vuren himself walks right up to Aioven and holds out his hand. Aioven takes it with a firm grip and shakes it.

Sam and Stark rejoin them as Aioven starts to redirect the fire. He waves his arms around whilst doing an exaggerated waltz by himself. Grand Master Koenig draws his sword but has allowed Aioven too much time. Aioven turns his hand to open a portal, which opens and moves over everyone on the stage like a magic net, and when he turns his hand over, it closes. The purple fire explodes in a shockwave, knocking almost every civilian back, whilst leaving the remaining knights and captains standing. As the tension leaves the coliseum, the buildings creak noisily as if being released of immense pressure.

"Commander?" A scrawny, greasy-haired boy in a captain's coat steps forward to approach Koenig. "Do we pursue? I can set my men on them immediately."

Koenig looks down at all the half-charred, groaning men wrapped in chains, spits on them, and turns to the adolescent captain. "That won't be necessary, Captain Iven. I'd rather you dedicate Squad Four to detaining and interrogating these people Aioven graciously bound and handed over to us. And then place them at the mercy of the people. Having failed to see them amongst us, I do not trust myself for this task."

The captain of Squad Four bows. "At once, Commander Koenig."

Koenig nods and snaps his fingers at his other serving captains. "The rest of you, assist Captain Iven in dealing with these traitors, and then return to me at the temple."

• • •

"Tell me his name again," Aioven says, walking toward the temple in his normal street clothes. Van Vuren, walking beside him, wipes his glasses with a cloth and hands them to him. "Horatio

Grizwald. A bit of a unique person—but pleasant to be around."

Aioven scratches his nose and adjusts his glasses before starting the climb up the temple entrance steps. "Do you believe he will reject our invitation?"

Van Vuren shakes his head. "As long as it's a request born from intellectual curiosity, no. He loves lore. The only thing he loves more is talking to people about lore."

As they enter the entrance hall, Aioven notices that the scorch marks, cracks, and other damages from his last visit are gone. The most notable repair being the absence of the hole in the floor that he had opened above Arthur's cell.

"Your architects and builders are very talented," Aioven slyly remarks.

Van Vuren glares at him but just says, "We have no builders. The temple services and repairs itself on its own. All it needs is power, which it gets from the sun."

"The Dark Temple had no such technology," Aioven says.

Van Vuren pats him on the shoulder. "Then I suggest you don't return to your decimated Imperial city anytime soon. Or you will find the temple in perfect condition, in complete defiance of your actions. Their temple is made of the same stuff."

"Who invented such materials? The architects?" Aioven asks.

Van Vuren stops speaking softly and replies aloud. "No, something much older. But I'm sure you will find your answers in the libraries, my apprentice."

Aioven almost breaks his own neck as he stares at the captain. "What?"

"Captain Van Vuren!" A man with circular, gold-tinted glasses and golden robes stands up, holding out animated arms and jazz hands. They hug awkwardly by leaning over the desk and bending themselves at their hips.

"And who is this dapper stranger?" the bejeweled gentleman asks.

Van Vuren pushes Aioven forward. "This is my apprentice, James Diarkis."

Aioven smiles and holds out a hand to shake and finds it being grabbed by both sweaty palms of the receptionist. "Welcome, Apprentice Diarkis. Tell me, have you ever been with a woman?"

Aioven blinks. "I, er …"

The gilded man claps his hands together and blows several loose pages away in a huge gust of wind. "A man then?"

Van Vuren smirks as the great Aioven is stun locked by the librarian's questions. "No, I haven't—"

The man sits back down, pulling off his golden captain's cloak. "Surely not an animal? A goat? I'd be tempted to judge you for that, sir."

"No, sir," Aioven says.

The captain shrugs. "These days geology is all I really have. Oh, to be young."

Aioven looks back to Van Vuren for help and only receives a head shake as he looks away, hiding his smile.

Aioven shakes his head. "No, captain, just one woman so far."

The captain strokes his bushy ginger beard. "Damn, must be a wild woman. You have an animal's eyes."

"Um…" Van Vuren interjects to move the conversation forward. "Apprentice, this is Captain Horatio Grizwald, loremaster of the Genesis temple and captain of Squad Five."

Aioven bows. "A loremaster, the perfect man to speak to for a man with many questions."

Grizwald raises his eyebrows, staring into Aioven's eyes. He frowns for a moment as if he sees something that perplexes him. "Tell me, young apprentice. What information can an old man share with you?"

"Who built this fine place? Our ancestors?" Aioven asks.

Grizwald rubs his hands on the ornate altar he uses as a desk. "In a way, yes. Before the architects, there were many powerful and less powerful entities fighting to control the universe. The architects won that fight, but the primaries set the stage for it."

"The primaries?" Aioven asks.

Grizwald holds out his hand. "Yes, come with me, boy. And I will share the powers of the reds, blues, and the golds. The ones who made the first and most powerful decisions when the universe was denser than any black hole could ever be."

Captain Van Vuren nods to give them his blessing as they step into the main annex of the temple library.

• • •

"Quiet!" Lee shouts, as all the people who stepped through Aioven's door look for him confusedly. Sam and Leo help some of the people to their feet as they recover from the effects of teleportation for the first time.

Arthur circles around them, inspecting them like cattle. "It's all right; they need a few moments to gather themselves. Even captains sometimes struggle their first time."

A girl with dirty blonde hair stumbles forward and stands up straight, teetering back and forth like a drunk, ready to timber.

"Whoa, there." Leo grips her shoulders and lets her steady herself before releasing her. "What's your name?" Leo asks.

"Senna Soleil," she says, bowing.

Sam beckons her to raise herself back up. "We don't really endorse that sort of thing here."

Leo crosses his arms. "That's a hell of a name though," he says.

She shrugs. "I'm no Dalkanos Aioven."

"I doubt he'd want anyone else to be like him anyways," Lee says, "but there are few who follow him with an Imperial accent like yours."

Senna Soleil smiles at them. "None I expect, but I am here all the same."

Sam steps into Senna's personal space. "We'll be asking everyone this question, but I'll start with you. Why do you want to join us?"

"I don't know much about you, so I can't honestly say I care about working with you," she says, making everyone fall into an uneasy silence. "Your leader, Aioven, or whatever his actual name is, came into my city and burned it to the ground without the help of any armies or atomic weapons. Then he came forward and offered a world I'd very much like to be a part of. I've heard about gods all my life; many of my fellow Imperials have as well. We've always been *told* about the great power they possess. I'd rather believe in a real person. Faith that is earned through action, and faith that is reciprocated."

"He believes in us, cares more about our own improvement than his own," Leo says.

Senna exhales with relief. "I want that too. In return, I want to be strong—not like a knight or an angel, or even a god. If he keeps his word, then I will strive to be as strong as Aioven, so I can shoulder his burden."

Sam looks at Lee and Leo, who both nod. "Then we will find a way to set you on that path. You may even meet Aioven himself along the way. But try to withhold any expectations you have of him."

"To save myself from disappointment?" Senna asks.

Sam smiles. "To save yourself from blindness. He will meet you before you meet him. If you're smart enough, maybe you'll meet each other together."

CHAPTER 14

THE FALL OF AN ANGEL

"So, tell me, apprentice Diarkis. What do you seek?" the librarian asks as he stands before large, wooden, iron-reinforced doors.

Aioven, or in this case, James Diarkis, smiles at the old man and says, "When I first discovered my powers, I was set down a path it appears no one else can walk—not without me at least."

"What kind of path?" Grizwald asks, the goofy old wizard now becoming quite serious.

Diarkis pulls his ring from his finger and allows the lorekeeper to gaze upon the glowing stones of power. "I gained the Red Gem of Energy when I was reborn. The good wise men of the Elder Temple guided me in acquiring the Blue Stone of Mind, saving me from certain madness should I ever lose control of my power."

Horatio Grizwald stares in uneasy silence as a supposed apprentice confesses to wielding power that would make almost each and every captain question their own strength.

Diarkis hands the ring to Grizwald, who gasps when it touches his skin. "And then there is the eternal Green Rock of Matter. My armour is made of some of the densest materials in the universe, and my sword is unlikely to ever break or dull, even under the weight of the world."

He examines the now-silver ring, turning it over in his hands, his face dimly illuminated by the glow of the four stones set into the band. "Four stones?" He looks up, his voice shaky.

"My latest accomplishment. Arthur showed me the inversion machines. Whilst my friends studied stars and singularities, my curiosity was piqued by the architect technology the Order revitalized. You see, it is my understanding that the architects designed the original quantum gates. Why invent them? Is it because they do not have the power to fold and tear space themselves? Or is it because they needed them because they wanted their followers to travel without having to learn one of their secret powers?"

"You . . . are a master of space?" Grizwald asks, to which Diarkis nods.

"Drop the ring, but hold out your other hand."

The old captain holds out both hands, palms facing upward, with the ring sitting on the right one. He slowly turns his right hand over and lets the ring slip away. He thought he was keeping a close eye on the artifact, but it vanished from view without a sound. A good five or seven seconds pass before the ring lands in the bookkeeper's left hand. He teleported it to his other hand and kept it from falling. Diarkis leans forward, still facing Grizwald, and reaches through a portal behind him to pat him on the back. In amazement, the man expected to know all there is to know about the world has just been patted on the back by the floating arm of James Diarkis, a master of energy, mind, matter, and space—more forces than even Captain Koenig.

His arm returns to him, and he becomes whole again. "Even if I am a terrible teacher, I am a quick learner. I understand now that I am quested to unite all nine cosmic forces within myself. I will then share my insights with the world, so that any who can be worthy can learn. In turn, they will share and pass on these gifts to others."

"And what do you plan to contribute?" Horatio Grizwald asks.

Diarkis returns the ring to his finger and closes his hand into a fist, staring at the IX on the back of his hand. "I want to make a world where power doesn't matter."

"And yet you seek power," Grizwald says.

Diarkis laughs softly through his nose. "No. I only seek a horizon that makes me smile."

Grizwald puts his arms together in his sleeves. "And where will you find this horizon? On Mars?"

"Maybe, I don't know. My best guess is that I need to find out what comes after Phobos and Deimos, fear and dread." Diarkis looks into the loremaster's eyes to gauge his response.

"You don't need to test me. I'm probably the only person alive who is old enough to know what you speak of," the loremaster says.

Grizwald begins walking Diarkis away from the large wood and iron doors at the center of one wall in the annex, arriving at an ornate door of solid gold nestled in the corner.

Diarkis places his hand on the opulent entrance. "I cannot proceed without your help. Behind these doors is the answer to my most important question."

Grizwald opens the door by placing his hand just above its handle. The door slowly swings ajar on its own. "What you seek, my friend, is the third moon of Mars: Mortis. Though that is not my interpretation of it."

Diarkis bows and walks through with the librarian's permission. "Share your wisdom with me, Master. Spare me from my assumptions."

Grizwald points upward, and when Diarkis looks up, he can't help but be surprised by the strange sight. Four walls of bookcases stretch miles up into the sky, a golden chandelier glowing at the top like a weak yellow sun. Books flap from wall to wall like odd birds with no songs to sing but the sounds of pages constantly turning.

The librarian gently nudges Diarkis's head to look where he is specifically pointing. "At the top of this tower sits a text as old as Mars itself, created by Mars himself. A red king, one of the last primaries. A manuscript for the planet itself."

A hidden doorway opens in one of the bookcases, and the darkness inside is so rich that the light of the room doesn't show where it leads. Nevertheless, Grizwald escorts Diarkis through it and into the darkness. Like leaving a fog cloud, the darkness peels away, and they are at the top of the tower, standing before a golden lectern with a book almost as thin as a few pieces of paper sitting atop it.

"I expected it to be bigger," Diarkis says, somewhat disappointed that it wasn't as grand as he expected.

"I suppose as a recent master of space, even you wouldn't be able to detect the reality-bending nature of this tome. It defies natural laws of matter and spatial containment. Otherwise we'd have nowhere to keep it where it will fit. A book with its mass and no exotic properties would be bigger than most stars."

James stands over the tattered book. "Well, how does it work?"

Grizwald shrugs. "I can't say for sure. We just know that if you're thinking clearly about what you want to know, it will show you when you turn the page."

Diarkis focuses on his desire to find the Mother Temple and slowly turns the golden foil parchment. The surface turns to a weathered, yellow colour, and words sprawl across the pages. Forgetting his guise, Diarkis responds as Aioven would, in a confident and commanding tone. "The universe continues to astound me. If I can be humble and recognize my profound ignorance, I can ask better questions. Ones that allow her to reveal the true nature of our reality."

"What do you mean, Diarkis?" Grizwald asks.

Aioven points to the page. "You weren't kidding in the way the 'moon' is described."

Grizwald nods. "Under the guise and shadow of the void, hidden away is a garden that harbors innocence and roots out evil. A vessel for those who would sail the universe like a calm and violent sea."

"An odd way to describe a moon. I must agree with you," Diarkis says, staring into the pages.

Grizwald again looks into Diarkis's eyes. "You are quite a contradiction. You are a man of great wisdom, but your curiosity is greater still."

Diarkis relishes the chance to engage with Grizwald, but treads cautiously. "An astute observation. The powers that I have gained came to me too easily. I do not understand the nature of power. Or how they might make a difference in our society. There have been so many powerful people in our history that have achieved so little. I hope to understand why that is and make a bigger impact for myself."

"Is that your destiny?" Grizwald asks.

Diarkis continues reading. "Probably not, but it's what I want to do. It's what Aioven wants to do." He closes the tome. "It says the entrance to the garden is buried beneath this temple. A quantum gate, I imagine, left by the architects since it doesn't function anymore."

"I believe the gate you speak of is the arch. A stone doorway that has stood the test of time, even if the walls around it have not aged. So now it sits as an unnatural stone archway to nowhere. We haven't been able to activate it. If we knew how to do something like that . . ."

Diarkis rubs his hand on the cover of the tome and turns back to the door leading to the bottom of the library tower. "Then you'd also be able to enter the architect throne room itself. But unfortunately, we do not have that power."

As they leave, Aioven hears Grand Master Koenig's voice. "I understand, old friend. I only hope that as you work with him that you remain a leader here too. There are many who depend on you."

"My loyalty to the Order remains, but I do believe it is important we understand and befriend this Dalkanos Aioven. He has enormous potential and an intense desire to do good. But he is conflicted and needs our guidance," Van Vuren says.

When they reach the main entrance hall, they find Captains Van Vuren and Koenig. Diarkis grabs and shakes Grizwald's hand and looks him in the eye with a soft smile. The loremaster's eyes widen. He felt for sure his sanity was leaving him, but he could've sworn he saw James's eyes flicker a deep purple hue before remaining their natural dark brown.

Grizwald watches as James Diarkis exits the temple. "Under a purple prince's sky, eclipsed by Eden, all those judged will die. A queen of green will exact her wrath with powers the gods have not foreseen. And a final war of red, violet, and blue will spawn a world anew. For all entities cower in his shadow of eerie amethyst. Angel's wings wither in his sight, and the heavens fall before his might. Kneel or stand before the eternal master, the will of the primaries."

"An old prophecy?" Van Vuren asks.

Koenig shakes his head. "Sounds more like a warning to me."

Grizwald nods. "The primaries are thought to be the most powerful entities to have ever lived. They created this universe. The architects just moved in when they left. And yet, these precursor beings left many messages about purple princes and violet doom. And now this Dalkanos Aioven has come among us, powerful and wise and growing faster than a quasi star. Within the year, he may rival you, Master Koenig. And within a decade, he is on pace to surpass even the old emperor. He turns skies purple, rains fire on his enemies and is reputedly beyond death's reach. And it is still early days in his development!"

Koenig looks to the horizon, somehow knowing that despite

the fantasies of legend, there is some truth in Grizwald's words. "So what is your counsel, Horatio? What would you have your grand master do?"

Grizwald adjusts his golden glasses. "He is powerful. As an enemy he could turn most of our world into mere memories, like he is doing with the Empire. But he is a man of legacy. He wants to leave something behind. I believe we share this goal with him. So I think we should work with him. Our chances are far better with Dalkanos Aioven and his knights as allies than with them as our enemies."

Fully aware of their conversation, Aioven walks away from the temple smiling at how well his first impression has gone with the people of the world.

"What did he want? Isn't he one of Aioven's men?" Koenig asks.

Van Vuren and Grizwald look at each other. The looks they give each other allow them to come to a silent agreement not to spill.

The old man bows and starts inching away, hoping to retreat from any more questions. "Indeed, that was James Diarkis. A man under Aioven's command, but he is also the curious apprentice of Captain Van Vuren."

Koenig sighs. "And what was our latest knight-to-be curious about? Awfully ambitious to enter the temple as if it were his right."

"Prophecies and legends, from all time. Then, now, and legends still to come," Grizwald says with a stammer.

Koenig steps forward, inches from Grizwald's face. "I'd appreciate it if you just said you weren't sure, my friend."

The old man's bones creak under the weight of the grand master's question. "I don't fully understand why, but he wants to find the hidden moon of Mortis. He thinks it's the key to mastering all the cosmic forces and making them known to us."

Van Vuren frowns, his face full of twisted doubt. "If Captain Koenig here told me he planned on hunting an invisible moon to gain ultimate power, I'd call him crazy and foolish."

Koenig nods in agreement. "Diarkis might be both of those things. To describe such a quest as impossible would be putting it lightly."

Grizwald shakes his head, his lips quivering as he speaks. "Grand Master, how many cosmic forces do you command?"

Koenig crosses his arms. "Three. Energy, matter, and information."

Grizwald bows to his leader. "I applaud your superiority, but I must also acknowledge his. I saw four stones of power on his ring. When was the last time in recorded history a single person wielded more than three?"

"I sense that's a trick question," Van Vuren says.

Horatio nods. "It is not. None have done so. In all recorded history, few have even tried. Despite their committing many years and vast resources to their efforts—all failed! And yet, this Diarkis describes his own successes as being 'effortless.' Like breathing for him."

Koenig stares into nothingness for a long moment, before arriving at a decision. "Prepare the gate. I'm convinced that our path lies in joining forces with him. Despite my reservations about his methods, he is progressing too fast to be left on his own."

Grizwald bows. "Yes, Master."

As the temple doors close, Koenig walks away, and Van Vuren notices Grizwald in deep thought. "Everything all right, Horatio?"

Grizwald shrugs. "I don't know yet. But keep an eye on your 'apprentice.' I doubt this is the last time he will surprise me or any of us."

• • •

Aioven strolls down the sidewalk, heading towards his car. He needs a chance to think carefully about his next steps. As more people join up, they will need to be more properly vetted than what he did with Victor. He'd prefer to keep their membership anonymous, so that they can infiltrate other organizations without undue resistance . . . and he's not likely to be the only one employing this strategy. In order to undermine the current leaders of the world, he will try to turn the population majority against them without them even knowing. He'll need people across all sections of society—from the most powerful to the most humble. When the time comes, a new social order will take hold smoothly and peacefully.

People who want to fight for Aioven will not be his apprentices. They will train just like anyone else would but with his Order as their secret sponsors. The Order of Genesis will do him the favour of training his people and in return, unbeknownst to them, share the inner workings of their society with him. Those who will remain by Aioven's side will wear standardized robes and masks to hide their identities so their lives aren't threatened. Slowly but surely, Aioven will have an Order of his own.

As he is about to turn over the engine in his car, he feels his ring tugging on his finger like a magnet being pulled somewhere. He looks around for an obvious source but realizes what's happening when he sees the black stone on his ring, calling him somewhere as it glows white around its edges. Closing his eyes, expecting a trap, he focuses for a moment on how and who might help him before closing his hand into a fist and disappearing from inside his car. If anyone had noticed, they'd think they were imagining things.

The sound of waves crashing into hard surfaces and salty air give little hints as to where he is, but when his eyes adjust, what he sees confuses him even further. An island of emerald, surfacing just at sea level somewhere in the ocean. Pillars of the precious stones spear high into the sky above the clouds, turning the sun green as it moves behind the decadent monoliths. "So it really is you. I never thought I'd get to meet you."

Aioven sees a cloaked figure standing in a large valley of emerald, holding out their arms to them. Instead of enduring the long walk, James opens a portal and arrives face-to-face with the speaker in a single step.

The mysterious speaker takes a step forward in response to Aioven's teleportation. "It would seem the Shade was truthful when warning us about you. You are as talented as we were told you'd be. Difficult to forget who you are, no matter how many times you are reborn, though you chose a good name." He removes his cloak, his tan skin filled with black cracks starting at his eyes—eyes with galaxies spinning at their center instead of pupils.

Aioven transforms into his masked persona, his armour and robes whipping through the air as they form onto his body and his sword extending from nothing into his hand. "You . . . you're an architect," he says.

"You'll need more than that to beat me." The god places his bare hand on Aioven's sword and snaps the tip off, making it explode and knocking him back several feet. Chunks of his mask and armour fall to the ground, exposing parts of his human face and body. Aioven regenerates his sword and points it at the deity. The god's face remains expressionless. "She didn't tell us you'd be playing dress up."

Aioven advances slowly, with his sword in his left hand, watching as burnt chunks of the architect's skin peel away to reveal cobalt-blue skin. "You're a primary; I thought your kind was extinct," he says.

Golden armour and robes are revealed as his dark cloak burns away. "No, just rare and above the secondaries and the tertiaries."

Aioven holds the tip of his sword just over the god's heart. "Tell me about yourself. You already seem to know a great deal about me."

With a finger he pushes the blade away. "I am Nomor, the

architect of law. Here to pass judgment on the apparently aptly named Dalkanos Aioven."

"You're here to kill me?" Aioven asks, pushing his sword through the architect's chest, only to have it pass through his like he has no mass at all.

"I'm not here, and I'm not going to kill you. He is." Nomor points over Aioven's shoulder and disappears. Aioven turns to face his executioner and grips his sword tightly.

"What do you think of the place?" Darius asks, sitting upon a dark green throne.

Aioven jams his sword into the lavish ground, causing cracks to snake everywhere like they're standing on top of a frozen lake. "Is this place yours? I like it. Not quite my colour, but I appreciate the simplicity."

Darius leans back in his chair and crosses his legs. "I appreciate that, coming from a man of style like yourself."

Aioven raises his eyebrows. "I can't tell if you're being sarcastic."

Darius puts up his hands. "No, no! I've seen some of your cars. I like your taste. I've never been much of a Ferrari guy either. More of a Chevy guy myself, always wanted a C6 ZR1. Sorry about the Lambo Lana blew up."

Aioven shrugs. "Don't worry about it. I still have the SV and a few others."

Darius laughs and claps his hands. "You live such a lavish life, don't you, Dalkanos?"

"Says the guy who built himself an emerald island." He stomps his foot, each thud solid and heavy, making it clear the entire foundation goes deep to the seafloor.

Darius nods. "A good point. Well, between you and me, my masters gave me this power, but I'm still limited in what I can hold. So, I figured, rather than cast all that extra matter into space, why not just make something with it down here?"

"Your masters didn't give you a temple themselves?" Aioven asks.

Darius sighs. "No, a secondary god can't rule from a temple made of primestone."

Aioven frowns. "The temples the Empire and Order of Genesis use are made of it, aren't they?"

Darius rises from his throne, holding a dark green wand with a glowing green stone set into the bottom of the hilt. "Yes, and they continue to serve their interests."

Aioven pulls his sword out of the ground. "And what are your interests?"

Darius squints at him. "My interests haven't mattered for a long time. Why do you care?"

Pointing his sword toward the sky, he asks, "Do your masters care?"

Darius twirls his wand through his fingers. "I don't remember what I cared about before they saved me. I was doomed to die. I was building a temple for them, got sick, blown up, and was given cancer from breathing in the dust of the primestone as we cut it."

Aioven takes a deep breath. "But what if we break your palace? Will it regenerate like the other temples?"

"No," he says, "but I'll be able to build something new and exciting whenever something breaks."

Aioven looks at Darius and sighs. "I'm getting the feeling you and I aren't that different. We both should be dead, yet here we are—doing things that we would have found unimagineable."

Darius looks at his wand, holding it in both hands. "We serve things greater than ourselves. I serve a duty and debt, and you serve life and her legacy."

Aioven holds out his hand. "You can join me too. They wouldn't have picked you without a good reason. I believe they thought you'd be useful even without their help."

Xenos laughs a little, thinking he must be joking. "And I can be useful to you?"

Aioven keeps his hand extended. "What I'm offering isn't the same. They felt that they owned you. They dictated your actions."

The new god of strange smiles, wishing he could accept Aioven's offer. "Death doesn't even hold a candle to what they could do to me if I betrayed them. You paint a pretty picture with your words, but I'll take my chances fighting you."

"Just me?" Aioven asks. A blue bolt of lightning blasts apart Darius's throne, spraying shards of emerald glass everywhere that slice up Darius's skin and Aioven's face. The god whips his wand through the air and sends a bubbling storm of strange matter into the sky. Another bolt breaks apart the matter and strikes the young deity in the chest but doesn't even knock him down; it just stuns him.

Leonidas Stark lands beside Aioven, with his own sword drawn and glowing blue with electricity. "You two are pretty loud—hard to miss your distinct cosmic pressures."

Xenos raises his wand to strike again but suddenly the sun is blocked. They all look up to see what is overshadowing them just in time to see a large meteorite of some kind falling toward them. The object vaporizes on impact, turning a huge amount of the green island into verdant mist.

Aioven and Stark land miles away, quickly joined by Sam with her body-sized sword drawn.

"You know a surprise attack isn't supposed to surprise your friends, right?" says Aioven.

"You dodged it," she says.

Aioven points at Darius. "He did too."

Darius brushes green dust off his armour and assumes a battle stance with his wand pointed at them. "Best get this over with, lest my masters lose faith in me."

With a single twitch of his wrist, a boulder-sized, glowing

green strangelet rockets toward them. The fight is on. Sam swings her sword, sending an arc of yellow plasma to collide with the infectious death rock. They crash together, spewing chunks of strange matter everywhere, converting and melting whatever they come into contact with.

"Scatter!" Leo shouts, as Darius assimilates the world around them. The ground starts dissolving and quickly turns into a swarm of hot corruption that, if touched, would mean instant death.

Aioven churns up a storm of purple lightning and stuns Darius with it, forcing him to defend himself with a wall of strange matter. "You guys, get ready! I'll keep him busy!"

"Ha!" Darius spews a fast-moving stream of glowing green liquid out of his wand at Aioven, who, in a desperate attempt to not be erased, thrusts his palm into the air to stop the strange matter in its tracks with a funnel of purple fire and black matter. The two jets of death remain locked for a moment before Aioven is quickly overpowered. Breaking away from the duel just in time to avoid assimilation, he points his finger in the air and hits the Stranger with a well-placed bolt of lightning in the chest.

"Grah!" Darius stumbles and starts bleeding what looks like liquid gold. Golden threads also appear and start to stitch the wound together. As the hole in his chest closes, he breathes raspy breaths and then takes a normal, deep breath through his nose once the wound is healed. Enraged, Darius moves faster than even Aioven can track. Inches away from his heart, Darius tries to jab his fingers into Aioven's chest. Instinctively, Aioven swings his sword wildly, but when it connects with the body of the god of strangeness, the blade melts away and joins the swarm of strange matter vortexing around them.

As the storm above their heads expands to the size of a hurricane and turns the sky green, Aioven backs away from Darius as fast as possible. He points his wand at him and starts rapid firing tiny rocks of strange matter at Aioven. Trying to escape, he starts running to the right, each shot just barely missing and exploding behind him. Time slows down as Darius and Aioven both focus their senses. The young god shoots at the ground ahead of Aioven's path. In the split second Darius takes a shot at him, with just the hilt left of his dissolving sword, he blocks the shot with his broken weapon and throws it away before it can infect him. But it's too little too late. Darius fires another dense funnel of strange matter at him like before. Aioven tries to stop it with fire coming from both hands, but the column goes straight through like there's nothing there and mows Aioven down like a soft sand sculpture.

The explosion blows Aioven's dissolving body away from the bubble of strange matter, prolonging his assimilation into Darius's influence. Wheezing and coughing up blood, Aioven rolls over and struggles to get up. When he tries to put both hands on the ground to get back on his feet, he collapses when only his right hand obeys. He looks to his left side to find most of his left chest, shoulder, and entire left arm are gone. The strange matter still slowly eating away at the left half of his rib cage, getting dangerously close to his lungs, makes Aioven panic. Roaring and tearing off his mask with his remaining hand, he transforms it into a black knife, with a similar zigzag design to his normal sword.

"You honestly think you can stop me with that?" Darius asks.

Aioven coughs up blood and chokes before growling his response. "Who cares about what I can do? It's about what we can do."

Darius's eyes widen with epiphany. "We?" Looking like someone who has just returned from a daydream, ribbons of bright, glowing-blue nuclear pasta wrap themselves around Darius's limbs and torso and pull him down to his knees.

Before he can conduct his green swarm, the hand holding his wand is severed and falls, and Stark appears from nowhere to catch it. Sam appears beside Aioven, clutching the grip of the cosmic lasso holding the god down. Aioven huffs and puffs as the world spins around him.

"Stop his thoughts," Aioven orders.

Sam lassos his neck and holds him still. Stark gets right behind him and runs his sword through the back of his head and out the middle of his forehead.

"Nngh!" Darius's eyes dart around. His body writhes and wriggles as his nervous system is pierced. Stark pulls out his sword and watches confusedly as Darius fails to immediately die. Stark cleans off his sword and sheathes it, stepping back to a safe distance as strange matter leaks out of the god's head.

"If only it were that simple," Aioven says, pulling off his belt, sticking it in his mouth, and biting down on it. He takes several quick deep breaths before plunging his dagger straight into the center of his shoulder, piercing the exposed flesh where his arm and shoulder should be. He lets go, tears streaming down his face as the knife heats up to a boiling, red-hot temperature. He allows it to melt into his body, making sounds like raw meat tossed onto a hot pan.

He lets out muffled cries and falls over. "Goddammit!" he shouts, as black threads of carbon grow out of his body like vines or fungi in a time lapse. As his missing body is replaced by the slick black tendrils, a gold metal pours over them until it all cools down and solidifies into the final product: a fully functional golden arm and shoulder to replace the corrupted flesh. Aioven breathes a sigh of relief and closes his new left hand into a fist, causing purple veins to appear in the arm and glow like neon lights in a red-light district.

Darius's head wound closes, and he quickly starts to regain his awareness. Aioven grips his sword with both of his hands. "Now!"

Behind Darius, Stark holds out both hands like he's holding an invisible ball. The sensation of gravity changes as he begins to slowly put his hands together, fighting an unseen force keeping his hands apart.

"Keep the mass in check, Leo!" Aioven shouts as he and Sam resist the pull of Stark's artificial singularity. Leo pushes hard against the space and matter around him, compressing it all together with his own power. Darius looks over his shoulder, panic in his eyes as he realizes what their plan is.

Aioven speaks with a calm, almost robotic voice, devoid of emotion. "Neutron stars are born when gravity fails to collapse the star as it dies. As a master of strange matter, you ought to know what happens when gravity wins."

Stark claps his hands together, and a singularity is born. Sam yelps and ties herself, Aioven, and Stark down to the ground as Mars becomes the former dominant gravitational force in its own planetary system.

Darius grits his teeth and conjures strange matter, managing to break Sam's nuclear restraints only to then be at the mercy of Stark's black hole.

Aioven, using his kinetic powers, holds Darius in place to keep him from falling into the tiny event horizon as it quickly grows bigger and bigger. "For what it's worth, I take little pride in killing you, a minor god with no will. But you are the greatest threat to my world right now. I can't allow you to live."

Stark wobbles like he's standing on a water bed. "Aioven!"

Aioven takes a deep breath. "Goodbye, Darius. I'd say 'make peace with your gods,' but that feels inappropriate. So, I wish you good rest in your oblivion."

Aioven raises his sword skyward, the ground and the clouds getting broken down and sucked up by the cosmic trapdoor. He simultaneously releases Darius from his grip and swings his sword down, sending a wall of black matter enveloped in purple fire barrelling down on the failed deity. Darius and his powers are knocked back, unable to escape the pull of the singularity as Aioven pushes him closer. His body is spaghettified as it crosses the event horizon and shifts to a red hue before disappearing.

Even amidst the chaos, the trio detects the complete disappearance of strange matter. Aioven looks over to Stark and nods at him, quickly becoming unable to speak as the wind is seemingly sucked out of him. Stark puts his hands together around the invisible ball again and starts trying to pull them apart in an attempt to speed up the radiating away of the black hole's mass before it feeds on too much of the planet. His arms start to get torn apart under the strain, and Stark screams as he keeps pulling on the singularity.

Aioven holds out his left fist. "Say when!"

Stark holds his breath as the black hole starts to noticeably shrink. "Wait . . . Wait . . ." he says.

Aioven looks over at Stark. "We don't want this thing here when it goes, Leo!"

Stark grimaces. "Wait!" Leo knows full well that if he doesn't push the singularity past the point of no return, it'll just start feeding again. More and more mass radiates away the faster it shrinks, until Stark feels it reaching the mass of a car and shouts, "Now!"

Aioven opens his hand and the black hole detonates like a supernova, but before the death bubble of the explosion can reach them, Aioven's portal closes over it. Gravity goes back to normal, and the world resumes its continuity almost undisturbed. The trio relaxes and deflates as the significance of what just happened starts to sink in. The wind on their faces feels cool and fresh. Each breath they take is deep and fills their lungs, and their thoughts slow down as their anxieties disappear.

Aioven looks onto the horizon, unsure how to feel, unsmiling. He looks at his ring and counts his stones. He frowns as a fifth space for a stone has appeared in the band, but no stone has appeared yet. "You know, even before I became . . . this, as I got older, one of the biggest things I learned over time was that the more time you spend being alive, the more you realize you'll always be a student and never a master. And after what just happened, I don't feel complete."

Stark rolls over onto his stomach like he's trying to get into a comfortable sleeping position.

Aioven continues to speak, "Not that I'm, you know, disappointed or anything, but I expected a god to put up much more of a fight. Did the architects care whether he won or not?"

Sam looks at her sword for the first time and begins to feel as though she will never want to pick it up again.

"For a fight I thought would last forever, that went by very fast," Stark says.

"Forever . . ." Aioven hears a whispering in his ears and shakes his head to silence them. "I hope not. No one should be fated to suffer forever." He sits down with his legs crossed in front of his friends and takes Sam's hand. Looking over to Stark, he grabs and shakes his foot. "You all right?"

"Yeah, I just want to take a long nap," Stark says, breathing into the dirt.

Aioven chuckles. "You and I can rest before long."

Sam massages Leo's back. Until then, we can make a difference." she says.

"Can I take a power nap first?" Stark asks like a whiny child refusing to get up for school.

Aioven creaks and groans as he stands up. "I haven't been fighting for long, but it already feels like I've been fighting forever."

"I'm pretty sure you're just old, James," Stark says.

Aioven looks back at the horizon and blinks confusedly. He could've sworn the sun was about to set, but instead it is sitting perfectly still, along with the rest of the world. As he inhales, he realizes the only sounds he can hear are his breaths, so loud he instinctively tries to make them quieter so the rest of the planet can't hear them. He looks over at his friends to find them completely motionless—and colourless.

"The Shaded Mother has bid me to carry out your execution, God Killer."

Unable to find the source of the voice but also not wanting to appear panicked, Aioven calmly removes his armour and repairs his robes and mask. "On what crime? he asks.

"Come to the Arena of Titans and hear your sentence and your accuser," the voice says before falling silent and returning the world to normal again.

"James?" Leo turns over and looks at his friend. "You all right?"

Aioven closes his hand into a fist, making all four stones on his ring glow. "I just received a court order from the architects."

All around the world, all ten billion people and all other walks of life abandon their daily lives to stop what they're doing and idle wherever they're at, as if entranced by some higher power. Everyone sits down whilst nine hundred and ninety-nine are transported from random places to seats in the stands of the Titan's Arena. Each person sits down involuntarily, staring blankly into the space in front of them until they're compelled to do otherwise.

The voice speaks again, filling the atmosphere. "Behold, a god's jury is being gathered today to witness the trial and sentence of Dalkanos Aioven!"

The people sitting in the stands surrounding the arena all turn their gaze to the center of the stage, where a portal begins to open. Every audience member's eyes glow gold as their vision zooms in on the action like high-powered lenses. Aioven steps through the gateway alone and looks around, seeing the hundreds of pairs of golden dots in the stands, like eerie lighters flickering at a silent rock concert.

He looks around to get his bearings. The arena is more of a ruined sandstone structure reduced to lumpy ruins than the grand stage he was expecting. More so, the surrounding area seems to be desert sands and huge rocks with a few cacti dotting the landscape.

He hears the beating of large, creaking metal swings and looks up into the sky, staring right into the sun as Rytram lands gracefully a few feet in front of him. The angel shakes his wings before closing them and drawing his sword.

Aioven remains unarmed and puts his hands on his hips. "Are you the accuser or the supposed executioner?"

The air cracks and sizzles as the faceless voice replies. "No one said anything about an execution." The angel smirks as a figure blurs into focus behind him. The sky turns dark red as the sun vanishes behind the horizon, the stars all turning red and pulsing in sync with a deep warbling sound in the air.

The angel welcomes his master with open arms. "Subjects of Mars, you stand before the projection of Exorsio."

The figure's form glows a gentle golden light before solidifying into a human shape covered in crusty black-and-red skin. When he steps closer, Aioven can't help but think that his skin and flesh have been burned in some sort of fire. The skin is blackened and peeling away, his flesh a dark cherry-red and in some spots held together by golden threads.

The charred god points his decaying finger at Aioven. "I, Architect Exorsio, come before you to mete out justice. Dalkanos Aioven, you stand accused of deicide. How do you plead?"

"I don't plead, and I don't have time for this." Aioven opens a portal like he is about to leave."

"You would dare attempt to evade justice?" Exorsio says.

Aioven slowly starts chuckling before finally laughing maniacally. "Ha! As if you give a damn about justice!"

Exorsio and Rytram look at each other whilst Aioven laughs

so hard he chokes and coughs. "Let me get this straight. You armed a man with doomsday powers, and then took away his free will to make him serve you, forcing us to kill him? Shouldn't we be calling out your irresponsibility?"

The architect's image shimmers and is briefly transparent. "The newborn god of strange was under our control. His thoughts were his own, but his will was ours, and so was his power."

"Oh, that makes it okay. You gave a man a cosmic nuke, but it's all right because you brainwashed him. I'm sure that sits well with everybody." Aioven looks around into the crowd, a little surprised by the lack of vocal reaction from the hundreds of listeners. "Tough crowd," he says.

The god tsks and folds his arms. "They will not respond. They are only here so others across the world can see your trial *through their eyes*. Through my power, all living things will witness what happens here."

Aioven smiles beneath his mask. "Well, just like you, I came here expecting my accuser to meet me face-to-face."

"Ha!" the god laughs. "That's hilarious coming from the man wearing a mask."

Aioven blows raspberries through his mask. "Oh, please. A basement dweller's blow-up doll is more real than you. Your image is less real than what a 200 projector can muster. Are the architects so afraid of facing me that they will only appear as an apparition? Do they fear being the first god to die at a mortal's hands?"

Rytram grips his sword, itching to attack Aioven. Aioven looks at him for a moment before finally drawing his own sword. "So, not only are you too scared to face me, you're going to sic this bloated pigeon on me in the hope that he—what? Pecks me to death with that gilded butter knife?"

Exorsio nods to his winged servant, and Rytram lunges at Aioven, who holds up his empty hand and flicks his fingers into the open air, smacking a thousand-mile-an-hour gust into the angel's body, yanking him into the sky like a kite that's escaped the grip of a child.

Aioven steps toward Exorsio. "Here's what I see: a god who refuses to face me. A coward laid bare. By hesitating you've already lost in the world's eyes. I'm glad that you've allowed them to witness this 'trial.'"

Exorsio steps closer too. "You think that you've won something? You know nothing. I hold the universe together! Without me, the very fabric of this reality will unravel. It is your actions that put their fates at risk."

Aioven shakes his head. "That's ridiculous. If the universe was so dependent on you for its survival, then why create a new god out of Darius Vaughn? You claim his death threatens everyone, yet the world and the rest of the universe existed long before he did."

Exorsio starts. "You have also destroyed a civilization—"

Aioven interrupts. "A society of sycophants placed by you to meddle with the world in case things got boring. Happiness and peace, for instance, are far too humdrum and uneventful god like yourself. I think that you incite these religion-based wars just to make things more exciting for you. Like a network producer."

Rytram lands again, beside Exorsio, and swings his sword down on Aioven hard, who stops it with his own blade with one hand. "Well, if you aren't going to do anything, your bird here is going to end up crispier than you."

Exorsio's smirk slowly vanishes before he puts his hand on Rytram's sword hand. "On this day and this day only, you will be my agent of justice. You will be granted powers upon powers until you can complete your task: execute the heretic, Dalkanos Aioven."

Aioven twirls his sword and assumes a one-handed fighting stance. The architect vanishes, not before pouring some of his power into Rytram. As the angel's cosmic presence intensifies, the strain on every civilian spectator in the audience deepens, pushing their minds close to a breaking point.

"Could we take this elsewhere?" Aioven asks.

The angel spits and bends down with his sword pointed at Aioven. "Your concern for them is silly. You all have us to thank for your lives. What's a few hundred dead to us?"

Rytram lunges, thrusting his sword at Aioven's heart. With an effortless swish of Aioven's sword, the attack is redirected, and somewhere in the distance, the terrain is obliterated by Aioven's parry. The dirt and rock disintegrate and get lifted into the atmosphere, with all the world to see.

"You know . . ." Aioven grips the angel's blade with his bare left hand. "I'm glad the universe is watching. I want you to try as hard as you possibly can. I want them to see how much you don't matter."

Rytram's pupils start glowing gold and suddenly he conjures the strength to push Aioven back and swing his sword again, this time locking blades as Aioven is unable to redirect the attack. The ground beneath them cracks and crumbles under the force of their duel. Aioven steps aside and maneuvers himself around the angel and swings at his back. He manages to slice away some of his feathers, but Rytram escapes with virtually no damage. Aioven pursues with a thrust of his sword into the open space between them. Suddenly, the angel's body jerks and the blade appears, protruding from his chest. Aioven's use of wormholes allowed him to stab the angel in the back whilst standing right in front of him. However, Rytram's life is far from threatened. He points an index finger at Aioven and unleashes a blast of golden gamma rays toward his opponent. Unable to open a portal to redirect the cosmic laser beam, Aioven drops his sword and absorbs the blast into his synthetic arm, hoping it will not spread to the rest of him.

As Aioven takes on more of the angel's newfound power, his

golden arm cracks and tarnishes. The fingertips turn black, and some of it even begins to melt away and expose the black carbon bones underneath. With his open, organic hand, he recycles the energetic radiation and shoots an elephant-sized boulder of black matter with purple fire leaking out of it toward the angel faster than the speed of sound. The black matter reaches Rytram and explodes into a tight ball of purple fire. Even as the concussion reaches Aioven, he hurls a superstorm of purple lightning into the ball to incinerate whatever is left of the angel.

A quick flash of golden light is the only warning Aioven gets before the smoke is blown away from the winds created by Rytram's wings, but it is too late. Aioven's senses completely lose track of the angel as he moves fast enough to jab his bare hand right into Aioven's chest. He let's out a gasp, but the angel's strike fails to pierce Aioven's heart. Still, Rytram chuckles like he's finally won. His celebration is suddenly cut short as chains appear and wrap themselves around them both. Aioven embraces the angel tightly and doesn't let go. The angel struggles and stabs at Aioven with a broken shard of his sword to no avail, and the chains yank his arms back so hard they both snap.

Aioven places two fingers over his chest. "You thought you found my heart?" he asks.

He burns a hole straight through the angel's body and pulls out the still beating heart of the Angel Rytram. The angel starts to hyperventilate as Aioven tosses the heart at his feet. Golden threads appear, connecting the heart to Rytram's body, trying to pull it back into where it should be. Aioven takes a few steps back, wondering whether he should ask him if he'd like to say any final words. But as he turns back to face the angel supposedly on death's door, he finds the angel holding a sword of pure, superheated plasma, as if he had brought a sample of the sun down onto the planet.

"And here I thought I'd ask you what your last words are, but you don't seem to be in the mood," Aioven says.

Out of the angel's mouth speaks a croaking voice not his own. "We won't use our full power to destroy this false deity."

Aioven picks up his sword, but as the angel swings his blade, he unleashes a tidal wave of apocalyptic proportions. Molten gold spews everywhere, but the audience doesn't react or even scream as the liquid metal floods toward them. Without thinking, Aioven pulls water out of the air and uses it in conjunction with sapping the heat away from the angel's attack to cool it down and stop it in its tracks. A massive bubble of water and freezing air surrounds the arena, bordering just in front of the stands looking onto the battle.

"You'll fight to protect our sandbox from us? You'll die for a few grains of sand?! We'll turn you all into glass!" The angel raises his arm to attack again, but Aioven is ready. He holds out his hands with his fingers spread apart, and spears of obsidian appear by the thousands, like a swarm in the sky waiting to pounce. Flecks of purple matter appear and begin sticking themselves to the angel's body, exponentially covering him faster and faster, obscuring his eyes, blocking his nose and mouth, and encasing him like cosmic cement.

Aioven makes sure both his feet are planted before continuing. "You want glass? How about an iron maiden with obsidian spikes?"

The angel squeals a desperate, muffled scream.

Aioven interlocks his fingers together, commanding the spears to rain down on him. The first few hundred go straight through him, allowing only his blood to escape the trap. But the angel cannot escape and is ground to a fleshy pulp under the sustained attack.

When the last spear squelches into the bubbling pile of hot flesh, feathers float everywhere, and the angel begins to leak the same red blood all mortals do, rather than gold.

Aioven raises his sword skyward. "You 'won't' use your full power? Or you can't? Are the architects afraid their full might won't be enough? That their defeat will lose them the faith of all those who fear them?"

The obsidian and gold around them breaks apart and begins to swirl in a shrinking vortex with the angel's remains at the center. Aioven smiles as cosmic energy gathers to revive and reconstruct the winged puppet. His skin wraps around his body, partially transparent and fully sunken with no blood to give the illusion of life persisting in the enslaved body.

"Look to your gods! See their desperation as they are challenged! For the first time in history, a god will suffer a loss against a mere 'grain of sand.'"

The angel raises his sword once again, and the tip of the blade begins to glow as the energy around them is sucked into it. A ball of thermal energy and some kind of material, possibly hydrogen, grows rapidly. From where Aioven is standing, it's like watching a star form, but on steroids, growing extremely quickly. As it gets bigger and brighter, everything that is capable of burning starts to burn. Eventually, it becomes so bright that the contrast in light makes it hard to make out anything surrounding the star. To human eyes it looks like the star is surrounded by darkness.

Aioven drains out all other sounds as he speaks softly to the universe. "Bear witness." In one final downward swish of his sword, he sews together violent torrents of nuclear pasta, purple fire, madness-inducing thoughts, and abyssal levels of pressure into the angel's body. His eyes squish like tomatoes, and the bones and flesh of his limbs splinter apart like table legs under too much weight. Unable to scream, Rytram throws his head back and lets out a dying breath as his body is shredded into actual ribbons. Thousands of golden threads appear, straining to hold him together only to finally start snapping, some of them reaching high into the sky like puppet strings before being severed too.

As the final thread snaps, the angel's powers explode out of his body in a flash of golden light. His wings burn away like flash paper, and he slumps to the ground like a street magician's magic trick coming to a conclusion. Aioven starts to breathe heavily through his mouth, dropping his sword as it disintegrates away. His golden arm is cracked and heavily tarnished, and his mask and armour slowly turn to dust as well. He kneels down on the burn marks where the angel once stood, who is still gasping for air.

In what feels like a feverish dehydration hallucination, Rytram grabs the collar of Aioven's shirt and pulls him in close. "You . . . you have to stop them. Before they get bored again. You ended their war. Give them a good show, or it's all over."

Aioven watches in shock as the angel's body ages rapidly before decomposing and leaving nothing but a skeleton behind. Just as his mask is half gone, he stands up and steps through a portal. It is just in time, as everyone in the world is having their senses returned to them. The world continues to rotate, but no one moves right away. Their minds were subjugated by the architects, allowing them to witness a battle between an angel and a mortal so that they may never again question the powers of the gods. But instead, billions watched as one of their most powerful servants died, helplessly.

Chapter 15

•

EDEN

With little power left in his body, Aioven is stalked by the crackling of thunder as he manages to complete an ungainly landing onto the roof of his apartment building back in Simeo. Unaided by the power, he stands uneasily for a moment before shedding his armour and then hobbling inside.

Not far behind him is Captain Koenig, whose mere contact with the roof blackens the gravel surface with immense heat, turning the closest stones and concrete structures red hot.

Blasting through the roof access door, Leonidas Stark arrives to the rescue. "That's far enough, Captain!" Leo zaps the grand master's shoulder with a bolt of lightning, burning a hole in his pristine captain's coat without harming the man at all.

Koenig draws his sword and growls through gritted teeth. "You dare?!" He swings his sword, white hot flames obscuring the blade from view, only to be stopped in its tracks by Sam's huge sword.

She blows cool air onto his sword, and the flames start to disappear. "You need to take a chill pill."

"Impossible! I wield the power of a thousand stars!" he shouts, conjuring more flames.

"Master Koenig!" Van Vuren stands behind him, seemingly unarmed. "Please! This is a bad business; it feels wrong to kill him."

Not completely turning his back on Sam and Leo, he looks at Van Vuren over his shoulder. "Aioven acts under his own authority. I will not have superpowered vigilantes on my planet!"

Victor shakes his head. "He doesn't mean us any harm. He has chosen to be an instrument of change. He strives against all that is wrong in the Empire. He pits himself against those we have not had the courage to challenge: the gods and their angels. His victory is far from certain. If we join forces, we can succeed."

Koenig grabs Victor by the wrist. "I will not ally myself with a terrorist!"

Unfazed by the crunching noises in his wrist, Victor continues. "He is no terrorist. He is in the open, calling others to his banner. I will join him."

Glaring, shocked at his own student's insolence, Koenig lets go of his wrist. "I thought I taught you better."

Victor sighs. "You taught me what matters most—to be a moral man."

Koenig's face softens and his shoulders relax. "Perhaps. Do we really know the he is a moral man?"

Aioven, dressed in street clothes and wearing new glasses, comes stumbling out onto the roof over the rubble where the roof access doors used to be. For a long moment he pauses, waiting. Does Koenig see Diarkis or Aioven? Will he attack or still his hand? Finally, Koenig sheathes his sword and exhales softly.

Senna Soleil, one of the recruits from Aioven's speech, comes out from under the rubble of the collapsed roof access door. She hops over the debris and walks right past Aioven. "He want us to believe and to act. Our world can be better. We few can make that happen for others. We must."

Aioven comes to stand beside her, nodding. "Yes, that's right. But it's a feeling, too. Everything is connected; it should be. There are those who withhold powers from others, creating unnecessary suffering in the world. They do so because they can; they believe they have the right to take more. This is not right. That way is darkness. It feels wrong."

Stark points at Senna. "This is Senna Soleil, a former Imperial. She came willingly after Aioven's speech."

"An odd decision for someone who had their home destroyed and survived," Koenig says.

Senna crosses her arms. "I didn't 'survive' Aioven. I survived the Empire thanks to Aioven."

Koenig presses further. "So now you're loyal to Aioven?"

Senna rolls her eyes and laughs. "Does that bother you? Do you want me to be loyal to you too because your bathrobe makes you special?"

Aioven stands between Senna and Koenig. "Look, we'd like to start small, lay the foundations for a society that allows us all to coexist and cooperate."

Koenig raises his eyebrows. "Something like that would take time, patience, and planning."

Aioven smirks. "Luckily for everyone, Aioven is capable of all of that."

The head captain stares at Diarkis for a moment, almost like he's trying to imagine what he might look or sound like in different attire and an alternate scenario. Koenig shrugs. "If you say so. How does he plan on getting started, Diarkis?"

Aioven holds up one finger. "Well, first, he would like you to welcome him into your temple, and with your supervision, open the gate to Mortis. And in return, he will share any findings with the Order, with Captain Van Vuren as an escort."

Before Koenig can speak, Stark interrupts. "Secondly, he would like Miss Soleil, Diarkis, and I to be inducted into your Order, following your traditions and rules to act as ambassadors. We would like to show you that we intend to respect your customs and values wherever we can in this alliance."

Stark and Sam look back and forth at each other. Sam looks visibly confused by this request. Stark gives her an inquisitive look to which she just looks flabbergasted. *Did Aioven not tell*

Sam? That's odd. Koenig holds James' eyes, "Do you think that you can abide by our rules?"

Aioven steps forward and holds out his hand. "Captain, I'm ready to do what's necessary for the future. I commit myself to try. So long as our purpose is served and your rules just, they will become my own."

Everyone looks at each other uncertainly, but Koenig appears bemused by Aioven's response.

The senior captain steps forward, "A sound reply. A promise made too lightly is too easily broken. I expect you to be committed to trying, and to learn. Perhaps, too, I will learn something from your efforts."

Koenig offers Aioven his hand, "I have already learned something, I think. In my haste to keep order, I judged you too harshly. For that I apologize. You are offering to try; so, too, do I."

Aioven smiles. "Then it is settled. Of late, I have had more bad days than good." He pauses and shivers. "With our alliance, I hope that is changing. Being a part of your Order means that things should go faster and easier. For good people, anyways."

Koenig holds onto Aioven's hand, "Good people? What about the bad?"

Aioven looks deep into Koenig's eyes and says, "We make sure the last day of their lives is the worst day of their lives."

"Then let's begin. Your star in the order will rise as quickly as you learn. I caution you against impatience. Though you hold as much power as a captain, you understand almost nothing about our beliefs. Be easy. When the time is right, you will be called forward for the Tests. And advancing, will be more."

Aioven wears a smile of gratification, "All you've done is tell me what my future holds, because there's no obstacle I won't overcome."

The captain releases Aioven's hand and nods. "Well, when Aioven is ready, we can begin."

Aioven bows respectfully. "He will be with you shortly, within the next hour." Everyone waits for the two captains to depart before everyone finally relaxes.

Sam groans loudly. "Jeez, James, did you have to take a risk like that without warning us? He could've guessed—"

Stark holds up his hand to shush her before she spills the big secret in front of Senna. "It doesn't matter. At least for now. What I'm more surprised by is that James just willingly agreed to go back to school."

Aioven looks at Stark with wide eyes. "Wait—I completely forgot! Their academy doubles as a college. And I HATED college! This is going to be more annoying than I thought."

Stark and Sam laugh together as Senna stands by confused, not privy to the context behind the apparent joke.

• • •

Somewhere in the darkness, shivering, dehydrated and unable to sweat to cool off is the forsaken heap of failure, Captain Smirnov. A metal door appears in the wall of her pocket cave and creaks open, scraping the uneven stone and sending sparks flying everywhere. Aioven and Leonidas Stark step into the room and close the door behind them.

Lana spits at their feet. "Just get on with it and kill me. I'm sure you've already decide how you're going to do it, you bastard."

Leo looks at Aioven to watch his reaction. He flinches at the sound of her voice before taking a deep breath and grabbing her by the throat.

"James . . ." Leo says, resting his hand on the hilt of his sword.

"Relax, man. I'm just standing her up," Aioven says. He brushes off her shoulders and pats her on the head. "You are correct. I have spent an unhealthy amount of time imagining ways to kill you, as payment for your misdeeds." He looks back at Leo, who still appears unsure about what Aioven is about to do.

Aioven draws his katana and rests the sharp edge on her shoulder, pressing it into her neck. "But as time goes by, faster and faster it feels like, the more tired I get of worrying about you. I can't get you out of my head though, and I can't allow you to have such a victory over me."

"Then kill me," she says.

Aioven shakes his head, "I wouldn't be able to forget you. You'd just haunt me more. If it weren't for the fact that time has passed, or that Leo here didn't want me to torture you any further, then yes I would have tormented you to the point of begging for death. Not before removing things like breathing or seeing from your skill sets."

Aioven forgets who he is and becomes someone else. "If I had caught you that night, the night you killed Patrick and his daughter Laura . . ." He presses the tip of his sword just below her abdomen. "I would've seen it as poetic justice to leave you to suffer for all eternity, tormented at the edge of reality where life begins and ends. A never ending death and rebirth."

Leo draws his sword slightly. "Which is a little over the top for my taste."

Aioven ignores his friend's warning and touches her face with an open palm. "Six months ago I might have made my hand into a branding iron and marked your face as mine to torture you forever. But, you see, the universe is a big place. Killing Rytram and Darius helped me see that."

Lana's eyes widen in terror, as she realizes that Aioven is speaking truthfully. Aioven nods in silent confirmation. "Now I realize the universe doesn't give a shit about you. And neither should I, but killing you would be a waste. The architects thought you were useful. You might be to me as well."

"As if I'd ever help you," she shouts.

"Technically you won't." He places the palm of his metal hand on her forehead and closes his eyes. His arm begins to glow blue as he reaches into her mind. "I know you don't fear me, but I know you fear failure. I know you cower at the thought of things you can't imagine. I can spare you the fear, remake you into something better. A whole new person."

Stark watches in awe, sheathing his sword as Aioven dives deeper into her mind. "You won't be leaving this cave as Lana Smirnov. You will leave as Mira Mikoto. A new life in a new world. The person who was Lana will be gone, unable to cause any further harm. Perhaps Mira will do enough good to redeem her. Be hopeful!"

He pulls out of her mind and lets her look around, confused about her surroundings. She looks at Aioven. "Wh-where am I?"

Aioven breaks her chains. "A prison. I just wiped your memory of your old self. You were evil and cruel and loyal to a theocracy of even more terrible people." Lana, now apparently transformed into Mira, massages her wrists and cowers in fear of Aioven.

Aioven holds out his hands. "Relax, you're a new person, unburdened by what you did before. You probably don't even remember. Some people may remind you if they recognize you, but Lana has been executed. I have no reason to hurt you. In fact, I want to help you. You are safe. Come! There is much for you to do."

She coughs as she realizes how thirsty and hungry she is. "Why not actually execute her? Why let her body live on?" asks Stark.

"Because her body is useful. It holds powers that could be used for good. That's what I want from you—Mira Mikoto is your name—and you will leave this cave to live in a world that needs good people like you." Aioven opens a portal for her to step through and holds out his hand to take hers. She does so and he helps her through it before closing it behind her.

Stark crosses his arms. "What? I didn't kill her," Aioven says.

Stark sighs and claps once. "James, you're the only person

I have ever met that has found a way to weaponize mercy, and quite frankly, it's a little scary."

"Well, you did teach me that everything is a resource," Aioven says.

Stark sighs. "That's not what I meant." He looks at where the portal Lana had walked through was. "Where'd you send her, anyway?"

"Back to the Order. She's ultimately their responsibility anyway." Aioven opens a new portal. "We should get going too. We still have plenty of work to do."

* * *

Sam, Captain Van Vuren, and Captain Horatio Grizwald are waiting on the other side. "Ah! James Diarkis! Welcome back to the temple!" Horatio shakes James's hand and looks at Van Vuren. "It's been hundreds of years since the last known person to use wormholes was recorded."

"Almost a thousand," Victor says, ushering everyone into the temple. "Horatio will be joining us on this expedition."

The old man does an excited hop. "Yes! I hope you don't mind. I wanted to be there first to grab some undisturbed samples of the terrain. I can't imagine the geology will be groundbreaking, but I'm hoping to find something to make a case for more space exploration."

"Is there anything specific that you're hoping to find?" Stark asks.

Horatio nods. "My hope is to come up with a commercially viable way of obtaining helium 3."

"Let me guess, to find a way to make a sustainable fusion reactor?" Aioven asks. The lorekeeper nods.

"Well, I imagine we'll be making all sorts of discoveries today, Apprentice Diarkis," Victor says.

Aioven nods too. "I wouldn't expect the landscape to be completely undisturbed though. This gate we're about to use is old; ruins are one of the most likely things for us to find."

"As long as they haven't been completely turned to dust. Nothing is permanent," Stark says.

Victor ushers them down a stairway lit by torches emitting blue light. "Can that happen?"

Horatio nods emphatically. "Oh yes, given enough time, evidence of our Type 1 civilization can erode away without a trace. It might last longer than most things, but eventually our entire history will be forgotten if we one day die out."

They all step into a huge chamber, composed entirely of basalt and decorated with gold shields and suits of armour along the walls. The walls are made of bricks, with symbols, hieroglyphs, kanji, and latin-derived characters sprawling across them. Near the center, however, are all the symbols and letters indicating the number nine, some of which are unrecognizable.

Grizwald runs his hand across the wall. "I'm seeing just about every language's symbol for the number nine. What's fascinating is that there are symbols here I don't recognize."

"Languages we haven't discovered? Ancient ones?" Sam asks.

"What is this place? Did the Order build it?" Stark asks.

Grizwald picks up a blue torch and taps the wall with it, causing all the golden elements of the room to glow like neon tubes. "This room was discovered by our ancestors during the first civilization. Under one banner, all members of the only nation to be formed out of multiple tribes, they built the Temple of Creation, the Temple of Genesis, and the Order that would be based out of it."

"What brought them to this place?" James asks.

Horatio looks at him. "Same reason as you: answers and power. They came here and meditated, learned about the cosmic forces for the first time, and used them to build this structure with this chamber at its heart. The powers they used made it so that any alterations to the building would be undone, thus keeping to the original design from tens of thousands of years ago."

"That's why no trace of Aioven's visit here remains," Victor says, nodding to Aioven knowingly.

"Indeed, this chamber spawned the modern world . . . and now Aioven has come among us with his followers and claims you can open this gate, Diarkis. Unless you find a way to build a Dyson sphere in the near future, your contribution to our society will be on par with the discovery of fire."

Aioven walks up to the dark stone archway and touches the cold stone with the open palm of his hand. He closes his eyes and tries to search for anything that reminds him of the gateway that took them to the space station: any energies, powers, or sensations that he can fixate on to activate it. He holds his breath for almost half a minute before gasping.

"What? What is it?" Victor asks, looking like he wants to see if Aioven is okay.

Aioven sits down with his legs crossed and stares at the golden symbols etched into the gate. "I don't sense anything. No energies, no unusual types of matter, no changes in space, and nothing that my mind can explore either."

Stark looks at the top of the archway. "I think you're on the right track. Look at the top." He gestures to the symbols at the top of the archway, pointing out the top four: a golden lightning bolt, a gold sun, a gold brain, and a black obsidian dot with gold swirls coming out of it.

The whole group stands beside James, gazing upon the archway. Victor crosses his arms. "They clearly represent something."

"I've always thought they represent the cosmic forces," Horatio says. "Look: the lightning bolt is energy, the sun is matter..."

Aioven stands up. "And the brain is mind. What about the rest?"

Horatio brushes off the left side of the gateway. "This top one is a scroll, representing information," he says, pointing at a golden scroll before gesturing toward a drawing of a clock. "We don't know of anyone that can completely control time, but we're pretty sure that's what it represents. My penchant only allows me to accelerate certain processes. Time itself is unwieldy."

"That's six, and there's three more," Stark says.

Aioven stands on the threshold of the archway, looking at the remaining symbols. On the left: a scroll, a clock, and a golden drawing of a stick figure. On the right: a golden figure eight and a hole going straight through the stone with the insides being covered in amethyst like a geode. Beneath it is a space that looks like it has been gouged out or mined away, leaving an impression that something is missing.

"Hmm." Aioven puts his hand in the hole. "A stick figure, a figure eight, and an empty hole."

"James!" Stark shouts. Aioven pulls his hand out and places it on his sword's hilt. "No, relax, my bad. But put your hand in the hole again and look at the symbols at the top."

Aioven frowns and puts his hand back in the hole, not even touching the amethyst stones lining the surface. When he looks up at the top of the archway, to his surprise, he finds that some of the symbols have started to glow purple, specifically the top four. The lightning bolt, the sun, the brain, and the black hole are all pulsing with purple light.

"Try focusing on the gate or your powers or something. Maybe you'll be able to sense something now," Stark says.

What happens next, Aioven can't even fully understand. One second, he tries to relax and meditate, and the next second he hears a female voice saying, "Remember, Aioven…" and is plunged into darkness.

To everyone else watching, a bubbling, purple film of strange ooze is filling the archway like a bubble wand dipped in soap. Aioven had disappeared into the portal, leaving everyone else to decide who would venture into the unknown next. It wasn't like an ordinary wormhole. The other side wasn't visible, so they couldn't peek through to see where they might be going.

"Well, Victor, captains first, I suppose!" The old man grabs Victor by the wrist and drags him into the portal. "Wait, hold on!" Victor says as he splashes into the portal and vanishes.

Leo walks up to the warbling doorway and groans. "Why me? It's not fair."

The moment he touches the purple substance a voice answers back. "Why indeed?"

Plunged into darkness, Leo feels like he is floating in bathwater, completely submerged but still able to breathe.

Inches away from his face is the pale, disembodied head of Patrick Reardan. "Reardan served a purpose: to find Aioven and to seek out a guide for him." Hundreds of golden wires appear around Leo, like a forest of jellyfish stingers. "See for yourself," the head says.

A complete image of Patrick Reardan shimmers into view for Stark to see. Stark is seeing a vision of his since passed friend kneeling before a female silhouette on a dark throne. "Find him before he remembers, choose a guide, and alter his course, or everything that I have built will be lost. And your family will have nowhere to go." The woman's voice sounds cold and calculating, but for some reason Stark feels comforted. An image flashes in his mind of his mom tucking him into bed, nostalgia washing over him.

Patrick remains kneeling but looks up all confused. "We don't want him to revert?"

The mysterious figure waves her hand dismissively. "No, or

this universe will suffer the same fate as all the others. We must break the cycle."

Patrick stands up and bows. "It will be done, Mother. I know just who to pair with him . . ." The scene bubbles and melts away like boiling wax, kicking Stark back into reality and dropping him onto a cold, metal floor.

Aioven's encounter is somewhat different, but just as cryptic. "What brings you here?" the voice asks Aioven, who is standing before the same dark throne, occupied by an unknown female figure.

Aioven steps forward. "I seek to understand the forces of the universe, so I may grant all living creatures the lives they deserve."

"You seek power then. Ultimate power at that," she says.

Aioven thinks for a moment before shaking his head. "If I'm honest with myself, that's not what I want."

The woman rests her head in one of her hands. "Indeed, it is what you feel you are meant to do. Destined to free the universe from the reign of the architects. The ones who took away your life, and more importantly, the life of a father and his child." She stands up from her seat, still a silhouette that doesn't reflect any light. "You seek what you had, what you don't think is possible anymore. An ordinary life and one day a family."

Aioven steps back, unnerved by her correctness in describing his inner thoughts. She holds out her hand. "It isn't out of your reach, but you can't seek ultimate power and legacy at the same time."

"I . . . can have a family?" Aioven asks, his voice full of hope and shock.

"You can, and you can't. The universe does not want you to have a legacy and sit on the throne at the same time."

"But with ultimate power, I can protect my legacy," Aioven says smugly.

The woman waves her finger at him. "If you fight forever, you will eventually lose something. If you wage war with everything, then you will eventually lose everything."

Aioven starts shouting. "I will avenge whatever I lose and destroy those who take what is mine."

The woman clicks her tongue. "Tsk tsk . . . you will kill those that deserve it, and you also won't."

Aioven feels dread washing over him, like his life is draining from his body. "What are you talking about?"

"You are both doomed and designed for one purpose. Nothing else you try to do will succeed. No universe will accept your bids for a legacy whilst you have any power, because you are the antithesis of legacy. You would have to discard your quests and live in peace. There is no peace to be found in fighting."

Aioven crosses his arms. "I'm a what? Any universe . . . what are you talking about?"

She places her hand on his shoulder and forces him to his knees. "Your bid for control, the powers you gain, the small victories that make you feel complete—all of it is for a purpose you cannot escape: The ruination of everything that is built to last. You are the unstoppable force that meets immovable objects. You will destroy everything, or watch the universe go dark with no one at your side."

"Why me?" he asks with a shaky voice.

"Because you are the master that is eternal. Your curse will not be immortality—but eternity."

His surroundings bubble and boil away, revealing a beautiful scene of Mars sitting tranquil in space, with satellites and solar foils orbiting the planet in awesome patterns. Aioven feels a tugging at his heartstrings as the sounds of millions of voices cry out in terror and panic. Women, children, men, adults, babies—all wailing in fear until they're suddenly silenced. A flash of purple light catches Aioven's attention as an eruption of purple fire blasts through the planet's atmosphere. The explosion destroys a third of the planet's surface, incinerating all orbiting man-made structures and turning anything green a black ashy colour. Very quickly, the whole of Mars transitions to a toxic, red-orange colour. The lights of civilization are extinguished, and the surface turns to sand and glass as Aioven hears his own voice echo through the stars. "I will avenge you. I'm sorry."

Aioven shakes his head. "No, I won't allow that to happen!" He feels the sensation of gravity suddenly change, and he spins around and sees a wormhole opening behind him. But before he can investigate, a large, humanoid monster with a decaying deer head and a single antler grabs him by the throat and tosses him through the portal. Unable to fight the momentum of the creature's throw, he falls into a black hole. As he crosses beyond the event horizon, he hears himself say, "I hope to see you again one day, brother."

The universe begins to speed up, like a film moving in fast-forward. Images flash by at a high rate of speed: A molten planet cooling down, covered in blue oceans and lush green lands. A white stone with billions of golden threads connected to it, sitting on a plinth in a strange chamber. And finally, himself, sitting on a throne with the architects and many others dead at his feet. But before he can feel pride in the image of his future, the scene changes one last time.

"If you try to fight the current of destiny, if you try to save everyone, you will in turn doom everyone, and everyone you will ever love." Two tombstones appear before Aioven, marking the burial grounds of his family in the orange desert, surrounded by ruins and corpses. Aioven collapses and starts to hyperventilate as the sand is carried away by strong winds to reveal the bones underneath: the skeletal remains of a woman and an infant child. He's not sure why, but somehow he knows they are meant to be his future wife and child.

The sight is seared into Aioven's mind. Even as it fades away, he cannot unsee it. He clenches his hands into fists so tightly his fingers almost break. "I will not allow that to happen."

The woman's voice echoes around him as he floats down toward a metal floor. "It's not your decision to make, or at least, you can't force the universe to provide what you want."

"The universe will do just that, or I will do what I must to make room for my desires," he says, as the landscape around him melds together like boiling wax. The orange sludge swirls into a vortex and at the center of the maelstrom a figure rises.

A man with cobalt blue skin and fiery golden eyes stares piercingly at Aioven, "Your journey will be the longest out of all of us, brother of suffering. You long for purpose, you think you can choose your destiny for yourself. If only you knew how little power you have. The mother is always especially cruel with you, robbing you of the knowledge that everything you are going to do . . . you've done before and will fall short of your grand aspirations. But go ahead and do it anyways. Slay gods, snuff out starts, atomize planets and sterilize galaxies . . . I'll be waiting. And when we met, I'll jog your memory. My only word of advice is this: Don't hope too much. Many will come to fear the name of Aioven. But you alone will know the truth, the next time you hear my name, the end of all things will come to pass. I will herald the end of all purpose."

"What is your name?" Aioven asks, eager to commit it to memory. The entity's azure skin begins to crack and flake away as it forces a smile, "Astamar. I will see you again, shortly after your greatest victory, to usher you towards your destiny."

"We'll see about that", Says Aioven, moments before landing softly on his feet, once again among his companions.

"Everyone all right?" Victor asks.

Stark pulls a dozy Grizwald to his feet. "We're all right," he says, looking to Aioven.

The woman's voice echoes for everyone to hear, as light

slowly enters the chamber from tinted windows. "If you wish to continue on your present course, if you wish to topple the architect throne, then you must ascend to a state of power no universe has ever seen. You must master all nine absolute cosmic forces. No more, and no less."

Aioven considers what he has been told and glances at all of his companions before looking up into the stars as they are revealed by the opening windows. "Tell us what we must do," he says.

"Very well," the voice says. "The first step is to master the initial eight cosmic forces: energy, matter, time, information, space, mind, existence, and infinity. You must master these to subjugate this universe in its entirety, and then you can move on to the second step."

"That's a hell of an oversimplification," Stark says. "Step one: become an all-powerful deity of literally fucking everything."

"What is the second step?" Grizwald asks.

"The second step is to learn how to travel to other dimensions beyond this reality," the woman says.

"Why is mastering eight forces necessary? Why not just go straight for interdimensional travel?" Victor asks.

"Because, in order to go from one reality to another, you must master the ninth cosmic force. Mastering all the forces of this universe is necessary because the final cosmic power is the nature of the void: the transitory ether that separates all realities. In order to be able to comprehend and traverse the void, you must first understand everything that is your universe, before trying to understand everything it isn't. Going to a place where physics doesn't exist without being prepared will doom you to a fate that is literally impossible to describe."

As the chamber floods with light, huge floating rings shrouded in shadow start to spin around them. "Has no one ever achieved this?" Sam asks.

The rings all stop. "No, no one, not a single entity in any

universe has ever come close to even attempting to master the void."

Aioven steps forward and kneels, drawing his sword and holding it out with two hands. "I pledge myself to this task, together with my friends and allies. We will succeed or die trying."

The rings are all illuminated by starlight, and on them hundreds of small and large monolithic eyes open at once, covering the rings completely. They all blink and stare at Aioven, whose sword begins to levitate.

"Very well," the woman's voice says again. "Then I, the Mother, bestow upon you the status of void knight, a warrior quested with the responsibility and upkeep of this universe. Your power will not be bestowed but earned through his own self-discovery, and yet will be second to none. Rise Dalkanos Aioven, knight of the void."

His floating sword taps both of his shoulders before returning to his hand so he can sheathe it. "Now, go forth, and sow the seeds of your future. Welcome to your Garden of Eden." The eyes on the rings all close and start to spin quickly. The group all gaze upon the sky above them in complete awe as the stars begin to move.

Aioven lets out a shocked laugh. "This isn't just a moon," he says as the sky comes to a halt with Mars taking up the horizon. "This is a vessel."

Horatio blinks and looks at Aioven. "Wait, did she call you Aioven?"

Victor takes him by the shoulders and shushes him. "We'll deal with that later," he whispers.

Sam watches in awe as the rings spin so fast they appear to be shimmering spheres. "So, now you've been quested with gaining enough power to usurp the architects. A quest like this is madness, and furthermore, the very thought of rebuilding the universe makes it sound like you'll be an architect by the end of this," she says.

Leo stands beside James, or Aioven—it's difficult to say at this point—and they both look upon the horizon at their home world.

"It's a beautiful sight," Leo says.

"From this far away, I suppose. But she needs work," Aioven says. "Hopefully, when we're done with all of this, I'll have a horizon to look upon and smile."

"What are we going to do to make you smile in the meantime?" Leo asks.

Aioven claps his friend on the shoulder and says, "How about a nice drive and some carbonara? And then we can all go to bed and sleep for forty-eight hours."

"Don't tempt me with a good time," Leo says, chuckling.

"Hey, if you're down, then I'm down," Aioven says with a yawn.

Stark fist-bumps Aioven's shoulder. "Dinner, a movie, a good night's sleep, and then we save the world."

"Sounds good to me. Gotta make the world you want to live in," Aioven says. The pair look past their planet, deep into the stars, losing themselves in this rare moment of peace and tranquility, unaware that hidden in the heavens the architects observe their endeavours.

The four architects rise from their thrones, with an army of a hundred thousand or more angels bowing before them. One architect steps forward and motions for the angels to rise to their feet. "So, Dalkanos Aioven. It has begun. Angelus, come here."

An angel materializes from nothing and kneels before him. "Yes, Lord Exorsio? I am yours to command."

"Do whatever it takes to destroy Dalkanos Aioven. Turn Mars to sand and glass if you must," the architect says.

The angel stands and nods affirmatively. "Death will rain from the heavens. A new Arkon will rise, and The Mad Architect Dalkanos Aioven will fall in the name of sparing the universe of Astamar's wrath. Even if he defeats all of us, he will still face The Mother's Apocalypse. I'll make sure of it. No one wants Aioven to win."

ABOUT THE AUTHOR

Hello! My name is Thomas Michael Wood (T. M. Wood sounds cooler) and I thought I'd introduce myself! I'm a natural born creative soul, a father, a driver of… vehicles big and small and I spend most of my time creating media to share with the world. Well, now I get to introduce you to an idea I've been wanting to manifest for years. You see, when I was in high school I had a moment during one of many routine physics lessons. This moment was like an epiphany, like when Doc Brown hit his head and invented time travel! I finally had an idea that felt original enough to pursue and develop into a story. Better yet, when I pitched the idea to my father he really liked it and that meant a lot because he's one of the smartest people I know.

After a few rewrites, several story edits, changes to characters and myself surviving a car accident or two… I finally have a story that I am proud of and have sufficiently poured my own soul into. If you pay close attention you'll notice themes that are very important to me. Doing your duty, being passionate about your endeavours and fighting as hard as you can to build a legacy worthy of celebration. I have privately known Aioven and his fellow characters for years, now I get to introduce them to you.